DIRTY BOYS

JOHN LIGATO

A POST HILL PRESS BOOK
ISBN (trade paperback): 978-1-68261-280-4
ISBN (eBook): 978-1-61868-869-9

Post Hill
PRESS

Post Hill Press
posthillpress.com

Published in the United States of America

This book is dedicated to the mud Marine and FBI brick agent: America's warriors who at this very moment are in harm's way. Whether on combat patrol in the Middle East or executing a search warrant in New York, they do America's dirty work and thus, the title of this book, "DIRTY BOYS."

ACKNOWLEDGMENTS

Writing is a solitary activity; however, it cannot be done in a vacuum. Most of us need the occasional encouragement or a ham sandwich. I'd like to thank the following individuals who provided me one or the other.

Lorri—my wife and best friend—the ham sandwich; Gia and Dani—my daughters—the gift of unconditional love; Florence, my sister and the "nicest" person in the world; Joe Pistone a.k.a *Donnie Brasco*—my undercover mentor and friend who provided me wise counsel such as, *"Don't **** this up!"*; Frank Weiman—simply the best literary agent in the business. He is also a man of subtle optimism. After reading my manuscript Frank's reply was, "I *might* give this a shot."; Anthony, CEO and "Capo" of Post Hill Press who always accepted my calls and was *always* positive; Bob Dupuis, Mike Williams, and Rose Eagan who doled out a steady stream of encouragement; Bruce "Bruno" Gombar for doing an initial edit, and Gary McKissock who informed me that my writing is *'very unusual.'*

My Marine Corps family who welcomed me back into the brotherhood as if I never left. And to the next generation of Devil Dogs who are the latest in the long line of warriors. To my combat brothers of Alpha Company, First Marines who distinguished themselves in the battle of Hué City Vietnam during the 1968 TET offensive, we fought our asses off: the late Jimmy Sullivan, Gordan Batchellor, Ray Smith, John Canley, Nick Carangio, Eddie "Alfie" Neas, Herman 'Buzzard' Watkins, Buck Stubbs, and our Medal of Honor recipient, platoon sergeant, Al Gonzalez. A "shout out" to my Geezer Golf Group who realize that we all suck at the game but love the Marine Corps brotherhood: William "Billy" Garret, Jerry Yanello, John Kopka, Efren Saenz, Dick Vercauteran, John Goodrich, Tom Cullison, Bob Dickerson, Bob Songer, Paul Lefebvre, and Jay "Princeton" Sollis. The boys and girls in the "Hood": Bob, Lois, Mike, Rose, Horace, Janelle, Dick, Dori, Frank and Flo, who welcomed the Ligato family into their lives and provided many ham sandwiches.

The opinions expressed in this book are those of the author's, are completely fictional, and not of the FBI's. The FBI has "vetted" the contents of the book in keeping with the confidentiality agreement I made as an FBI agent. The major characters in this book are fictional. Actual people and events of public prominence are included when relevant to the story. Individuals, whose names appear as characters, have given their permission to use their given names.

CHAPTER 1

"To kill the plant, you must first kill the root ..."
— An old Sicilian saying

"This is *bullshit*." Is my initial response. Lately it's been my *standard* comeback. I know I won't win the argument so I decide to push the career envelope.

"Matt," I say evenly. "I don't want to be here and you *really* don't want me on your squad."

"And why is that?"

"Because my last supervisor was demoted, and the one before that is selling insurance in Peoria. He's doing great actually ... as long as he stays on his meds."Matt Michaels is my new supervisor and the intel on him is that he is an empty suit. He covers his ass, doesn't back the troops, and can't make a decision which is pretty much standard operating procedure for much of the FBI hierarchy *after* the terrorist attacks on 9/11. He is the latest in a series of *"Boy Wonders"* skyrocketing through the ranks of the *new* FBI.

"Most agents would kill to get on the Joint Terrorism Task Force," Michaels whines.

It may not have been the most politically correct thing to say but he had a point. The JTTF has become the sexy assignment post 9/11 for a lot of the agents around here but I can't see myself staring at a computer screen all day looking for some hidden meaning to words beginning with the letter Z.

I'm a brick agent, a street guy from South Philly who had infiltrated the Italian mob and survived seven years in deep cover. After two hours in an office, I sprout hives. I recently surfaced from my latest Guido soiree in New York City playing the silent owner of a high-end gentlemen's club. *"The things one must do for their country ..."* is my standard comeback whenever someone questions my backstopping. I wanted the fun to continue but a few random corpses fermenting the local landfill had the bureaucrats scrambling for cover. Being assigned to the task force would put an end to my make-believe world of strippers, Cuban cigars, and Portobello mushrooms stuffed with crab meat and the most succulent lobster tail that government money could buy.

I grudgingly accept my fate and smile at my new boss. Supervisory Special Agent Matt Michaels gives me an uneven grin that resembles a stroke victim. He hands me a FBI Training Manual on Terrorism and recommends that I read it *thoroughly*. He calls it *our bible*. I find a desk and dump my cardboard box of job-related possessions. A quick confession here, I am not the poster child for the FBI in any way. I once arrested some drug dealer and charged him with *felony stupid* in addition to trafficking. The U.S. Attorney didn't share my sense of humor.

Most FBI agents come from Middle America with advanced degrees from private schools. I grew up in a dilapidated row home in South Philadelphia, enlisted in the Marine Corps, and barely graduated from Slippery Rock State College. This is *not* your typical FBI resume.

I make a promise to myself to lose the attitude and view this unwelcomed transfer as an opportunity. I'll make the best of my new assignment and this includes reading Boy Wonder's bible. It's entitled, *Terrorism in the United States*. The first paragraph alerts me to the requirement that *"the FBI investigates terrorism-related matters, without regard to race, national religion, or national origin...."*

I reread this opening mandate and suspect it's merely a disclaimer on racial profiling. I find the attempt at political correctness ironic. Radical Muslims have been attacking American interests for a hundred years. Perhaps we should target the French instead, who always struck me as arrogant snobs. But I read on, hoping to find *something* useful in the war on terrorism.

Chapter two chronicles the reasons *why* radical Muslims are angry with America. I read the entire chapter and *still* can't figure out why they view us as camel dung. What'd we ever do to them? But it is chapter six that really frost my ass. It consists of twenty pages on *my* responsibility to *understand* radical Muslims, so that the FBI can begin the process of changing their hearts and minds. I must have missed the memo on the FBI's role as social workers.

My view on radical Muslims is quite simple. As a Marine I spent a month training in the desert at 29 Palms California. There are more scorpions inhabiting that grid than human beings. I killed a minimum of three scorpions a day. The thought never crossed my mind on why a scorpion would bite me because that's what they do. It's in their DNA. I also never attempted to negotiate or reason with the little fuckers or get to know them better. I just killed them. I also came to understand that for every scorpion I killed, two more lurked nearby. So, I realized that I could *never* rid the desert of scorpions nor could I convince a jihadist to love America.

Chapter six concludes with the recent Headquarters policies aimed at not offending *any* group. *"Good morning Mr. bin laden, you look particularly dapper today. My name is John Booker and it's my honor to be your arresting agent. Have a nice day."*

I locate the nearest trash can and toss the bible. So much for my attitude adjustment. As I am counting my paper clips, I hear a familiar voice.

"Hey, if it isn't Johnny Booker."

Bruce Gombar is a Harvard law graduate who had made some pretty good corruption cases before his transfer to the task force.

Bruce is a decent enough guy but has an annoying habit of reminding the world he went to Harvard. He rolls up a chair and is joined by his partner, whom I call S.W.A.T. Boy.

I greet my two new squad mates and inform S.W.A.T. Boy that he is leaking testosterone all over my desk. I am just about to say *joke* when Steve Booth smiles and punches my arm. It hurt. S.W.A.T. Boy is capable of pulling my limbs apart like a Thanksgiving turkey wishbone.

Some men get excited by *Hustler*; S.W.A.T. Boy gets excited by the nomenclature of an MP5 machine gun. He spends workdays alternating between the firing range and gym though I've never seen the guy sweat. It's a good gig. S.W.A.T. Boy's official title is Firearms Coordinator.

Dirty little FBI secret: the new FBI has spawned a gaggle of coordinators such as applicant, informant, EPA, training, evidence, and the useless position of Media Coordinator. They exist in a parallel work dimension. These men and women are FBI gun-toting special agents who *never* leave the office, except for lunch.

I truly have no idea of what these coordinators coordinate, except that they don't investigate bad guys or make arrests. They are simply wasted manpower but project an air of royalty. They always say they'll get back to you. They *never* do.

I shoot the shit with Bruce and S.W.A.T. Boy for a while. Law enforcement partners spend a significant time of each day together. Eventually they take on each other's personality and behave like an old married couple.

The odd couple takes turns updating me on the latest office rumors, gossip and scuttlebutt. It reminds me a well-rehearsed Vegas lounge act.

"Matt Michaels is an asshole."

No surprise there, I think.

"Lucy, the squad nine secretary, is screwing the media coordinator."

I file this tidbit away for a more opportune time.

"Tim O'Leary's in rehab."

I had closed many a Bureau watering hole with Tim so I dismiss any self-incrimination on his alcoholism.

"And one last thing," Bruce says, "our squad secretary is different."

"You want to explain *different*?"

S.W.A.T. Boy chuckles and says, "You'll find out."

I enjoy gossip as much as the next guy but I'm more concerned with this entity called the Joint Terrorism Task Force. It will consume most of my waking hours. Lucy will have to wait. "How's the work here?"

Bruce shakes his head and explains, "This place is *not* a terrorist hot spot, John. We get some bullshit leads on a few Iranian students at Cleveland State, trace some Hamas money from the towel heads operating the convenience stores on the east side, and on a particularly thrilling day, we may do a surveillance on some visiting imam at the local mosque."

"So what you're telling me is that I will rot on the JTTF vine. Maybe I should request a transfer to Violent Crime or join Tim O'Leary on the rubber gun squad."

"It's not all that bad. Michaels never comes out of his office. He's busy with the *New York Times* crossword puzzle in the morning, and then inserts his nose up the SAC's ass all afternoon. The man is just cruising through Cleveland on his way to a desk job in D.C."

"Why does his name ring a bell?" I ask.

Gombar shakes his head and says. "Michaels was the informant coordinator in Idaho when the two agents were killed."

"That's the fucking guy!"

Whenever an agent is killed in the line of duty, the facts and circumstances are forever seared into the minds of our ranks. The episode becomes both a teaching tool at the academy as well as a reminder that we chase bad people for a living.

Two years ago, Boise, Idaho agents had a snitch who was a card-carrying member of a major domestic terrorist group. The National Force was your basic white supremacy group of militant yahoos who believed in the segregation of races, an obsession with assault weapons, and screwing a few second cousins. They were hunkered down in the hills of Idaho awaiting the revolution. You get the visual.

It was a Friday afternoon when the agents approached Michaels for $400,000 in *show* money. Show money is just that. Bad guys need to *see* the cash before they hand over the booty. The FBI informant had arranged a deal to purchase four M60 machine guns, two LAW rockets, ten Claymore mines, and five AR-15 rifles on Saturday afternoon.

The plan was to take down the entire National Force and eliminate their organization. Michaels refused to go through the administrative gyrations on such short notice. It would've required him to work a Friday night securing approvals and rounding up the cash.

The agents argued that they had been waiting nine months for this deal and the window of opportunity was *now*. Michaels reasoned that the deal would still be there next week and went home. His kid had soccer practice.

The field agents made every attempt to postpone the deal but the bad guys became suspicious and issued the ultimatum of '*now or never.*' On Saturday, the snitch along with two FBI agents acting in undercover capacities met with the white supremacists. Since they had no money to show, they pointed to a canvass satchel filled with newspaper. The deal went south fast and the two agents were shot and killed. One of them, Joe Falcone, had been my undercover mentor and friend who died needlessly due to Michaels's laziness.

"So they *promoted* him after he gets two agents killed?" I ask.

Gombar says, "Michaels argued that they should have waited for the money. Headquarters agreed and demoted the field supervisor and thirteen months later promoted Michaels and sent him here."

"So that's the fuckin' guy."

I thank my co-conspirators for their honesty but feel a sense of gloom. I joined the FBI *not* to protect and serve, which is the preferred reply during the job interview, but for the hunt—of being both predator and prey. As a self-proclaimed thrill junky, the Cleveland JTTF will deny me my drug of choice.

"So," I sum up, "what you're telling me is that the terrorists in Ohio are quiet and well behaved."

"Wanna go for a cup of coffee? We got a hook at the Galleria, coffee's on the arm," Bruce says.

Dirty little secret number two is that FBI agents are cheap. We get running shoes, clothes, and food at discount prices from contacts or, *'friends of the Bureau,'* as they prefer to be called. I once witnessed an agent on the verge of tears when he couldn't find a friendly jeweler and had to pay full price on an engagement ring.

"Nah. I wanna go through some case files and catch up on the players here," I say. "Where's the Squad 4 Rotor located at?"

"You know John," Bruce lectures. "At *Harvard* we *never* end our sentences with a preposition."

"Sorry Bruce, Permit me to correct my grammatical error," I pause, and emphasize each word. "Where is the Squad 4 Rotor located at ... asshole?"

Both Bruce and S.W.A.T Boy are cackling like schoolgirls on their way out the door. I didn't think it was *that* funny the first time I heard it.

I log onto my computer and see a message from my new supervisor. It is accompanied by a little red flag. I have no idea of the flag's significance but deduce that Michaels is kin to Chicken Little.

"John, welcome to the squad. I am assigning a lead regarding a concerned citizen claiming possible terrorist activities. It's an interview with a source of unknown reliability."

The attached lead had the usual FBI jargon with due dates, contact data, and a brief summary of the information alleged. I have handled hundreds of lead interviews and although most were a waste of time, every now and then one could lead to the Holy Grail. The source alleges some vague accusation that terrorists were opening up a charter school near Strongsville, Ohio.

The lead instructs me to: *"Interview complainant and determine validity. Recommend closure or further investigation."*

I give this lead some hopeful reflection, but conclude that ... *this is bullshit.*

CHAPTER 2

"The supreme art of war is to subdue the enemy without fighting."
— Sun Tzu

I drive south on I-71. The day is overcast and gloomy with smoke billowing from the rusty towers of the few remaining steel mills. The massive Cleveland Casting Plant at Ford Motors looks eerily abandoned. Grass and weeds claim much of the concrete parking lot which was once filled with three shifts of American made cars. It's been a tough run for a city that deserves better.

I have no earthly idea what a charter school is so I call my wife. Yes, I am a married man, though my undercover existence has muddied the marital waters of late. The former Lorri Olson is a beautiful human being in every regard. I often kid her that she is Martha Stewart minus the indictment. A social worker, artist, and gourmet cook all rolled into a five foot five inch frame of a perfectly proportioned Nordic beauty.

"What's a charter school?" I ask after a moment of idle chatter. Lately most of our communication has been reduced to either idle chatter or life-altering ultimatums, as in, *"If you're not happy, then leave!"*

Lorri offers, "Charter schools are public schools which operate independently from the local school board. They have their own curriculum and philosophy about education."

"Where do they get their operating money?"

"Can be from private donations or tuition, but mainly through public tax dollars."

This last bit of information gets my attention. "You saying that *anyone* can start a school, get some public dough, and teach *whatever* they want?

Lorri says, "Well not whatever, but almost. It's the wave of the future since city schools are basically day time juvenile detention centers. Not much learning going on at PS 108."

I ask, "So *almost anything* can mean teaching first graders abstract art or lesbian line dancing?"

Lorri sees where this is going and switches to her teacher *'voice.'* "Charter schools are neither good nor bad. Like most things, it's how the educational format is applied that can make the experience worthwhile."

"How about a course on 'Why I Hate America'? Do you think that's worthwhile?"

"I think that children should hear all sides, so they can make informed choices in life."

"That's just liberal drivel," I counter.

Lorri is now in full teacher mode, placating the third grade trouble-maker. "I'm not sure that course gets by the accreditation board, but you can and *should* teach alternative or historically different viewpoints."

"Give me some examples, Lorri."

"Okay, but I already know what your reaction will be." My spouse continues the tutorial.

"Some of America's most traditional and cherished beliefs are being questioned *and* corrected such as, could same sex marriage comprise the natural family unit, is Christianity responsible for American democracy, did Betsy Ross sew the first flag, will global warming destroy the planet in twenty years," Lorripauses and asks. "Should I continue or has your blood pressure reached critical mass?"

"You definitely have my attention."

"Okay John, but you asked for it." She continues with, "Did Lyndon Johnson have President Kennedy killed, is the CIA responsible for the 9/11 attacks...."

"Bullshit!"

I've long ago accepted our ideological differences. Lorri enjoys white wine and chick flicks, while I lean toward bourbon and gushing blood movies.

"Oh wait, John," Lorri taunts. "Here's two more of your childhood myths debunked: John Wayne was *not* really a Marine and there *is* no tooth fairy."

"Well there seems to be a lot of *other* fairies involved in this *fairy tale*."

"Touché, John, the daily double; both clever *and* homophobic."

"You're right, Lorri," I counter. "I am a smart ass, but I still worry about my country. It concerns me that our educational system is poisoning young minds."

"It's basically a good system, John, it adapts and evolves to the times."

"With the times," I challenge. "Is that why *our* colleges are offering classes on *The Jersey Shore* with a *Snooki* lab while other countries like Japan are offering boring courses in math and science."

"Goodbye, John."

"Hey what are we having for dinner?" I ask to dead air.

I find the house in the trendy Deerfield Woods development of Strongsville, Ohio. My complainant is a sixty-nine year old retired Army Colonel, Jay Sollis, whose son and daughter-in-law have enrolled his grandson in a charter school. We discuss the weather, the Browns, and our mutual military experiences. It's important to build some rapport when conducting interviews. I eventually say, "Tell me about this charter school, Colonel Sollis."

Jay nods and begins with, "My son and his wife both work, so I get to take my grandson to school. Tommy's a great kid. Public school is around the corner but his mother wants a different experience for their only child. So I take Tommy to a charter school twenty-three miles away. Seemed a little peculiar, the classrooms have no desks, chalkboards, or even windows, but I meet his teachers and they seem normal. Tell me how Tommy's gonna learn more than he would in public school, how the kids who go there score better on tests. I listen and nod and am feeling better about it until I meet the school's director."

I continue to take notes, though I have no earthly idea where this is heading.

"The director is a woman wearing a burka."

I nod again but realize that I just spent two hours of my life that I could never get back. That Colonel Jay is some curmudgeon patriot that sees terrorists everywhere. Six hours a day listening to Rush Limbaugh, Sean Hannity, and Bill O'Reilly can have that effect. Though I am in the same philosophical camp as Colonel Jay, I know this is a dry investigative hole.

Ever since the attacks on 9/11, I also feel a knot in my stomach whenever I see Middle Eastern garb. Intellectually, I understand that not all Muslims are gun-toting al-Qaeda, but emotionally that message gets interrupted en route to my brain. Could be a burka, turban, kaftan, dishdasha, or egal. Could even be a guy in a polyester leisure suit that "looks" Arabic.

I can't help how I feel, but it's definitely rooted in the televised images of thousands of Arabs in America jubilantly celebrating the horrible death of three thousand American lives following the attacks on 9/11.

Time for another dirty little Bureau secret. Most federal agents are fairly racist. '*Towel head*' and '*camel jockey*' are two of the more benign Muslim expressions floating around Bureau watering holes. But in all fairness to Muslims, FBI agents are equal opportunity bigots. We are also appalled by the hordes of illegal aliens and welfare commandos.

But, we *really* get lathered up at female FBI agents who get to count *modified* push-ups during the annual PT test.

I totally agree on the push-up issue. I hate to break it to the brass, but your ongoing required sensitivity training merely provides new material for our sexist and racist repertoire.

I ask all the follow-up questions to determine if there is anything *other* than the burka. There isn't. Truth of the matter is that I observe some form of Middle Eastern garb every single day, so unless the school director was waiving anthrax in one hand and pointing a Rocket Propelled Grenade in the other, my lead would enter the black hole of *'closed with no recommendation of further investigation.'*

I commiserate with Colonel Sollis, wish him well, and promise to look into the school. I don't have the heart to dismiss the old warrior's effort in his war against terrorism. As I am heading for the car, Colonel Jay says, "One last thing ... don't really know what it means but one of the teachers said something about the teaching of Waba or Whatism, something like that."

I thank the Colonel again and make a mental phonetic note of 'whatism.'

Back in the car, I fight the disappointment that my first investigation into the murky world of terrorism is a dead end. I need a smile so I call my daughter.

Nikki Booker has the distinct disadvantage of being my clone. The poor kid has inherited my skewed and irreverent humor much to the chagrin of her mom, teachers, and friends. A high school senior with good grades, Nikki is headed off to Ohio State in the fall to study Astronomy, though at times I swear she says Astrology.

"Hey sweets," I say. "Whatcha doing?"

"You don't want to know Pops."

"You're right. Gotta question."

"Shoot."

"You know anything about the Muslim world?"

"Not a thing except what you tell me ... that they're all psychotic killers who eat their young."

"I don't tell you that."

"I hear you and Uncle Russ talking."

"Well, try not to listen," I say. "Ever hear of Whatism or Whaba, something like that?"

"Nope but call you right back." Nikki's gone before I can utter a *never mind.*

I barely have time to scratch an itch when the phone rings. It's Nikki. She tells me that she searched her smart phone and may have solved the Wabash or whabis mystery. Twenty years ago, it would have taken a half hour drive to the library and three hours on the second floor scouring thick research books to do what a smart phone and a teenager could do in a nanosecond.

"Talk to me honey."

"Too much stuff for the phone Pops, I already e-mailed it to you."

"Thanks sweetie. You doin' Okay?"

"Gotta go, Pedro is calling...."

"Wait!" I say to dead air. "Tell me what's wrong."

Numerous attempts at reconnecting with my daughter are met with Nikki's voice mail ... *"It's Nikki, I'm either at the gym or have run away to Tahiti, leave a message."*

That's twice in one day that a Booker lady hung up on me in mid-sentence. It could be a trend. I am also left wondering who the hell *Pedro* may be.

It's been an interesting first day on the task force. I'm exhausted and need to reflect on my life. Or maybe I just need a Jim Beam neat. I decide on the bourbon over any self-reflection and change into my evening uniform of sweat pants and Marine Corps t-shirt. After a few sips of Mr. Beam, I sign onto my internet account and open up Nikki's smart phone research.

I read for less than a moment when a chill runs down my spine.

CHAPTER 3

"It's hard to lead a cavalry charge if you think you look funny
on a horse."
— Adlai E. Stevenson

I sleepwalk my way to the coffee pot. Mornings are my favorite time of the day, with false promises of new beginnings. I am a card-carrying pessimist, fatefully awaiting man's next inhumanity to man. Caffeine is one of my few addictions along with an occasional cigar and the swimsuit edition of *Sports Illustrated.*

Lorri and Nikki are asleep. It was business as usual last night when Lorri arrived home around eight. She casually offered the excuse of a glass of wine with a few *"friends"* after work. We exchanged pleasantries and I couldn't detect any residual effects from our earlier conversation.

I love my wife, I love my wife, I love my wife … is a genuine mantra which often runs through my brain whenever we hit matrimonial speed bumps or whenever Lorri stops for a glass of wine with *friends.*

Nikki's research would have been merely classified as interesting had I not met Colonel Sollis, but now it had been upgraded to disturbing.

I reread the material after a few sips of java hoping it would somehow read differently in the cold hard light of morning. It didn't.

"The extreme and uncompromising form of Islam known as Wahhabism is taught in virtually every Islamic charter school in North America."

And, that was the good news. Examples of how Wahhabist ideology permeates the curricula in these institutions include the following:

>*New York City:The New York Daily News* found that books used in the city's Muslim schools "are rife with inaccuracies, sweeping condemnations of Jews and Christians, and declarations of Islam's supremacy.

>*Potomac, Maryland:* The Muslim Community School imbues its students with a sense of alienation from the United States. One seventh-grader there told a *Washington Post* reporter in 2001 that "being an American means nothing to me."

>*Alexandria, Virginia:* A textbook that has been used at the Islamic Saudi Academy teaches first-graders to commit acts of violence such as taking of the lives and property of Christians and Jews. Ninth to twelfth grade curricula place heavy emphasis on jihad, and on Muslims' *religious obligation to kill infidels.*

>*Ashburn, Virginia:* The Graduate School of Islamic Social Sciencesgraduates commonly go on to become imams, academics, military and prison chaplains. The federal government has long suspected the organization of maintaining ties to Islamic terrorism.

No matter how many times I dissect the material, I cannot find a silver lining. When did American schools begin teaching anti-American values? Why wasn't I aware of something this blatantly treacherous? It's as if I had been living in a cocoon of blissful ignorance as a member of the premier law enforcement agency on earth. But, I am determined to find the answers.

A quick shower and shave and I'm a new man. I enjoy getting to the office before the masses arrive. You can actually generate complete thoughts, minus interruptions from bored co-workers.

I query the Bureau intelligence files on Wahhabism. An hour later it becomes painfully obvious that the FBI's secret intelligence network contains the identical information as my daughter's Wal-Mart purchased phone. So much for the FBI being the end-all oracle of super-secret shit.

I grab a copy of the U.S. Code -Title 18- Crimes and Procedures manual and jot down possible federal violations. After an hour, I draw a blank and reduce my scribblings to two sentences.

1. Charter schools teach anti-American propaganda.

2. Propaganda is *NOT* a crime — End of story!

This conclusion hits a note of discord with both my common sense and sense of patriotism. Something smells here but it could just be the odor of changing times. In the past few years many school districts had bastardized this nation's cultural traditions with such idiocies as eliminating our pledge of allegiance, Easter Bunny decorations, and nativity scenes. A few schools had even tolerated illegal aliens stomping on the American flag at a school sponsored activity. I am repulsed by these actions but they are still *not* criminal.

I need a legal opinion so I dial extension 147. Scott Bradley is Cleveland's principal legal adviser and a good man. An attorney by education, he counsels agents whenever we venture near touchy legal waters. Scott is also a scratch golfer who in all probability paid for a room addition with my double bogeys.

I explain my charter school dilemma and ask if any laws are being broken, insisting that there must be a horde of them.

Scott listens patiently as I spew out what I've learned. I finish my rant with demands that he tick off the litany of federal laws that have been violated.

His reply consists of two words: "First Amendment."

I wait for some additional pearls of legal wisdom but there are none. When I begin to repeat my case, Scott interrupts and repeats. "First Amendment," then he adds, "Free speech."

Bradley explains that "Under the First Amendment, Muslims have a constitutional right to express ideas, even ones that the government consider dangerous or unpatriotic. That's why the Supreme Court struck down a law banning flag burning. In that case, the court said prohibiting people from mutilating the American flag was an illegal attempt to restrain speech."

"When did our country go commie?" I wonder aloud.

Scott says, "I don't like what's going on in this country any more than you do, but as FBI agents we can't pick sides; we can only enforce the laws on the books. You have to accept that we are now a nation of political correctness."

"You know something, Scott," I offer seriously. "Political correctness is something devised by liberals who feel that it is entirely possible to pick up a piece of shit by the clean end."

Scott laughs in the same odd manner that he does after making birdie putts. It's a combination wheeze and snort. This is usually followed by my handing him gobs of cash and a hollow threat to beat him next golf match.

I am not about to give up on my logical position. "What about laws that state you can't yell 'fire' in a movie theatre?" I protest.

Scott explains, "The Supreme Court has ruled that speech which directly incites violence or some kind of physical retaliation is *not* protected under the First Amendment. *But* while this is true in theory, the court has rarely banned that kind of speech or conduct."

"Fuck you," I say good-naturedly.

Scott laughs and says, "I gotta tee time at Pine Hills on Saturday."

"Can't make it, but if I could, I need four more strokes a side."

I sit at my desk and think that America is transitioning into a period of political correctness that doesn't *correct* anything. Radical Muslims have been at war with America for over a hundred years. I love this country with a passion but *our* government scares the shit out of me.

We recently received a directive from Headquarters, which prohibits *any* type of racial profiling at airports. So TSA workers are waving bin Laden look-a-likes through airport security while strip-searching granny.

This charter school thing has afflicted me with a case of work related impotence. I need some background information from an expert on Middle Eastern customs, so I rifle through a stack of business cards. A few years ago I caught a case which required me to interview an Egyptian Professor at Case Western Reserve University. Her colleague was dating a Mafia wannabe, who was shylocking to the wrong folks. The interview lasted two hours past any information I required.

Dr. Suehad Fasaid is a Rhodes Scholar from Cairo, Egypt. She is also an ethnic beauty whose wardrobe encompasses short skirts, cleavage exposing blouses, and Victoria's Secret lingerie. The lingerie is simply an assumption on my part based on the Victoria's Secret catalogue on her desk *and* an errant purple bra strap.

I guess she didn't get the Muslim memo on proper dress and demeanor for women. She is an expert on all things Muslim, which is the primary purpose of the call. A secondary motive of a personal nature lurks in my subconscious.

Although the topic was never directly broached, I gather that Suehad is a moderate Muslim who took the good from the Koran but saw past the bullshit in the more extreme teachings. As a Catholic, I understand this religious paradox.

Suehad took her progressive convictions one step further. Five weeks after the 9/11 attacks on New York and Washington, D.C., she created and maintains *"The Jihad Watch"* website. It's sort of a daily terrorist scorecard of Islamic attacks around the world.

A moment after providing my name, rank and serial number to the secretary, I recognize the voice of Dr. Fasaid.

"I'm gonna have to cook up an official reason for this call," I say.

"Nonsense, John Booker," Suehad says. "You're just an incorrigible flirt."

"Maybe a flirt, but *never* incorrigible."

Of course she is right. If a woman is attractive and I'm in a frisky mood, it doesn't matter is she's single, married, infirmed, pregnant, divorced, or attending her husband's funeral. Maybe that's because I never go past the 'flirting' stage.

We catch up on our lives. Suehad is dating but no one seriously, she just returned from a conference in Holland where she presented a paper entitled *The Role of Muslim Woman in Emerging Democracies* and she lost five pounds on a new diet involving seaweed.

We reminisce about the mob shylock and Suehad's associate who was indicted as a co-conspirator in my case. Monica, the co-worker, pled guilty and was sentenced to probation. Shortly after the story appeared in the newspaper, Monica married the shylock, was promoted to department chairwoman and given tenure. Suehad laughs and explains that just last month, "Monica divorced the mob guy and is now having a lesbian relationship with a stripper."

Dr. Monica's lifestyle may seem decadent to some but it triggers some fond memories of my college days at Slippery Rock State.

We take a moment to examine the political landscape, and I share several tactless jokes involving sex and terrorism. Not an easy thing to do. My most juvenile attempt is a riddle. I ask. "What do you call a radical Muslim who owns both a camel and a goat?"

"Haven't the slightest, John."

"A bi-sexual."

Dr. Suehad offers a polite chuckle, and says, "I'll make sure I tell that one at our next sensitivity committee meeting."

"Suehad, I know you're busy. What do you know about Wahhabist ideology?"

"Bad stuff, John. A form of brainwashing that is especially effective on children. It contains most extreme radical Muslim anti-American propaganda that promotes intolerance and violence."

"I just learned that it's being taught in American charter schools. How can these schools get away teaching that crap with public funds?"

"It's not just charter schools, The Omar Ibn Khattab Foundation donated hundreds of copies of *The Meaning of the Holy Quran* to the Los Angeles city school district. Within months, this book had to be pulled from school libraries because of its anti-American commentaries. It called for the end of the United States of America by *whatever* means."

"I know it's all legal but it sure as hell shouldn't be," I say indignantly.

Suehad patiently explains, "Freedom of speech is constitutionally protected in *our* country, Mr. FBI agent. Just last year a U.S. Muslim Congressman officially proposed that American public schools be modeled after Islamic schools and the system called Madrassas with a foundation in the Koran."

"So I guess I should just suit up in sandals and a dashiki, score some dynamite hash and just chill."

"No," Suehad scolds. "But you need to realize that my adopted country is resilient and can withstand some random discourse. You, my friend, should spend your time chasing down guys named Mohammed waiving box cutters at airports." Suehad pauses and her voice becomes playful. "It's my turn for a joke. What is a *real* man's idea of group therapy?"

"I give up."

"World War Two."

"Very funny," I respond with a tinge of mock anger.

Suehad explains. "John, you are a warrior in mid-life crisis. You need to fight another war, knock somebody over the head, or break something. It is commendable, but emotionally dangerous. Most men join a bowling league but you need to slay the dragon. Forget about any Muslim influence in our schools, and concentrate on the dragon."

"You are a wise woman," I say, now weary of the entire charter school mess. "When can we grab some lunch?"

"I'm free tomorrow."

"Frymans at noon?"

"My last class is over at four," Suehad suggests. "Let's make it dinner and drinks." A pause. "Lazzara's at six?"

I am momentarily speechless. "See you there." I mutter, and rationalize this *date* as work-related research. The Catholic side of my brain immediately disputes this fragile supposition. You see the Catholic religion operates on guilt and I am a card-carrying member of that cult.

As I am attempting to digest the *true* meaning of Suehad's invitation, a red flag appears on my computer screen. "See me — URGENT" accompanies the flag. I knock on Boy Wonder's door.

My supervisor seems anxious as he points to an empty seat. "You are going TDY (temporary duty) to D.C." Michaels announces in his official voice. "You leave within the hour."

"What's the case?"

"Assistant Director Anthony Daniels requested you by name," Michaels says, now irritable. "Why you?"

"Tony and I were new agent roommates at the FBI academy." I explain. "He would cheat off me in Forensics class."

Michaels shakes his head and declares, "I doubt that."

"What's the case?" I ask again.

"The Chief Justice of the Supreme Court has been murdered."

CHAPTER 4

"Round up the usual suspects."
—Casablanca

I arrive at Dulles on the last flight from Cleveland and am met by the FBI Assistant Director, Anthony "Tony" Daniels.

Tony is a *'good shit,'* which is actually high praise among law enforcement officers. We were roommates at the academy and have been friends ever since. Tony understands his role with the field. Most officials begin sentences with, *"What's the liability"* but Tony always asks, *"How can we make this work?"* He is more concerned with the greater good and will accept the occasional stain of a career shit bomb for the good of a case.

Another dirty little secret is that many FBI bosses are frightened of failure and thus evolve into decision-avoiding obstructionists. Their primary goal is the continued advancement through the puzzle palace in D.C. One bad decision can delay or terminate their journey.

They can no longer articulate the reason they *became* part of Federal Bureau of Investigation. It certainly wasn't for the repetitive thrill of scribbling their initials on the reports of brick agents. Maybe they just enjoy the endless stream of tedious pointless meetings. At some point in their bureaucratic journey, these boy wonders actually believe that paper shuffling is not only important, but also terribly challenging.

I have an ongoing love-hate relationship with the FBI. It is the finest law enforcement agency on earth and if my daughter was kidnapped, I'd want them on the case. But, like any large institution, we recruit from the human race and it has evolved in directions which now threaten its very identity.

We hug and exchange pleasantries but there is a sense of urgency, so Tony briefs me on the case.

Douglas Michael Williams has the distinction of being the *first* sitting Chief Justice of the United States Supreme Court to be murdered. A simple mugging 'gone bad' is the *unofficial* police verdict. The *official* report is couched in police verbiage, diagrams, crime scene photos, CSI reports, and fifty-two interviews resulting from a neighborhood canvass, all concluding with … *subject(s) still at large.*

At approximately 8:47 P.M., the seventy-three year old judge was walking his west highland terrier, Ollie, short for, *Oliver Wendell Holmes Jr.*, when he was allegedly approached by two black youths who demanded money. The judge refused and began to lecture the delinquents who promptly 'shived' him in his carotid artery and ran off into the night. Ollie, being a typical terrier, gave chase and has not been seen since.

Agents establish that Williams had no items of value on his person. His housekeeper was adamant that Williams left both cash and wallet at home when walking the dog at night. She explained that he was fearful of being robbed.

The Chief Justice died on scene, though the EMTs would never make such a hasty medical diagnosis on a nationally known dignitary. The frantic ambulance ride included every piece of resuscitation equipment in the bag. Justice Williams was finally pronounced dead at Georgetown University Hospital *after* ER doctors spent an additional hour of basically beating up on a corpse.

'*A robbery gone bad*' in Washington D.C. is about as common as a fart in a chili emporium. But when the victim is a Supreme Court Chief Justice, it becomes an extraordinarily unique event.

Tony drives me to the crime scene so I can get a visual "feel" of the scene. I always place myself in the role of both victim *and* suspect, looking for any inconsistencies in the general consensus. There weren't any. We visit the mobile command post where introductions are made. I review some reports and briefly speak with the case agent. Fred Gregory is a former Georgia State Trooper and the biggest black guy I've ever seen. With his shaved head, intimidating glare and muscular body, I am ready to confess my theft of ice cream in the third grade. But I get a really good vibe from the no-nonsense Agent Fred. At this point in the investigation everyone is in a chaotic reactionary mode. This is normal.

I ask Tony, "Why Gregory?"

Tony smiles and explains, "His nickname is Thumper."

"Thumper? Okay, I'll play. How'd he get the moniker Thumper?"

"Well Fred was one of the first black state troopers in Georgia and it seems that the bubbas didn't like being pulled over by a big black guy with a badge. So, Fred had to *thump* a bunch of rednecks." Tony smiles and adds, "*And*, a former Marine." A reference to my alma mater.

"I like him already."

I couldn't figure out my presence here since locating two inner city thugs is child's play for someone of Thumper's pedigree. Offer a twenty grand reward, roust some snitches, and the tip hotline will burn out.

"You got hundreds of agents, as well as the resources of the entire government at your disposal, why me?" I ask.

"Thumper is a good man and *you* are a pain in the ass, but you see things differently, think outside the box, *and* will do things most agents won't."

I understand the Assistant Director's meaning. Tony may need someone who will occasionally color outside the lines, disregard a few guidelines, break several policies, and if need be, bend a law or two. That someone would be me.

Dirty little secrets continued. I am *not* the only federal agent who would smack around a kidnapper to find the child. Twenty years ago this behavior caused a wink and nod from the bosses but in today's Bureau, you will be fired, indicted, and possibly face a firing squad.

The lone witness is Loretta Gould, an eighty-two year old great grandmother, also out walking her dog in the trendy Georgetown section of town. She wasn't sure of much more than ... *two black boys*, and a *scuffle*. Nothing about their age, height, or weight, but, "*Two black boys* ... and, *scuffle.*" Mrs. Gould was also positive that "*They just stabbed the poor man and ran off.*"

No matter how many complex conspiracy theories I mull over, this killing is basically your everyday robbery gone terribly wrong. It seems to involve two ghetto thugs already high on some controlled substance and looking for more drug money. It is their misfortune that the victim is one of the most powerful men in the United States.

I watch the sun rise above a Starbucks and realize that I am exhausted. Tony points to a car and provides directions to a hotel in Northern Virginia. Before I pass out I remember to text Suehad and cancel tonight's, *dinner, drinks, and* ... whatever.Even at this early hour, she responds within minutes with regrets and suggests a rain check.

I immediately reply with, '*Can't wait!!!*'

Congress should pass a law restricting the use of electronic devices for men who are either drunk or tired. It should include, but not be limited to, cell phones, texts, e-mails, and even fax machines. The three exclamation points had crossed the line. Real men just don't put exclamation points on text messages. I rationalize exhaustion and realize that I am behaving like a stalker. A pang of guilt triggers images of Lorri and Nikki and I promise myself *not* to have dinner with Suehad. I recognize that we are auditioning for an affair but I love my wife. I resolve to stay faithful, but a minute later my mind strays to the image of Suehad's purple bra strap and my little meat puppet sits up and begins doing calisthenics. So much for good intentions.

I awake and find my way to the Washington FBI field office. An agent from the crime scene recognizes me and directs me to the conference room, which has been reconfigured for a major case. It is a beehive of activity with dozens of video screens, frenzied phone conversations, and analysts pecking away at computers. I head straight for the table with the coffee and bagels. The killers had not been located during my four-hour nap, but there were plenty of *'black boys'* in the hood who had been hassled and threatened.

Each FBI case is assigned a case agent. That agent calls the shots and their authority is sacrosanct. This system has worked well for many years, so I feel like a gatecrasher who had scalped a ticket to the game. Being a *'friend'* of an Assistant Director should not entitle me to front row seats, let alone calling plays from the sidelines. Special Agent Frederick Gregory is competent, professional, and *busy*. He is covering all the bases and the killers *will* be located, arrested, and convicted in short order. Gregory did not need nor *want* my help so I excuse myself and find an empty computer.

An intelligence analyst directs me into the case files, which examine the Justice's cases over his entire career. Gregory had ordered this particular database to possibly identify a disgruntled defendant that Williams may have pissed off from the bench.

The file contains subsections on Williams' judicial journey, beginning with his first job as a Philadelphia city prosecutor. It cataloguess stops as an Assistant United States Attorney, magistrate, common pleas judge, state appeals judge, federal judge, and finally an appointment to the Supreme Court by Republican President Ronald Reagan.

There can be no confusing Williams' ideological leanings. Having served as a Marine Corps company commander in Vietnam, Captain Williams won the Silver Star for his actions during the Tet Offensive. Upon his discharge he enrolled at the University of Pennsylvania law school and began his climb through the judicial ranks. Williams was a strict constitutionalist who viewed the Constitution as the basis for each and every judicial decision. A two-fisted law and order enthusiast, he adored the second amendment. His decisions were consistent and in my humble opinion, impeccable. I take notes as I review the report.

Forty-seven cases involving civil rights. Nineteen decisions involving abortion cases. One hundred and five cases involving search and seizure issues. There were hundreds of other cases pertaining to a wide variety of legal issues. But throughout, Williams was consistently tough on criminals and remained judicially unswerving in his basic belief of God, family, country. His *official* bio included altar boy, Eagle Scout, and life member of the American Legion. Basically, the judge was my kind of guy.

There are *always* two sides to a case so *any* judicial rendering will infuriate *somebody*. With this in mind, I conclude that the conservative judge had pissed off *thousands* of people, making it problematic to point a finger at a specific suspect, *or*, group.

I find Tony sitting behind a desk large enough to land a Cessna airplane. He asks me what I think.

"I think I should go back to Cleveland," I say.

"Going with the simple robbery scenario?"

"That's the one," I confirm. "It fits."

He relents. "Well, give my best to Lorri and Nikki."

"Will do. Tell Nancy I got a great seaweed diet for her."

"You know, it *could* be a radical domestic group. Williams has pissed off those yahoos," Tony muses. "Like ELF, PETA, or even a Nazi skinhead group."

"Doesn't fit," I counter. "What about the eyewitness ... try visualizing two black gangster rappers doing '*seig heils*' at a Neo Nazi meeting."

Tony laughs. "I'll take you to the airport, and...."

A heavy rap on the office door followed by the entrance of Special Agent Fred Gregory who announces, "We may have something."

Thumper explains that the police found the bodies of two young black males in a crack house a mile from the murder.

"And why is this unusual?" Tony asks.

"They both had OD'd on some bad heroin," Gregory explains.

"Still doesn't tie them to Judge Williams." I throw in my two cents.

Gregory barely acknowledges my presence and says to Tony, "There's more. A bloody knife consistent with Judge Williams' wounds was found in the crack house."

"Get it to our lab ASAP for a DNA match!" Tony orders.

"Already en route." Gregory confirms. "But the lab did a quick typing. Came back as AB negative, which is relatively rare. And it just so happens that Williams also is AB negative."

"Good stuff," Tony offers. "But we'll need more to close *this* particular case."

"There is another bit of evidence," Gregory nods and smiles like a man about to throw his full house onto the green felt. He says, "There was a West Highland Terrier gnawing away at the deceased eyeballs. Gregory turns and looks me straight in the eye and finishes with. "In case you don't know, *John*, that is *not* your typical ghetto pet."

Gregory earned that shot at my bow.

"This is sounding better and better," Tony prompts.

"The dog's ID tag came back to the Chief Justice of the Supreme Court."

"Glad the *dog* survived," I say in complete sincerity.

Tony and I spend the remainder of the day tying up loose ends. The two black males are identified as eighteen-year old Ronald Jones and nineteen-year old Reginald Thomas. They have lengthy rap sheets graduating from general mopery to aggravated assault and drug trafficking. I personally believe that Ronald and Reginald's exit from the human race is terrific. Sorry to say so, but they were *never* going to be productive members of society or evolve past the primitive state of pillaging and plundering. And, they are *not* victims in any sense of the word but predators who will rape your daughter and feel nothing but smug success.

Another dirty little FBI secret—*most FBI agents were rooting for Charles Bronson in those vigilante movies.* And anyone who feels differently is probably against childhood obesity but loves Michael Moore.

Tony takes me to his favorite Italian restaurant in D.C. We are heading in the general direction of the airport for my return trip to Ohio. He recommends the Linguini with red clam sauce, topped off with the best Tiramisu this side of Calabria. Assistant Director Daniels takes off his official cloak and becomes Tony *the roommate:* a down-to-earth, irreverent, and funny guy who was victorious in a farting contest as a rookie agent at the academy. But rather than forget such a classless act, the Assistant Director mentions it whenever he can. He once began a speech using the disgusting contest as an example for bonding and team building.

We clink glasses and toast the quick resolution to such a historically significant homicide case. He says, "I guess you were right and I was wrong. You had the botched robbery motive from the get go. I was looking for some grand conspiracy."

I laugh out loud and say, "So nothing's changed since the academy. I was *always* right." I pause and get serious. "Tony, your agents did a great job. They solved this horrendous crime in thirty-six hours. It's got no loose ends."

As soon as I utter these words, a little warning bell goes off in my brain. It's like a weather advisory interrupting the regularly scheduled program. The scroll at the bottom of the screen is warning me that the case was *too* neatly wrapped in an investigative bow. Why kill an old man, *before* robbing him? According to the eyewitness, they never patted Justice Williams down even as he lay on the ground. Killing him seemed to be their sole purpose, but I am the paranoid undercover, so I congratulate my friend and confirm. "Case closed."

We spend some time gossiping about our classmates. Ken Dole was killed in the Miami shootout in 1996, Tommy Norton had been fired for theft, Tonya Kowolski opted for a sex change, Brad Candlless quit the B for the priesthood, and Tony Daniels made it to the number four man in the entire Federal Bureau of Investigation. Not your *typical* new agent training class.

Tony sips from a vodka tonic and enters evangelical preaching mode. "This death translates into some real bad shit for us."

"How so?"

"Our President gets to nominate the justice's successor and that idiot is sure to pick some far left weenie. Got any idea what that means?"

"It can't be good," I reply.

Tony shares some inside the beltway scuttlebutt. "Williams was the swing vote in a moderate court. The guy, gal, or *whatever* who replaces him will tilt that court to the left for decades to come. Law enforcement will have their hands tied with precedent cases giving the bad guys more rights than the good guys. "

Another dirty little FBI secret is that most federal agents *and* Marines are conservatives. They will lay their life down to protect the *office* of the President but wouldn't lose any sleep if a liberal president croaked from syphilis.

He says, "Have any idea what cases are on the docket this term?"

"Haven't the slightest," I confess. I don't like this guy any more than you do, but we're stuck with him. We survived Jimmy Carter and we'll survive this one."

Tony smiles and agrees. "Yea, I always suspected that Rosalyn had the balls in that family."

We finish our meal, have a second cocktail, and head to the airport. Tony is off on another diatribe as he maneuvers through Washington traffic. I hear every fifth word as my mind meanders through images of my wife, job, the Pittsburgh Steelers' chances for the playoffs, and Suehad's boobs. As we pull curbside next to the Delta departure, Tony fires off one final rant. "They're going to rule on racial profiling, expedited search and seizure, and granting military status to terrorists. A bad decision on any one of them will put a knife through the heart of our war on terrorism."

As I board the plane to Cleveland, I think about Tony's angst concerning our President. Our government continually cycles through divergent ideological leaders. When things get too extreme, one way or the other, then the citizens balance the ship and we sail on as the greatest country on earth. I could never envision America destroyed by some court decisions, or a few ideologically skewed officials.

That is what my heart told me, but similar to a minority jurist in Supreme Court decisions, my brain is slowly forming a dissenting opinion.

CHAPTER 5

"They're not gonna catch us-we're on a mission from God."
— The Blues Brothers

"Corpsman up!" someone screams.

The voice sounded like mine but that just couldn't be. This desperate cry had always been reserved for the *other* unlucky soul who'd forever walk with a limp or be zipped into a dark green body bag.

"I'm hit!" the same voice says.

"Don't look too good, Booker," Doc Ker says after a quick inventory of my body.

"Fuck you," I spit back, needing to irrationally lash out at *someone*. The smell of cordite and singed flesh is in the air. My instincts on this one are bad as I somehow know the worst is yet to come.

The pain arrives in waves replacing the initial shock as Doc's mud covered hands push and pull at my torn burnt flesh. An Improvised Explosive Device more commonly known to the troops as a *fucking IED* had exploded some eight feet from me. Silver cylinders of morphine are injected somewhere below my gaze and the pain in my legs slowly dissipates. The usually familiar words in the Act of Contrition suddenly become a mystery so I opt for an unscripted conversation with God, "Just let me live."

My impromptu chat is interrupted by an al-Qaeda rocket-propelled grenade which sends shrapnel through Doc Ker's head. The deal with God is off. I attempt to propel myself backwards until I discover the lifeless body of the corpsman across my numb legs. From somewhere off in the distant chaos of battle I hear more screams and I *know* that it's over.

My squad was ambushed by a company of al-Qaeda regulars during a routine patrol. They had us in a crossfire killing zone and were now maneuvering into position for the grand finale as I lay as helpless as a turtle on its back. A rash of M-16 fire signals our last gasp. I had seen what terrorists do to captured Marines and resolve not be paraded through the streets dragged by a rope while being spit upon and ultimately beheaded on camera.

Instead, I claw open my holster and aim the pistol at the approaching doom. I boost my torso to an upright position and am startled at the apparition before me. It is my daughter. Nikki is dressed in her immaculate white confirmation dress, walking calmly in my direction. Standing over my leaking body, she smiles and offers her hand. "Let's go home daddy." Nikki says. As I reach for her hand, I hear a panicked scream.

It's Lorri shaking me. The bedside clock indicates it's five in the morning, and my poor wife has been through this drill before. For some reason I apologize though I have no control over my demons. It takes a moment to gather myself before I head to the kitchen for some coffee and alone time. The bed is soaked with the sweat of my recurring nightmare. Iraq always seems to push its ugly recall button in times of doubt and uncertainty. Something bad is lurking within the shadows of my brain.

I turn on the television to breaking news. The European and Asian stock markets are in the midst of a meltdown. They plummeted some four hundred points and financial experts are scrambling for an explanation. Predictions on its effect of the U.S. market are dire. CNN reports that our dismal unemployment figures just released will fuel further decline of Dow Jones. Fox News feels that the continuing subprime housing debacle combined with tax hikes will cause a deep plunge in the U.S. market.

I switch to Sports Center because in this day and age, one becomes immune to *"breaking news."* The sun always comes up in the morning and no matter how you feel when looking at images of children in Africa with distended bellies and circling flies, as soon as you walk away from the television screen, everything is normal again.

I take a shower and pack my bags. It has been six months since my transfer to the task force and so far I've been on nine interviews and twelve surveillance operations. I'm fairly certain that I had not come within two hundred nautical miles of a terrorist, but who knows.

The remainder of my time is spent requesting a transfer. The problem with doing nothing is that you don't know when you are finished. The Special Agent in Charge (SAC) wants an experienced criminal investigator on that squad. That would be me. Jack Bell is an old school organized crime agent who earned his bones on the streets of New York chasing gumbas.

Bell is sympathetic but does not mince his words. *"You're staying on the JTTF, John, and that's that."*

Prior to 9/11, there was a clear line in the sand separating a criminal agent from a Foreign Counter Intelligence agent. A large part of that divide was their intended mission; criminal agents put people in jail and FCI agents gather intelligence. An FCI agent will get an erection by simply determining the color of socks worn by a subject, but a criminal agent's orgasm can only be achieved by slapping cuffs on bad guys. The two sides rarely spoke unless it was at the FBI Christmas party.

I always maintained that a terrorist is your basic garden variety scum bag criminal. It took the worst tragedy on American soil to get the FBI hierarchy to realize this simple truth. Terrorists are in reality, dumb, ruthless, religious hypocrites who go to strip joints, watch pornography, and treat women with contempt. Just like Italian men.

Today, I head to the FBI academy at Quantico, for in-service training on Counter-Terrorism. It is the right of passage for JTTF agents. The training consists of a weeklong series of stimulating lectures given by counter terrorist experts from both the FBI and CIA. Given the choice, I would rather be water boarded than sit sedentary in a windowless room for a week.

One hour had elapsed since my very vocal nightmare and Lorri is still awake as I approach our bed. I whisper, "Gotta go, I'll call when I get to Quantico."

She leans forward, kisses my lips and asks, "Are you alright, John?"

"I'm fine," I lie.

"Are *we* OK? You've been distant, John."

"Just need a mental enema."

Lorri sometimes surprises me with little flashes of insecurity. If I were a more manipulative man, I would promote this insecurity as a means of keeping her attention, if not her affection.

"When I get back, maybe we can get away, just the two of us."

"I'd like that."

I occasionally need an injection of Lorri Booker. It makes me bolder and more self-assured. We may not be the perfect married couple, but that couple didn't exist, except on old television shows. All married couples experience relationship speed bumps, though every now and then a gas tank explodes.

The FBI academy at Quantico Virginia is a self-contained city with glass-enclosed gerbil-like tunnels connecting banks, chow halls, a gym, and living quarters. It's a secure womb surrounded by the Marine Corps base and plush pine forest. I arrive after the dinner hour and settle on a vending machine chicken salad sandwich, and peanut butter crackers. I find my dorm room and fall fast asleep. I awake to a crisp October morning and head to the mess hall. Contrary to what you may hear, the food at the academy is first-rate and plentiful. Anyone who complains must either be a militant vegan or a Kardashian.

I glance at my course outline over scrambled eggs and bacon, and learn that my primary instructor is Grant Beck of the Central Intelligence Agency. Grant is the operations officer in charge of the Egyptian desk at Langley. You've probably heard all the stories about how the FBI and CIA don't share information and can't get along. All true. After 9/11, the CIA announced that they would *now* cooperate more openly with the FBI. They just haven't told the FBI yet.

I arrive at my stadium-style seating classroom with a cup of coffee and bagel in hand and sit squarely beneath the sign prohibiting food or drinks. It's a test. Grant Beck stares in my direction, checks my name on the seating roster, and says pleasantly, "Good morning, Agent Booker. You must be the class anarchist."

I smile and raise my coffee cup in a toast to the victor of round one. This quick and clever aside leaves me with a deep appreciation of a fellow sarcastic prick. I couldn't *help* but like the guy. I will now have to raise my bantering level to keep pace. Beck smiles back then addresses the class providing a brief intro to the course. And thus begins my education into the fascinating world of terrorism.

"Radical Islam's kinship with terrorism and its willingness to use violence is spelled out in the Koran. An Islamic government would never be established *except* by the bomb and rifle. Islam does not coexist or make a truce with unbelief, but rather confronts it. The confrontation that Islam calls for with these godless regimes, like Americans and Jews, does not know Socratic debates or diplomacy. It only knows the dialogue of bullets, assassinations and the sword."

Beck glides back and forth across the floor occasionally pausing to regroup. He has a pleasant voice and I think I detect a New England accent.

"Radical Islamists tend to gravitate toward three major methods of achieving their objective. The first is to fight the Near Enemy who is anyone inside Islamic lands. The second is to fight the Greater Unbelief — the major enemy, which today is the United States. And the third method is to fight the Apostates, which are the false Muslims."

I barely glance toward the clock as morning turns into afternoon. We take a few coffee breaks and a short pause for lunch. After lunch, I ask a question. "You use the term 'radical Islam,' and 'jihadist' interchangeably, but can we also add the term, 'radical Muslim' to that group?"

Beck takes a few seconds to digest the question and says, "The general public seems to group the three together, but it's important to understand that most Muslims are *not* radical."

"Agreed," I say. "But most Muslims *contribute* to the radicals agenda."

"How so, Agent Booker?"

"Because there's no such thing as a peace-loving Muslim."

He smiles and says, "I can't wait to hear this explanation."

"Muslims, whether they be radical or meek, will become our enemy since their religion will never accept any type of Christianity and the Koran encourages Muslims to kill the unbelievers by whatever means. You said so yourself."

Beck smiles and nods his head in assent, "Continue."

I nod back and say, "These non-radical Muslims have also been made irrelevant by their silence and one day soon they'll find that the fanatics own them, and the end of *their* world will have begun."

"So you've studied the Muslim culture and the Koran?" Beck challenges.

"Not really," I reply. "But I *am* a student of history and millions of Germans, Japanese, Chinese, Russians, Rwandans, Serbians, and Algerians, have died because the peaceful majority did not speak up *until* it was too late."

FBI Agent Jerry Yanello jumps in with, "In the U.K and Paris, the Muslim communities refuse to integrate and there are now dozens of "no-go" zones within major cities that the police force *dare* not intrude upon." Agent Bill Garret adds, "Sharia law prevails there, because the Muslim communities in those areas refuse to acknowledge British or French law, *and* there are actually civilian Sharia courts in Texas and other American cities."

This nugget produces several minutes of comments and asides among the class. Beck maneuvers the conversation back *'on point'* with questions and comments. I'm not sure he welcomes our departure from his lesson plan but the CIA spook seems to be enjoying the mild debate. When we students exhaust our editorial asides he asks, "Any more questions?"

There are none.

"Well then," Beck says. "See you tomorrow."

Following class, I take a leisurely three-mile run on the tank trail. The sounds of Marines training with small arms fire, helicopters, and howitzer rounds fill the air. It is music to my ears. A quick shower and it's off to the Board Room which is actually a beer hall where the actual learning of the FBI academy takes place. FBI agents, police officers, and the faculty gather at day's end for a bullshit session. Friendships are forged over popcorn and beer.

I spot Mr. Beck holding court with several classmates. There are pitchers of beer on the table, along with a basket of half-eaten chicken wings. The conversation sounds a bit animated.

Beck is dressed down in khakis, Dockers, and a perfect haircut. I usually steer clear of this type. He greets me as I sit.

"Just in time to break a tie, Agent Booker."

"At your service."

"We've been continuing our class debate and Agent Yanello believes that we have basically won the war on terrorism, but I beg to differ."

Yanello adds, "There'll always be some type of terrorism aimed at America, but we basically destroyed their infrastructure. We've isolated their cells and killed off their leaders. There have been only two attacks on American soil since 9/11, so I rest my case."

"But can we look at terrorist in the same way we viewed the Nazis or Japanese in World War Two?" Beck challenges. "That war had a beginning, middle and end. They surrendered with the understanding that to continue the war meant the annihilation of their homeland, culture, and way of life."

Yanello counters, "That proves my point, Grant. Terrorists don't have the advantage of a government that can produce weapons, ships, airplanes, and troops."

"I agree with Jerry," Bill Garret adds. "You said yourself that terrorists are divided into cells and that the cells operate independently. So how can they organize into a sizable credible threat if they're a bunch of isolated rag tailed thugs?"

Beck asks, "Remember the January 2015 terror attacks in Paris when 13 people were killed at that magazine Charlie Hebdo?"

Garret adds, "*Then* the three suspects in the attacks were killed by police."

"Correct, Bill," Beck says, "but what the public *never* heard was that Saida Kouachi, one of the brothers involved in the attack, fought for al-Qaida in Yemen."

Garret wonders, "So if I'm hearing you, Grant, although terrorists operate independently, they can and *do* communicate."

"All good points," Beck agrees. He looks my way and asks. "What say you, Agent Booker?"

"Terrorists are dumb shitheads who do not present a military threat."

"But are they *all* dumb shitheads?" Beck challenges.

I offer, "Terrorists are untrained goat fuckers living in caves. They pretend to be religious fanatics and a few will strap explosives on their balls and take one for Allah but they're basically dumb shitheads who can never organize enough past some isolated murder and mayhem. They got lucky on 9/11 but will *never* present a serious threat to the American way of life.

Yanello laughs and says, "Right on, Booker."

CIA operations officer Grant Beck gives a sly smile and asks, "Possibly, *but*, what if a few terrorist were both brilliant *and* organized?"

"Then the United States would be in a world of shit."

CHAPTER 6

"Pain is inevitable, but misery is optional."
– L/Cpl Eddie Neas at Hue City

I've come to love the city of Cleveland. It offers all the amenities of a New York City minus the attitude. You can enjoy major league sports, live theatre, receive topnotch health care, *and* actually find a parking space.

But the sad reality is that Cleveland is slowly dying and all the doctors at the Cleveland Clinic can't save the patient. Residents are deserting the ship in droves for warmer climes and employment opportunities.

Cleveland has the highest foreclosure rate in the nation; its neighborhoods are being abandoned, and crime is rampant. Once-proud areas such as the Flats now feature toothless hookers with herpes offering twenty dollar blow jobs.

I return from my terrorism indoctrination at Quantico with a slightly better attitude. Grant Beck and I had become buds. We convened nightly in the Board Room over beers and argued a wide range of topics including but not limited to sports, movies, married life and midget wrestling. Beck's favorite grappler was a Chinese dwarf with the moniker of Pee Wee Lee.

Beck also convinced me that I can make a difference in the war on terrorism *in* Cleveland. He encouraged me to think outside the box and constantly review the top secret intelligence bulletins. As we were saying our goodbyes on Friday, Beck became serious and said. "John, you have a gift for this, an ability to think like them."

"Them?" I ask.

"Don't take offense, but yes, them ... *bad people*. You understand *them*. All bad people have one thing in common. They do *bad* things. Whether it's a tax cheat, drug dealer or terrorist, you have an ability to crawl inside that brain."

"Thank you, I think?" I mutter.

Beck reminds me for the fourth time to read the intelligence bulletins. Since I am new to the world of counterintelligence I ask him how we gather the information contained in the bulletins.

The CIA spook smiles and provides me the abridged version. He says, "There are four different collection *disciplines* of intelligence."

Beck explains that HUMINT or **Hum**an **Int**elligence is the collection of raw intelligence from agents working in the field. IMINT: **Im**agery **Int**elligence is the interpretation of photographs from aerial units or satellites. SIGMINT: **Sig**nal **Int**elligence consists of radar intelligence and, COMINT which consists of **Com**munications **Int**elligence which deals with electronic signals which contain speech or text.

Beck finishes his mini lecture with, "COMINT is a very valuable asset since it picks up chatter from cell phones, radio transmissions, and the Internet. Our computers then kick out certain buzz or red flag words and analyze them for patterns or specific threats."

I thank him again and we promise to keep in touch. I intend to keep my end of the bargain. Beck will be a terrific resource *if* I ever catch a case involving an actual terrorist.

It's a cold and dreary Monday morning back in Cleveland. I log onto my Bureau computer to discover sixty three e-mails.

I punch my delete key on most messages, reply with several electronic "Okays" and glance at the seven with red flags. Boy Wonder has struck again with urgent communications to yours truly. His most recent e-mails combine some new guidelines and a request to see him *immediately* upon my return from Quantico. Neither of which seemed critical to the survival of mankind. My personal standard for anything *urgent* requires the presence of gushing blood.

My Marine Corps service spoiled me. I witnessed inspired leadership under the most intense conditions. Matt Michaels views the troops as pawns in his personal chess game. Another FBI dirty little secret is that many FBI supervisors have never made a *single* arrest. They make the leap into management after a year or two of being *co*-case agents on a major case, and then it's off to the puzzle palace in D.C. for some seasoning and back out into the field as supervisors. They are now in a position of supervising field agents minus any experience of *being* a field agent.

I need a hug so on my way to Michaels' office I make a stop at our squad secretary's cubicle. Peggy Munson was hired under the umbrella of the American Disabilities Act. She is a chunky black woman with Tourette syndrome. Peggy is competent, smart, industrious, and didn't require any government bonus points. She wears a perpetual smile, sings in her church choir, and curses like a drunken sailor, compliments of Tourette syndrome.

I approach Peggy and say. "Hi sweetie, miss me?

"You're my favorite John Booker," Peggy says. "Ain't the same here when you're gone." She pauses and screams, "Shit!"

I generally ignore her unintended profanities but every once in a while, I can't control myself. Peggy also has this endearing quality of addressing everyone by both their first and last name.

"Boy Wonder wants to see me," I say. "Is pecker head available?"

Peggy smiles. "Now don't go making me laugh John Booker," she pleas. "He's just an anxious soul."

"You've seen them all, Peggy. This new crop of agents seem a somber group to you?"

"Not like the old days. No practical joking, no laughing, no characters. They just come in and stare at the computer all day then go home." You are a dying breed, John Booker." After a brief pause Peggy adds the addendum of three cuss words.

"A flawless trifecta of vulgar language," I say. "I am impressed with your range."

Peggy laughs and says, "Now you know I can't help myself, John Booker."

Just as I am about to slander Michaels again the power goes out. The overhead lights, computers, and everything else that depends on electricity go 10-7. A moment later, the emergency generator kicks on and restores most of the power. It's amazing how much law enforcement depends on electricity. In that brief period I realize that our communication system is gone, wire taps discontinued, our armory locked down, and access to sensitive areas severely compromised.

Michaels sticks his head out the office door, looks around, and says to no one in particular, "Lights went out in there." There, being his office. He notices me, shoots his practiced grimace. "Come in my office, John, let's *chat*."

I follow my leader into his inner sanctum and slouch into a chair. Just for the record, men don't *chat*. We *talk, speak, discuss, consult, confer* and occasionally, *shoot the shit,* but we *never* chat.

I have a bad habit of slouching in chairs. It originated in grade school as I attempted to avoid eye contact with teachers. I realize that my behavior is a notch above holding my breath on the passive-aggressive scale, but Boy Wonder pushes all my buttons.

Michaels actually lowers his head to make eye contact and says. "So tell me about the training.

As I am about to provide an extremely abridged version the phone rings. Michaels rolls his eyes at me and with just two fingers, he daintily picks up the receiver. "Michaels here," he announces in his official voice.

A few ... "*ah has,*" followed by, "*that serious, huh?*" He finishes with a flourish of "*Yes sir, I'll get right on it.*"

"That was Jack Bell," Michaels announces. "There is a regional power outage and the entire office is being mobilized."

Michaels wonders. "Why is the FBI involved in a power outage?"

I say, "The Perry Nuclear plant is a few miles east of here, we've got international airports, and a U.S. Mint around the corner. I pause and add a cynical, "And that's just for starters."

At eleven o'clock, an all-office meeting convenes in the operations center. One hundred and forty three individuals comprised of agents, intel analysts, and an array of support staff make small talk while awaiting Bell. The SAC enters the room and all talk ceases. He climbs the stairs to a stage and stands before a floor to ceiling screen with a color map of the United States on display. The affected area of the blackout is outlined in red and federal installations marked with a blue X.

"Gentlemen *and* Ladies," he begins, "the news is bad. Half of the population is without power as the grids covering nineteen states broke down. The power loss includes grid failures on the entire eastern seaboard and as far west as Michigan. It is the biggest power outage in U.S. history."

I sit in the back of the room with Bruce and S.W.A.T. Boy attempting to absorb the enormity of the situation. The news goes from bad to worst. Bell continues while pointing at the map. "The outage affected a wide swath of territory in the U.S. and Canada including New York City, Albany, Hartford, Toronto, Ottawa, Detroit, Cleveland, and Ontario."

"Right here in Cleveland, the loss of power also means a loss of water as there is no way to continue pumping water to 1.5 million people. We have reports of store owners engaged in price gouging for water and other items, including batteries. Wall Street has suspended trading. If the power outage continues for any length of time an already fragile U.S. economy could go on life support."

Bell pauses and checks his notes. "Subway and train systems in the major east coast cities are down. Meteorologists forecast frigid temperatures tonight and officials fear over flowing shelters and fires as citizens use faulty fireplaces to keep warm."

Our SAC presses a computer key and assignments appear on screen. I am to report to Captain Ray Kopka of the Cleveland Police Department as the FBI liaison. This is a critical role since local police have a healthy paranoia of the Feds. It is a somewhat deserved reputation since many FBI agents treat *locals* as second-rate law enforcement officers. My father was a Philadelphia police officer so I grew up among the Philly coppers. Some real tough hombres. They were an irreverent, boozing, hard charging band of brothers who could *never* be considered *second* to anyone.

My job is to support the Cleveland Police Department during the blackout and provide any federal law enforcement assistance they may require. It is a critical assignment since police are the true first responders.

Michaels raises a scrawny hand and asks, "What about our precarious nuclear plants?"

Bell says, "Good question Matt." and explains that nine nuclear power reactors—six in New York and one each in New Jersey, Ohio and Michigan—were shut down because of the loss of offsite power, according to the Nuclear Regulatory Commission in Bethesda Maryland.

An hour ago my supervisor had no idea Ohio had nuclear power plants so his question is pure ass lick. In a strange way, I have to admire his total lack of self-respect.

Gombar wonders. "Any time frame to get power back on line, and is terrorism suspected?"

Bell begins a nervous pace. "Utility experts have no time frame on restoring power since they have no clue what caused the blackout, and regarding the second question, there is no indication that this was a terrorist act. No group has claimed responsibility and our intelligence did not have this on their radar."

Gombar follows up with, "Could our intelligence have missed something?"

"Possible," Bell muses. "But I doubt that our intelligence could have missed something this big. We would've definitely had *some* indication."

"Any other questions?" The SAC wonders. A few hands jerk up and Bell answers the remaining questions. He finishes with, "You are agents for the Federal Bureau of Investigation. Now go do your jobs."

As I am leaving the conference room Michaels intercepts me and says, "Thank you for the 'heads up' on the nuclear plant."

"My pleasure," I say with all the cheerfulness I can muster.

I gather my handheld radio, battery, cuffs, extra 9MM magazines, and for good measure check out an MP5 from the armory, because as Bob Conile once said, *"If you find yourself in a fair fight, your tactics suck."*

CHAPTER 7

"Hell is empty and all the devils are here."
— William Shakespeare

Day one of the blackout. Traffic lights are out throughout downtown Cleveland, creating havoc at the beginning of rush hour. A wet snow began a steady assault on highways and sidewalks. People who normally use mass transit are hitchhiking, walking across bridges, or trying to find open bars and restaurants. At this early stage of the blackout the hot rumor blames terrorists, along with a promise of additional mayhem at any moment. People are on the verge of panic, attempting to vacate the downtown before a second strike. Wailing ambulances can be heard on a continuous basis as pedestrians are struck by motorists frantically rushing home to their families. The police radio spews non-stop emergency calls ranging from theft of flashlights to cold-blooded murder.

It's now around ten at night or so, and I'm sitting in the passenger seat of a Cleveland Police car rolling through the heart of Cleveland. Captain Ray Kopka is a big man of few words who exudes a quiet confidence. We go through the customary whooping crane ritual, verbally circling each other in an attempt to establish trust. We find some common ground with the Marine Corps. Kopka is an old Gunnery Sergeant who fought in the final days of Vietnam. Marines tend to give other Marines the benefit of the doubt when first introduced. It's a brotherhood and one must prove to be a real asshole to screw it up. My additional ace in the hole is my father. He spent twenty-five years as a Philadelphia police officer, so I'm aware of how that generation of street cops view the world.

It is a moonless evening with a light snow falling. Streets usually bathed in light and marquees are pitch black and seem empty, although they aren't. A closer look reveals someone walking or standing in the darkness, wondering what to do next. Some people hold blackout parties in restaurants, on sidewalks, or gather in circles around candles stuck in bottles. Alcohol lessens fear and the unknown but not for long. Eventually you must face the demon and do so with a hangover.

We pull the black and white to the curb and I say to no one in particular, "How's it going?"

"I'm scared," Lois Dutchman answers. "It's creepy. Everyone's panicking. The city's shutting down. What's going on?"

The patrol car is suddenly encircled with concerned citizens. They want answers. The questions and comments come in rapid fire.

"When's the power coming on?"

"Somebody tried to rob me and I tried to call 911 and couldn't get through."

"Who did this?"

"Is the city running some more buses?"

"You fuckin' assholes need to fix this shit and quit bullshitting with us."

Following this last comment, I turn to Kopka and say. "He must be talking to you."

A smile barely creases the Captain's lips as he pulls away.

Along several blocks of St. Clair Ave., some deli, grocery and restaurant owners bring their suddenly unrefrigerated food out on tables, iced in buckets. "Half price on everything," reads one sign.

Power company officials have spent the day speculating on the cause of the power outage. One theory is a power transmission problem from Canada as the most likely cause, said a spokeswoman.

However, Canadian authorities said it appeared lightning had struck a power plant on the *U.S. side* of the border in the Niagara Falls region, setting off outages that spread over an area of 9,300 square miles with a population of roughly fifty million people. This initial mishap may have set up a domino effect, resulting in a perfect storm of lights out for an additional hundred million people. The bottom line is that they've got no idea why citizens are bumping into each other in the dark.

The President declares that people affected by the huge blackout may not see their lives return to normal right away, but "slowly and surely we're coping with this massive national problem." The president also told reporters in San Diego, "I have been working with federal officials to make sure the response to this situation is quick and thorough, and I believe it has been. Terrorism is *not* the cause of the outage."

National Guard Units are eventually mobilized and assigned perimeter duty for sensitive locations such as the U.S. Mint, nuclear power plants and government buildings. The number of heart attack victims in the affected major cities triple as overweight and out of shape workers caught at work in skyscrapers have to descend up to seventy flights of stairs. The blackout closed the Detroit-Windsor Tunnel, which 27,000 vehicles use daily, and silenced the gambling machines at Detroit's Greek town Casino. Patrons filed into the afternoon cold carrying cups of tokens.

Emergency lighting flicker at government buildings as officials dust off their disaster plans. There seem to be plenty of questions but not many answers.

I finally get through to Lorri using a government satellite phone and detect concern in her voice, though she assures me that everything's alright.

"How's Nikki?"

"Nikki is surgically attached to her iPod. She'll resurface when the batteries die."

I suddenly feel in a reflective mood. Perhaps a national emergency elicits that type of emotion. "Hey Lorri, remember Nikki's first steps? She had that Frankenstein walk—sticking her arms out in front of her, knees locked, and staggering around stiffly. She couldn't figure out why we were laughing so hard." I smile at the image of my daughter and ask, "You guys keeping warm?"

"Wrapped up in sweatshirts, ski caps, and blankets. We're fine, John, but how are you? The radio reports are scary."

"The Cleveland Police have this blackout stuff down. We got all the food, pop, toilet paper, and bullets needed to survive on Mars."

"You always make me smile. When can you come home?"

"When it's over. Remember, my off duty pistol is in the bedroom nightstand. Just point and squeeze like I showed you."

"We live in a safe neighborhood. Some of the neighbors got together earlier and they know you're not home. They promised to check in."

"That's great, honey. Just make sure you don't shoot Arnold the accountant. Probably make his wife happy but it'll cause us some heartburn."

"I love you, John Booker."

"And, I love you, Lorri."

Five minutes later Captain Kopka announces, "We gotta go."

Looters have seized the Wal-Mart at the Steel Yard. Food, batteries, blankets, other miscellaneous items have become a major concern. Hoarders have depleted much of the inventory, leaving the shelves sparse. Any attempt at civility vanished in direct proportion to the loss of Captain Crunch and diet Pepsi. *"Every man for himself"* has replaced *"Thou shalt not covet thy neighbor's goods"* as the mantra of many citizens who have banded into gangs looting, robbing, and assaulting. Reports indicate "shots fired" between the looters who currently occupy the

Wal-Mart and the looters who want some of *their* loot. If you think about it, these super Wal-Mart's stock every conceivable item one would require to indefinitely sustain life.

Four patrol cars with lights and sirens wailing arrive at the parking lot. This is all the manpower we can spare with a city in chaos. The less hearty crooks scramble in all directions as we screech tires to a dramatic stop. Many of those exiting the area are lugging boxes, mostly containing electronic items. Their notion of survival goods pisses me off. I can understand pilfering frozen pizzas or cans of chili but these urban opportunists have crossed my personal line in the survival sand by toting televisions and iPods.

Kopka sends Sgt. Tommy Shoulders around back, though I sense no one will be beating a retreat. I tell Kopka, "You realize that we are probably outmanned and outgunned."

The beefy cop smiles and says. "We usually are. This is Cleveland."

I grab my MP5 submachine gun. I'm expecting Captain Kopka to make some elaborate tactical plan but instead Kopka walks nonchalantly into the building as if expecting to be welcomed by the Wal-Mart greeter. He has a bullhorn and calmly announces. "This is Captain Ray Kopka of the Cleveland Police Department, the building is surrounded.Everyone in this store has five minutes to come out into the parking lot with their hands up."

I am crouched behind cash register number 12 admiring Kopka's audacity but guessing his ultimatum won't work. It doesn't. Shots ring out from somewhere in sporting goods. Kopka merely shakes his massive head in disgust, looks at me, and walks slowly out the front door.

"You know they ain't coming out," I offer. "They were firing pistols, rifles and I believe I saw an arrow sail over our head."

Kopka smiles and says. "I saw the *fucking* arrow. We're the Cleveland police department, not the Texas Rangers, and my obituary ain't gonna include the word *arrow*. Let me think about this." Kopka takes a step, stops and turns toward me. He asks, "Did you know Wal-Mart sold arrows?"

"Nope."

"Me neither," He mumbles, "fuckin' arrow."

Kopka thinks about the situation for a full minute. He asks to borrow my MP5, flicks the selector switch to full auto and strolls back into Wal-Mart. A full magazine of 9MM rounds is loudly expended inside the building. Kopka strolls out, hands me the MP5 and says, "You need some more bullets."

A moment later seventeen men and ten women surrender. During the subsequent interviews we discover that it was a fat plumber who attempted to impale us with arrows. We immediately dub him *Cupid* and single him out for additional harassment.

On day three, the governor of Ohio declares martial law. Looters are to be shot on sight. A somewhat harsh order but after the Wal-Mart stand-off, I am warming up to the idea. "A fuckin' arrow" has become our new battle cry, which brings immediate laughter so whenever things become tense or we are in need of comic relief someone brings up the arrow.

There are confirmed reports of armed gangs roaming the city and barging into private homes. They take not only food and drink, but also scoff money, jewelry, and other valuables. Several of these home invasions have included rape of women and children as the citizens of Cleveland seem to be reverting to savages. The sun rises but hides behind dark snow clouds. Lake effect snow dumps an additional seven inches overnight and the temperature drops down dramatically. We have been sleeping a scant few hours a night on lumpy cots in the Justice Center. My back is aching, and I have a head cold, sniffles and diarrhea.

On day four, the National Guard and police department begin to experience desertions as a trickle of soldiers and cops go home to care of their family. The trickle becomes a steady rain, with a torrential downpour predicted soon. The one constant in Kopka's world is Sgt. Tommy Shoulders. The two have shared a decade of urban warfare.

Refrigerated and frozen food items in many homes had thawed and were contaminated with Ecoli, bacteria, and maggots. But people ignore the risks and chow down on the spoiled food. Most hug the porcelain princess but a few pay for the feast with their lives. Hospital beds *and* hallways are filled to capacity with blackout-associated ailments and new patients are being triaged in the parking lot. Only life and death emergencies will get you through the front door. Hospital janitors fulfill the duties of registered nurses, and nurses are performing minor surgery, thus freeing up the few doctors for the *really* serious stuff.

Insurance companies are predicting billions of dollars in claims, and some have threatened to go Chapter 11. Companies that survive have already predicted significant increases in insurance premiums. I personally feel that Insurance and IRS agents should have masks and guns anyway, so this news pisses me off on a personal level.

In Washington, the Health and Human Services Department list the biggest health concerns associated with the blackout. They include people not receiving essential home health care, and a scarcity of life sustaining equipment and medicines such as oxygen, insulin, kidney dialysis, chemotherapy and the ever popular ' *freezing your ass off.'*

The President provides a daily blackout update and pep talk on television and radio, but most televisions and radios are useless pieces of plastic and metal. Social media such as Twitter and Facebook provide essential emergency updates during the first few days, but the batteries on phones, laptops, and iPads have long since conked out.

Those lucky souls who had been off the grid with solar power or windmills are fat and happy. I make a mental note to buy stock in alternative energy once this is over.

And on day seven, in somewhat of a parallel biblical story, the cause of greatest blackout in U.S. history is solved. Workers immediately begin to slowly reconnect the country's power, and optimism fills the American people.

It seems that problems began when electricity reliability coordinator Southwest System Operator failed to use two vital software tools properly.

One, called a state estimator, makes intelligent guesses of the voltages in lines that are not monitored. Information from the state estimator is fed into the second device called a Real Time Contingency Analysis, which calculates what would happen to voltages across the grid if a particular line went down.

On day one of the outage, a shutdown on a line went unreported, causing the state estimator to make a false guess. The incorrect data was entered into the RTCA, which consequently failed to pick up on the looming problem. To compound things, when the shutdown was finally entered into the software and a new estimate obtained, an analyst forgot to switch on the RTCA and promptly "went out to lunch."

So, one of the greatest tragedies in American history was a combination computer glitch and human error. There always seems to be 'human error' in any catastrophe, because human beings are basically *fuckups*.

I arrive home and feel like a conquering hero returning from the Crusades. I'd been gone for much longer periods during our marriage but for some reason, these seven days felt like seven years. Perhaps it was the element of uncertainty and the interruption of *their* routine that had my family hugging on me.

The home seems fine with only a few visual reminders of the bedlam. Blankets are strewn throughout the house and the remnants of candles litter most of the flat surfaces. Other than that and the candy wrappers, it is back to normal. But I had learned long ago that *normal* is a relative term. Two hours later the television, refrigerator, and hair dryer come to life and the entire nasty blackout episode begins to recede within our memory bank. That is, all except for my cold and diarrhea which attack my bowels with a vengeance. I had been occupying the couch, taking a few days off. I'd lost some motivation since discovering that the blackout didn't involve terrorism. It somehow bummed me out that it was patriotic Americans and not a slimy foreign terrorist that had fucked up on such a grand scale. No, I can't provide a rational explanation for this feeling other than wanting to arrest a psychotic jihadist.

Peggy calls every day providing a *Michaels Report*. About every other call involves several Tourette-induced cuss words. I usually respond with heavy breathing and ask, "What are you wearing?"

"Now you stop that smut, John Booker," Peggy laughs.

It seems that my supervisor had *somehow* taken credit for saving the Perry Nuclear Power Plant and added this fictional tidbit to his existing fictitious list of achievements. At this rate he will be promoted within the hour and whisked off to the puzzle palace on a chariot. And the public wonders how we choose our leaders.

CNN News is reporting that the East Coast is functioning splendidly considering the toll the blackout had exacted on our daily routine. The broadcasting babe gives several anecdotal examples of how Jane Doe or John Smith became heroes during the crisis by saving lives or simply being good neighbors. I can't help but feel pride in my fellow Americans, though *my* eyes witnessed looting, assault, larceny, rudeness, and murder. Being a caustic pessimist is a job requirement in law enforcement. We are well-balanced individuals, having a cynical chip on *both* shoulders.

The babe hands off to a veteran newsman who stares intently at the camera and offers a commentary. *"It is a triumph of the American spirit to handle crisis in our usual indomitable manner. Americans simply roll up their sleeves and adapt to calamity as did their fathers and grandfathers before them in the depression and the Great Wars. We Americans are a tough, resilient lot who view adversity as simple obstacles to hurdle. It is part and parcel of our DNA and though we may, on occasion, stumble, we always get up and complete the race. Yes, this blackout tested our mettle and, ladies and gentlemen, our mettle is indestructible. This is Eric Kent wishing you safe journeys."*

We are one tough country I think. But I would soon discover just how fragile we *really* are.

CHAPTER 8

"In time of universal deceit, telling the truth becomes an act of rebellion."
— George Orwell

It's a sunny cool December Monday morning and my first day back at work following the blackout. I took five days of sick leave with symptoms that can only be diagnosed as a "funk." Every few years I go into a funk. It only lasts a few days and disappears like a rash.

Michaels is sealed inside his office tomb. We have reached an unspoken truce. He's now fully aware that I find him a worthless piece of dung so we barely speak. It works well for me. The coward even attempted to *"back door"* me while I was abusing the government sick leave policy. He went to Bell and called me names like "incorrigible," recommending that I be transferred to the Bank Robbery Squad. Peggy called me even as Judas was making his case as I sat home *funking* and munching on pizza with anchovies and watching Dr. Phil.

But the SAC simply informed Boy Wonder to *"figure out some way to get along and that if he transferred anyone, it would be Michaels."*

I grab a cup of coffee, give Peggy a hug, and log onto my government e-mail account. When computers initially became standard fare in government offices there was a noticeable reduction in productivity. It took four committees and a two-hundred page report before they realized that many employees were spending thirty-five percent of their day playing solitaire. It then took the bureaucrats an additional year to develop a program to block the fun and games.

One e-mail does get my attention. My CIA buddy Grant Beck sends a pleasant "catch up" note. The first few paragraphs inform me that he has just returned from Cairo, his daughter Gia was accepted to Dartmouth, and he asks few pointed questions about the FBI's role in the blackout. The final paragraph takes on a more mysterious tone. Beck inquires if I had been checking the top secret intelligence bulletins, *"as I promised."*

These bulletins provide the latest worldwide intelligence gleaned from a combination of human and electronic assets. These days, most of it is specific to Middle Eastern radicals but unless the intelligence poses a threat to U.S. soil, then the FBI has no jurisdiction. The general public is not aware of the mission distinction between the FBI and CIA. Simply put, the CIA is responsible for gathering intelligence on *foreign* soil, and the FBI is responsible to counter *other* countries' efforts to gather intelligence on *our* soil. So they *spy,* and we *catch* spies. Prior to 9/11, the CIA and FBI simply didn't speak, let alone share information. Imagine two prom queens with only *one* prom.

The CIA and FBI employ hundreds of intelligence analysts whose sole responsibility is to connect the dots. They have at their disposal the specialized training and electronic tools needed to descramble the most complex and obtuse ramblings. I, on the other hand, am a "hands-on" agent who takes their findings and does the dirty work in the field.

Just for the record, I had skimmed a few bulletins that seemed to be written with alphabet soup. The bulk of the information include tedious double talk and refer to names and places that sound like the expulsion of phlegm by an elderly Italian man.

I congratulate Grant on his daughter's Ivy League acceptance, briefly describe man's inhumanity to man during the blackout, throw in a complaint about my asshole supervisor, and confess to breaking my promise on reading the intelligence bulletins, then hit *"Send."*

S.W.A.T. Boy struts by and proudly informs me that during the blackout he arrested ten people and had rappelled down the side of an office building to disarm a raging lunatic who had taken *himself* hostage.

"Good shit," I say. "But did anyone shoot a fuckin' arrow at you?"

S.W.A.T. boy is speechless.

"I thought not."

Four minutes had elapsed since I had sent Beck the e-mail, but there was already a response. The CIA head of the Egyptian desk at Langley wrote, "*I want to remind you of our conversation in Quantico. I feel that you have an ability to see things most of us can't. It's a gift. Review the intelligence bulletins from April through November. Let me know if you see some pattern.*"

My initial reaction is that the reply seems stiff and almost scolding. Perhaps I misjudged Grant in the less pressurized environment of the FBI academy. Maybe he is just another intelligence squirrel. But there's something about the tone of Beck's request that prompts me to input the additional clearance code required to access SCI level information such as the intelligence bulletins.

There are three basic government clearances: confidential, secret, and top secret. Information *above* Top Secret is called Sensitive Compartmented Information or SCI. SCI information has strict controls on dissemination beyond all others. In order to gain SCI Access, you are subjected to severe additional background checks. Most FBI agents receive a top secret status but only a few receive SCI status. As a member of the task force, I am SCI-cleared.

Compartments of information are identified by code names. This is one means by which the *need to know* principle is formally and automatically enforced. Only persons with access to a given compartment of information are permitted to see information within that compartment, regardless of the person's security clearance level. I top off my coffee and adjust my reading glasses. Beck's admonition to look for "patterns" repeats in my cranium.

I write the words *"pattern / 3 months"* on a pad and begin to catalogue the list of the towel head super stars. I add a few of the minor league prospects along with their counties and affiliations. In addition to the known terrorist hot spots such as Iraq, Iran, Syria, Afghanistan, and Libya there seems to be significant terrorist buzz in the lesser known locations of United Arab Emeritus, Dubai, and Morocco. North Korea is mentioned both as a traditional military threat with possible clandestine ties to al-Qaeda, or, *some unaffiliated cell.* Interesting.

There also exists a communication system between certain groups, which dispels the myth that *all* terrorist cells operate independently. Proof of links between some cells occurred in the September 11, 2012 attack on our embassy in Benghazi, Libya with a simultaneous attack in Egypt. Both of these attacks were coordinated and connected.

Sometime in the late 70s our intelligence community became captivated with artificial assets such as satellites, internet, radio, and drone imagery. Big Mistake. They neglected good old-fashioned snitches. The dependence of electronic assets over human assets caught us with our pants down in the 1993 Gulf War when a massive troop movement from Iraq through Saudi Arabia en route to Kuwait went undetected by our satellites.

Had there been a good old fashioned informant, some CIA field officer would have received a call from Abdul the snitch who reported that his Republican Guard cousin Private Nasar was mobilized and headed south with ten thousand of his friends.

The intelligence bulletins also include a section on words and seemingly nonsense phrases that have been intercepted. There are several gibberish words and phrases, but one peculiar idiom appears on three occasions during the three month span: "The DARK BIRD MADE THE SON SICK."

The bulletins offer no conclusion on the nursery rhyme refrain, advising the reader that *"preceding is intercepted chatter and considered raw and singular in nature. Analysis is inconclusive."*

The dark bird made the son sick. The dark bird made the son sick. I have no earthly idea of its meaning and feel that Beck may have an inflated opinion of my abilities. Riddles leave me frustrated.

I might relate to the depraved mind of a career mobster but was never good at parlor games. Nikki, at nine years old, trashed me at Clue and my one Mystery Dinner had me falsely accusing the butler when it was the socialite.

It's time for a coffee refill and a mind dump. Maybe I need to reevaluate my theory that terrorists are basically low level thugs. Perhaps my Neanderthal approach to law enforcement has reached its expiration date. Maybe the new FBI needs *more* Boy Wonders and less John Bookers.

Or *maybe*, I'll just call Grant Beck and demand the answers to my take-home exam. I dial Beck's direct line.

"Hey Grant. It's John Booker. How are you?"

Beck asks. "Have you looked at the bulletins?"

"I have, and that's why I called, there's a ..."

Beck interrupts, "Look John, call me back in two hours. Go to a drug store and buy a disposable cell phone. Pay with cash and destroy the phone after we speak."

I ask, "Call this number?"

"Yes. It'll be rerouted and scrambled."

He hangs up.

I sit at my desk and attempt to make some sense of this conversation. I don't know Grant Beck all that well, but I *can* recognize the unmistakable smell of fear.

"You heading out, John Booker?" Peggy asks as I tug at my winter coat.

"Spy stuff," I say. "You want me to bring you back a sandwich or something?"

"No thank you, don't want to be a bother."

"No bother."

"Then I'd really like a Reuben." And adds a Tourette-induced, "Shit."

"Got it, Peggy," I say. "One Reuben with a side of shit."

I head toward the Galleria, which houses a variety of retail stores and restaurants. There is a plethora of disposable phones at the CVS. I choose a ten-dollar model with four hours of battery life.

I grab a diet Pepsi and meatball sandwich and sit in the food court. The echo created from a few hundred noisy people in an enclosed area makes for an excellent background diversion from prying ears.

My brains wonders, *"What the hell is going on here?'* Could Beck have gone mental and require a trip to the ice cream factory? Does the CIA know that the head honcho of their most critical foreign desk may be in the midst of some great conspiratorial breakdown? I dial his number and hope we'll keep the conversation limited to sports, the weather, and perhaps the ingredients to a secret CIA potion that will cause Michaels a slow agonizing death.

"John," Beck begins in a hushed tone. "Sorry for all the cloak and dagger stuff."

"You okay?"

"Fine." A pause. "Okay, maybe not so fine, but I may need your help."

"Absolutely ... whatever I can do, Grant."

"About ten weeks ago, a reliable asset provided information to one of my field agents in Cairo that some terrorist act was imminent. That it would occur within the next sixty days on American soil."

"Well thank God the informant got it wrong...."

"No listen, John. The asset says it happened."

"What happened?" I ask. "Nothing of a terrorist nature happened here. No unexplained bombings, assassinations, no biological or chemical release."

"The blackout," Beck says.

"I think I heard you say *blackout,* but that was caused by a combination of a computer glitch and human error. Do you have *any* evidence that terrorists blacked out most of America?"

There was a silence that prompted me to say. "You there, Grant?"

Beck explains that his field agent documented the informant's assertion that a terrorist attack would occur on American soil within the next two months, but the source couldn't provide any specific details. The assets handler was one of the best field operatives in the intelligence business.

"Trust me on this one," Beck says adamantly. "Mike Vickers was not only a colleague, but also my friend."

Protocol was followed. Beck contacted all agency stations *and* also alerted his FBI counterpart, who followed similar protocol with our field offices. The disseminated communication clarified that the information originated from a confidential informant of excellent reliability and requested that all agents query their informants for verification.

I'm an FBI agent and in many ways as naïve as most civilians on the most sophisticated electronic programs in the CIA and NSA's arsenal. So I ask Beck, "So you covered all the bases, what else could you do?"

Beck patiently explains that we employ a variety of cyber and *other* programs. "One program is designated as PRISM, which scans every single internet conversation in America. Major browser sites such as Google provide the government easy access to this information."

"Isn't that an impossible amount of data to review?"

"Our computers are just looking for key words, or specific subject matter. Let's say for example that our computers program the words, 'Ricin" or 'Anthrax' as trip words. If we get a hit then an intel analyst will review those interchanges to determine if it's some college kid doing a paper on biological warfare or two terrorists planning an attack."

As I listen to Beck, my mind rationalizes that we receive similar warnings weekly, if not daily. The American public would be unable to handle the stress associated with endless threats of Armageddon. Most of these alerts prove to be false alarms, and the few with teeth are never as bad as advertised.

Grant explains that some alerts originate with information obtained from human assets and some are merely the result of "flagged" buzz words intercepted during "chatter" in known terrorist regions.

I interrupt him with a dose of reality, "But Grant, nothing of an *unexplained* terrorist act occurred recently on American soil. Certainly nothing linked to the great American blackout, which was investigated by every government agency and deemed an unfortunate series of unforeseen events."

Beck ignores my logic and tells me that the source information was the reason he pushed the intelligence briefings with me at Quantico. That somewhere within the raw data was the answer. But after a few weeks, even Beck began to doubt his best field agent. He was about to suspend the alert and label the threat as *not credible* until two days ago.

"What happened?" I ask.

" Mike Vickers died."

"How?"

"Car accident."

"Suspicious?"

"Still being investigated, but the initial report from Cairo has a seventy-year-old man swerving and hitting Mike as he was crossing the street. The man has no ties to any political group and his family checks out. The driver has narcolepsy, which was verified with medical records. Doctors suspect he had an episode while driving."

"Was Mike completely covert?"

"No. As you know, many of our field operation officers have cover jobs within our embassy. Allows them to mingle with the populace."

"Any leaks or suspected double agents?"

"No."

"Then why are we having this conversation," I ask rhetorically. "*Why* do you feel that our blackout was an act of terrorism?"

"I owed Mike more than a 'case closed' stamp, so I poured over the intelligence bulletins. Last night I think I found something."

"I'm all ears."

He asks, "In the intel briefings, did you notice the phrase '*The DARK BIRD MADE THE SON SICK*'?"

"Hard not to, but I couldn't figure how many rats were involved in *Three Blind Mice*."

"That phrase was electronically intercepted by a drone. It was repeated one week *before* the blackout. It originated somewhere in the southeast region of Egypt. On the day *before* the blackout, intercepted communication originating in North Korea used the phrase '*DARK DAY IMMINENT ... BIRD SERVED NEXT.*'"

The beginnings of a headache form as I attempt to follow the covert bouncing riddle ball. I'm hoping that Beck is about to conclude this complex saga with some rational explanation. I would hate to think I am having a conversation with a high-ranking government lunatic.

"Grant, I have a lot respect for you but all this talk about '*dark birds*' is not computing in my brain. I want you to tell me, in the most direct language possible, what the hell is going on."

"I believe that a sophisticated and evil terrorist group is destroying America from within."

"Glad I bought the four-hour phone battery."

CHAPTER 9

"You can't handle the truth!"

— A Few Good Men

"Okay, Grant," I say calmly. "Let's begin with why."

"Several reasons. Ideologically, America is viewed as the world bully. Our Christian beliefs, military power, and affluent society are interpreted as an arrogant superiority. Not only in the Muslim world but now even the citizens of Western Europe view America with contempt. They don't want us settling disputes where we don't have standing. This goes back to Vietnam and also applies to Iraq, Afghanistan, Libya, Egypt, and Beirut."

"The world has always considered the United States as upstarts," I interrupt. "We're constantly in some skirmish or war. From the Revolution to Afghanistan, some asshole nation always wants to mix it up with us. Why is this any different?"

"Because we are the last super power standing."

"Wouldn't that *discourage* attacks?"

"Our enemies realize that they can't win a traditional war with us. And, they now understand that terrorism or shadow wars are ineffective. America is too resilient. The attack of 9/11 was devastating to America. So what happens? Do we surrender to al-Qaeda? No, we strike back. America adapts, improvises, and overcomes. There have only been two credible terrorist attacks since 9/11 within our borders."

"Grant, so how can they destroy us from within *and* who the hell are *they?*"

"I'm not completely sure I have the answer to either question, but I think that America is extremely vulnerable to a *combination* of catastrophes. Think of a science project when you mix several chemicals. If you keep adding corrosive elements, eventually the test tube will explode from within. That tube is the United States."

"Cut the analogies. Give it to me in English!"

Beck pauses and his voice becomes reflective. "Have you had periods where things go wrong?"

"Of course."

"So let's say that your car's transmission goes and the next day you sprain your ankle. A week after that, the roof leaks and your insurance policy has a $5000 deductible. Two days later your wife is involved in a minor traffic accident with some guy who pulls out a neck brace and his lawyer is talking big money." Beck pauses and asks, "All plausible, right?"

I agree and say, "I've been down several of those roads, but things usually level off and your ankle heals, your insurance company settles with the asshole, you find a friend of your cousin to fix the roof *and* the transmission. Two months later we're laughing about our run of bad luck with a few beers at the bar."

"It's only normal to believe that the seemingly unrelated setbacks are just a series of misfortunes that will run their course. But," Beck presses, "what happens if the bad stuff continues and someone steals your identity and wipes out your bank account, your father is diagnosed with stage four cancer and you lose your job?"

"Then, that scenario seems overwhelming," I conclude.

"But what *if,* you discovered that your misfortune is *not* just a string of bad luck. What *if* some person, or persons, was orchestrating these events with the purpose of destroying you?"

"I think I see where you're going," I say. "Then I *might* be able to stop them *once* I find out who *they* are."

"Our country is just like that individual," Beck explains. "We can handle a few random catastrophes but a continuous chain of disasters weakens our economy, our military, and eventually our will. They will ultimately destroy our collective psyche."

"I am trying to wrap my brain around this but it seems so far out there."

"Take the recent blackout," Beck pushes. "It literally crippled America. Our financial institutions were teetering, our commercial supply chain was broken, and normally decent citizens were reduced to predators," Beck pauses, and his voice rises both in tone and volume. "Imagine a *series* of disasters that hit in succession. Catastrophes that cause massive loss of life, major economic loss, and force us into a bunker mentality while awaiting the next shoe to drop. And then it does and our water supply is mysteriously tainted, epidemics like Ebola hits and wild fires destroy chunks of five western states!"

"Calm down, Grant," I scold, then wait a few seconds for Beck's breathing to regulate. "I'm not sure I agree with you, but if you're right, then the question becomes, can we prove any of this and have you told your superiors?

"No."

"What about the informant?"

"Disappeared."

"Well, Grant. *If* we are going to save America, and that supposes it *needs* saving, we need to identify the '*who*' and get the big guns working on it."

"Can you push something from your end, the FBI?" Beck asks.

"What do I push?"

Beck mumbles an understanding and calmly says, "Have you lost any loved ones to cancer?

"My dad, colon cancer."

"Then you know the drill. I lost my wife to cervical cancer. When you first get the diagnosis, the doctors offer *some* hope. They order chemo, radiation, they discuss statistical success rates, and you grab onto that hope like a life preserver in a storm. But the cancer has no conscience or mercy. It proceeds slowly but surely. It literally eats away at your loved one's organs, tissues, and muscles. If I'm right about this, John, then America has terminal cancer."

"Very visual," I say. "But since you made this diagnosis, what's the prescribed treatment?"

"If the blackout was a planned event, then the next catastrophe is about to happen. I'm convinced the answer lies within the intercepted phrase … *DARK DAY IMMINENT … BIRD SERVED NEXT.*"

"And *if* you're correct, then the *dark day* was the blackout so the question becomes … what's the *bird?*" I wonder aloud.

"Not sure but we better find out soon."

We promise to study the intelligence briefings and get back in touch tomorrow. Same time and same disposable cell phone routine.

I walk north on Ninth Street toward Lake Erie. The wind coming off the lake is gusting and adds to the wind chill that is teetering in single digits. Lake Erie seems like the ideal location to dispose of a disposable cell phone. As I toss the phone into the murky waters I chuckle and think that I probably just provided Jimmy Hoffa with his first cellular communication device.

CHAPTER 10

I am sitting across the table from Lorri at our favorite restaurant. It is date night. Santos has hand rolled their gnocchi and added a secret Sicilian ingredient with an addictive zest to their gravy. Our marriage requires some alone time. The blackout had somehow drawn us closer, and we wanted to parlay that feeling back to our courtship days, when she thought me handsome and funny and I found her gorgeous and sexy. It's ironic how chinks in the human armor appear in time and erode any perceived perfection. Of course, none of us are perfect, which is why most relationships fail.

I met Lorri Olson in a college bar. It was a decade before the internet when many relationships started in saloons. I was a senior at Slippery Rock State College and she was a sophomore at Westminster University. The "Rock" may have not been Ivy League but it provided an outstanding education to a kid from South Philly.

The Shed was a loud dilapidated college joint on Route 8, and I was in the midst of impressing a rowdy group with magic tricks. I actually had only one trick in my repertoire, which involved a coin, tequila, and a willing participant. Lorri volunteered and it was love at first sight. We married a week before I graduated.

I joined the Marines, went to OCS, and commanded a rifle platoon in Iraq. The IED was not part of my long-range plan. I spent a few weeks in the hospital with shrapnel wounds on my face and chest. I was lucky since my wounds healed and left me with a great conversational scar that ran down my right cheek. "Sword fight," I would say when people stared a little longer than necessary.

After my discharge, I returned to Slippery Rock and received a Master's in Educational Psychology. I applied to the FBI and was accepted to new agent training eleven months later.

Lorri became my best friend and confidant. She encouraged me through the dark days in the VA hospital, wrote my admission essay for grad school, limited my alcohol intake, and received a Master's in School Administration herself along the way.

I usually don't discuss my work with Lorri but today's conversation with Beck left me troubled. On one hand I thought Beck a delusional spook, but there was too much sizzle in his tale to ignore. My wife is a level-headed Swede who wouldn't tell me what I want to hear.

Another FBI dirty little secret is that *many* agents disclose confidential information to their wives, girlfriends, or both. They discuss active cases, name names, and even solicit advice from their civilian squeezes. Some FBI agents have taken family members on interviews and even surveillance.

I give Lorri the Reader's Digest condensed version over salad. She listens, nods, and offers a few *"uh huh's."* I finish up as the gnocchi is served and say, "So whatta you think?"

"Do you trust this Beck?"

"No," I say too quickly, then add, "I'm not sure. He's a professional and I *like* the guy, but the jury's still out on the trust issue. I am sure about one thing though."

"And what's that?"

"Beck *believes* that our nation is in peril."

"Can *you* do anything to prove or disprove his theory?"

"Been thinking about that," I muse. "About the only thing I can do is go to my bosses and ask that...."

"Ask what?" Lorri says, finishing my thought.

"Well that's just it. I don't know what to ask. The FBI already queried their FCI sources after the blackout, so about the only thing I can do is ask that they do it again."

"Not a good move since you can't offer anything new," Lorri advises.

"As of this moment, Beck believes that the recent interception of *Dark day imminent,* which occurred the day *before* the blackout, actually predicted that event, and he's convinced that the rest of the interception ... *bird served next,* means that more bad stuff is coming soon."

Lorri asks, "What about the *bird served next* riddle. It seems that if you can decipher that phrase, then it could help prove Beck right."

"Easier said than done without knowing *who* they are," I pause. "Remember Sammy the Bull?"

"Yea, Gotti and Sammy ran one of those mob families."

"The Gambinos," I add. "Well, Sammy whacked twenty-one guys, but was never indicted or convicted for any of those murders. He *was* arrested for killing the Dunn brothers."

"So?"

"So," I explain. "He had never even *met* the Dunn Brothers. He didn't order their deaths or pull the trigger, so when the FBI arrested Sammy and asked if he wanted to make a statement, Sammy said. *"Who the fuck are the Dunn brothers?"*

"I know that there's some moral to this story, John."

"There *probably* is, but right now I have no idea what it is," I say to end the official portion of the program. "Can I pour you another glass of Chardonnay, Mrs. Booker?"

My strategy, though simple, was well tested. I would get my wife tipsy, go home and do things to each other that sober people normally wouldn't do. Men are simplistic living organisms with simple plans.

The more liquor we consume the simpler our plan. We also tend to hide behind an invisible cloak when drinking which we believe shields us from disgusting behavior. So when I thought I *whispered* … "I'm getting horny honey," Lorri kicked me in the shin and gave me *the look.*

Lorri, ever the adult, drives us home. Nikki is doing an overnight at a friend's home. We arrive safe and sound at the Booker mansion which is actually a heavily mortgaged split level and I begin chasing Lorri around the house chanting, "The bird served next … the bird served next… "

I do believe that I am about to discover the meaning of at least one version of that phrase.

I hit the snooze button the next morning with a sluggish finger. I usually get my coffee at the Flying K Gas station, but stop at the first caffeine location I spot. It's the local Starbucks.

"Can I help you?"

"Yes please, a large coffee."

"We have on special Cappuccino, Latte, and Mocha Cafe, Con Leche and Caramel Macchiato."

"Just a large coffee."

"A grande or venti?" asks the male clerk who bears a striking resemblance to Donnie Osmond.

"The biggest you got."

"We have three sizes, tall, grande, venti."

"The *biggest*," I repeat.

"Would you like to become a member of the Starbucks club?"

"No, thanks."

"Do you have a gift card?"

"No."

"And what's your name?"

"Look Donnie, I don't want to swap spit, I just want a big cup of coffee."

"Room for cream?"

As I am reaching for my gun I decide that a nod will suffice.

I arrive at the office with a Venti double caramel latte. Donnie Osmond proves to be a born salesman.

Boy Wonder is actually strolling around the office. He must feel particularly vulnerable to be out in the open and interacting with the boys, *and* girls. At present Boy Wonder appears to be chatting up Special Agent McNulty.

Several of us have noticed that Michaels has taken a fancy to our latest female G-man. Gwen McNaulty represents the new era of female agents. When I first joined the Bureau, most female agents resembled members of the East German shot-put team, only with more facial hair. Ten years later the transformation was amazing. Gwen is a blonde-haired, green-eyed beauty. She is also an attorney, wine expert, tells raunchy jokes, and sports a natural pair of classic 36 Cs. The near perfect woman. I met her at mandatory sensitivity training and bestowed her the moniker of, *Agent 36.*

"Hey Gwen," I shout out. "Still have that nasty rash?"

She smiles and replies with, "Gone; how's your case of genital herpes?"

"Having a breakout," I say and scratch my crotch.

Boy Wonder turns his head toward me and I can actually see his cretin brain attempting to determine if Gwen and I are fucking with him or if he's witnessing a major ethics violation.

I smile and sit at my desk as Gwen says, "Oh by the way, Booker, you left your shoes under my bed."

My plan for the day includes reviewing the intelligence briefings prior to my call to Beck. Our latest intel seems a rehash of the past few weeks, with one exception. Intercepted chatter originating in Cairo overnight contains the words *"BIRD COOKING."*

It's obviously related to Beck's prediction that this *"bird"* somehow represents an impending crisis on American soil. Some immediate word associations come to mind and none of them good. A *'cooking'* bird can be a dirty nuclear device, or some type of airborne method of destruction. But how can we anticipate a where, how, or who when we don't know the what?"

My phone rings.

"Booker," I say.

"Do you usually stand up your dates?"

I recognize the distinctive voice of Suehad Fasaid. It had been several months since I'd cancelled our dinner get together. There were several times in the interim when I reached for the phone but somehow knew that calling Suehad was the prelude to *mortal sin* as we Catholics like to say.

Most men, including married ones, will verbally probe the lines of an attractive female. If the feedback is positive then men either retreat or advance. Most will advance. Even our most religious president, Jimmy Carter, admitted to "lusting" in his heart. Had his lower half become involved, then he would have morphed into Bill Clinton.

"Duty called," I say but want to say, *Meet me tonight and wear the purple bra.*

"The Bureau did a fantastic job on Judge Williams' murder," Suehad offers.

There is an awkward pause since we are both unsure of our end game.

Woody Allen once said that relationships are like sharks: if they ever stop moving, they'll die. Lorri explained that sharks move at all times, even when asleep. It makes perfect sense since all relationships are constantly evolving.

It was her dime so I wait until she finally says, "I'm calling for that rain check."

"Anytime."

"Tonight?"

"Sure."

"Lazzara's at six?"

"Sure."

Another awkward pause and I say, "Till then."

Who the hell says *till then* besides some Shakespearean actor in tights? Why does Suehad turn me into a bad cliché machine?

I notice that it's almost time for the Beck call. I stop by Peggy's desk and ask, "Want another Reuben, Peggy?"

"That was one delicious sandwich, John Booker. But since you won't let me pay for my own Reuben, I will suffer my hunger in silence and pray for you and world peace during my lunch break."

"Quit the martyrdom, Saint Peg. Give me the money."

She hands me a ten-dollar bill and asks. "Can you also get a pickle and a bag of barbeque potato chips?

"Not a problem." As I exit the squad area I place the sawbuck into the pocket of Peggy's winter coat on the rack and smile.

I find the same store, same clerk, and same cell phone and head back toward the Galleria food court, order two slices of pizza and a diet Pepsi. I realize that I have nothing new to report other than the words, *Bird Cooking.* Perhaps Beck has a better take on its meaning. Maybe he went to some high-up spook and as I chomp on my pizza the entire intelligence community is busting down doors.

I dial his number and hear a high pitch squeal. I redial the number three times, and get the same annoying screech. It is louder and more annoying than fax machine feedback. Maybe while transferring the call between five time zones the transmission hit some electronic feedback in Budapest.No problem. I wait ten minutes, same result, fifteen minutes and more ear-splitting racket.

I grab Peggy's Reuben and head back to work hoping Beck will call me at the office. I arrive winded and confused. Beck did not seem the type to stand up a fellow fed on such an important issue.

After a brief exchange with Peggy I check my voicemail. The third message is an anonymous male who informs me that "Grant Beck is dead."

CHAPTER 11

"Reality is the sanctuary of the dull"

I hang up and dial the switch board at Langley.

"Central Intelligence Agency."

"Grant Beck, please."

"One moment, sir." A click followed by a repeat of the voice mail greeting.

This shouldn't be so difficult I think. Beck is not in a covert status and openly conducts the governments business, albeit for a secret organization.

Could the anonymous call be a joke? Not likely. Even I have limits.

Boy Wonder is back at his desk and I walk in unannounced. Michaels prefers that Peggy *announce* all entrances to the throne room.

"Mike," I say. "I need you to make a call for me."

"Who and why?"

"CIA and inquire if one of their bosses is alive or dead."

"Who and why?" Michaels repeats in his condescending whine. The asshole is enjoying his unexpected role in my dilemma.

Instead of strangling Boy Wonder to death, I patiently explain that I received an anonymous call that Grant Beck is dead.

"Who is Grant Beck?"

"My instructor in the basic terrorism in-service at Quantico."

"Why am *I* calling; don't you know if the guy is dead or alive?"

I am running out of patience and take a step toward Boy Wonder. "Look Michaels, do me a favor, just call your fuckin' task force contact at the CIA and inquire about the health of one Grant Beck."

We have just entered into a schoolyard staring contest. Michaels is giving me his best glare but he and I both know he'll blink first.

Boy Wonder caves, presses the intercom and asks Peggy, "Can you get Richard O'Mera at the CIA on the line." He stares at me with a face full of contempt and adds, "Tell him it's urgent."

A moment later Peggy's voice informs Michaels that... *"Mr. O'Mera is unavailable."*

I turn to leave but Michaels orders me to stay.

I stop, turn and face my supervisor. Boy Wonder glares at me and in an attempt to save face and reassert his authority says, "Look Booker, I am your immediate supervisor and will *not* tolerate this type of behavior."

"You are also a lazy incompetent fool who got two agents killed in Idaho," I say calmly.

Michaels stands and raises his whiny voice. "Special Agent Booker, I would strongly recommend that you find a dictionary and look up the meaning of the word *insubordination!*"

I take two steps toward Michaels and lean over his desk. Our faces are inches apart. I hiss, "And, *I suggest* you look up the meaning of .... *getting your ass kicked.*"

Okay, I think as I exit the throne room, not exactly my *best* come back.

Back at my desk I call the personal cell phone of Assistant Director and former roommate, Tony Daniels. Tony regularly meets with his CIA counterparts both formally and socially. They regularly do the Georgetown pub crawl in a show of agency solidarity. His rank and Rolodex guarantees an immediate human response. I provide an abbreviated version of the Beck saga and Tony informs me that he'll call back in twenty minutes.

I am in the process of logging onto my computer to check the latest intelligence buzz when Peggy's announces over my phone intercom, "Jack Bell desires your presence as soon as possible. He sounds somewhat bothered."

I check my watch and determine I have seventeen minutes to placate the Special Agent in Charge of the Cleveland office, and be available for Tony's call.

Bell is a good guy. He's a former Army Ranger and worked Organized Crime in the New York Division. Although he probably knows that Michaels is an incompetent troll, he also is a stickler for chain of command issues.

I enter the SAC's office in apologetic mode, "Sorry boss, but ..."

Bell waves a dismissive hand and points to a chair. He begins calmly. "I can't have you threatening bodily harm to FBI supervisors. It may start a trend."

"You *do* know that Boy Wonder should *not* be in law enforcement, let alone leading troops. He's afraid of his own shadow and can't make a decision."

"I know, but he *is* an FBI supervisory special agent and as a fellow member of *that* club, I have to pretend that he's a steely eyed G-man."

"Okay," I relent. "I'll be nice to him."

"Thank you."

"Why don't you just get into management, then you get to make the decisions?"

"I don't play well with others. Besides, all you guys do is lie to each other at meetings."

Bell smiles. "I do miss the field."

"We good then." I say standing and checking my watch. Five minutes until Tony's call.

"Not really, John," Bell offers. "Michaels wants to officially write you up for insubordination, and if he goes on paper, I *have* to kick it over to OPR. Those boys have no sense of humor. Probably cost you a week."

"Asshole!" I spit. "What's this Bureau coming to?"

"I told him that I would issue a verbal reprimand and counsel you on appropriate interaction with supervisors."

"Okay." I say and smile. "I consider myself counseled and reprimanded, and, will offer up a Novena up to those poor souls in Headquarters."

"And," Bell continues ignoring my sarcasm. "You will probably like to offer up an apology to Michaels."

My immediate reaction is '*I would rather stick toothpicks in my eyeballs than apologize to that weasel,*' but I have about two minutes until the call, so instead I say, "Consider it done."

Back at my desk with over a minute to spare, Ten seconds later the phone chimes.

"John," Tony begins. "Got ahold of the Deputy Director for Middle East Affairs. Yep, this Beck is dead alright."

"How?"

"No signs of foul play. A brain aneurysm. It happens."

"It may happen," I say. "But two mysterious CIA agents are dead in the span of a week and both chasing the same conspiracy. Seems more than coincidental."

"There's nothing mysterious about a traffic death in a third world country and an aneurysm to someone in such a high stressed job like Beck."

"You know how you say that I'm usually right about things." I ask Tony seriously. "Well, something ain't right, and I'm calling in the roommate chit. I need an HBO and that'd be you, roomie."

"What do you need John?" Tony asks.

CHAPTER 12

"You can check out anytime you like, but you can never_leave."
"Hotel California" — The Eagles

Tony schedules a meeting at the SOP (Seat of Power) as J. Edgar referred to FBI HQ. The attendees will include the JTTF Section Chief, a deputy director of the CIA, Unit Chief of the Intel Unit, two Homeland Security reps, and an ad hoc member of the National Security Council.

My roommate attempts to downplay this three-ring circus by telling me, "John, don't worry. These headquarter types have forgotten that they exist to support the field. They'll ask a lot of questions that may seem condescending and off topic and many more that have no answers. It's nothing personal, that's just what we do in headquarters. Keep your cool and let me be your wingman."

My roomie agrees to pick me up at Dulles on judgment day. "I owe you Tony," I say.

"Consider it payback for the forensics exams."

"That slate will be wiped clean."

"You are a pain in my ass, John," Tony laughs, "But this one's on the house, because on the outside chance that you're right, then America will *owe* you. See you at Dulles."

Something's been bugging me about Beck's death. Most of us are familiar with the term brain aneurysm. It brings about images of a brain imploding or something equally gross.

When I was deep cover with the Italian Mafia in New York, there was a neurosurgeon who removed a tumor from the brain of my capo. Dr. Enrico Grisoni is the best head cutter on the East Coast and we hit it off as I spent plenty of hospital time guarding the boss. We bullshitted about sports, politics, and nurses' butts. He once commented that I seemed like too nice a guy to be hooked up with '*these particular Italians.*'

After I surfaced as an FBI agent I called Enrico and we continued our friendship long distance. I scroll down my cell phone contact list and dial his private cell number.

"Giovanni," Enrico shouts. "How's my favorite G-man?"

I decide to skip the details of my chaotic existence and simply say, "Great, and you?"

We make some small talk and catch up on old times. Dr. Grisoni successfully removed the tumor from Don Vito's brain but three months later, some guy named Tony the Chin simply replaced it with a bullet. Enrico chuckles and offers. "The brain is not designed for objects going in and out with such frequency."

"Hey doc," I say. "Gotta question."

"Shoot," Grisoni says and adds, "I suppose one should not say that to an armed individual."

I laugh and ask, "In laymen's terms, explain a brain aneurysm."

"Are you okay, John?"

"I'm fine. Its case-related."

"Glad to hear that. A brain or cerebral aneurysm is a bulging, weak area in the wall of an artery that supplies blood to the brain. In rare cases, the brain aneurysm ruptures, releasing blood into the skull and causing a stroke or death. The rupture is called a subarachnoid hemorrhage."

"So it's like a bicycle tire that has a bubble. It eventually leaks air and you get a flat, but sometimes it explodes and you get a blowout. End of tire."

"That's a good analogy."

"Can a brain aneurysm be induced through artificial means?"

"Yes," Grisoni confirms and adds. "In all other aneurysms such as abdominal, aortic, or thoracic aneurysms there are associated symptoms, but a brain aneurysm has no symptoms and goes generally unnoticed until it burst."

"So," I ask. "An individual with knowledge and opportunity can kill someone simply with a syringe filled with air?"

"Yes."

We say our goodbyes with promises to get together. I sit at my desk and suddenly have pangs of uncertainty. I had huffed and puffed my way into this *save our country* meeting but I basically got squat for facts. Vickers and Beck are dead, but thousands of people die every day from car accidents and aneurysms. An informant, currently MIA, alleged that terrorists had caused the blackout, but government investigations chalked it up to a computer glitch and human error. Both Beck and Vickers believed that America is in peril but neither will be attending the meeting.

What exactly *did* I want? I understand that I would only get one shot with the suits. It was no secret that Tony Daniels is indulging his eccentric undercover friend a favor. I also understand that I am painting Tony with my erratic paintbrush and should things go south, my friend may resemble an abstract Picasso.

My 'wish' list is similar to my first letter to Santa, which also included a slew of unreasonable demands such as:

Exhume Beck's body and examine it for needle marks that could indicate an induced air bubble into his blood stream. Torture the old man in Iraq to determine if he murdered Vickers at the direction of some sinister group. I realize they wouldn't torture the old man, but perhaps they can smack him around a bit. Request that the CIA and FBI form a task force to explore Beck's theory that America is about to implode. Assign twenty additional intelligence analysts and twenty agents as well as a request for CIA liaison personnel. Find the missing informant who provided the initial information on the blackout. Concentrate on deciphering the phrase, *"Bird served next...."* Award John Booker an increase in pay and a better company car.

There was also one more question that gnawed at me. Who was the anonymous guy informing me of Beck's death? Why didn't he leave his name and how did he know to call me? I had checked with our switchboard providing them the time of call, but eighty percent of all incoming calls are "withheld."

I make an executive decision not to mention the mystery caller during the meeting since alerting the CIA may dry up this valuable information hole. They wanted to give me a "heads up," but why?

Peggy strolls by my desk and wishes me a good night. She adds something about being *a cock sucker*. I thank her and realize that I am meeting Suehad in an hour.

I call my spouse and provide a sanitized version of the truth. "Honey, I have a meeting."

"Do you want me to keep dinner warm?"

"Naw, I'll just get a Subway sandwich." I realize that I had crossed the line of truth with that one.

"Well, be careful John."

"I will.... Bye.",

Lazzara's is one of the latest in upscale chain eateries in the area. It specializes in Italian food served family style. This culinary approach consists of twenty plates of vittles doused in red sauce being politely passed around. The only difference between Lazzara's and Sunday dinner at Nanna's is the addition of a few obese cousins tugging at the brazzoli plate and having your Uncle Vinny belching and farting.

I arrive first so that I can request the proper law enforcement seating which is back to the wall. Having your back exposed to the room makes law enforcement officers squirm because we arrest bad people who occasionally go out to eat.

Suehad arrives and looks sexier than I remember. We engage in an awkward combination of a grope and hug, then peck European style on both cheeks. Just for the record, men do not like the two cheek peck.

Suehad reveals some spectacular cleavage in a bright red blouse and compliments the package with tight black leather pants and three-inch heels. My eighth grade teacher, Sister Alberta Marie, never came close to this ensemble.

"You look great, Suehad," I offer.

She eyes me slowly from head to toe. "Not too shabby yourself."

"I clean up nice."

I pull out her chair and proclaim with a bad French accent. "Madame, the house wine tonight is a very vintage 1968 Boones Farm. Goes well under viaducts or while studying for Art History exams."

"I've heard tales of this rare wine. It's rumored to be carbonated and sports an easy twist-off top."

The thought *does* cross my mind that most Muslims lack any sense of humor. Generally, they seem a glum, serious, and perpetually pissed-off group. But Suehad somehow comprehends the subtle irony of Western humor and can banter with any smartass. She smiles with her big brown mesmerizing eyes, which rarely stray from my eyes.

I do realize that no wife can compete with a girlfriend. It's an unfair competition since wives have pimples, furry slippers, and stuffy red noses, while girlfriends always look great and never ever fart.

The conversation begins with the usual generic topics of politics and the economy. As we order a second drink, Suehad is regaling me with hilarious examples of student behavior. "John, you wouldn't believe when I give exams. The students Skype the test to friends with their smart phones who are back in the dorm room with the text book."

"That sounds like some high tech cheating," I say. "My primitive Catholic school method consisted of writing answers on the back of my tie."

We pick away steadily at the variety of plates before us. My white shirt suffers some collateral red gravy damage and I make a mental note to clean it later. I am also aware that Subway serves meatball subs in case the gravy stain proves stubborn.

It is sometime after my third glass of bourbon, when I broach the Beck matter and *only* after Suehad asks. "So tell me John, how are things in the Bureau, any interesting cases that you can discuss?"

"There is a matter that I can probably use some civilian perspective. I've been struggling over a case with some agents at the office."

Suehad laughs and says, "You really need to talk with people who have opposing views."

"I do, I'm married."

Suehad smiles and I say, "So I need to run this by you, but I'd appreciate if it stays just between us."

I launch into the Beck matter in the most general terms. I rationalize my security breach preferring to view Suehad as an unofficial government consultant. We hire civilians to act as linguists, photographers, intel analysts, and janitors, so why not a middle eastern expert. Suehad couldn't be a terrorist, because terrorists rarely wear Victoria's Secret undies.

"So, Suehad," I conclude. "Could a group of super terrorists exist?"

"Not likely, John. But shortly after the 9/11 attacks, there *were* rumors of some shadowy collection of individuals who were not your garden variety terrorists"

"Whatta you mean by *garden variety?*" I ask.

Suehad explains that "Most terrorist leaders lack any formal education; they don't understand the subtleties of warfare and lack resources, training, and money to sustain any consistent long-term strategy. But this ghost group is rumored to be educated and partnered with an industrialized nation. They are both brilliant and ruthless. The word is that they vow to bring Sharia Law to the western world and America to its knees."

"I know the basic principles," I begin. "Under Muslim Sharia law, the clothes you wear, the music you listen to, and the television you watch would all be censored. Behavior in public is legally restricted and controlled. Right so far?"

Suehad nods and continues. "Sharia is an Arabic term referring to a legal framework to regulate public and private aspects of life based upon specific Islamic teachings. Sharia is an intolerant system that threatens the Western ideals of liberty and justice for all. It views non-Muslims as second-class citizens, sanctions inequality between men and women, prescribes cruel and unusual punishments for crimes, and promotes a restrictive business environment that strangles the freedoms of capitalism."

"So how can they achieve this lofty goal of destroying America?"

"Nothing specific, but the rumors were consistent that they will destroy America without firing a single shot."

"That just doesn't make sense," I conclude. "We have the most powerful military in the history of civilization, and they have barely evolved past Fred Flintstone. Are they going to stone us into submission?"

"Imagine Fred in the role of David and America playing Goliath."

"You sound like a friend of mine. He believed that some evil enemy is attempting to destroy America from within through a series of disasters. So could this phantom group be responsible for the recent blackout?"

"That would be your area of expertise John, but the newspapers concluded that the blackout was caused by a computer problem." Suehad looks at me and asks, "That *is* what caused it. Isn't it John?"

"There's no evidence to the contrary. So does this group actually exist, Doctor Fasaid?"

"My doctorate dissertation referenced that possibility, among others, but I concluded that the group never existed and has evolved into an urban myth."

"How did you conclude that?"

"It's been well over a decade since the terrorist attacks in America. During that time there has not been *one* credible piece of evidence that this super terrorist cell exist. They'd *have* to interact with other human beings."

"You have a point there." I agree. "They would have had to piss off a wife or girlfriend by now who would have ratted them out. And these scumbags usually brag about their barbarism, use it as a recruiting tool."

"We both sound as if we are trying to convince ourselves."

"You mentioned some *other* possibilities. What *exactly* was the topic of your dissertation?

Suehad sips her wine and sighs. "It is very technical and I'm afraid it will bore you."

I smile and say. "Just pretend you're teaching a remedial course on secret terrorist cells for dummies."

Suehad chuckles and says, "If you insist. Much of my research originated from *The Jihad Watch,* which I created right after 9/11. It is a website that collects data on radical Muslim activities around the world."

"I ran your name through our computers when I first interviewed you. Standard procedure—so I knew about your blog. We actually have FBI analysts who monitor your site.

"I'm flattered that the FBI finds my work worthwhile."

"Don't be. We also monitor porn sites. But tell me more about your doctorate research."

"My basic premise was that radical Muslims were making significant inroads into imposing their culture on traditional democratic societies. Muslims now control sizeable areas of France, England, and Spain. They hold the elected offices, dictate the curriculum in schools, appoint law enforcement officials, elect judges, *and* enforce Sharia law."

"I heard that parts of England resemble downtown Tehran."

"Yes, and using statistical data to predict future trends, I concluded that this Muslim invasion shows no signs of slowing down."

Suehad pauses in her mini lecture and sips her wine. The waiter takes his cue and refills her wine glass from the bottle chilling in the ice bucket. She actually frowns and says, "They have basically begun an occupation of the civilized world minus the threat of any violent invasion."

"And you don't have to tell me that America is on their wish list."

"You are a quick learner," Suehad says. "During the last midterm elections 47 Muslims ran for U.S. Congress and 21 actually won their district."

"Surprising, but certainly not proof of terrorist activities."

"Correct, John. But I researched their campaign strategies and finances, and none of it adds up."

"Whatta you mean?"

"They received significant funds from shell corporations and PACs. And, all of their campaigns used similar tactics of smear and destruction. They play dirty John, employing private investigators who ruin lives...."

Suehad pauses and confirms, "We analyzed everything from their billboard ads to their stump speeches at the Rotary Club. The words and message were in many cases, verbatim."

"You could probably chalk that up to communication among the campaigns, or maybe some Muslim political organization that provides Muslim candidates a standard message."

"There is no such organization and when we dug deep enough we found that their campaign monies were filtered through four or five corporations, *but* approximately 80% of the campaign funds originate in North Korea."

My brain immediately associates Suehad's reference to North Korea and the pertinent intercepts from the intelligence bulletins.

"Did you provide the Justice Department this information? Seems like several campaign funding violations."

"They are *officially* investigating. It's been several years and I am not expecting a call any time soon. But there is something far more ominous tied to these attempts to place Muslims in control of our legislative branch of government."

"And that is?"

"Just imagine when these Muslim Congressmen become political appointees in the executive branch and control *two* branches of the government."

"Tell me."

Suehad explains. "The IRS scandal is a great example. An agency with unlimited power and the ability to marginalize individuals with opposing views through audits, fines, and even imprisonment." Suehad leans forward and locks eyes with me. "And, what about our third branch of government?"

"Our Judicial branch is fragmented into 94 separate court districts," I counter, "the majority of which are very conservative."

"Yes, John." Suehad says about to make a point. "But there is only *one* court that matters, and that's the Supreme Court."

My brain flashes back to D.C. and the murder of Chief Justice Williams, with Tony Daniels warning that *"A liberal Supreme Court will destroy this nation...."*

Suehad seems to read my mind and challenges me with,"You're thinking like the typical government employee. Imagine Muslims with anti-American agenda holding posts in all three branches of government. Think of the damage they could inflict on America."

I give this sobering notion some thought and dismiss it with, "There's too many checks and balances for any government agency to go *completely* rogue."

She counters with, "Jihadists have a long-term vision regarding their plan for world domination. The United States is the new kid on the global block. We feed, shelter, and educate foreign nationals, many of whom have a deep hatred and distaste of the hand that provides their very subsistence."

"Those two Chechen brothers who planted the bombs at the Boston Marathon were receiving scholarships, food stamps and other government goodies, yet despised everything America stood for." This topic always pushes my hot button so I ask, "Anything else in your doctorate research that would support a conspiracy theory?"

Suehad leans across the table as if she is about to share a secret.

She says, "Hosni Mubarak was the President of Egypt for twenty years. He was America's ally and provided critical support such as allowing Egyptian military air bases to act as staging areas for American jets."

"He was no angel," I counter. "He often played both sides."

"Correct, John, but in a region filled with devils, Mubarak had the smallest horns. Anyway, America could always count on Mubarak to do the right thing when push came to shove. Sometime in 2008, America abruptly made it known that Mubarak lost his favored leader status in a geographical powder keg where America has *few* friends." Now here's where it gets interesting ..."

"Fast forward to 2010 and America is supposedly shocked when Egyptians revolted against Mubarak's government and demanded elections. A major faction that initiated and supported the uprising was the Muslim Brotherhood."

I sip on my bourbon and add, "And the Muslim Brotherhood has made it perfectly clear that they view Israel and America as their sworn mortal enemies and vow our destruction by whatever means."

"Correct. And shortly after the forced elections, an Egyptian Islamist was invited to the White House by the name of Hani Nour Eldin. Eldin was a newly elected member of the Egyptian Parliament who belongs to an officially designated terrorist group, the Gamaa Islamiya. That terrorist group is closely aligned with the Muslim Brotherhood."

I observe, "Our government meets with terrorist groups all the time. Look at the PLO and Arafat. We'd want a say on who rules Egypt due to its strategic position in that region."

"I'll get to that. The newspapers reported that Eldin promised the U.S. that the Muslim Brotherhood wasn't behind the Egyptian uprising and that they wouldn't start a political party, wouldn't run for parliament and they definitely wouldn't put up a candidate for president."

"But," I say, "Everything we were told they wouldn't do, they *did*. And I have a feeling that it gets worse."

"Much worse," Suehad warns. "Somehow, the newly elected parliament is dissolved and miraculously Mohammed Morsi of the Muslim Brotherhood becomes the President of Egypt."

"Then we immediately sent the new Egyptian government several billion dollars in aircraft, tanks, and *other* weapons, but," I add, "the Egyptian people overthrew Morsi shortly after they received the weapons and eliminated the Muslim Brotherhood threat."

Suehad actually shakes her head and says, "John." She scolds, "You, along with the entire American government, must begin the process of understanding your enemy. This is a flaw that will eventually prove fatal for the free world. America's *only* ally in the Middle East is Israel. The remainder of that region possesses a deep seated hatred for the United States. It makes no difference what political faction controls a government since they are all Muslims who believe in Sharia law and want to destroy America."

"So," I say. "We have essentially armed our sworn enemy with weapons that will probably be used on Israeli and possibly American troops in the Iraq or Afghanistan region, or even on American soil." I wonder. "Are you implying that our government could be part of a conspiracy to assist terrorists?"

Suehad shakes her head and says, "Not at all, John, and that's the scary part. I believe that our government is being duped. America's electorate has demographically and radically changed within the last fifty years. We have become more dependent on government for our survival."

"How does that tie into the Muslim Brotherhood?"

"This new American electorate has voted into office those who share their vision. Consequently, our current administration is more sympathetic to European socialism and Marxist teaching."

"So," I surmise, "Whoever is pulling the global terrorist strings has used this opportunity to make a move in the U.S. of A, just like they have in Europe."

"I believe so."

This seems the right time to further probe the possibility of a super terrorist group so I slip into investigator mode. "You said a few minutes ago that there were *rumors* of a super al-Qaeda group. When did you hear these rumors?"

"Maybe a year after the terrorist attacks in New York. I was born and raised in Cairo, but went to NYU for my undergraduate studies in 1997. I returned to Egypt three months before 9/11. I taught primary school for two years before returning to the states for my doctorate work at Stanford University."

So you first heard the rumors while in Cairo, teaching school?"

"Yes."

"Can you recall the context in which you heard the rumors and who told you?"

"The context?" Suehad asks.

"Where and how did the conversation occur, but more importantly was the person who mentioned this phantom terrorist group a reliable human being?"

"The person who told me was very reliable, although we both were very intoxicated.

"Did they tell you as fact or as rumor?"

"It was told in a matter of fact manner, perhaps bragging fueled by the alcohol."

"Did you ask how they knew?"

"Many times and in different ways, but after a while he started to recant and called it idle gossip."

"So who was this person and could they be in a position to know if a super terrorist organization existed?"

"His name is Mansur El-Quadir. His father is an imam connected to the Muslim Brotherhood." Suehad pauses and lowers her eyes to the table. Her words were barely above a whisper. "John, you asked me where I was."

"Yes, it may help me determine how much weight to give his words."

"We were in bed and Mansur is my husband."

CHAPTER 13

"A nation of sheep begets a government of wolves"
— Edward R. Murrow

So, Suehad had a past. Who'd have thought? I escort her to the parking lot and she seems subdued. The evening went south after the *terrorist husband* thing. Funny, how something so trivial can put a kibosh on a fun time.

"I don't often share such personal information," she says.

"You can trust me, Suehad. FBI agents are like priests, minus the pedophilia stuff; we take an oath of silence at the FBI academy."

A smile and she stops and locks eyes with me. "I hope so, John Booker, because I *do* trust you, but if you choose to betray me, the FBI can do me great harm."

"You lost me, Suehad."

"I am in this country on permanent resident status. Two more years and I will apply for citizenship. If the INS knew that my husband's family had ties to the Muslin Brotherhood, they could deport me."

"I must be slipping," I say, "'cause that thought never crossed my mind."

"Thank you for that *non* thought."

We both laugh and I ask the obvious, "You still married to that guy?"

"Legally, yes, we communicate, but he feels I betrayed Allah."

"Because Sharia law believes women are a subspecies?" I ask rhetorically.

Suehad smiles and says, "That, and my conversion to the West including my wardrobe, views on equality, my education, and my belief that our universal supreme being, whether it be called Jesus, Buddha or Allah, is a good and just God."

"What's he do to make a buck?"

"Mansur owns an import/export business."

I like where this is going and ask, "What and where?"

"A variety of items such as electronics, jewelry, clothing. He travels to China, Vietnam, and Korea."

"Is that North or South Korea?"

"North, John. Egypt has normal trade relations with North Korea."

"Didn't you trace campaign funding for Muslim Congressional candidates back to North Korea?"

"Yes, but North Korea is a large nation."

"Maybe," I say. "But all roads seem to lead back to North Korea. Do you keep in touch with your husband?"

"Mansur claims that he still loves me and wishes Allah will show me the light. He calls me daily."

"Can you write down his name and any other identifying information for me?

"That part of my life is done. What would be the purpose of this information?

"Curiosity," I say not too convincingly. "I want to run this guy and see if he's connected but if you prefer me not to, then I won't."

This was a fib since I have every intention of running Mr. El-Quadir.

Suehad pulls a pen and business card from her purse and scribbles something on the back. She hands me the card, opens her car door and says, "This was nice. Your call if you want a do-over."

"I'd like that." But with four bourbons my meat puppet is saying
... *I want to stick my tongue down your throat and take one for Allah.*"

Instead we repeat the awkward combo hug and grope followed by
the European two cheek peck. "Goodnight, Suehad."

"Goodnight, John."

As soon as I get home I douse my gravy stained shirt with industrial
strength stain removal. I know evidence when I see it.

It's the day before the Washington summit and Boy Wonder sends
me an e-mail that is disturbing. "Will meet you at the airport at seven."

I should have guessed that Michaels would never send me to the
puzzle palace alone. His motivation to accompany me was twofold.

First off, *all* Boy Wonders view the opportunity to stroll the halls
of FBI HQ in the same manner that children view Disney World. They
get to meet Mickey, Donald, and a slew of Goofys as well as lobby
the seven dwarfs for their next rung up the beanstalk. Occasionally
a boy wonder will hop aboard the boat on *It's A Small World* and fail
to disembark. They can be found staggering around HQ like zombies
with a thousand-yard stare.

And secondly, Boy Wonder simply did not trust me to play nice
with HBOs. It would be a reflection on his management skills if a
lowly brick agent wreaked havoc with the same people who ran the
promotion boards.

I call Bell, though I already know his reply. "Does Michaels have
to go?" I ask anyway.

"Yes," Bell says. "He's your supervisor and any decisions will
affect *his* squad in terms of manpower and resources; besides, someone
needs to apologize for your behavior."

"I'll be good."

"No you won't but that's alright." Bell pauses and offers. "John, I
read your agenda and attachments for the meeting. Looks thin."

"It may not have a lot of meat, but when I was twelve some skinny
kid beat the crap out of me. Look, boss," I reboot. "I'm an intuitive
agent. I play my hunches and so far I've always been spot-on."

"The only reason people put up with your shit is that you get results, John. But the Bureau is changing and agents like you are on short leashes. The stuff you pulled five years ago will get you fired and the crap you pulled ten years ago will get you indicted. Be careful."

"I appreciate the sentiment, boss."

Bell laughs and says, "Now leave me alone; you give me a headache."

As I am about to hang up, Bell adds, "And one last thing Special Agent Booker."

"Yes."

"Be nice to Michaels. He's itching to get you suspended or fired so don't make it easy for him."

"I will sincerely try, Boss, but that man pushes *all* my buttons."

As I am reaching into my pocket to pay Peggy for our squad coffee fund, I pull out Suehad's business card. On the back is the pedigree information Suehad provided on her husband. Back at my desk, I log onto the intelligence SCI site containing known suspects and associates of terrorist individuals or groups. I further limit the search to Cairo, Egypt, and input the name Mansur El-Quadir.

Several *'hits'* appear on my computer screen that credit reliable assets for the information. The sources report that *Mr.* Suehad operates an import/export business that has extensive dealings with the North Korean government. I'm beginning to hate that shithole. But more importantly, my gigantic jigsaw puzzle is slowly piecing together and all roads seem to lead to North Korea.

Mansur's father, Jabar, is a spiritual advisor to the Muslim Brotherhood, which according to the liberal media is the equivalent of Scientology. In actuality, the Muslim Brotherhood is a group of Jihad radical extremists whose avowed goal is the destruction of America and Israel. I'm not exactly sure of Scientology's goal but I know it's also sinister.

The next morning I arrive at Hopkins International Airport with a Venti double latte. I am now an official card-carrying member of the

Starbucks cult. I swapped the stale coffee and hostile sneer of Bruno at the Special K gas station for the Stepford smile of Donnie Osmond.

Michaels is waiting at the gate area for the early flight to D.C. I force a smile and he immediately starts with, "Listen up, John. I know we have our differences but I need you to be a team player at this meeting." He looks at me to make sure I am sufficiently awed by the pep talk. I stare straight ahead.

He continues anyway. "I would appreciate if you show the proper respect, to me *and* the higher ups at the meeting, so under no circumstances should you swear or raise your voice. If you disagree with them on an issue, just smile and explain your position in a polite voice. And make sure you thank them for taking the time to listen before we leave. We good with all that?"

I take a sip of my Starbucks and stare straight ahead. "Okey dokey."

My cheeky response is an attempt to placate Boy Wonder's Napoleonic complex. He nods with smug satisfaction and says, "I'm glad we had this conversation.

I think *'what an asshole'* but say, "Me too."

As we are deplaning at Dulles, Michaels turns to me and says, "I rented a car."

Using my most pleasant voice I say, "I've arranged for our transportation, Matt."

I thought the *"Matt"* may have been a bit much, but Michaels actually smiles and cancels the rental. My twisted sense of payback is kicking into high gear. He follows me outside where a large black government SUV awaits. A.D. Tony Daniels paces the curb smoking a cigar. He gives me a hug and asks, "How are you roomie?"

"Never better," I can feel Michaels's eyes staring in disbelief. An HBO in a public display of affection with an insubordinate subordinate seems to upset his world. What is the Bureau coming to? I turn toward Boy Wonder and say, "Mike, this is Assistant Director Anthony Daniels."

To someone like Michaels, an assistant director of the FBI packs the same starstruck awe that Elvis had on 13-year-old girls in Tupelo, Mississippi. Boy Wonder's first inclination is to bow, kneel, or kiss Tony's ass. Instead he mumbles, "A pleasure to meet you sir. I've followed your career."

Tony, being ever the gentleman, shakes Michaels' hand and says, "Nice meeting you, Matt. John has told me *all* about you."

I did call Tony last night and made him promise to say those *exact* words. A very childish but subtle and effective form of mind fucking. Boy Wonder understands that Tony already received the heads up that he is a total asshole. Even with that understanding, Michaels starts with the predictable ass licking line, "We have some mutual friends, Director Daniels."

Boy Wonder is adept at twisting every sentence into a subtle cataloguing of his qualifications for upward mobility, including saving the Perry nuclear power plant during the blackout. He is a master at pushing round pegs into square discussion holes. I punish Tony by claiming the back seat that allows Michaels unrestricted access to an HNO. I close my eyes and allow their conversation to fade into background noise as we crawl through D.C. traffic.

The J. Edgar Hoover building gives me the creeps. After you clear security and begin trekking down the hallways, it reminds me of those Halloween straw mazes where kids get lost and begin sobbing. I truly have no idea how the business of the most powerful law enforcement agency on earth is conducted in such a stilted environment.

Tony directs us to an empty fourth floor conference room. There's a tray of coffee and donuts, so I make myself at home. Boy Wonder seems surgically attached to Tony with no more than two feet of separation since the airport. I strongly suspect that my roomie is getting tired of the blatant brown nosing, because I am feeling a bit nauseous just listening.

Tony begins in a more formal tone. "Let me give you a rundown of the players."

We give him our undivided attention and he says. "The main player in the room will be the Deputy Director, and *my* boss, Edward Batcheller."

"Eddie the Exorcist?" I ask. "Did he really transfer twelve guys to Butte, Montana for some bachelor party at a strip joint?"

"That's him," Tony chuckles. "But in his defense, he had to do something when it hit the newspapers. The groom never made the wedding. He called his fiancé, broke off the engagement, and a month later married the stripper."

"How's the stripper like Butte?"

"Another major player is the JTTF section chief, Elizabeth Lewis. She's a law school classmate of our president and worked previously at some liberal think tank."

Sometime around the late eighties, the FBI began hiring civilians for high-level positions at Headquarters. Brick agents were forced to seek approvals from non-law enforcement types to conduct field operations. Not good.

Tony continues, "The only other major player at the meeting will be the CIA deputy director of Middle Eastern Affairs, John Burke. John's a good guy and was Beck's boss, although some steps removed."

"So," I ask. "We make our pitch to those three and basically ignore the bench players?"

Tony confirms that. "The rest of the attendees will *pretend* to take notes but will be deciding on where to have lunch."

Much of my ability to peacefully coexist with Mafia mopes comes from family gatherings with thirteen Italian aunts and twenty-one cousins. But unfortunately, these skills never translated to bureaucrats who are considerably more treacherous than psychotic mob guys.

I suddenly realize that I am overmatched!

CHAPTER 14

"You have no respect for authority. You're dangerous and
depraved, and you ought to be taken outside and shot!"
Catch-22 by Joseph Heller

Introductions are made and I attempt to size up the players using Tony's scouting report. FBI Deputy Director Gordon Batcheller sits at the table's head. The CIA deputy and Tony frame Eddie with the remaining faceless minions filling up the seats according to the professional size of their dicks *and* vaginas.

Michaels and I are seated at the far end of the conference table. It brings back memories at being vanquished to the children's table during family Thanksgiving dinners. I pay particular attention to Elizabeth Lewis, sensing some seething hostility just below the surface. My guess is that Ms. Lewis views law enforcement with a jaundiced eye and her assignment to the FBI was our liberal President's attempt at oversight. She wears a pants suit, subtle makeup, practical shoes, and is about fifteen pounds north of Oprah.

Tony begins the meeting. "Appreciate everyone taking the time out of their busy schedules. Being perfectly honest, this meeting would never happen unless the subject matter was not of such significant national security. The issue at hand is at a very preliminary stage and not even an open case."

When Tony mentions my name, the entire table of suits and skirts snap their heads toward me. It was their first overt indication that I existed. I give the group a slight nod and some weird facial gesture that resembles a botched plastic surgery.

Michaels can't help himself. He says, "My name is Supervisory Agent Michael T. Michaels of the Cleveland task force, and Special Agent Bookers's immediate *supervisor.*"

"Was just about to introduce you, Mike," Tony says almost apologetically. Tony looks at me and says, "John, it's all yours."

My vibe within the room is that I am wasting my time. This group of the supposed best and brightest is already bored. But I plunge ahead with, "I met Grant Beck at an in-service on terrorism."

I provide a rehash of the intelligence bulletins with the strange nursery type rhymes, and then launch into Beck's suspicions. I follow with CIA operative Mike Vickers's belief that the blackout was a terrorist act then build the foundation of the existence of a super terrorist organization connected to the North Korean government. I toss in Vickers's traffic death, Beck's frantic calls to me just prior to his own death by an aneurysm, the bizarre telephone sounds, and finally the admonition that the *"BIRD IS COOKING,"* which Beck and I believe may predict another catastrophe on American soil.

"Questions?" I ask

Ms. Lewis comments, "A very frightening scenario, Agent Booker, but as an attorney I can assure you that none of it rises to the threshold of probable cause. Lots of circumstantial happenings, but not one concrete piece of evidence."

"'Ms. Lewis," I counter. "This is *not* a court of law, and as an investigative agent of the FBI, all I'm asking is that we investigate."

"Investigate what, investigate who?" Lewis asks with an impatient edge. "What exactly do you want?"

"For starters, exhume Beck's body and check for any evidence that the aneurysm could have been induced by an air bubble. While we're at it, take another look at the old narcolepsy guy who played bumper car with Vickers's head. Find the source who provided Vickers the information that the blackout was a terrorist act, assign some intel analysts to review the past two years of intelligence bulletins and determine if the intercepted chatter is connected to actual disasters, and *finally*, we need to get ahead of the phrase, *"BIRD IS COOKING."*

CIA Deputy Director Burke says. "I cannot in good conscience ask Beck's family to approve exhuming their father's body. They're still in mourning and no exigent circumstances exist to warrant such an extreme act."

I make a counter offer. "How about if we turn up the pressure on the old man who killed Vickers?"

Burke getting agitated, "Mr. Jihbard was investigated by both my agency and the Egyptian police. He had been a cobbler for over forty-five years with no ties to any suspicious group or individuals. And besides that, he passed away six weeks ago."

"So now the old man is dead," I say incredulous. "Can I ask how he died?"

"You can. He died of kidney failure," Burke back in official mode. "And just as a precaution, since he was involved in the death of a CIA field operative, I had an autopsy performed. His kidneys were operating at eleven percent capacity. Had Mr. Jihard been eligible for kidney dialysis, he still wouldn't have survived much longer."

Eddie the Exorcist finally chimes in with, "Agent Booker, we all have heavy schedules today. Is there anything else that you can add? Something not of a hearsay or third party nature?"

I hesitate and feel the meeting slipping away so I swing for the fences. "Yes sir. I have a reliable informant who can corroborate Vickers's source."

"That a super terrorist cell exists?" The Exorcist asks.

Lewis immediately jumps in. "You didn't mention this source till now, and you certainly didn't include it in your summary," she adds while waving my written summary.

Eddie the Exorcist looks at Michaels and asks, "Supervisors have to approve the opening of all sources and sign off on each and every contact. So, Agent Michaels, assuming that you have done *your* job, then I will ask *you*, does this source exist?"

Boy Wonder looks like the proverbial deer in the headlight. He glances at me, then back at the Exorcist. He finally says. "Agent Booker never opened a source that provided anything close to what he alleges."

My view from under the bus is not promising.

"I never *officially* opened the source," I counter. "But I have an informant who can corroborate what Vickers asset told him about the existence of a super terrorist cell. Isn't *that* the more important issue?"

My mind is racing. I had decided to pull the rabbit out of my hat and now Bugs is crazily running out of control. There is no way that I'll front Suehad since she would be subject to intense scrutiny followed by deportation. Besides, I'd given her my word *and* she has big tits.

The Exorcist is all over me, about to go in for the kill shot. I suddenly see myself in Butte Montana guarding Moose preserves, and sharing Sunday potluck dinner with the Chicago agent and his stripper wife.

"It was a hip pocket source," I finally say.

Ms. Lewis asks. "What in the world is a hip pocket source?"

Tony *finally* enters the arena with, "It's not uncommon for agents to have hip pocket sources. These are individuals who do not want to go on paper but provide valuable information. They understand that by not being official snitches, they'll never have to testify in court, and their identity will never be revealed. It's worked well for decades."

"But," Lewis counters, "The regulations mandate that *all* FBI informants be *officially* opened on paper. Our liability is off the charts if we allow informants to run around ignoring our guidelines. As you may or may not know, Agent Booker, the FBI maintains a sacred trust with the public, and phantom informants erode that trust."

At this point in the lecture, Ms. Lewis glares at me as a crocodile would a fat squirrel. We're also behind on the scoreboard again. She continues the regulatory symposium, "Informants act as government agents and sign agreements that they will not engage in criminal activities while working with the government. If you eliminate this official understanding, then informants can kill or sell drugs and when they get caught, simply use the FBI as their alibi."

Oprah has a point, and I can counter that point if it wouldn't further paint me as an irresponsible, regulation-ignoring, rogue agent.

Another dirty little FBI secret is that the more successful agents *all* operate hip pocket sources and should the snitch go off the reservation, then we would simply disavow any connection to the scumbag. In other words, two can play at a deceitful relationship. Of course, I couldn't exactly wink and nod this gray area to this particular group.

Tony attempts to jump in front of the bus by saying, "I realize that hip pocket sources are not *officially* permitted but it's a well-recognized law enforcement technique, and ..." My roomie looks directly at several FBI agents sitting at the table including Eddie the Exorcist. He continues with "... and, I'm sure that many agents in this *very* room have used hip pocket sources."

But Ms. Lewis is on firm regulatory ground and pounces with, "So Agent Booker, since this is a matter of national security, I will give you the opportunity to reveal your *hip pocket* source. Our counter terrorism experts at Headquarters will debrief the source and determine if their information is reliable. We will also ignore your blatant violation of government regulations provided you cooperate. How does that sound?"

It sounds pretty shitty and my mind is calculating damage control. I realize that I had put myself in this pickle by demanding a meeting so ill prepared. Then I parlay my initial bad judgment by casually mentioning eight pages of regulatory infractions to the exact people who write those regulations.

I stand and head toward the door. Ms. Lewis says, "Agent Booker if you walk out that door, you leave us no choice but to consider disciplinary action against you."

I stop, turn back toward the group, and say, "Roomie, I'm sorry I got you involved in this mess." I look Ms. Lewis in the eye and announce, "As far as me leaving the room,I feel that it is currently in *your* best interest that I exit now."

"And why would it be in *my* best interest?"

"Because if I stay I'll probably tell you that you have no idea what's it like to spend twenty hours freezing your ass off in a surveillance, or busting down a door to a drug house, or rolling around on the ground trying to cuffsome idiot on PCP. I will probably tell you that civilians have no place making law enforcement operational decisions, and I will strongly suggest that you try this great seaweed diet I know. And last, but certainly not least, I would highly recommend that you get laid. You seem very uptight."

I find my way out of the straw bale Halloween maze and breathe the fresh air of the late February morning in our nation's capital. I grab a sidewalk vendor hot dog, walk aimlessly for an hour, and then hail a cab and head toward the airport.

I feel like a cross between Chinese toothpaste and the hunter who shot *Bambi*.

CHAPTER 15

"Human salvation lies in the hands of the creatively maladjusted."
— Martin Luther King, Jr.

I arrive in Cleveland and awake my cell phone from airplane mode. Fourteen voice mails and six text messages. Two from Bell, six from Boy Wonder, three from Tony, a few unidentified numbers, and somehow the *'Christian Mingle'* date group has targeted me. Perhaps, they know something that I don't. I can guess at the general theme of the Bureau messages.

The Office of Professional Responsibility is manned by the FBI headhunters. That office seems to attract agents who had pulled the wings off flies as children. One or two of them probably even put their cat in a microwave.

If an FBI agent steals, kills, or violates a few other commandments, then they should go to jail. I understand that line in the sand, but OPR has ruined lives over a free lunch. Another dirty little secret is that *most* FBI agents violate some rule, regulation, guideline, or policy on a daily basis. There is actually a guideline on the number of paper clips permitted inside our desk. A particular favorite is the misuse of our *'official use only'* government ride. Agents use their government ride from everything to picking up laundry to picking up hookers. Just ask the Secret Service.

The FBI car provides transportation to soccer matches, little league games, and dance classes. If bosses ever bothered to inspect the cars, they would find an assortment of items ranging from infant car seats, golf clubs, beach umbrellas, and an occasional pair of lace panties.

I conduct a quick damage control of my situation. Not too good for yours truly, but my schoolyard behavior also affected the *one* individual in the entire Bureau that I both respect and love. I dial Tony's personal cell phone.

"*I would highly recommend that you get laid ...* " is Tony's opening salvo. He continues, "Great exit, John. The group recommended that you be shot by a firing squad. The vote was nine to one."

"Thanks for sticking up for me."

"I voted for the firing squad."

"You mad?"

"Fuckin' right I'm mad. I put my ass on the line and you shove a load of immature bullshit right up it. Lewis has probably already informed the President that the FBI is running fast and loose. And our President is just looking for a reason to castrate the Bureau."

"Sorry, roomie."

After a few seconds of awkward silence Tony says, "Okay, John, here's what went down after you pissed off the entire hierarchy of three government agencies. Lewis demanded an immediate suspension, without pay, pending an OPR investigation, *which* will in all likelihood recommend termination."

"So I stepped in it pretty good," I say.

"No shit, Sherlock. And in case you didn't know, your supervisor Michaels wanted you fired immediately. Said you were an insubordinate, foul mouth excuse for an agent. And your behavior did nothing but reinforce his opinion."

"So give me the bottom line."

Tony continues. "After the meeting I got with the Deputy Director alone and basically blackmailed him to back Lewis off."

"Deception has always been your strong suit. I remember the forensics exam."

"Look, Eddie the Exorcist is a good guy. He worked the streets and loves brick agents. He told me that he operated hip pocket sources for years."

"That's nice, but get to the blackmail stuff."

"We went to a law enforcement symposium in Copenhagen last year and all I'll say is that Eddie had a good time. You can fill in the blanks. Now back to your little problem."

"How bad?" I ask.

"You're assigned to the office pending the outcome of the OPR investigation. You are to completely drop this entire matter of a super-secret terrorist cell. Desk duty and you better not pull any of your shit because I'm way out on a limb for you on this one."

Tony pauses and his voice subtly changes. "But here's the out. Eddie said that if you give up your hip pocket source, providing one exists, then OPR disappears and you're back in the saddle." Tony pauses and asks, "This source does exist, don't they?"

"They do."

"And you will identify them?"

"I'll think about it."

"Listen to me, Booker," Tony says angrily, "you better fuckin' give up this source, or I'll …"My roommate is at a loss for a good threat.

Before he concludes his ultimatum I say, "Call you later."

I head home and tell my wife that I had a wonderful and productive meeting in Washington. "That's unusual, John." Lorri says suspiciously. "You usually come back from meetings in a foul mood."

"Got to see Tony, had a great lunch, and met with some really interesting folks."

"Somehow, you don't sound too convincing."

"I'm gonna go take a bubble bath," I change the subject." Is the rubber frogman in the closet?"

The next morning I stop to see my favorite Donnie Osmond at Starbucks. I have some idea of what's awaiting me at the office, so I decide on a holding pattern. First would be the notification by Bell that I am officially chained to my desk. He will order me to cease and desist *all* investigations but especially anything to do with Beck's death, super terrorists, and probably forbid me to eat anything with curry. I will be effectively neutered and Michaels may actually hang my balls on his wall like a small game trophy.

All my cases will be reassigned pending OPR's investigation, which will recommend immediate termination, *unless*, I give up my source.

I finally reach Donnie who smiles and says, "The usual, John?"

I nod and ask. "Hey Donnie, you always seem in such a great mood. You ever break a shoelace, have a girl dump you, or have some boss be an asshole?"

"All of the above, but it was a guy who dumped me."

"Whatever," I continue. "So how do you handle all the bullshit?"

Donnie seems to give my question some thought. He says. "I *choose* to be happy."

"That's it."

"When you wake up in the morning," Donnie all sincere, "it's your choice to be happy or sad. I choose happiness."

"Thanks for sharing, Donnie."

He takes a step toward the counter, scoops up my Starbucks card and adds, "I *also* smoke a lot of pot."

Peggy knows my fate when I walk into the office. I can see the pity in her eyes. There *no* secrets in the Bureau and if you want to know where the bodies are buried, ask a secretary.

"SAC wants to see you." Peggy says and then lets fly an involuntary string of profanity. She retains control and adds calmly, "Michaels wants to see you right after."

"It's okay, Peggy." I tell her. "I'll live."

"You're my favorite, John Booker," Peggy says sincerely. "This outfit sometimes eats their own."

I pat Peggy on the shoulder and say, "Very true, but *I* will cause them severe indigestion."

My meeting with Bell went as predicted. He chews my ass out, repeats a few, "*I told yous*, and then lays down the official terms of my grounding. He sounds like a parent who is about to spank their kid and says, "This is going to hurt me a lot more than it will hurt you."

Then his mood lightens and Bell tells me that my comments to Ms. Lewis in Washington are being quoted Bureau wide and garnering a cult-like following. "The internal FBI computer e-mail system almost shut down this morning."

"You went viral," Bell laughs. "Evidently you struck a blow for all the brick agents who always wanted to tell some head honcho to '*fuck off*.' Bell asks, "So you actually suggested to a high ranking Bureau official that she had no business in law enforcement, *followed* by a recommendation of a seaweed diet and sex."

"That about covers it."

"I've operated a slew of hip pocket sources," Bell confirms. "You're a good man John, do what they ask and get this behind you."

"So you know about the ultimatum to give up my source."

"They're not asking that you disclose the source *outside* the Bureau, and, *if* you had *followed* Bureau regulations, we would have the identity anyway. This is not the fight worth risking your career over. It's just some snitch, John."

"How long will the OPR investigation take?"

"Usually, five to eight months. OPR has the luxury to turn up the heat by playing the waiting game. Agents who are guilty of even *minor* infractions become more paranoid with each passing day. But you're already a ten on the paranoid scale so the wait may work to your advantage."

"I appreciate your unyielding confidence and support," I say. "But what am I going to be doing for the next six months?"

Bell says. "Basically, you're going to be Michaels's gofer. I counseled him to treat you fairly and back off. Warned him that I would not tolerate another cat fight, and now I'm *warning* you."

"I'll be good."

"You said those exact words *before* the meeting." Bell gets serious. "Look, John, I got my twenty-five in and they can't hurt me, so I really don't give a crap about what went down in D.C. I actually agree with you that these civilians have no business in operations. But I can't have you being a dick to your immediate supervisor. Besides, that's *my* job."

I laugh and ask, "So, how's Boy Wonder going to get even with me?"

He told me that he wants you to analyze every closed case for the past five years and make recommendations."

"The old *dead dog* punishment. That idiot couldn't even get creative."

"Get the hell out of here," Bell laughs.

Upon my return to the squad area, Gwen McNulty and her perfect 36 Cs stand and begin applauding. S.W.A.T. Boy, Bruce, and the rest of the task force rise in unison and start clapping. I bow at the waist and wave like Queen Elizabeth greeting her subjects. "Thank you very much," I say and take my seat.

"Hey Booker," Gwen laughs. "I need to get your advice on a very sensitive issue." She pauses for effect. "I've been a little uptight lately, what do you recommend?"

"Either the seaweed diet or sex," I say.

This brings howls from the peanut gallery who evidently had a verbatim copy of my comments to Oprah. Peggy's voice interrupts the fun and games to remind me that Michaels desires my presence immediately.

I decide to get the Boy Wonder lecture behind me so I can begin my new exciting career in reviewing the cold cases of the Bureau. There usually is a good reason that a case is closed, and scrutinizing discarded case files is similar to reading the Dead Sea scrolls. I actually have no idea what the Dead Sea scrolls entail, but they probably won't be basing an action film on their content.

Michaels is sitting behind his desk as I enter, minus a knock. I may have to eat crow but I need to maintain some shred of my testicles.

"Well, John," He begins. "Needless to say, I am very disappointed in you. Your childish behavior has reflected negatively on this office."

I say "Understood" but think *'You are only thinking about your own ass.'*

"Now this is just between you and me, but after you left the room the consensus was to terminate you entirely." Michaels pauses to allow the gravity of his words to sink in. "But, I went to bat for you. I personally stopped them from firing you."

"Thank you for that," I say, but think, *'You lying bastard.'*

Boy Wonder continues his 9AM reprimand lecture. *"We* decided that you will be restricted to desk duty. No leaving the office and no contact with the public. Your active cases have been reassigned and OPR will conduct a thorough investigation into your blatant disregard for regulations involving our informant program. Questions?"

"No sir," I say because I need to exit the room pronto. At present I am merely having a bad day at work, but this conversation could easily degenerate into murder one. "Anything else?" I ask while gaining my feet, and walk out as Boy Wonder says "No."

My next few months are spent chained to my desk assessing closed cases. My mission is to decide if a particular case deserves some additional investigation. It is the perfect punishment for a brick agent who believes that agents need to be in the field since there are usually very few criminals in the office. I take coffee breaks, an occasional walk, or lunch at the Galleria with Bruce and S.W.A.T. Boy.

The clock is ticking on my OPR investigation. Tony and Bell regularly encourage me to "give up the informant." OPR will eventually interview me and demand I disclose my hip pocket source. Since this is not a criminal matter, I cannot refuse to answer. In administrative matters, FBI agents have no constitutional rights against self-incrimination. If I refuse, they fire me for insubordination, failure to follow the Bureau regulations of operating informants, and insulting my superiors. Guilty as charged.

My cell phone rings and it's Nikki. "Just letting you know that I'm going to the mall with Jenny."

I check my watch and ask, "It's noon; shouldn't you be in school?"

"They closed all the schools in the county. Haven't you heard?"

"No."

"Something about ovarian flu."

CHAPTER 16

"If at first you don't succeed ... failure may be your style"
– Quentin Crisp

I didn't give Nikki's mall trip much thought. Schools are always shutting their doors for reasons ranging from broken heaters to teachers' conferences. But I did inform Nikki. "Honey, it's probably *not* the ovarian flu."

"Well, it's something *like* that; gotta go." End of conversation.

I forget all about the *ovarian* flu, due to my current life-altering predicament. I could either continue earning a paycheck to purchase food and shelter, or I can destroy the life of someone who had put their trust in me.

Michaels keeps his distance as I await the call from OPR. We communicate electronically, which is part of his strategy. Boy Wonder is playing the '*gotcha game*' which consists of assigning me impossible tasks with unreasonable completion dates. Since everything is reduced to writing, Michaels will be armed with the documentation of my incompetence to fatten up OPR's case.

He glides around the office with a perpetual smirk on his face as if he is about to win the lottery. The rumors are that Boy Wonder is expecting *the* call up to the puzzle palace. Another promotion for a job never done.

It feels like a game of Russian roulette every time my phone rings. Because once OPR corners me into the interrogation room, my options become extremely limited. I can give up Suehad and hope she antes up her hubby or remain silent and hang out in soup lines. If I do divulge Suehad as my *'hip pocket'* source the outcome is written in stone. After they debrief Suehad, they'll wire her up and fly her back to Cairo with orders to *'patch up the marriage.'* Regardless of what happens after that, Suehad's idealist academic life in America will cease to exist. If she escapes deportation based on perjuring herself on her visa application, she can no longer stay in the states, and she *definitely* won't be welcomed back in her homeland.

I consider calling Suehad just to connect and get a temperature but feel that now is not the time. The conversation would be stilted, so I opt for the path of least resistance. Let her think that our dinner left me not wanting to break bread again.

The only good to evolve from my troubles is that I now work bankers' hours. I am home by five-thirty and spend an hour in the kitchen gossiping with Lorri about trivial matters. Our time together, though, is darkened by the cloud of job uncertainty, so our conversation lacks any real enthusiasm. Although I've given my wife the basics, we never mention the elephant in the room. The Jim Beam, which I consume in a stadium cup, dulls the anxiety and alternately provides me false courage or plummets me into despair.

Peace and quiet is not a natural state for a brick agent who is also a thrill junky. Although I'd sometimes complain about the constant interruptions to my free time with work-related calls, the sudden silence makes me feel insignificant. My government issued cell phone *never* rings.

Several times during the workday I draw a line down the middle of a paper and furiously scribble numbers. One column consists of our monthly expenses such as mortgage, utilities, insurances, food, internet, cable TV, cell phones, and bourbon. The other column tallies our income. Lorri's salary can't carry the load, and like most working humps, my savings may amount to five or six months of survival expenses. No matter how many times I reconfigure the numbers, I couldn't stay unemployed for long.

Following dinner, my new nightly routine includes a few horizontal hours on my recliner in front of the flat screen. Talk about a mind diversion. My primary distraction is the cable news talk shows. A CNN special report catches my attention this particular evening.

It's a report on Nikki's *ovarian* flu or more accurately the avian flu. I've heard of the avian flu but only in the most general terms. The news anchor provides the latest on what he terms, "*A frightening epidemic.*"

My first inclination is that this bird flu epidemic is merely a coincidence with my terrorist group. After all, the word '*bird*" is very common and I presently reside in an extremely paranoid state.

What do I know and what do I *think* I know?

The intelligence bulletins first indicated that "*The DARK BIRD MADE THE SON SICK.*" This jumbled sentence contains two of the four words, "*Dark*" and "*Bird*," which may indicate the existence of a grand terrorist conspiracy. But who is the "*SON*," and how did he get "*SICK*?"

"*DARK DAY IMMINENT ... BIRD SERVED NEXT,*" was followed by the great American blackout that resulted in anarchy, rape, and murder. It also promised that some bird will be served, *next.* Could that be the avian aka '*bird*' flu?

This particular communication also linked Cairo and North Korea. That geographical *and* ideological connection may seem odd at first blush, but the common thread is their mutual and overwhelming hatred of the United States of America.

And finally, "*BIRD IS COOKING.*" Could the avian flu epidemic be the latest nail in America's coffin? I realize that I require information, before my head implodes with visions of neighbors flapping their imaginary wings and foaming beaks. I need to know how a human become infected with avian flu. Is it merely close proximity to an affected bird or some type of physical contact? And, once a human is infected, how is the disease transmitted?

And finally, can I connect the bird flu epidemic and the blackout with my phantom terrorist cell? Doubtful, so I refill my cup of bourbon.

I am visited by the exploding IED in my sleep, but my dream includes a new twist. A large black bird resembling a crow keeps pecking away at my head as I lay helpless on the ground. No matter how hard I twist and turn, the bird's beak is relentless and on target.

The next morning at *Starbucks*, I order a double espresso instead of my usual Venti Latte. Donny Osmond is in his usual manic state and I envy his seemingly uncomplicated existence. Smoke a little dope, play hide the salami with some male fitness instructor, and entertain the masses at *Starbucks*.

As an investigator, I need leads. Solving a case is similar to pulling on a loose thread of a large knit sweater. If you keep pulling, eventually the sweater dissolves and becomes transparent. My first step is to find that loose thread. Calling Tony Daniels or Jack Bell are options but I can already predict the conversation. I rehash the Beck and Vickers alleged murders, and surmise that the blackout and now the bird flu are all connected.

My hunch is that *if* I can access the *current* intelligence bulletins perhaps I'd discover some reference to the bird flu. And, if I examine some of the *older* bulletins there may be a connection between intercepted chatter and previous national disasters. Instead I spend my days staring at old dog cases and daydreaming about purple bra straps. My frustration level forces me to regularly leave the office and take walks. I buy cigars at the Galleria and pace along the street like an angry steam engine. An hour later, I'm usually back at my desk. The walks do little to sweeten my sour disposition.

It's a particularly gloomy Thursday afternoon when I return from one of my strolls. While in the office, FBI agents place their weapons inside their desk. I slide open my drawer and see a yellow stick 'em note paper with a series of handwritten numbers. They appear to be an access code for the SCI compartment housing the intelligence bulletins.

I scan the room to see if anyone might be watching. My first thought consistent with my paranoia is that I'm being set up. My second thought is that one of my squad mates may have reconsidered, but desires the plausible deniability of, "I didn't give Booker the access code." If I am caught accessing *eyes only* information without authorization, the penalty is immediate termination and possible criminal charges. It takes less than a second for me to decide and peck the code onto the key board and chuckle to myself thinking that they can just add this violation to my existing felony tab.

I make an arbitrary decision to begin my historical trek six months before 9/11. It takes about an hour before I notice an odd radio interception originating in Cairo just one week before the terrorist attacks on the World Trade Center. "CANADIAN HOLIDAY ENDS."

The terrorists who commandeered the plane in Boston entered the US from Canada. A coincidence? Perhaps.

Two days later a second interception from the same region declares ... "APPLE FESTIVAL." The big "apple" is synonymous with New York City.

The day *before* the attacks, a communication intercepted in a region near Cairo declares, "FAT - WAH."

The significance of *this* interception is that it originated in the same geographical area as the most recent communications concerning "BIRDS," "SON," and "DARK DAYS." I had learned a few things during my time on the task force and one of them was that the word *fatwahh* is an absolute ruling on Islamic law.

The intercepts really get interesting in April of 2013. Three days before the Boston Marathon Bombings, there is chatter on a suspected web site used by radical Muslims and monitored by our intel analysts who flagged a message, *SON RUN NOW*. Three hours later there was a response posting stating, *AND FERTILIZE GARDEN*.

On April 14th two Chechen brothers set off bombs at the Boston Marathon touching off a week of national panic. On April 15th a large fertilizer plant in Texas blew with the earth quake force of 2.1 on the Richter scale.

Aside from the needless deaths and casualties, both events had a profound effect on America's collective psyche. Citizens felt extremely vulnerable and wanted to strike back, but, the final Marathon investigative conclusion was that the brothers acted alone and had no outside assistance. So the United States couldn't exactly attack Chechnya to exact some revenge.

The fertilizer accident in Texas was deemed an *industrial accident*. Three months later a propane plant blew sky high and four major wild fires erupted west of the Mississippi, resulting in billions of dollars in damage and hundreds of lost lives. All of the fires were *also* deemed 'accidental.'

There seems to be plenty of serious *"whoopsies"* occurring in America. A coincidence? Perhaps.

"Hey handsome," Gwen McNulty says. "What are you doing?"

Ms. Perfect 36 Cs is walking my way so I slide the cursor and make the screen disappear. She leans over my desk and asks. "Hear the news?"

"What news."

"The President just appointed the new Chief Justice to the Supreme Court."

"I've got the feeling that it's not good."

"Couldn't be much worse," Gwen chuckles. "It's the former executive director of the ACLU. Ms. Eleni Atwabi, though born in San Francisco, converted to the Islam religion in high school. She was educated at Berkeley and received her Juris Doctoris at NYU. How's that for a radical pedigree? Ethnically, she's half Lebanese and half Irish."

"She must have some vicious arguments with herself."

Gwen laughs and continues with, "Atwabi was appointed to the federal bench ten years ago, and recently ruled that Muslim prisoners in California State Prison Solano have the right to a full-time Muslim chaplain, prayer oil, attend Friday prayers, *without* losing good time. *And*, they get to wear beards up to one inch."

I slowly gain my feet, look Gwen in the eyes and say, "I'm feeling ill, Gwen, and I think it's time to head home."

"You haven't heard the worst," Gwen warns. "Chief Justice Atwabi is going to fast track cases on racial profiling, expedited search and seizure, and granting military combatant status to terrorists."

As I enter the elevator I seem to remember that Tony Daniels had predicted this exact judicial scenario with the warning, "*A bad decision on any one of them will put a knife through the heart of our war on terrorism.*"

CHAPTER 17

"All generalizations are false"
— Mark Twain

I feel surprisingly refreshed after a night's sleep minus exploding IEDs. Iraq evidently wasn't on my dream itinerary.

Several people standing in the Starbucks line are wearing surgical masks. They're supposed to prevent the spread of bird flu, but I seriously doubt that one-sixteenth inch of fabric can stop a plague. The hot conversation in the line concerns the epidemic's death toll. The elderly seem to be dropping like flies, followed by people with prior health issues, then children.

Donnie Osmond, by virtue of his unlimited informational access to the masses, becomes the burning bush of wisdom. He announces to his audience that sufficient vaccine to inoculate three fourths of the population is ready to be shipped. This pronouncement creates a ripple effect of comments throughout the line.

I notice that Donnie is sporting a rainbow colored surgical mask accessorized with glitter.

As I reach the counter he asks, "How do you like my mask?"

"Colorful, Donnie. Is that some kind of gay statement?"

"Is that a yes?"

"Yes."

"I wanted to offer a special bird flu latte, but the corporate types thought it tasteless. What do you think?"

"I'd wait for the bubonic plague. It has a better caffeine ring to it."

"It's scary, John, this whole epidemic. You can't stay cloistered in your apartment, 'cause you gotta work. Some guy sneezed in line yesterday and I stopped breathing until I reached the bathroom where I scrubbed down with near scalding water."

I obviously wouldn't share my theory that the bird flu is a terrorist act. There were moments when I thought this possibility so farfetched, that I wanted to throw the net over my *own* head. Yet, my intellect knew that terrorists were plotting and scheming our demise every second of every day. So perhaps my theory is *not* so extreme. And my instincts have kept me alive through a war with both the Iraqis *and* the Mafia.

"At least with the AIDS epidemic, you got to swap bodily fluids."

"Great visual," I say. "I couldn't quite hear your comments on the flu fatalities."

"As of today the CDC reports that for every ten persons infected with the flu, two will die." Doesn't seem like much until you do the math. Twenty thousand infections equal four thousand Americans deaths.

I commiserate with Donnie, then grab my coffee and beat feet from the guy behind me who suddenly appears contagious. I could almost feel the tickle in my throat and wonder if that's a symptom of the avian flu.

Boy Wonder has two new assignments awaiting me at the office as part of his campaign to prove me an ineffective FBI agent. It's working so far. I decide that Michaels is a vicious petty individual so I reflexively delete the assignments, pull out the secret code, and access the prohibitive SCI site.

This simple action constitutes additional counts in my indictment of unauthorized access. I also realize that as soon as the "eyes only" site is audited, they'd match the individual codes and dates with the authorized agents. Since all paths would lead to me, it would be game, set, match, Mr. Michaels. I have to act fast.

Due to my ticking time bomb of an existence, I attempt to narrow my searches to specific gibberish phrases that possess the same tone and feel of the "BIRD" series. If Michaels discovers my electronic fishing or OPR calls, then the jig is up. Though I can't articulate what I am looking for, I feel that I'll know it when I see it.

Five hours later after two coffee breaks and a salami hoagie with mayo, I have several promising idioms. The second part of my exercise is to match these phrases with a previous catastrophe, which on their surface, seem unrelated. If the time period coincides with the intercepted phrase, then I have what is called in law enforcement, *reasonable suspicion* – nothing firm but simply a gut instinct based on circumstantial events.

Whoever is pulling the strings of this operation understands that if a calamity *appears* to be an act of terrorism, then the U.S. strikes back with a vengeance. I have to grudgingly admire their creative and diabolical evilness. These guys are good.

My final list includes:

"CRUDE." This intercept occurred a few days before gas prices soared in 2004 to an average of $4.75 overnight. It had a crippling effect on interstate commerce, the airline and transportation industry, and caused the layoff of thousands of workers in industries ranging from manufacturing to tourism.

"TOP NOW." This intercept occurred the day prior to Chief Justice Williams' murder in a supposed simple mugging gone bad. The Judge's murder resulted in a Supreme Court tilting dangerously to the left, which will turn the judicial tide in favor of terrorists.

When I add these pieces to yesterday's research, I actually feel nauseous. My puzzle may have a thousand pieces, but the few that *are* connected are cataclysmic. But the possibility still exists that this plot is one giant coincidence.

Feeling a sense of urgency, I query the bulletins for the current week. A few of the intercepts seem interesting but the one stands out is *"SON SICK WITH VIRUS."* This phrase was intercepted two days ago and includes two interesting references. It originated in North Korea and it referenced a "SON."

The first suspicious intercept of *"The DARK BIRD MADE THE SON SICK"* also originated in North Korea and was followed by a major blackout, thus the word *'DARK.'* And the reference to *'BIRD'* most likely refers to the "avian" flu. But I am still wondering who the hell the *'SON'* may be.

So if I'm correctly connecting the dots then this latest intercept is a prelude to some major American disaster. I just have to figure out who, what, where, when and how.

My cell phone interrupts my mental impasse. Caller ID indicates *"Wife."*

"John," Lorri says slowly and in a tone that is usually followed by some tragic announcement. "Nikki wasn't feeling well at school today, so I picked her up and took her to the Urgent Care Center in town."

I hold my breath awaiting the worse and I'm only slightly off the mark.

Lorri announces, "The doctors think she may have the avian flu."

After getting the basics of, *"not currently life threatening,"* and *"she's on a regimen of antibiotics,"* I jump up and grab my coat just as Boy Wonder is making his way to the bathroom. A classic case of imperfect timing.

He looks at the clock asks, "Going somewhere?"

My default mode is to lie since my grounding stipulates *'office only'* but my daughter's health overrides the usual bullshit. Michaels actually seems ecstatic by catching his main antagonist in an act of open defiance.

"My daughter is sick."

Michaels forces a look of concern and wonders. "Hope it's not serious, John."

"Not life threatening, but could be the bird flu."

I continue my exit but Michaels says. "Lot of people *think* the sniffles may be the bird flu. My son stayed home from school today with a slight fever."

"Hope he gets better," I offer, but somehow know this conversation is going somewhere bad.

"Is your wife with her?"

"Yep."

"Well," Boy Wonder whines. "You need to finish up some of the leads I've assigned you. Don't you think?"

"Look Matt, I'll get on that stuff tomorrow, I promise."

The entire squad is watching this Greek tragedy unfold. They are sitting motionless and staring without the slightest pretense of looking elsewhere.

I'm not interested in having this particular discussion at this particular time, so I head toward the elevator. Michaels takes two steps to the side and physically blocks my path. I attempt to walk around him but Boy Wonder grabs my arms and screams, "You will not leave this office until I tell you."

I instinctively snatch my immediate supervisor by the throat and shove him against the wall. I lean into Boy Wonder's face and hiss, "Look asshole, I'm going to see my daughter." As I tighten my grip above his Adams apple, his eyes begin to roll back into his head. "Is that okay with you, Mr. Michaels?"

Michaels nods his head and I release him. He slumps to the floor in a slow motion montage and begins to gag. I feel no remorse for my actions, but only the angst of a parent with a sick child.

As I drive towards my family, I believe that my latest behavior may be the proverbial straw that broke the camel's back. It's not likely that assault with twelve eyewitnesses added to insubordination, unauthorized access, and violating Bureau regulations on operating informants will result in, "*Hey Agent Booker, just don't do that shit again, We good now ...?*" I can only hope that the FBI decides on a pink slip in lieu of a cyanide capsule.

As I speed to the hospital a quite different thought enters my brain matter. This secret fucking terrorist group had just made this personal.

CHAPTER 18

"Speak the truth but leave immediately after."
                                        – Slovenian Proverb

I sprint down the hallway to Nikki's room but am denied entry by my wife, who is wearing a surgical mask. She points to a box of masks attached to the door and provides a mini lecture on contagious disease. I affix one to my face and sidestep past her to see my daughter.

"Hey Pops," Nikki says. "Wanna see me fly?"

It may have been a lame reference to her 'bird' flu diagnosis, but its effect down shifted my panic needle from red to yellow. My daughter's flippant comment was classic Nikki. As a ten year old, my Nikki jumped on a rusty nail and instead of tears, she looked me straight in the eye and said, *"Nailed the landing, Pops."*

Lorri attributes Nikki's caustic wit to my defective DNA. I used to deny that claim but now feel immense pride. The bottom medical line is that Nikki is a healthy teenager who should fully recover with rest, isolation, antibiotics, and follow-ups. We get to take her home immediately since hospitals are basically germ factories. Lorri and I are encouraged to wear the masks when in the presence of our daughter, and be alert to symptoms. The three of us walk to Lorri 's car wearing our masks and looking like a street gang about to rob a gas station.

I follow our minivan home and use the alone time to take the temperature back at the office. I dial Agent 36 A's direct number, "Hi Gwendolyn." I begin in as if my supervisor had not recently been flapping around the floor like a decapitated chicken. "What's up?"

"What's up?" Gwen repeats incredulously. She pauses, laughs and continues. "Nothing much going on here. Actually been a boring day at Club Fed." She hesitates for effect and finishes with, "Oh, wait a minute. I seem to remember a stretcher and ambulance carting off your immediate supervisor, who accidently ran his throat into your hands."

"Ambulance? I barely squeezed his scrawny neck."

"The asshole is fine," Gwen confirms. "Michaels's a drama queen. He'll probably write himself up for a Purple Heart."

"So," I ask nonchalantly. "What are you hearing?"

"Well John, you seem to have a knack for verbally and physically assaulting Bureau authority figures. The one saving grace is that you've picked pathetic excuses for human beings, so you've got a sympathy factor going for you."

"You think."

"Look, Booker. You're a great FBI agent, but you really have to work on your people skills. Michaels wanted to file a police report but Bell told him we'd handle it internally."

"Boy Wonder went along with it."

"Not at first, but Bell played the bad publicity card and explained to Michaels how'd it reflect negatively not only the Bureau but also on Boy Wonder."

"So I kicked the punishment can down the road for now."

"I wouldn't count on that. Maybe twenty years ago you could slug it out with a boss then go have a beer, but, this is the *new* Bureau." Gwen laughs and adds. "OPR is probably sharpening their number two pencils as we speak. You may have set the unofficial Bureau record for infractions by an agent in a short film."

"Look Gwen, I won't ask you to put yourself in a line of fire, but I'd appreciate if you could keep your eyes and ears open. I'm going to take a few days leave."

Gwen immediately asks, "Did you put in a leave slip?

The FBI has so many rules, regulations and procedures that a cloistered nun could violate a page full before morning prayers. Leave request had to be submitted and approved twenty-four hours prior to the leave.

She answers her own question with, "Duh, I guess not. Well I'll fill it out and back date it. Then I'll slip it under Michaels's pile of shit and get Peggy to swear you handed it to her this morning."

Agent 36 speaks fast. It's more like a filibuster than a conversation. Though I appreciate her ingenuity, falsifying a government document would get her suspended. I say, "That's nice Gwen, but I'd rather not get you involved." "Already done," She counters. "Call me tomorrow. Gotta go, I've got a Zumba class in an hour."

"I owe you, girl."

"You don't owe me shit, Booker. I'm living vicariously through your miserable life, and choking out Michaels is a gift to me that will keep on giving. Bye Booker."

I feel as if my world is caving in on all sides. My daughter has the bird flu, my supervisor wants me arrested, and OPR is lurking somewhere in the shadows ready to pounce. It can't get much worse, I think, until my phone rings. Caller ID indicates that Jack Bell wants a word with me. My world is about to get a whole lot worse.

"John," he says in an official tone. "You're suspended without pay immediately. I warned you to stay clear of Michaels, but you wouldn't listen. I need your car, badge and gun by morning tomorrow."

"I understand. See you tomorrow morning."

I have no intention of being unarmed. My private arsenal includes two shotguns, an AR 15, three 9mms, one 357 Magnum, and a Walther PPK. I was considering a cross bow until the shootout at Wal-Mart. The fuckin' arrow thing.

I decide to call Suehad. It seems like the right moment to follow up on her allegedly terrorist spouse. It was time to shit or get off the pot in terms of trusting Suehad. My decision is to push my chips all in and disclose the top secret intercepts. Suehad can offer an insider's perspective into a culture that I no longer had access. Anyway, what are they going to do to me, suspend me and take my car, badge and gun?

"John!" Suehad excited. "I was wondering when you'd call. Did I offend you in some way?"

"Nothing like that. My life has had some twists and turns lately."

"Would you like to talk about it?"

"What's your schedule tomorrow?"

"Thursdays are my morning classes. I can be free by one."

We plan to meet at Fryman's Deli at one thirty.

I pull into my driveway and head directly to Nikki's room.

I knock and say, "It's dad."

"Enter, Pops."

Nikki is propped up in bed by a dozen pillows and surrounded by ten stuffed animals. The kid has always loved pigs and we have had an ongoing battle on her desire to own a Vietnamese miniature potbellied pig. She is in the process of aiming the remote at the television.

"Pops, you forgot your mask."

"Don't need it," I say.

"But you can get sick from me."

"Honey," I say, "I could only hope that this bird bug flies from you to me, and you get all better. That's what dads are for."

"Noble, but not too bright," Nikki rationalizes. "More likely we'll just *both* be miserable."

I sit on the edge of her bed and we talk about things. Important things, silly things, and *thing* things. Sometimes it takes a life crisis to appreciate the people and *things* in your world. Nikki and I rarely take the time from our busy days to just sit and talk. I have no idea of how long we sat there until Lorri appears and announces, "Nikki needs her meds and some rest."

My wife joins us on the bed and we give a group hug, all without masks. We tuck our daughter beneath her Cinderella quilt and I follow Lorri to the kitchen. I decide on the spot not to mention my little career issue. My wife could do nothing but worry and I got that covered for both of us.

Lorri sticks a frozen pizza in the oven and I pour two glasses of white wine. We are feeling optimistic about Nikki making a full recovery. I take a sip of wine and realize that Nikki's health scare has put my own career issues in perspective. I am a former United States Marine and wouldn't starve if that meant digging ditches. Option two could always involve a life of crime due to my unique insider's knowledge.

Sometime after our second glass, Lorri asks. "What's up with you, John? You seem anxious and preoccupied with something."

"The usual job stuff," I say offhandedly. "Asshole supervisor, but nothing I haven't been through before."

Lorri has one of the best bullshit detectors on earth. She stares me straight in the eyes and says. "Somehow I don't buy that."

I deflect any further probes into my job perimeter and hit the sack.

I rise my usual time since Lorri is already on a John alert. The passing of my government issued badge, gun and car is scheduled at 0830 military time so I decide to kill some time at my new hangout.

As I wait in line, some of the regulars at Starbucks are discussing the arrival of the avian flu vaccine. Although I don't encourage conversations, my habitual presence, same time, same station, breeds familiarity. For example, I know that the pretty lady directly in front of me is going through a nasty divorce, and the guy behind me, Bill, is an insurance salesman considering a career change. I have been successful in dodging questions on my profession so far but in a few hours I can honestly claim to be, *currently unemployed.*

As I reach the counter I pull my own surgical mask from a breast pocket, raise it to my face, and in a low threatening voice tell Donnie Osmond, "Give me the secret caffeine formula or I'll do something terrible to you."

Donnie is still wearing his designer mask and unflappably answers with, "Promises, promises."

I grab a newspaper and find a seat by the fireplace. The newspaper becomes a prop since the next hour or so is spent trying to decode the phrase, "*SON SICK WITH VIRUS.*" I also make a mental list of questions for Suehad. I check my watch and arrive at the FBI office in time for my defrocking. I hate scenes and lingering around the office today could take on the emotional aspects of an Irish wake. My ten minutes with Bell is frosty. His only sign of compassion was a final combination handshake and pat on the back. "I hope this all works out for you, John. You are a fantastic agent, but a *lousy* employee."

Peggy does nothing to hide the tears as I say my goodbye. "The Bureau is in cahoots with the devil, John Booker," Peggy sniffles. "That man...." She points toward Boy Wonder's office, "is not like any real FBI agent I ever knew."

I hug her large shoulders and say, "Shush, Peggy. Don't let him hear you."

Peggy actually raises her voice and tilts her head toward Michaels's closed door. "I want him to hear me, 'cause I'll be here long after Mr. Michaels is gone." She pauses and I can see it coming like the prelude to a sneeze. "Cock- sucking shithead turd."

I smile at Peggy and ask in all sincerity, "That last barrage of cuss words had nothing to do with Tourette's, did it?"

S.W.A.T. Boy, Bruce, and Agent 36 gather around me and say all the right things. S.W.A.T. Boy vows some future revenge on Michaels involving a chokehold, Bruce opines that Boy Wonder could have never cut at Harvard, and Gwen promises to go sexual harassment on Michaels using her two best assets. It's actually touching and reminds me of circling the wagons in the *old* Bureau. It also demonstrates that the FBI could be the family it once was.

But the reality is that the moment I walk out the door I will be yesterday's *crazy guy* anecdote. There'll be no choking or boob enticements. I understand this simple reality but give hugs all around and promise to be in touch. I can almost hear tomorrow's refrain of, *'John who?'*

I leave the FBI office a badgeless and gunless suspended Special Agent, *but* I do have a plan. Well not exactly 'gunless,,' since I now have my .357 Magnum tucked into my waistband holster.

Fortunately Fryman's Delicatessen is a mere eight blocks walking distance from the FBI office which is fortunate since I had also forfeited my government ride. Somewhere around 19th and St. Clair, I try to remember if I removed Nikki's roller blades from the trunk. If not, OPR will add *misuse of government property* to my already crowded rap sheet. Perhaps this will qualify me for OPR's *serial* offender program.

Winter tends to linger in Cleveland, Ohio. It sometimes sticks around until May, so residents develop a fatalistic attitude toward weather. Statistics indicate that the sun shines less than a hundred days a year in Cleveland. Most people in the area are familiar with the acronym SAD, which stands for Seasonal Affective Disorder. I may not have SAD, but my current disposition certainly could not be classified as sunny.

I locate a corner table at Fryman's which is always a beehive of activity between the hours of usual lunch time. It is the type of place where you can find judges, criminals, plumbers, strippers, cops, mobsters, and priests sharing a confined space. It reminds me of a church sanctuary where the unwritten rules render the occupants off limits from the outside world.

The cuisine is Cleveland legend, especially for those with discriminate taste palates for food groups containing massive amounts of carbs and Trans fats. Their specialty is corned beef, pastrami, and crisp home fries. The waitresses are cut from the same mold: chubby, middle age, and flirtatious.

Bunny approaches my table, sits squarely on my lap and says, "Where you been sweetie, I've been cheating on you with a rodeo clown from Albuquerque. And I have been having an affair with a Bulgarian trapeze artist."

Bunny howls and asks, "What can I get you, darling?"

"How about some coffee? I'm waiting on someone."

Suehad arrives and even her winter wardrobe showcases spectacular cleavage. I wonder if those puppies ever get chilled like a frozen daiquiri or margarita. Just for the record, ladies, if you wear stuff that is sexually enticing, then men will gawk. Not just *some* men but virtually *all* men.

We go through our greeting ritual and Bunny appears carrying a coffee pot in one hand and menus in the other. She looks at Suehad and offers, "Nice work Johnny."

Suehad gets to the point with, "You seemed troubled on the phone, John."

"You're right Suehad, big troubles, and I may have indirectly involved you in it."

Bunny returns and takes our order. I select the super corned beef on rye with home fries and coffee, while Suehad decides on a cheese omelet with green tea. Bunny informs Suehad that Fryman's tea is brown but that she could probably get it green if she tried hard enough. Suehad opts for water.

I spend the next thirty minutes disclosing everything from the secret intelligence briefings to my job problems. I babble on about Beck's aneurysm, narcolepsy man plowing down Vickers, missing CIA snitches, and even throw in Nikki's bird flu. I finish my confession with the specifics on how my big mouth threw Suehad into the murky mix. She immediately understands her tenuous continued residency in the US and my dilemma of potentially outing her to save my own ass.

As I wind down from my opening verbal salvo, I pull out a piece of paper and finish with the *really* bad stuff.

I announce, "I feel that we are both in great physical danger, Suehad."

"I can understand our employment problems and my possible deportation, but why *physical* danger?"

"It's like a math formula," I explain. "Follow me on this, Suehad. An Egyptian CIA informant claims the existence of a super-secret terrorist cell whose goal is to destroy America from the inside out.

Without firing a single shot, hijacking an airplane, or planting a bomb. Pretty ambitious undertaking."

"Yes it is, John, but their existence is still conjecture."

"But these are the *facts*," I counter. "That CIA informant is now missing. Their CIA handler, Mike Vickers, is dead. The old man who *accidently* killed Vickers is dead. Vickers' immediate supervisor, Grant Beck, who believed in the existence of this cell, is *also* dead!"

"A pattern, yes, but using your math analogy, it still doesn't add up to murders. All of the deaths are explainable as either an accident or illness."

"Seems so on the surface," I say. "But there's more numbers to add. Supreme Court Justice Douglas Williams was killed by two street thugs. They in turn go belly up a day later. Williams's replacement on the court is sympathetic to radical Muslim views and is a Muslim herself."

"I see where you're heading, John," Suehad says. "I think."

"Add to that mix your own theory that Egyptian President Mubarak was inexplicably replaced by a junta that may have had American support and the new president of Egypt just happened to be a member of the Muslim Brotherhood. How does my math add up now?"

Suehad appears to be digesting more than the home fries. She frowns and says, "So you feel that this secret terrorist group is killing off people who are a threat to their existence *or* to advance their cause."

Suehad pauses when she realizes, "That group now includes us."

CHAPTER 19

"Don't corner something meaner than you."

We remain at Fryman's to discuss options. The much-discussed *'fight or flight'* response suddenly seems like a viable choice. But if we *are* the target of a *secret* terrorist cell, then how does one fight *or* run from ghosts?

I often refer to my badge as the *'gold card'* since it opens doors which normally slam in your face. My badge has been my shield protecting me from the barbarians at the gate. It dawns on me that I no longer wear that armor. As much as I bitch and moan about my job, being an FBI agent provided me with a protective shield that bad guys rarely penetrated. It was the highest step in the law enforcement ladder and the longest arm of the law.

"I think we need some help," I inform Suehad.

"But who can we go to?"

"That's the weird part. The FBI is the logical choice but they're currently not taking my calls."

"So what do we do?" Suehad whispers.

"I spent my entire adult life in government," I say. "And the one thing I know for sure is that *if* we can get some proof, then the FBI will act. *Especially* if they figure we'll go to the press if they blow us off. God forbid we warn them of a pending disaster and it happens. They'll spend the next five years testifying before Congress."

I motion Bunny for a coffee refill. The lunch crowd has thinned out while we were discussing weighty life and death issues.

I sip on my java and say, "We'll need solid evidence that these deaths and disasters are connected and part of a conspiracy."

"Tell me how, John. How can we get that evidence?"

"By predicting a disaster that *actually* happens. We document our prediction and get it in the hands of someone who has both authority and credibility. But our proof *has* to be ironclad."

"Can we do that?"

"Maybe. Just yesterday, I analyzed the latest intelligence briefings. There was one particular satellite radio interception that could help us."

I lean forward onto the table toward Suehad. We had discussed the previous intercepts that either originated in the same region of Egypt or seemed connected to an American calamity. The additional wild card linking North Korea with Cairo is both particularly troubling as well as baffling.

Suehad scoots forward in her chair until we are inches apart.

I whisper, "*SON SICK WITH VIRUS.*" Does that mean anything to *you*?"

Suehad wonders if, "The virus could refer to the avian flu somehow."

"Not likely. They, whoever *they* are, used BIRD for that one. What's a really lethal virus?"

Suehad offers, "There's the AIDS virus, tuberculosis, Ebola..."

I fill in Suehad's pause with, "West Nile virus, small pox virus, and, my personal favorite, the disturbing, flesh-eating virus...."

"We need to examine this puzzle using standard research techniques. There are computer applications which can analyze the key words.

"Suehad," I interject, "You just said we can use the *computer* to find the *virus*."

We look at each other and Suehad wonders, "*Could* it be a computer virus?"

"Well," Suehad muses. "A computer virus can be devastating. America is totally dependent on computers."

I agree. "Have you ever been to a McDonalds when the computer registers go bonkers? Teenage cashiers can't make change for a dollar."

"It has the possibility to inflict severe chaos. Think about it, John. Nuclear plants, Wall Street, interstate commerce, law enforcement, the military — *all* depend on computers of some sort."

"Which makes it difficult for us to predict just how they may introduce a computer virus *and* which vulnerable area they'll target."

We're silent for a while as we struggle to wrap our brains around the magnitude of a virulent computer virus' effect on America.

"Let's not get fixated on the computer virus," I muse. "In fact my money is on small pox. Maybe we first need to figure who the *SON* might be."

"Perhaps it is a religious reference to the Christian belief in the holy trinity of the Father, *son*, and the Holy Ghost."

"Good thought. How *do* Muslims view Jesus?" I ask.

"Jesus is named ninety-seven times in the Koran. Even the prophet Mohammed thought very highly of Jesus and affirmed his virgin birth. He believed that Jesus raised people from the dead and was a miracle worker. The Koran calls Jesus pure and sinless."

"I'm shocked. I would've thought there'd be a gaping spiritual divide."

Suehad shakes her head and continues, "Not really, John. Muslims view Jesus as prophet, teacher, healer, mediator, and miracle worker with great power. They have even named shrines after him."

"Do we have something here with the *SON* Jesus thing?"

"Perhaps, but what is the connection to this virus phrase? Will a holy man or the church somehow transmit the virus?"

"Hell, Suehad," I say all frustrated. "We aren't even sure it's a computer virus. I'm leaning toward smallpox. It fits the criteria of a natural calamity that can't be traced to any person or group. No one knows how an epidemic starts and I would bet our current small pox vaccine supply is nonexistent. And, that *particular* epidemic has already wiped out chunks of the world's population at different periods in civilization."

"We need to take a break. Our brains are trying to process too much information."

We're silent for a moment and sip our coffee. Bunny visits to refill our cups. She asks. "Dessert, anyone?"

Suehad thinks about it and says, "Some vanilla ice cream please."

"Ice cream sounds good," I say. "I'll have chocolate with some nuts."

"You two-timing me with this pretty woman?"

Suehad smiles at Bunny and says, "I could only hope it true, Bunny, but I'm afraid he remains loyal to you."

"Good answer, pretty lady. Good answer."

After Bunny walks away, I say, "Got an idea. Let's make a game out of it. I'll say one of the key words, and you say the first thing that pops into your mind. You do five words, then we'll switch."

Sue had nods and says, "I'll give the first clue. Ready?"

"Ready."

"Virus."

"Aunt Lena."

"Cairo."

"Pyramids."

Suehad laughs and says, "Perhaps we need to modify the rules to our game. Your thought process is not linear."

"Linear?"

"You know, if I say '*A*' most people say '*B*', but you seem to be a free thinker, which is a kind way of saying scatterbrain. It's actually an endearing quality on you."

"Thank you, I think. But my Aunt Lena was constantly sick with either the flu or virus. She automatically flashes into my brain if I hear those words. But let's continue this exercise with your *linear* mind. *I'll* give the clues. Ready?"

"Suehad nods and I say, "secret terrorists."

"Terrorists are inherently secret. It is the nature of the beast."

"That is *not* a one word response," I scold Suehad. "Let's try this again. Stick to the first thing that comes to mind."

I say, "Cairo."

"Home."

"Sick."

"Plague."

"Son"

"Father."

"North Korea."

Suehad gives me a strange look and tilts her head the way a puppy does when they hear a distinctive sound."John, the last sequence, actually the last three. Did anything register in your brain?"

"What was the sequence?"

"Son, Father, North Korea."

"I think I got it. The first thing that pops into *my* brain is that crazy dictator of North Korea with the Elvis haircut who died a few years ago, and his equally crazy *son* who is the new president."

Suehad says, "I just thought of something. Kim Jong Il died in 2011, which is the identical time frame to Egyptian President Mubarak's death. Probably a coincidence, John, but our theory combined with several of the pertinent intercepts originating in North Korea *and* Egypt may be too much to ignore."

"All I remember about Jong is that it seemed that he and Sarah Palin bought their eye glasses at the same drugstore."

"Kim Jong II was America's sworn enemy but predictable. But his son is a certifiable sociopath *and* the supreme commander of the Korean People's Army, which, in case you didn't know, is the fourth-largest standing army in the world."

"Interesting. So two of the world's most brutal leaders die at about the same time and their successors are even crazier and *more* anti-American."

"If this sleeper cell of terrorists exists and partners with North Korea's unlimited resources, it is a terrorist marriage made in heaven."

"You're right," I observe. "North Korea has scientists, academics, money, and the technical expertise to support terrorist operations in America. The radical Muslims act as the operational arm of Korea."

"It really is diabolically brilliant. North Korea is an acknowledged enemy of America. It is a sovereign nation with defined geographical boarders, a government, and citizens. They understand that they'll lose a traditional military war with the U.S."

"But," I finish her thought, "if they join forces with a terrorist group who operates in the shadows and can't be tied to North Korea, then they get the best of both worlds. Destroy America minus any risk of American retaliation."

A chill runs down my spine as I suddenly recall a conversation with Grant Beck at Quantico. I had maintained that the average terrorist cell did not have the resources or organization to hurt the U.S.

Beck had asked me, "*But* what if a few terrorists were both brilliant *and* organized?"

"Then we'd be in a world of shit."

CHAPTER 20

"A prophet is without honor in his own community."
— The Bible

Suehad and I make a tentative plan. She'll use her resources to identify the Egyptian end of the terrorist puzzle, and *I'll* identify a trusted individual to act as our front man with the FBI, as well as scan the new intercepts from the intelligence bulletins.

My firm belief is that the intelligence briefings foreshadowed past disasters and will provide the clues to any *future* ones. Without this information we are helpless bystanders to misery and chaos. I realize that I lack access to both the intelligence briefings as well as any individual with authority."

"Suehad," I say, "you said that Mansur calls you almost every day."

"Yes."

"Next time he calls, I want you to be especially nice."

"I have no feelings for my husband." Suehad counters. "Why?"

"Pretend you're an American wife. They're skilled at faking emotions and orgasms."

Suehad couldn't comprehend the use of deception in a relationship so I explain. "Both your husband and father-in-law could have information about this secret super terrorist cell. Your Egyptian hubby has business ties to North Korea and has mentioned the existence of this group, *while* your father-in-law is an imam for The Muslim Brotherhood. There's lots of smoke there."

"But what can I do?"

I explain, "We approach this like an undercover operation. Hubby would be suspicious if you suddenly saw Allah's light. So when he calls you, just express some very general doubts about your life in America."

"Like what?"

"Nothing major. Maybe, *'My students are rude and lack motivation.'*"

Suehad laughs and says, "I thought you were instructing me to be deceptive."

"Sorry, I got carried away with the student thing. How about, 'I miss my home. America is very violent'. Maybe tell him you got mugged."

"He will simply tell me to come back to him. That's how he ends each conversation."

In the operational planning of long-term undercover cases, one of the primary goals is to establish a strong and dependent link between the undercover operative and the target. The stronger this link, the easier to infiltrate a criminal organization. Every group, whether it be the Rotary or al-Qaeda, has a need. If you can supply the organization with what they *need,* then they're toast. From our conversation, it seems that Suehad's return to Cairo would somehow fulfill a need with Mansur, so we are way ahead of the undercover curve.

"Can I ask a personal question?"

"Of course, John."

"Why does Mansur want you back?"

"I've asked myself that many times. When we were living as man and wife, he constantly complained about my desire for an education, my doubts about Shariah law, and my progressive views on wardrobe and the equality of women."

"So why would he want you back if nothing's changed?"

"This is difficult for me to say," Suehad pauses and lowers her eyes.

"You don't have to say anything that makes you uncomfortable."

"I need to tell you this John. It may help us." Suehad looks me straight in the eye and says, "Mansur is a sexual deviant. So, though he protested my progressive views, he was also excited by my clothes and independence. He invited other women *and* men into our bed. That is the real reason I fled Cairo."

My first thought was a visual of Suehad participating in an orgy but my *second* thought was the hypocrisy of many supposedly devout Muslims. On the surface they appear deeply committed to their faith and the teachings of the Koran but an inch beneath that surface, they are your run of the mill pervert.

"I'm sorry," I say. "And actually, it *could* help us."

"How?"

"The next time he asks you to come home, tell him that you're considering it. Nothing more or he may get suspicious. Just that you've been giving it some thought and if he presses you then back off."

"He will push hard if I say those words."

"Listen to me, Suehad, it's important that he believe you, and most human beings don't make impulsive life-altering decisions. He'll wonder why the sudden change of heart. It's a process and Mansur must genuinely believe that he is *part* of that process. Allow *him* to convince *you*."

"I understand."

I ask Suehad to drop me off at *Chuck's Saloon* in Parma. My cell phone interrupts our conversation in the car. Caller ID indicates *FBI*. I debate whether to answer, but take the chance that it could just be a fairy godmother calling to tell me '*everything's okay, come home*'. It isn't.

Bell informs me that "OPR wants to interview you the day after tomorrow. Now John, I have to warn you, if you fail to show, you will be terminated immediately."

"See you then, Boss," I assure him.

Suehad and I spend the remainder of the trip going over safety issues. *If* we are now the target of ruthless terrorist, some precautions are in order. Suehad rationalizes that she has an alarm system and a shotgun but both are useless against professionals. I convince her to bunk with Monica and her lesbian stripper girlfriend. I wonder if they have room for a third.

As we arrive at CHUCK'S we engage in a brief goodbye hug and I offer one last warning, "Suehad, they won't come at you head-on so you must be aware of your surroundings. Keep a low profile until we can figure this thing out."

Charles A. *"Chuck"* Peters, better known as Rock, was a Marine Corps helicopter pilot in the first Iraqi War. When I abruptly met Mr. IED, it was Rock who landed in a hot LZ to transport my leaking body back to a field hospital. Somehow we kept in touch and when Rock retired from the Corps, he took over his father's saloon in Ohio.

Parma is the gold standard for blue-collar towns. It is situated on the western boarder of a Cleveland ghetto and has more than its share of churches, bars, and bowling alleys. The Professional Bowling Association hosts one of its major bowling tournaments at The Parma Lanes.

CHUCK'S is a typical Parma, Ohio joint. A classic shot and beer emporium with impressive chicken wings, two-pound hamburgers, and pickled hard boiled eggs which sit on the bar in large glass jars. It is populated by a group of colorful neighborhood characters.

The lovely Jackie is pouring a draft as I stroll in and take a seat at the far end of the old mahogany bar. Jackie happens to be Rock's wife and one tough broad. CHUCK'S will *never* need a bouncer as long as Jackie is around. If she likes you, then you could shit on the bar and Jackie would likely laugh and call you an asshole. If she didn't care for you, Jackie could be your worst nightmare.

"Well if it isn't Johnny Booker," Jackie says as she runs around the bar to give me a hug.

I have always graded hugs and believe that you can determine a person's personality, ethnicity, and perhaps their soul by the *quality* of their hug. If you are attuned to hugs then you know that people hug for various reasons. Some hug in self-defense, some hug tentatively, some hug out of habit such as Italians *and* some hug because they understand the subtle *nuance* of the hug. These individuals are capable of communicating love, affection, sorrow, sadness, joy, and even hatred into a *simple* hug.

Jackie's hug is a combination of, *'Hi John,'* and, *'Damn, I missed you.'*

She says, "You must be back from one of your little government vacations. Who were you this time, The Duke of Earl or Mussolini?"

"Actually, I spent the last few years as Madonna."

Jackie laughs and mutters, "Asshole," which is actually a term of endearment for the fast-talking lady from Brooklyn, New York.

"Where's that piece of shit husband of yours. I can't believe you're still married to his sorry ass."

Jackie smiles and says. "Rock's at mass at St. Ed's."

"You're kidding me, right?"

"He got religion about a year ago. He attends church three days a week and prays before he goes to bed."

"That won't save him from eternal damnation."

"Yeah well, those days are gone. Rock has arthritis, an enlarged prostate, and a bad back. He constantly reminds me that he is *'circling the drain.'*

The place has about twenty thirsty patrons given the dinner hour and a few are vying for Jackie's attention. She says, "The usual?"

I nod and she informs me, "Rock should be back in half an hour. Stick around, Johnny, I know he'll be disappointed if he misses you."

I order some chicken wings and a bowl of chili. Perched on a nearby barstool is a typical Parma girl. She is about thirty but looks forty, probably works as a waitress somewhere, plays the lottery, has a tattoo on her shoulder, smokes Menthol cigarettes, and her mother is presently babysitting her two kids. She refuses to accept the fact that life is not going to get any better although she has not yet uttered a single word.

She smiles at me and says. "My feet are killing me."

"Why is that?" I ask.

"Worked all day. Just got off." She holds up her drink and finishes the thought. "I come here to take the edge off. Haven't seen you before."

"My name is John. Buy you a drink?"

"Sure, John. I'm Sandy."

I hold up two fingers to Jackie who nods. She sets our drinks before us and gives me the *look*. "Watch him, Sandy." Jackie warns. "He's a heartbreaker."

Sandy giggles and we touch glasses. She asks. "No really, why are you in this joint?"

"I am actually a deep covert agent for the FBI and am on the trail of a super-secret terrorist group who plan to destroy the United States."

Sandy giggles again and says, "You're crazy."

"That's the consensus, Sandy."

"So you came to *here* to save the world?"

"Well, I have to start somewhere."

Sandy playfully punches my arm and says, "You *just* may be a secret agent because just last week, in that *exact* seat, I met the Green Hornet."

I hear Rock before I see him, "Booker, you wimp. A few pieces of shrapnel and you're sucking dirt in the fetal position. Two fuckin' band aids would've taken care of that bullshit wound."

"Talk about wimps. At least I was a real mud Marine. You pampered air wingers had a nightly hot and cot, and the scuttle butt was that half of you wore your skivvies backward."

Rock saunters up to me and gives me a bear hug. He says. "I miss the hell outta you, Booker."

The Marine chopper pilot's hug is pure love and no bullshit. He is a bear of a man. The term *strong like a bull* generally comes to mind when meeting him.

Rock turns to Sandy and says, "This man is a degenerate bullshitter, so everything he told you is a lie."

Sandy says, "I figured, Rock. Johnny here told me he was a secret FBI agent here to save the world."

Rock shakes his head, grabs my arm, and while leading me away says, "Excuse us Sandy, we've got some shit to discuss."

Sandy looks at me and asks, "Will you be back?"

I nod and blow her a kiss. "The day after I save the earth."

Rock and I settle down at a corner table. He laughs and warns, "You need to cut that FBI shit out, Booker, my customer base is a combination of low-level felons, tax cheats, and an occasional fugitive or two."

"You have gone to seed, Rock," I observe. "What's with the pot belly, three-day whiskers, and pizza stains on your gnarly sweatshirt. And, in case you didn't know, cigar smoking in an eating establishment is against the law."

Rocky takes a puff on a cigar that resembles duck poop and says, "I am the fucking law here."

As all combat veterans seem to do, we rehash our shared combat experiences which grow in direct proportion to our memory shrinking. But Rock's daring rescue needs no embellishment. He was monitoring our radio frequency as al-Qaeda ambushed our undersized patrol. Rock disobeyed a direct order to abort my medivac and descended into the middle of an old fashioned fire fight. The al-Qaida bullets riddled his C6 aircraft as Rock calmly landed his bird.

As they threw my shrapnel ridden body into the chopper, Rock turned toward me and said, "Welcome aboard, Lieutenant. Here are the rules on my bird. You are not permitted to die while aboard my aircraft. That is a direct order and if you violate said order I will throw your carcass off this chopper into the desert where your remains will be shit upon by camels for eternity. Enjoy the flight."

I could barely see due to a shrapnel-peppered face but I believe my response was, "Just my luck. I get the fuckin' comedian pilot."

Rock received non-judicial punishment for disobeying a direct order, but I wrote him up for a Silver Star and the award became a Mexican stand-off until my Battalion Commander reminded his Air

Wing commander that we grunts often protected *his* perimeter. Rock received the Silver Star and I have never paid for a drink or pickled egg here since.

"I heard you turned religious, Rock. Where's your Christian spirit?"

Rock chuckles and says, "Fuck you Booker, I'm hedging my bets."

So we catch up on our lives. It seems Rock had a health scare about a year ago. High cholesterol, high blood pressure, enlarged prostate, and some pre-cancerous *"shit all over my body."* He made an attempt to get healthy with a proper diet, exercise, and no cigars or scotch, but that lasted a total of a month or so. That's when Rock rationalized that he could continue eating, drinking and smoking as long as he went to mass and prayed real hard.

"God will either kill me or cure me," He explains. "But I ain't giving up food, liquor, and cigars." Rock has always pronounced cigars as *see-gars*.

"I'm glad you got this whole health thing figured, Rock. But your religious conviction seems an illogical combination of fatalism and spiritualism. And, you *do* realize that God may strike you dead for being both lazy *and* insincere."

"Enough about me, Booker. What's happening in your world?"

"Nothing earth shattering — work problems, marriage problems," I say. "Probably just going through your routine case of mid-life crisis."

"You wanna quit the bullshit and get to the point. I tell you about my fuckin' prostate and you give me *'routine mid-life crisis'* crap. I can tell you got some major shit going on in your life; now tell Uncle Rock."

I smile and provide Rock the major brushstroke version of my current world. He is a perceptive soul and can fill in the blanks. When I finish Rock asks, "So let's reduce this to the basics. *Do you feel your life is in danger?*"

I begin a rehash of the Beck saga but Rock holds up both hands with the universal *'time out'* sign and says, "Whoa, Booker, just answer the fucking question with a *yea* or *nay*. Do you believe that your life's in danger?"

"Yea."

"Question two: do you trust this broad with the big tits?"

"Yea."

"Question three: "will you tell the headhunters that she's the snitch?"

"Nay."

"Question four: do you have a primary and alternate plan to square away the job issues and stay alive?"

"Nay."

"Then," Rock concludes, "that's what we need to do."

"But I need you to promise me something."

"What?" Rock says sensing a serious request.

"Promise me that if anything happens to me, you take out the people responsible."

Rock smiles and says, "Goes unsaid, Booker, my pleasure."

"So, let's begin." Rock says. "It seems to me that step one is to get access to those intel briefings."

"They're critical but I can't get close to the Bureau computer."

"You still have the access code."

"Yes."

"But none of those idiot pals at the office will go out on a limb?"

"No."

"Where will OPR do its number on you?"

"At the office, but I'll be escorted, and they won't let me near me a computer."

Rock is thinking hard when an idea dawns on me. Agent 36 C won't risk *giving* me her access code, *but* I don't need her code. The question is would Gwen allow me some time '*unescorted.*'

I say, "Be right back."

I exit the front door and pace the sidewalk. I turn my back to the cold wind and call Gwen on her personal cell phone.

"Booker," she says. "How you doing?"

"Been better, Gwen. Gotta question for you."

"All ears, Booker."

I explain that OPR will be interviewing me the day after tomorrow. Would she volunteer to be my escort *and* would she allow me to disappear for about twenty minutes?

"No problem. If they make a stink I'll tell the prim and proper boys in the front office that my period started and I had to use the bathroom. That'll short circuit any bureaucratic penance."

I return to the bar and tell Rock that stage one of a plan will be operational soon.

"Good," He says. "That wasn't so hard now, was it?"

Jackie calls me a cab and as I am leaving I remind Rock of his promise. As I am hugging Jackie goodbye she whispers in my ear. "I don't know what you and Rock discussed, and I don't wanna know. Just be careful, asshole. We both love you."

"It's good to be loved."

CHAPTER 21

"It's good to shut up sometimes"
– Marcel Marceau (famous mime)

I am fully aware that I *should* wear my best suit and tie to impress the OPR goons but I am a stubborn fellow. We had a saying in Iraq whenever we bent some rule, *"Whatta they gonna do to me, shave my head and send me to Iraq?'* Consequently, I choose black jeans and a turtleneck sweater. I throw in hiking boots to complete my Woodstock outfit.

Due to my current status in professional limbo, it wouldn't matter if I show up naked. My fate is preordained, because the fix is in. OPR and I will do a choreographed two-step rumba for several hours. They'll question me on each charge and dutifully record my replies. The only answer that really matters is to the question, *"Who is your hip pocket source?"*

My interview is scheduled at nine but it's important that I get there at least an hour before. Agent 36 C and I work out our plan the night before.

I arrive at the FBI compound but somehow it no longer feels like a home game. Gwen greets me with a hug and informs me that I have to process into the building as a visitor. I am basically required to shuffle into my building doing the equivalent of the perp walk. Pam is the receptionist and a casual friend. We usually shoot the shit about her boyfriend who is a Marine. It had always been a pleasant experience until today.

"I'll need your driver's license and a second form of ID," Pam monotones.

"Pam," I say. "You really gonna to make me go through this?"

"I'm sorry John, but Michaels insists I follow procedures."

Gwen leads me into one of the interview rooms and I tell her, "I need to find an empty office where I won't be bothered for about thirty minutes."

The building has three floors in addition to a sub-basement. All supervisors occupy private space while agents function in communal squad bays. But there are also many rooms which are use designated such as EAP (Employee Assistance), Intercept rooms, and Polygraph. I ask Gwen, "Any polygraphs scheduled this morning?"

"Give me a second," Gwen says while grabbing an office phone.

I hear her ask the question and say, "Okay, Lucy, I have an important report to get out by noon. I need some peace and quiet girl. Yea, I'm going to Zumba tonight. See you then."

Agent 36 C announces, "Polygraph."

I wonder, "Is Lucy the secretary screwing the media coordinator?"

"*And* the informant coordinator."

I make a mental note that should I somehow survive this ordeal, I will apply for some coordinator position.

Gwen and I head to the polygraph room that is located at the far end of the building to avoid outside noise interruptions when someone is strapped to the box.

I tell Agent 36 C, "I'll call you in a bit. Come back here and knock a three, three, one, tap on the door."

"This is getting complicated, Booker," Gwen laughs. "Just don't step on your dick."

I lock the door and punch my mysterious gift code into the computer. I hold my breath as the screen gyrates through the preamble just prior to either granting access or being denied. BINGO! I'm in.

The last few days of bulletins seem sparse. Perhaps the terrorists are on holiday in Atlantic City. I read every word afraid that I'll miss the brass ring but equally worried that some unexpected interruption will shorten my search. I check my watch and can't believe that twenty minutes have elapsed. I can probably go another ten or fifteen at most before OPR comes looking for me. If they discover me inside an office minus my escort they will surely check the computer and that will cause Gwen some severe aggravation.

I am about to bag my search when I hit gold. At 2237 hours yesterday an outgoing communication was intercepted from North Korea which reads, *SON CRITICAL WITH VIRUS,* then at 2347, an intercept originating from our now familiar region in Cairo states, *FINANCE CURE.*

I have no idea of their meaning but I do know that they are part of our puzzle. I just need to find where these particular pieces fit. There is an emphatic rap on the door and I literally leap to my feet. It's Gwen who tells me that "OPR just called for you. They're in the SAC's conference room."

As I walk past Gwen she off handedly tosses out. "Probably nothing to worry about, but they asked me where we keep our rubber hoses."

I laugh and then say seriously. "Thanks for helping me out, Gwen."

"No problem, Booker. I *always* root for the underdog."

We head toward Bell's suite and knock on the door to the conference room. It is opened by Tweedle Dee, who is the partner of Twiddle Dumb.

"I'm Special Agent Robert Gering," he says while offering a limp handshake. "And this is Special Agent Peter Bailey."

I smile and say, "I used to be *special* myself, but at the present time I seem to be quite ordinary."

Neither OPR guy even so much offers me an awkward smile. Had I been in their shoes I would at least acknowledged the gallows humor with a polite laugh. I feel it deserves at least a seven on the spontaneous sarcastic comeback scale. I often joke in tense situations.

It's my coping behavior and I've done it ever since the eighth grade when Sister Alberta Marie caught me looking at Carlo Ciccini's math test. The good sister screamed "You were cheating, John Booker!" to which I replied, "So how's 'bout I say a few Hail Mary's and we forgive and forget?"

Gering motions me inside the lion's den with a wave of his arm and Petey stands to offer an equally weak handshake. They strategically position me in a corner chair with the two administrative hit men on each side. I've actually performed this technique myself, albeit with *real* bad guys. The two OPR agents are right from central casting in roles requiring two arrogant slick Wall Street types. Gering probably practices his condescending smile before a mirror. Bailey seems to have refined a glare similar to UFC fighters meeting in center ring. It didn't quite intimidate me as much as amuse me. I dub him *Pissed-off* Petey and Gering *'Herman'* in memory of the Nazi general.

"How can we help to get this behind you?" Herman asks before any pleasantries are exchanged.

"Just jot down that I am indeed sorry for all my sins and apologize to Ms. Lewis for inferring that she is fat and sexually frustrated."

Pissed-off Petey *almost* smiles, but pretends to cough as a diversion.

"Well, there's more to the inquiry than just Section Chief Lewis's insubordination charges. Let's start down the food chain a little, and deal with your supervisor, Agent Michaels. You seem to have difficulty accepting his authority and actually assaulted him."

"Have you met the guy?" I ask.

"Yes we have. We've interviewed him regarding your behavior."

"Well then, I rest my case. That guy is a coward and a worthless piece of shit."

Pissed-off Petey's glare suddenly seems genuine. He says. "Matt Michaels is an outstanding supervisor and a friend of mine."

The word *'whoopsie'* comes to mind. It's the same feeling I had when I asked a plump bank teller what month her baby was due, only to have her say, "I'*m not pregnant.*"

Gering attempts to get us back on track. He says, "We're all FBI in this room and Peter and I have worked the streets like you, John. We understand that street agents take certain short cuts and occasionally have to massage a policy. Just explain why you didn't *officially* open up your informant?"

"Let's cut the little gamesmanship from interrogation class." I counter. "If you actually worked the streets then you *know* what a hip pocket source is and *why* I didn't open her up."

"*Her.*" Petey suddenly interested. "We didn't know it's a she. So could the problem be that you have something going on with *her*? Maybe an intimate relationship and you're afraid that she'll spill the beans if you ID her?"

I realize that I just blurted out the gender of my phantom source. So, I award one point for the home team. I smile and say. "Nothing like that, though I'm sure if you saw her, both of you would love to jump her bones."

I am also irritated off that these OPR idiots have gone directly to the sex card, though the thought of having sex with Suehad *has* crossed my mind. Any normal male could not gaze at her melons and *not* have impure thoughts.

Time for another dirty little Bureau secret. The statistics indicate that FBI agents have three main problem areas. They are sex, booze, and theft. A close fourth is misuse of the Bureau property, which often dovetails with the first three, like when a drunken agent uses the Bureau car to hump some informant *after* cashing a voucher for source information. Although I have never personally scored that particular hat trick, my conservative estimate is that 60% of all agents could check at least *two* of those blocks.

"No," I say back in control. "I have *not* been intimate with my source."

They write furiously on their legal pads as my cell phone chirps Suehad's special ring. I ignore the call since we communicate several times a day per our safety agreement. This does *not* seem the appropriate time to speak with the '*hip pocket*' phantom source.

"You're a patriot, right John?" Pissed-off Petey asks.

I merely nod sensing the question both rhetorical and a prelude to some bad television dialogue. Unfortunately, I am right.

"So a patriot would do the right thing for the country. If some snitch can *really* help identify a terrorist cell, then giving up her name is a patriotic act. Isn't it John?"

I am suddenly *very* angry. These two junior G-men were on their high school debate team when I lay bleeding in Iraq. They were celebrating spring break when I was undercover with gangsters and killers. Now they are challenging *my* patriotism in such a juvenile and flippant manner.

I immediately default to caustic "Hey, speaking of sex scandals, did you guys hear about the OPR agent who got caught screwing a drug-dealing crack whore?"

Gering and Pissed-off Petey offer identical disapproving frowns.

Gering says. "C'mon John, no OPR agent ever got caught up with a drug dealing crack whore."

"No, really," I say earnestly. "And when asked how it felt to get involved with someone in such a sleazy business," I pause for effect, "the drug-dealing crack whore said, '*I didn't know he was OPR.*'"

Sometimes I just can't keep my pie hole shut even when I *know* I should. Probably some undiagnosed medical condition which would qualify me as a victim in today's society. My phone chirps Suehad's special ring again and the timing of the two calls cause me some concern. I am about to excuse myself by evoking the classic law enforcement alibi of, '*Gotta take this, case-related,*" but I no longer have cases, so I go to plan B and say, "I need to answer this, family issue."

I leave Tweedle Dumb and Dee in the conference room and find the men's room. I hit redial but the phone is *not* answered by Suehad.

"John, this is Monica. We've met a few years ago when you indicted me."

A little awkward opening but I am sensing her previous legal issues are not on her current agenda. I ask. "Is Suehad alright?"

"Suehad's been in an accident. The doctors say she's hurt bad. She's in surgery but begged me to call you before they rolled her away. Suehad wanted me to warn you."

"Where is she?"

"Cleveland Clinic."

"I'll be right there."

CHAPTER 22

"If you want to achieve greatness stop asking for permission."

I break the land speed record getting to the Cleveland Clinic. The hospital is a maze of buildings stretching five square city blocks. There is a series of tunnels that connect the complex at the best hospital in the world. Monica actually gives me a quick hug which surprises me given our past. It is a hug that screams relief to be sharing the burdens of grief and fear. She explains that Suehad was driving her car northbound on I-77 and lost control. She rear-ended a tractor trailer hauling steel. Some cop grabbed Suehad's cell phone and reconnected with the last number called which was Monica. She actually arrived at ER before the ambulance and briefly spoke with the police officers who accompanied the ambulance to the Emergency Room. Eyewitness statements clearly fault Suehad, basically describing her car as *'accelerating'* into the back of the semi, which had slowed down due to the morning rush hour traffic.

Suehad suffered major head trauma and requires surgery to relieve pressure on the brain. The doctors also discussed the possibility of a medically induced coma if tests indicate more serious complications.

I ask Monica, "What *exactly* did Suehad say to you?"

"She was barely conscious in the ER but begged me to call you. Tell you that you were in grave danger."

"Look Monica," I say. "I really appreciate your calling me and letting me know what's going on, especially," I hesitate as I try to find the right words. "… I'm sorry I involved you in your boyfriend's legal mess."

"Don't apologize, John. I got *myself* in that mess. And as for calling you, well, Suehad trusts you and believes you are a good guy, that's good enough for me."

Monica is an interesting individual. Any bi-sexual doctorate level academic who is equally attracted to Mafia mopes and female strippers certainly qualifies as fascinating. Monica is the embodiment of sixties hippie with long straight jet-black hair, blue eyes, and granny glasses. She is relatively tall at about 5'8 and skinny as a rail. As chairwoman of the Sociology Department for a major university, Monica is smart as a whip although ideologically challenged.

I give Monica a supportive pat on her slender shoulder and announce, "Gotta make a quick call."

I wonder who I can trust at the Cleveland Police Department. A smile creases my lips as I scroll down my contact list and press *call*.

"Captain Kopka."

I say, "A fuckin' arrow."

Kopka laughs and says. "How's it hanging, Booker?"

"It's *barely* hanging, and you?"

"Busy but at least, no fuckin' arrows lately."

We laugh like two old war buddies who once shared a foxhole. I need to get right to the point. "Look Ray, I'm currently jammed up."

"I heard. One of my coppers is dating an FBI secretary, Lucy I think."

"Lucy gets around. I need a favor."

"You got it."

I run down the specifics of Suehad's accident and ask, "Can you check and see if anything was fishy with her brakes, brake fluid, steering mechanism, accelerator cable, and anything else that would cause someone to lose control of their vehicle." "So you think this may be an attempted murder?"

"I do."

Captain Kopka tells me that Suehad's car was probably towed to the city impound lot off Superior Avenue. He ends the call with, "I'll get back to you."

I return to the ICU waiting room and ask Monica for any update on Suehad. "She's still in surgery." Suehad has been in surgery for over three hours and one can interpret that in several ways. Most of them are not promising. Monica informs me that Suehad has no family in America and asks my opinion on contacting Suehad's husband in Cairo.

"So you know about her husband," I say.

"Suehad's my friend, John, and whatever you think of me for the choices that I've made, that girl is a kind and compassionate human being. We talk often and I know she discussed her *situation* with you."

"Of course," I respond. "Everyone needs a confidant, but let's wait till the doctors get done doing their thing before you call Mansur."

My cell phone is chirping incessantly ever since I bugged out on Agents Tweedle Dee and Twiddle Dumb. I am not in the mood for the predictable threats and verbal gymnastics, so I place the phone on vibrate only.

I'm not good at waiting. There is a subtle difference between being patient and being adept at waiting. I can endure time spent in a movie line or awaiting a restaurant table. But, there is a certain endgame with those situations *and* a certain amount of control. I can choose to leave at any time or eat at the bar.

'*Waiting*' for something to happen, of which I have no sway or ability to influence, leaves me frustrated. Alpha males are control freaks and generally need to manipulate a situation and '*fix things.*' We are not good *waiters*.

Two more hours pass before the phone on the wall rings. This phone is the only line of communication between doctor and the patient's family and friends. There has been a river of tears shed on this particular phone, both of sorrow and joy. Monica grabs the phone and mumbles replies. She hangs up and gives me a fragile smile.

She says, "The surgery went well. Suehad has a fractured skull and will need rest followed by rehabilitation. Some of her motor skills have been damaged, but the good news is that they feel she'll make a full recovery."

"When can we see her?"

"Maybe tomorrow. She'll be out of it at least until then and it could be longer."

"Where will she be?"

"A few hours in the recovery room and then to ICU."

"Okay," I tell Monica. "You square away her personal issues like getting someone to teach her classes, paying bills, and stuff like that."

"Been thinking about that, John." I can cover most of her classes and handle insurance matters and anything else she needs. But what about her husband? Should we call him?"

My brain ticks off the pros and cons of a Mansur visit. This doing the *right thing* is turning into some type of complex Machiavellian strategy. I make a decision. "Call Mansur, and tell him Suehad broke her jaw and can't talk. Then go for the guilt with, '*Suehad's gonna be laid up a few weeks, lucky girl, bad concussion, but no one to care for her, could've been a lot worse,*' got it?"

"So if Mansur asks me if he should come to the US, *what exactly do I say?*"

"Tell him that Suehad would love to see him and could use his help while recuperating."

"Anything else?"

I was about to ask Monica about her ex-Mafia husband and her current lesbian relationship with the bi-sexual stripper, but felt it the wrong time and place.

"Not for now," I say and add. "Suehad is lucky to have you as a friend."

Monica smiles and says. "I've got to get back to the university and arrange for Suehad's classes, call Mansur, and cover her student advisory schedule."

"Go ahead Monica, I'm staying right here for a while. Call me later."

Monica cocks her head and offers. "Suehad is right, John. You *are* a good man."

"You probably say that to all the guys in law enforcement who indict you."

Monica smirks and gives me the middle finger as she turns and walks out the door.

I need some time to reflect on things. It has been just a few hours since I blew off the OPR guys and now I have a new clue to the terrorist puzzle. Add Mansur's possible visit stateside, the mystery of Suehad's car, *and,* I just remembered a routine colonoscopy scheduled the day after tomorrow. I'm supposed to be drinking some concoction that makes you crap every twenty minutes. My dance card is getting filled so I call Gwen to find out exactly just *how* filled. Agent 36 begins the conversation with, "Well if it isn't Richard Kimball, the fugitive."

"Very funny Gwen. I had an emergency."

"I heard, Booker," Agent 36 begins. "The oft- used but never believed, *'family emergency.'* They want to put your photo up at the Post Office."

"That bad?"

"Worst. Michaels's contacted your wife and daughter trying to verify a family emergency. They both dimed you out and said they didn't know anything about an emergency."

"Did I jam you up, Gwen?"

"Not a problem. Once OPR had you in their web, the chain of custody was theirs. I'm also an attorney, Booker, so I know how to twist the truth."

"Any creative thoughts on my family emergency?"

"I'd find some distant cousin who'll fall on his sword for you."

"Thanks."

"Oh, and by the way. The OPR guy with yellow tie was cute. In a creepy sort of way."

"So you go for the dark brooding type? Then, Pissed-off Petey is your guy, but remember, Gwen, that guy is so uptight he probably steps outta the shower to pee, and he's *never* going to bind you to the bed post with that yellow tie."

"That's gross, Booker, but so in character" Gwen says and then hesitates a moment and her voice becomes serious. "Listen up, whatever they're gonna do to you, will take weeks for the paperwork to reach the Director's desk. So you better pull the rabbit out of your hat, the sooner the better."

I see Captain Kopka's name on my *call waiting*, so I bid Agent 36 goodbye and ask Ray, "Did you get to look at the car?"

"Car wasn't at our impound lot Booker."

"Where could it be?"

"Well," Kopka explains. "Sometimes we contract with local towing companies, and sometimes the accident victim or their family calls some towing outfit."

"So is that what happened?"

"I checked with our contract boys and it's a no go. I had two of my detectives call all the independents and they didn't tow it. The patrol guys on scene requested only one tow truck. The tractor trailer sustained minor damage and after a brief interview drove off to Indiana."

"So." I wonder. "Where could that Toyota be?"

"No idea."

"The tractor trailer. Was it some national trucking outfit or a fly by night?"

"According to the accident report, it was a U.S. Steel truck. Can't get more legit than that."

"Can I get a copy of the accident report?"

"No problem. Where are you?"

"Cleveland Clinic ICU waiting room."

"You hiding or hurting?"

"Presently hiding, but I'm anticipating some pain real soon."

Kopka laughs and says. "I'll send someone over in about an hour, okay?"

"I really appreciate this. I realize that this is off the books."

Captain Kopka fills in my pause with. "No fuckin' problem, Booker. We *are* the Cleveland Police Department and we usually operate *'off the books.'*"

"When this shit is over, Ray, let's get together and have a pop."

"Or," Kopka laughs, "maybe we can go to *Wal-Mart* and shoot some fuckin' arrows."

I find an ICU nurse and ask about Suehad. She's still in recovery, and if her vital signs remain stable, should be in the ICU ward within the hour. Suddenly, I'm hungry and head to the cafeteria. I owe my wife an explanation for the aggravation I caused her and dial Lorri's office.

"Family Services." The secretary is Allison Milovitz. I had met Allison at several work functions and we hit it off since we are both Pittsburgh Steelers fans.

"Hi Allison," I begin. "It's John Booker, how 'bout them Steelers?"

"Hey, John. They need a linebacker, nose guard and wide out. Won't get to the big one again unless we can beat the Ravens and Patriots."

I agree and ask, "Don't want to interrupt Lorri, but can you get a message to her?"

"About the family emergency?"

"So you know?"

"Some hard nose from the FBI called and wanted to speak with Lorri *immediately*. Told him she was with a client and I'd give her a message. This guy goes into his official threat mode. I tell him that unless it's an emergency, or he can prove he's FBI, then I won't interrupt her."

I smile and ask, "Evidently there's more to this story."

"You bet," Allison says. "This guy threatens me with insubordination and asks to speak with the director. I tell him that she's busy and he goes ballistic. Says he's sending two agents to *speak* with me about my attitude and demands my name, rank, and serial number."

"Sorry if I caused you some problems, Allison. I seem to be doing that a lot lately."

"Actually, I just followed agency guidelines about dealing with calls from unknown individuals. And, it was fun to tweak this asshole's sense of importance."

"So did agents show up?"

"Certainly did. I have their cards here. Agents Gombar and Booth."

"Bruce and S.W.A.T. Boy," I interrupt.

"So I called Lorri and we all went into the director's office. They asked if there's some type of family emergency."

"I think I know where this is going."

"Lorri looked baffled and immediately asked if you were okay. They explained that you left the office for some family emergency. At that point, Lorri called Nikki's school, and confirmed that she was okay."

"So what, then?"

"Well," Allison continues. "The two agents left and Lorri went back to her office."

"That's it?" I wonder.

"Not exactly, John. As Lorri was leaving she *may* have muttered something about, '*that bastard better have a good explanation involving my work in his shenanigans.*'"

"And who might she be talking about?" I ask rhetorically.

Allison chuckles. "If I was a betting woman, and I am, I'd say the odds are that you are that *bastard*."

I head back to the cafeteria and grab another cup of coffee. My instincts are on high alert since I am next man up for assassination. I had two loaded weapons in my car when I left home this morning and both were currently residing on my person.

Although the two weapons make me feel somewhat secure, I doubt that any attempt on my life would involve a shootout with a masked terrorist. Their strategy wouldn't involve a frontal assault. It is critical to their plan that my demise appears accidental, so I mentally tick off a list of deaths that would not arouse suspicion. Maybe poison, traffic accident, aneurysm, botched robbery, and unfortunately there are many others that even *I* could not fathom.

Grant Beck believed I held a special ability to think like the bad guys. That process had always come natural before, so I ask myself how I would off myself and *not* make it appear murder. Who the hell am I? I think. Well presently, I am a suspended FBI agent whose bizarre behavior can be documented by the highest officials within the FBI. I have marriage problems, job problems, and as a combat-wounded vet, a splash of PTSD, with the addendum that my last few years were spent undercover with a psychotic mob."

That seems to add up to an erratic, unpredictable, and dangerous individual. So how would I take out this particular character? It dawns on me that I really wouldn't have to lift one murderous finger. The individual I just described is so unstable that they would kill *themselves*. The bastards are going to kill me and make it appear a suicide. It was fucking brilliant, and given my present circumstances, not the least bit suspicious. My friends, and co-workers would probably observe, *"We saw this coming."*

So my radar is up for some type of suicide scenario. To be successful, the bad guys would have to kidnap me so that they could control the scene. There seemed only two options. They can either drug me or put a gun to my head. On the surface it seems simple enough to avoid either alternative. Be careful of everything I ingest and *never* place myself in a situation to be snatched. I can do this, I think.

But, I have no way of knowing how wrong I am!

CHAPTER 23

"The world has always been fragile ... just ask the dinosaurs.."
 – Michael Shannon

I arrive back at the ICU waiting room and am greeted by a familiar face. "Hey John," Detective Tommy Shoulders says, "Captain Kopka wanted me to give you this."

Sgt. Tommy Shoulders had played a pivotal role in the great Wal-Mart shoot out. Like his boss, he's a dinosaur who refuses to be emasculated by liberal judges. Shoulders is a doer and operates under the old cop credo of, *"I'd rather be judged by a jury of twelve than carried in a coffin by six."*

"Tell the Captain I said thanks."

"Hey John," Tommy smiles. "The Captain wanted me to tell you that they are having a special at *Wal-Mart* this week."

"Let me guess."

"A dozen fuckin' arrows for a dollar."

Tommy hands me an envelope and I can hear him laughing all the way to the elevator. I am about to open the manila envelope when a nurse enters the room and informs me that Suehad has been transferred.

"You can visit but *only* five minutes," She warns.

Hospitals are depressing entities under any circumstances, given their antiseptic smells and the air of desperation that permeates every square inch. But the ICU is in its own unique category. Motionless patients have arms and orifices attached to various tubes that are in turn attached to walls and metal stands. There's not a lot of meaningful conversation and voices are generally subdued and severe.

Suehad is surrounded by a gaggle of medical equipment, which blink colored lights and ever changing digital numbers. As I approach the bed her eyes are closed and bandages engulf her head and most of the right side of her face. She seems fragile and vulnerable. I touch her hand and her left eye opens. It takes a few seconds for her to recognize me and then she smiles.

I say, "What's the other guy look like?"

Suehad attempts to say something but can't move her lips."

"The doctors say you're going to be alright."

She squeezes my finger and the smile disappears, replaced with a look of dread. Suehad seems coherent but wounded both physically and emotionally.

The doctors feel that the severe bolt to the brain temporarily impaired some motor skills. I lean over and kiss her forehead.

Suehad grabs my shirt and pulls me close to her. She struggles to form a word, repeating the same garbled sound. Eventually the word takes form on her lips and she enunciates in the clearest manner, "Danger."

The brief warning seems to have expended whatever energy she had in reserve. Following this solemn warning, Suehad loses consciousness in what I hope is a deep sleep. I press the *call* button and a nurse hustles into the room.

"Can you check and see if she's okay? She just suddenly conked out on me."

The nurse says nothing as she first checks the machinery attached to Suehad and then pulls her eyelids back and looks intently while shining a small light into her pupils. The nurse pronounces, "She's fine. Been through a lot and the body is basically demanding rest for healing. You'll have to leave."

"I'll be in the waiting room," I say. "How often can I come see her?"

"We need to play this one by ear. Check with the duty nurse first."

I thank her and as I am about to leave she asks, "Are you her husband?"

"Good friend," I say. "She has no family here."

"Well, she's lucky to have you."

I make myself comfortable in the waiting room and dial my wife. "Hi honey," I say as nonchalantly as possible as though two FBI agents had not grilled her in her bosses office today.

"Tell me what's going on and don't start with, '*nothing's going on.*' You embarrassed me at work and scared the crap out of me with some pretend family emergency."

"It was an informant, Lorri. My source was almost killed in an accident that was NO accident."

"There's a lot going on with you, John, and I need to know what."

"You're right. We'll talk about it."

"Okay." Lorri softer. "I'll put a couple steaks on the grill and open a bottle of wine. What time will you be home?"

I conduct a quick mind inventory of my recent lies and omissions to my wife. Lorri is aware of some *minor* work problems involving an a-hole boss, but I omitted the suspension without pay. She knew about my suspicions of a super terrorist cell, but I occasionally discussed cases. The *family emergency* visit today by my co-workers would require some fancy word-smithing but that dialogue was well within my verbal toolbox.

"Lorri," I explain, "this source is in critical condition and whoever tried to kill her today may try and finish the job. I am working a late shift at the hospital. We'll talk soon."

Lorri is a pretty stoic individual. Our arguments over the years have followed a similar pattern of my basically shooting from the verbal hip while Lorri is a hesitant and thoughtful passive-aggressive. She states her position or voices criticisms after careful thought and *only* says what she actually means, while I have no verbal filter. I generally spew forth whatever impulsive thought enters my cranium.

So it is somewhat out of character for my wife to tell me, "You had better get your shit together, John, or else there will be no '*soon.*'

It might be my imagination, but it seems that everybody I speak with lately threatens me.

My plan is to protect Suehad until I can figure out a long-term solution for her safety. If she had been an *official* informant, Suehad would be surrounded by U.S. Marshals. But, as a *hip pocket* source Suehad is basically a bastard child of the FBI. One option would have been to document her information and even at this late junction provide her government protection. But since I am no longer a card carrying member of big brother, I can't exactly open informants. It's a classic, damned if you do, damned if you don't situation.

My phone vibrates in my pocket and I am definitely screening my calls. It's Monica, who asks, "How's Suehad?"

"In ICU. She's stable and I spent a few minutes with her. Weak but actually spoke a few words."

"That's good news, John. I've arranged to cover her classes, reassigned advisors for her students, and called Mansur."

"Is he coming?"

"I think so. Said he'll call me back. Needs to make some arrangements."

"Tell me about him."

"What do you mean?"

"Did he sound concerned, what exactly did he say, did you sense sincerity, or was he just giving you canned responses?"

"Hard to say," Monica muses. "I can't account for cultural differences in handling bad news, but I'd say he was worried."

"Did he ask questions, did he act surprised? Tell me how you started the conversation and what he said. This is important, Monica."

Monica is silent for a brief moment and finally says, "You're freaking me out John. Why these questions? You sound like Mansur is the enemy."

"Monica, Sorry for coming out of left field on this but it's possible that Mansur is a bad guy and it's also possible that Suehad's accident was no accident."

"Holy shit," Monica utters. "You have to fill me in, John."

"Glad to but it's too involved over the phone. I don't think we should leave Suehad alone. Can you get some of her students to work in shifts?"

Monica is silent for a second as she digests my request. She says. "That's not a problem. Suehad has devoted students."

"Great." I say. "I'll stay here till morning. Get someone to relieve me around eight. Just tell the students that Dr. Fasaid needs some emotional support. Have them read to her. I'll spend the overnights with Suehad, so schedule the students till ten or so."

Monica wonders, "If you really think Suehad's husband is trying to kill her, then why did you have me call him?"

"That is a very long and complicated story, but trust me on this," I pause and finish with, "I have Suehad's best interest at heart."

"Never believe a man when he asks that you *trust* him on something."

"Aw c'mon, Monica. I would never do a thing to hurt Suehad."

"You'd better not." Monica says in a stern but teasing voice. "You men are all fuckin' con artists, *and* that's why I switched to women."

"Talk to you later, Monica."

I befriend the night nurse who allows me to sit by Suehad's bedside. She explains that if her vitals remain steady for the next few days, Suehad will be moved to a regular room. The various visual displays and sounds of the life-sustaining machinery eventually retreat to the background of my senses as I grow sleepy off and on throughout the night.

At 7 AM, I run down to the cafeteria for coffee and a bagel. When I return I meet John Goodrich, who is a student in Suehad's Arab Culture and Society course.

He asks about her prognosis and then launches into the story on how Dr. Fasaid has changed his life. John is an Irish kid from Atlanta who became fascinated with Middle East culture after watching the animated version of *Aladdin*.

I marvel at how this latest generation can disconnect the 9/11 attacks from the Muslim world. Ever since the attack on the World Trade Center, my perspective is that *Aladdin* was probably some radical Muslim kid who attended an al-Qaeda training camp.

I explain to Goodrich that he will remain at Dr. Fasaid's bedside until a student relieves him citing the importance of his presence to her emotional recovery. I was reaching for some reason why Suehad should not be left alone and this line of bullshit should suffice for college kids. He nods his understanding and I gently touch Suehad's forehead and leave.

Although my wife will be at work when I arrive home, my groveling plan includes flowers, candles, and her favorite wine. That was my plan but to quote a popular saying on bumper stickers … "*Shit Happens!*"or in my particular case, *Some REAL bad shit happens!*"

CHAPTER 24

"Humpty Dumpty was pushed!"

I pull out of the hospital parking lot and make a left on Euclid Avenue. Since terrorists have me at the top of their dead pool, I carefully scope out nearby cars and their occupants. It is amazing how everyone looks suspicious when paranoia is running wild throughout your veins. That little old lady in the Ford Taurus just glanced my way and that seemingly happy family in the Chrysler minivan is just *too* pat.

I first notice the Cleveland police car at around 67th street, as it falls in behind me acting as an escort providing me safe passage. As I am approaching 55th street I am startled by a siren. I slow down and maneuver my car to the curb expecting the police vehicle to swerve around. I glance at my rear view mirror and realize that the police car is now bumper locked with my vehicle.

A couple of quick thoughts ramble through my brain the first of which is that Captain Kopka or Detective Shoulders are having some fun. I have been guilty of hitting lights and siren on my FBI car upon seeing an unsuspecting friend. A week after Nikki passed her driving exam I followed her as she drove a little too fast to the mall. When I *"lit her up"* she reacted instinctively by swerving the car into a concrete mailbox. That little exercise taught me a lesson *and* cost me $450.

My second thought is that I may have been so preoccupied with spotting assassins that I probably ran a light or tweaked the speed limit.

Two police officers approach my car from each side with weapons drawn. *'What the fuck is this all about?"* I think while placing my hands on the dashboard. Any armed individual should follow this procedure if stopped by the police. It avoids confusing and often misinterpreted actions. You move your hands only when instructed by law enforcement officers.

I turn slightly and say, "I'm armed."

This statement has the opposite effect of my intended purpose as both cops raise their weapons in my direction and scream conflicting commands. One cop orders "Hands up," while the other cop screams, "Hands out the window."

Finally the robust older cop instructs me to, "Exit the vehicle." As I open the door I have no idea on *what* to do with my hands so I place them on my head.

"FBI," I say.

This seems to relax them somewhat as their shoulders visibly slump.

"Show me your ID." The older cop demands. He is clearly in charge as the younger cop just glares at me while aiming his weapon center mass on my body.

I automatically reach for my credentials, which are obviously elsewhere.

"I don't have them on me," I say and their shoulders instantly tense again.

"Place your hands behind your back."

I realize it futile to begin a long explanation until these two cops control the situation so I assume the position and offer my hands for cuffing.

"Where is the weapon?"

"One in a belly band holster and the other in a coat pocket, front passenger seat."

"Do not move!" The younger cop speaks his first words as he roughly pushes me over the hood of the police car. He holds my head against the car metal and gives it a slight shove for emphasis. The older cop conducts a thorough search of my person and removes my pistol. He straightens my bent body and guides me to the back seat of their patrol car.

When the cuffs had been on *other* wrists I felt like a big game hunter who had just bagged their prey. I really never envisioned *myself* being the one strapped to the roof of a car and driven around like a trophy buck.

The junior cop says, "I'll get the weapon in the car." He looks my way and asks. "Anything else in that vehicle I should be aware of?"

"Just the gun," I reply.

The senior officer is ready to begin a dialogue with the threat neutralized. In the police defense, many a patrol officer has been killed during a routine traffic stop, thus, police officers are taught that there is no such thing as a *routine* traffic stop.

"Name?"

"John Booker."

"*Special* Agent John Booker," The senior officer taunts. "I am going to call the FBI office and see if you really are a fed."

"I'm suspended."

"So you're not really an FBI agent."

"I'm technically an agent," I explain. "Just not active."

"Do you have a concealed carry permit?"

"No. Never needed one since I'm law enforcement."

"But," the cop reasons, "You are presently *not* law enforcement 'cause you're suspended."

"I guess."

"So, Mr. FBI agent. Let me ask you a simple question. Since you do not have a badge and you do not have a concealed carry permit, why are you carrying *two* pistols?"

"Can I ask a question?"

"I can't wait."

"Why did you stop me?"

"We received information that a person meeting your description, driving *your* particular car, would be leaving the parking lot of the Cleveland Clinic sometime this morning and would be armed." He pauses and finishes with, "*And,* that this individual is going around town impersonating an FBI agent."

I'm really thinking fast here since I *am* technically guilty of carrying a concealed weapon.

"Do you know Captain Kopka?" I ask.

"Yes, I know the Captain."

"Can you give him a call? He'll vouch for me."

I reason that half the population of Cleveland are illegally toting weapons at any given time, so a simple, *He's okay, you can let him go,* should be sufficient.

"If Captain Kopka says you're alright, then you can get on your way."

As the senior cop reaches for the radio microphone his partner taps on the window and motions him toward my car. They have an animated conversation and both lean into the back seat for several seconds. The older cop casually walks back to the patrol car and stares at me as I sit cuffed in the rear seat.

He asks. "What are you doing with an official accident report if you're suspended?"

I breathe a sigh of relief since accident reports are public documents, and though I didn't go through proper channels, this is a bullshit issue that would go nowhere.

"My friend was in an accident," I say. "Why such a big deal?"

"No big deal," he says in a manner that promises a *really* big deal is on the next horizon.

"It's just that next to the accident report is a bag which seems to contain five kilos of cocaine."

CHAPTER 25

"Badges! Badges!....We don't need no stinking Badges"
—*Blazing Saddles*

The *Cleveland Plain Dealer* leads with my arrest in two-inch block letters on their front page. It must be a slow news day. There are no words in any language which could describe the embarrassment I've caused my family and friends. The damage seems irreparable and no matter the legal outcome, my reputation will always include the footnote of *drug dealer*.

A law enforcement officer involved in large quantities of illegal drugs is viewed by *others* in the fraternity as toxic waste. Although I am extremely familiar with the process as arrester, being *the* arrestee did not prove to be as much fun. I did not receive the usual professional courtesies extended to fellow members of the law enforcement community. In fact, my booking included a few rough shoves when a simple '*move forward*,' would suffice.

My protests of innocence are met by the incredulous stares of seasoned detectives. If I had been sitting on their side of the table I would also be furrowing my eyebrows and thinking, '*bullshit!*'

I initially waive my rights since I have nothing to hide and am one of the good guys. This is a big misunderstanding and at any moment I expect someone will apologize and say, "Sorry ... our bad."

The lead detective is a big guy with a bulging belly hanging over a rodeo belt buckle. His polyester tie is sprinkled with old gravy stains and is wide as a Buick. He positions a well-used tape recorder in front of me and states the time, date, and location.

Before we begin the formal interview he rhetorically wonders. "How could an FBI agent and former Marine get involved in cocaine dealing?"

I have a good explanation but realize it may sound like the ramblings of a mad man. *'You see, the cocaine was planted by a super-secret terrorist cell that are in the process of destroying the United States."*

Since I can't state the truth, I say something that I imagined would never pass my lips. These words when said to me, always made me want to puke. I looked at the two detectives and say, "I want an attorney."

After *"lawyering up"* the Cleveland Police detectives go through the entire law enforcement repertoire of threats.

"You lawyer up and we can't deal, you go to the pen for the rest of your life."

"And you know what they do to cops in the pen."

"Give up your supplier and we get you sent to some country club for a few

years."

This dialogue could go on indefinitely if I did not interrupt with, "I appreciate your offer of help, but I want to speak with an attorney."

Both detectives take turns telling me that I am a piece of low life shit who betrayed the badge and would be buggered regularly by weight lifting black guys named Bubba in the Lewisburg Penitentiary shower.

I decide not to speak another word since it would be misinterpreted as a willingness to continue the dialogue. My silence does not dissuade them as they badger me for another fifteen minutes until I remind them that "You guys do know that *after* I request an attorney, even if I do confess to something, it'll be thrown out in court."

My knowledge of the system seems to anger them more. The big cop grabs me roughly by the arm and leads me to the holding cell. He pushes me inside, mutters 'asshole,' and locks the door. Three men sit on concrete benches and give me the 'fuck you' stare as I find a space to sit. The two black men continue the intimidation glare but the white guy actually smiles and says, "How you doin'?"

"Fuckin' wonderful, and you?"

"Not too good."

I avoid any follow up dialogue since the first rule of survival with bad guys is to remain quiet and appear deranged. Tough guys can deal with *other* tough guys but never want to start a beef with *crazy*.

My silence only seems to encourage Dick Scaeffor.

He says, "Can't believe I'm in here."

I nod but look straight ahead.

Dick slides closer to me on the bench and begins his story. He speaks quietly so that the two black guys can't hear. Scaeffor is a middle school teacher who likes little boys. He explains that he is a member of NAMBLA, which is the *North American Man Boy Love Association.* This group feels that there is nothing wrong with having sex with young boys since the boys are willing participants. He was snagged on an internet police sting when he went to meet an eleven year old who was actually a fifty-year old cop.

I nod occasionally but really want to smack Rick around. I finally say, "Get the fuck away from me, you pervert, before I pluck your eyeballs out."

He actually seems offended but slides away into no man's land between me and the two black guys. Just like politicians who vote along party lines, jail follows the color-coded system for survival. Blacks hang with blacks, Hispanics with Hispanics, pedophiles with pedophiles, and so on. I seem to be a few members shy of my particular team.

Three hours pass until a cop appears and says, "Booker!" I stand and the cop opens the door. He motions to follow him, and as I am leaving I turn to the two black guys and say, "Two things."

They stare at me with mild interest.

"First off, ol' Dick here is a pervert who likes to bugger little black boys."

Criminals can forgive almost any crime including drugs, murder, and even killing a grandmother or two, but, *not* pedophilia.

"And secondly," I continue, "Dick also told me that, '*the two niggers smell.*' I believe he was referring to you two."

The cop tells me to "shut up," but he is smiling as he leads me down the hallway.My initial phone call post-interrogation was to my friend and former Assistant United States Attorney Steve Sazzini. Steve is a former federal prosecutor who tried several of my FBI cases until he was offered triple the salary to defend the scumbags that he once prosecuted. It seems that at this moment in time, I'd be one of those scumbags.

Our meeting is brief and to the point. Like any good defense attorney Steve never asks about my innocence or guilt. He merely asks, "What happened?"

I tell him that the drugs were planted and rattle on how I would never be involved with cocaine. This is not the time to discuss the secret terrorist plot. Steve ask questions about my Marine Corps experience, my job, family, any community or volunteer work, then simply instructs me not to say a word during the bond hearing.

The process following arrest and booking is called the initial appearance. At this hearing, the judge reads the charges against you, determines bail, and asks how you plea. The courtroom is packed with my wife as well as the media, cops, gawkers, and Agent 36. I nod at Gwen who smiles and gives me a thumbs up. Lorri and I are permitted a brief hug and I can tell from her red eyes that she has been crying.

The judge asks how I plea and Steve answers with, "The defendant pleads not guilty, Your Honor."

The County District Attorney then goes for my throat and demands that I be remanded without bond based on the seriousness of my crime and the fact that I had *several* guns and drugs in my possession.

I suppose two guns could qualify as *several* and am reminded that the government is a vindictive exaggerating entity, though I never minded their half-truths when I was on their team. The combination of drugs and guns usually guarantees, no bail, and a mandatory five-year prison sentence unless there is some persuasive mitigating circumstances. I can only hope that my attorney can come up with some good shit.

Steve counters that I am not a flight risk, nor am I a danger to the community. These are the two criteria the judge must consider when determining bond. Our Constitution guarantees a fair and righteous bond. Steve explains that I have lived ten years at the same residence, am married and have a child. I am a life member of The Veterans of Foreign Wars and have raised money for wounded veterans. Since this is such a high profile case, the district attorney himself is getting the face time. He is a theatrical asshole who is eyeing the governorship and needs to hit a publicity home run.

He screams, "Even a suspended FBI agent is adept at disappearing, and since he is facing a long prison sentence, he is more *likely* to disappear."

Steve calls this speculative since I have not yet been convicted of anything and have distinguished myself both as a Marine and an FBI agent. He lists my Purple Heart, Silver Star and I believe he even awarded me some medals not noted on my discharge papers.

Judge Anthony Perry is a cantankerous old law and order man, but also a former Vietnam Marine who will either throw the book at me for betraying my oath or give a brother Marine the benefit of the doubt.

Perry stares down at me from his perch and says, "Whenever a member of law enforcement goes bad it sickens me to the stomach. You have disgraced yourself and your profession, and as a former Marine I am personally offended by your behavior. I am setting the bond at two million dollars secured."

The judge stands and stalks out the side door. I suddenly realize that a two million secure bond is basically no bond. Steve tells me that he needs to speak with Lorri and will get back to me within the hour. I am shell-shocked as officers lead me back to the holding cell.

I am in no mood for conversation and when Dick Scaeffor approaches me screaming, I hold a hand up like a school crossing guard and say, "Not now!"

Pedophiles must not understand a simple request since ol' Dick continues advancing with his fists balled. He is screaming something about me being *"not funny."* When he is about a foot away I knee the pedophile in the nuts. Seems like the appropriate body part to gain his attention. Dick falls to the ground gasping in pain.

One of my black cellmates informs me, "That was pretty *funny?*"

An hour later a jailer tells me, "Your lawyer's here."

He leads me into a room with a small metal table and two low bid government chairs. Steve rises when I enter and shakes my cuffed hand. The jailer instructs Steve to knock on the door when finished and cautions that the room is being monitored.

"The judge hammered you."

"A blinding flash of the obvious," I shoot back. "Now what?"

Steve sits down in a chair and opens his brief case. He extracts some papers and says, "I have some good news and some bad news."

"Bad first. I hate unhappy endings."

The former federal prosecutor sighs and says, "They caught you in possession of five kilograms of cocaine. Field tests were positive on the cocaine. As you know, the government will pile on the charges and hope you cut a deal. They are also charging you with carrying *two* concealed weapons and conspiracy to distribute the cocaine. The amount of the drugs along with the guns makes your minimum prison exposure at eight years."

"This is pure bullshit. I am a former Marine and an FBI agent who carried a weapon my entire adult life."

"At the time of your arrest, you were not an active duty FBI agent and *not* authorized to carry a weapon."

"C'mon, Stevie," I almost scream. "This reeks of a setup and you gotta be able to smell it out a mile away."

Steve looks me in the eye and says, "I believe you, John, but right now they're holding all the cards. You've got to help me. Is there any possible explanation on how the drugs ended up in the back seat of your car?"

"I was set up!"

"By who?" Steve demands. "Someone you arrested? The Mafia? An FBI agent makes a lot of enemies, and an undercover agent makes even more. Think, John."

"I have a hunch but just that. You're right, Steve, I have a lot of enemies."

"You need to think long and hard about who may have planted the drugs. We need to go on the offensive," Steve pauses and adds. "I've spoken with your wife and even if she puts up the house as security on the bond, you're still some one point eight million shy."

"Have we got to the good news yet?" I wonder.

Steve smiles and says. "Well, on the bright side, we know the prosecution's entire case. They found five kilos of cocaine in your possession. We don't know about prints, but that seems to be the extent of their evidence. They'll run your phone records, try and find some corroborating witnesses, and paint you as a rogue agent. Judging from what you've told me about the past year, that won't be too hard to do."

"I thought we were on the good news," I say. "I need to be on the outside to prove my innocence. But you're telling me that I can't make bond."

In the majority of bail hearings, the plaintiff needs to come up with ten percent of the total amount. But Judge Perry specifically ordered that I post a *secured* amount which means that I either had to lay down two million in cash or like collateral in a house, jewelry or other assets worth two million. A bail bondsman can usually cover the ninety percent on most reasonable bonds, but none will go out on a financial limb for this amount.

My high bond is the judge's way of keeping me under lock and key. The Eighth Amendment of the U.S. Constitution states that excessive bail shall not be required. Though the judge could argue that two million is not excessive, a reasonable person would throw a penalty flag. By remanding me *without* bond, he would be vulnerable for a reversal on appeal. But the brilliance of offering me an exorbitant bond, is that he *knew* that I could not come up with two million dollars, thus he could defile our constitution through the back door.

Steve has a weird smile on his face. He shoves some paperwork in my direction and says, "After I spoke with Lorri, some woman approached me in the hall. Introduced herself as Bonnie the Bail Bond Babe. Ring a bell?

"Yea. The girl on late night cable who looks like a drag queen."

Steve says, "He *or* she, *is* a drag queen. But Bonnie runs a top notch agency."

"Where is this going?"

"Do you know her?"

"Never met her *or* him, why?"

"She's posting your bond."

CHAPTER 26

What we got here is a failure to communicate."
— Cool Hand Luke

A few hours later, I meet Bonnie the Bail Bond Babe in her office on Prospect Avenue. Standing a shade over six feet tall with four-inch spike heels, Bonnie makes an immediate impression. Born Bernard Smith, he began hormone treatments and traded jockey shorts for silk undies eight years ago. I notice hair extensions, red lipstick, stretch pants, and lots of jewelry. Although Bonnie wasn't my type, I may have bought her a drink during my Marine Corps days.

She explains, "Here's the deal. Sign the paperwork and be a good boy. Rules are, can't leave the county, you must surrender your passport, random piss tests, and show up for court dates. Got it, honey?"

I nod my head. "Got it."

"Any questions?"

"Yea, who put up my bond?"

Bonnie the Bail Bond Babe looks down at me and smiles. She says, "I've been in this business for twenty-three years both as Bernard and Bonnie. Thought I saw it all. This morning two point two million dollars is wire-transferred into my account. The instructions are simple. "Bond out John Booker and keep the two hundred grand as your fee."

"Who from?"

"No idea, but their money is green. Easiest dough I ever made. So thank you, John Booker."

Bonnie leans down, hands me an envelope and gives me a hug. I am smothered in fake hair, hormonal boobs and cheap perfume.

"Thanks Bonnie," I say sincerely, "you're a class act."

Steve drops me off at home. We plan to get together tomorrow and strategize, but it seems hopeless. I've had plenty of time to consider who may have planted the cocaine and it all comes back to international phantom terrorists. How does a trained investigator minus badge, gun, and access to intelligence data find such a group?

My reunion with Lorri and Nikki is emotionally agonizing. Tears flow down all our cheeks as I attempt to soothe their pain. I proclaim my innocence and rationalize that the truth will eventually prevail. I try to sound convincing but lack the belief to pull it off. If I had been the investigating officer on my case, the fat lady would be singing and I'd be smoking a victory cigar.

Lorri demands to know, "Tell me, John, tell me you're not involved in drugs, tell me!"

I look at Nikki first, then Lorri. Their eyes are wide as they await my answer. There are many thoughts flying through my brain but it's important to find just the *right* words. I fail miserably.

"I swear on my daughter's soul that I am not a drug dealer."

Nikki maintains her stare until a smile slowly forms on her lips. Being ever her father's sardonic daughter she says, "Well that's a relief, Pops, but you could've left my soul out of it."

My daughter gives me a hug and tells me that she loves me. Then it's off to her room for this generation's version of electronic homework. It fascinates me that my bizarre assertion of innocence is sufficient for my daughter. She'll handle the taunts and glares at school as long as "Pops" said it *ain't so*.

Lorri, on the other hand, is a tougher sell. She demands a lengthy dialogue and my legal problems are but a small part on her agenda. I pour a white wine for my wife and a Jim Beam straight for me. Lorri deserves answers and although I am prepared to bare all, I'm not so sure that it will suffice.

She opens with, "You have been a complete idiot, John. Distant, moody, drinking too much, secretive, and my instincts tell me that you're fooling around." Lorri looks directly in my eyes and challenges me. "Are you having an affair, John?"

My immediate instinct is guilt, as in, *'I'm caught.'* But then I remember that I have *not* been unfaithful. Although my mind had strayed to purple bra straps and Egyptian cleavage, my body had remained at parade rest. So why the guilt? Perhaps I subconsciously subscribe to the premise that cheating in the mind is being unfaithful.

"I am not having an affair, Lorri."

There is an awkward silence as Lorri's bullshit meter measures my sincerity. Most married individuals have an innate sense of spousal infidelity. Their intellect screams *cheater*, but their heart will muffle the brain almost every time. Lorri maintains an appraising glare before her face softens.

"Then I need to know what's going on in *our* life, John. In case you forgot, this is a partnership."

Men's DNA can be downright combative when confronted on the battlefield, the ball field or a bar, but when the venue is your kitchen table and the opponent is a loved one, most males would rather stick toothpicks in their eyeballs than have a *'discussion.'* The next hour is painful as I maneuver through an emotional mine field. Since I could not deny or dismiss my bizarre behavior, it's time to come clean. Perhaps clean, but certainly not *squeaky* clean.

The truth of the matter is that I am a thrill junky. If this were a medical condition, the symptoms would include risktaking, being a loner and a resentment of authority. I actually view most individuals as assholes who attempt to hide that condition from the rest of society. Unfortunately, I am correct in my assessment of the human race.

But I truly love and *like* my wife. It's easy to *love* someone who has shared your life for many years, but it is much more difficult to *like* that person. Just look at married couples in restaurants who spend two hours staring at their water glass. I explain my job problems and we discuss all the options of life with one paycheck. Then it's on to the more ominous legal issues which threaten our very existence as a family. I explain that I have one of the best attorneys in the business and how we'll save fees by me acting as my own investigator.

We move on to the entire Suehad relationship and how an Egyptian Rhodes Scholar figures into the equation. I admit to an infatuation, but adamantly deny any physical contact. Realizing that most females require specific details, I tell my wife that "All that ever happened was a simple hug and a European two-peck cheek kiss."

My wife actually nods her head as if grasping some complicated math formula. It's classic Scandinavian Lorri behavior of evaluating a situation in a calm demeanor and making monumental decisions minus any rancor.

I tell my wife, "Those drugs were planted and I *will* find out who planted them."

Lorri stares at me minus a response and my immediate reaction is that she doubts my innocence. I ask, "You *do* know that I'm innocent?"

My wife smiles and says, "I have lived with and loved you for over twenty years John and I know two things."

I wait for her reply.

"You are not a drug dealer, and you will find who did this to you." Lorri pauses and corrects, "Who did this to *us*?"

We embrace and although I am facing a long prison sentence, I am suddenly filled with hope. I know how to do this investigative stuff, and it is time to stop feeling sorry for myself. It is time to go on the offensive. I promise my wife that things will work out and actually believe my pledge. Someone once said that *"Life is a journey and not a guided tour."* It is important to have the Booker women behind me as I begin this particular part of my journey.

My man cave is located in the lower section of our split-level home. It is a ten-by-twelve room situated between the garage and laundry room. The usual memorabilia of life consuming my walls, shelves, desk and tables. You can tell a lot about a person by their '*I love me*' room. Even the most unassuming person enjoys life's special moments. Whether it be a family vacation photo, a diploma, or a Purple Heart, they represent your path from past to present. Their cumulative effect is a road map to the person we have become.

I dial Monica's number hoping for some good news on Suehad.

She begins with, "Oh my God John, are you okay?"

"Fine," I lie, "a big misunderstanding."

Now that could be classified under the heading of an *understatement*. My arrest has been the top story on the news.

"How's Suehad?" I ask by way of changing topics.

"Better," Monica explains. "Doctors say that she's out of danger and the next step is a rehab facility."

"Students showing up?"

"More than enough. Once the word got out, we sometimes have two and three students with Suehad."

"I'll be by tomorrow," I say and then remember, "I hope you haven't mentioned my legal problems?"

"Not a word, John. I don't know *exactly* what you two got going, but I *do* know when to keep my mouth shut."

"Give her my best."

"I will," Monica says.

"Bye."

"Hey John," Monica says with a mischievous inflection.

"Yes."

"Now that you're an outlaw, like me. Maybe we can start a gang?"

Since I had provided Monica her felony record, she deserves that note of irony. It was actually pretty funny. I say, "I'd be honored to be a member of your gang."

My next call is to Captain Ray Kopka. I trusted this Cleveland cop the second I shook his beefy hand. He was a throwback to a bygone era when cops understood that the world was black and white with no shades of gray. They built a giant blue wall to shield them from the remainder of society.

These guys may have massaged a few laws along the way, but *always* for righteous reasons. They drank tons of whiskey, fooled around with strippers, and would occasionally duke it out with a brother cop. But they always remained steadfastly loyal to each other and to the brotherhood.

Thus, it was important that Ray Kopka believe me when I told him that I was *not* a drug dealer. His approval would connect me to the law enforcement community and though a reluctant member, I'm like the wayward son who occasionally needs to come home.

"Ray," I begin tentatively. "You gotta second?"

"All the time in the world."

"You've probably know what's going on?"

"No shit, Sherlock. You're big news … *'FBI agent goes bad.'* I even took some shots from the boys since I had put the word out that you were an okay Fed."

"Sorry about that."

"Don't be. I've got big shoulders. Now what the fuck's up Booker?"

"All I can say with certainty is that I am not involved with drugs in any way."

"I figured," Kopka answers matter-of-factly.

I wait for more but when none is forthcoming, I ask. "Is that it? So you believe me?"

"About fifteen years ago," Kopka explains, "I was a hard-charging narcotics detective. Balls to the walls and I made a lot of enemies. A few of the bigger drug dealers got together and set me up. Somehow deposited cash in my bank account and for the grand finale, planted cash in my personal vehicle. Then they called Internal Affairs who found the cash. The goons conduct an investigation and get four dope dealers to swear under oath that they've been paying me protection money for years."

"What happened?"

Well," Kopka continues, "things looked bad. Grand Jury indicted me for bribery. Most civilians and half of the people at the Justice Center believed every fucking word in that indictment. I was looking at ten years hard time. But the coppers I worked with knew I was set up and things got worked out."

"Whoa!" I interrupt. "Whatta you mean, *'worked out?'* How did *things* get worked out?"

"When you trust guys to cover your back every stinkin' day, when you stand beside them at their weddings, kids communions and funerals, you get to know them. You would know if they went bad. My friends knew I was being framed so they did what they had to do."

"And what was that?" I ask.

"Well," Kopka chuckles and then offers. "The only thing *I* know is that one of the dope dealers who set me up, *somehow* got religion. He wore a wire and recorded a long conversation with the other three dirt bags on how they framed me. How they put the money in my bank and car, and how they wanted me off the street so they could sell their poison."

I knew not to push for the details and say. "That's great, Ray. Happy it all *worked out* for you."

"Anyway, when I heard about *your* problem it had the same stench of *my* problem, and since *I* knew you weren't a dope dealer, I'm currently looking into your particular situation on the street. I'm shaking the branches and stirring up the snitches. Nothing yet, but I don't give up easily."

"I really appreciate your vote of confidence. You have no idea how much that *means* to me. But, the people who did this to me are not on the streets of Cleveland."

"Well," Kopka grumbles, "then I'll do my best to help you in *other* ways."

"Thank you."

"Nothing to thank me for … *yet*."

"I'll be in touch Ray."

"Booker?

"Yea."

"You wouldn't listen to me."

"I'm not following."

"You got hit in the ass," Kopka now laughing, "with a fuckin' arrow."

"I certainly did, my friend."

I hang up feeling almost normal though my life is anything but status quo. Kopka's sharing his own personal legal mess gives me hope. A moment later my brain mulls over on something he said. At the time I had thought it curious. Maybe it wasn't exactly what he said, but *how* he said it. When I dismissed that anyone in Cleveland may be behind my troubles Kopka promised that he'd do his best to help me, 'in *other* ways.' This seemed an unusual offer of help, but knowing the man, it wasn't just a hollow *'feel good'* empty pledge.

I am wondering what these *'other'* ways implied.

CHAPTER 27

"Success is simply a matter of luck. Ask any failure."
— *Earl Wilson*

I felt that there are three nagging questions. *Who* called me confirming Grant Beck's death? *Who* put up two point two million dollars in cash for my bond? *Who* provided me the access code for the intelligence bulletins? It is quite possible that they are all the same person since the actions appear to be an attempt to help me. But, who is this person and how do they figure into my secret terrorist theory? Do I know them or are they simply using me as *their* instrument? I can only guess at the *why*, which is some type of common goal. Yet, *my* most pressing goal at present is to stay out of jail.

If my fairy godmother wanted me dead, I'd be dead since it's easier to kill someone in jail than on the street. So, I figure, I have at least one member of the Booker team, albeit an invisible one. I also figure that my cohort must have some connections *and* money, which is an extremely useful twosome.

Iraq returns in my dreams with a vengeance. This particular nightmare includes some new footage. While lying in my own pool of IED-induced blood, al-Qaeda overruns our position and I am repeatedly bayoneted in the back. Since al-Qaeda soldiers are not known for bayonet warfare, I can only deduce that my savage death is some type of symbolism. Maybe I need a shrink to interpret this latest episode of John Booker's nightmares.

I head to the kitchen for some coffee and a bagel. My *'to do'* list for the day includes visits with my attorney and Suehad. Some other objectives include attempting to trace the money wire transfer to Bonnie and scrutinize the outgoing communication from North Korea which read, *SON CRITICAL WITH VIRUS,* with the reply from Cairo of … *FINANCE CURE.*

Tracing a wire transfer is difficult even for a trained financial analyst of the FBI. They'd have no difficulty locating the originating sender but would get immediately mired in a quicksand of uncooperative foreign financial institutions and confidentiality agreements. It really is a mute issue since I have no official standing to issue subpoenas. My conclusion is that my only realistic option for the day is to figure out the intelligence bulletin chatter and visit Steve and Suehad.

I realize that I'll need some help in interpreting the riddle. The person would have to be creative, bright and be able to think outside the box. My list is short. It includes Chuck, Suehad, and my daughter Nikki.

Since my daughter is closest in proximity, she becomes my default choice. Nikki will be down for her coffee and cereal in about two hours. I'll spend the time developing an investigative plan.

When the IED exploded and my platoon was about to get overrun by al-Qaeda, I prayed. Many fallen religious types turn back to God in times of crisis. Since we usually break our deal with God, it's fortunate that the big guy is not in the Mafia and retaliates by *breaking* our legs. I could endure prison. I wasn't going to be anyone's *bitch* and would adjust by going into survival mode. Any Marine who had been to basic training knew the drill. Keep your mouth shut and when confronted with force, strike first and hard. Thus my prayer is simply to spare my family both the emotional and financial burdens of my being gone.

I hear Nikki before I see her. She is definitely not a morning person and requires caffeine for efficient operation. Nikki has been drinking coffee since third grade. Initially, Lorri and I forbade this addicting habit, but when your eight-year-old daughter is stashing coffee beans in her *Cinderella* lunch box, it's time to cave.

"Hey Pops," Nikki mumbles. "Coffee done?"

Lorri tells me that I always smile when Nikki enters the room. It's a similar sensation to opening a bottle of Champagne. I wait until she settles at the kitchen table and the coffee makes its way into her system.

"Nikki," I say. "I'm working on my case and need your opinion on some stuff."

Nikki takes a sip of her coffee and asks, "A *real* FBI case?"

"Yep," I nod and discuss the case in general terms. Nikki asks a few questions and sips her coffee. I am particularly interested on her take on the latest intel briefings. The average high school senior of today routinely solves complex puzzles and riddles on their Samsung tablets. They are not intimidated by the most convoluted mosaics.

"Okay, Nikki." I conclude. "Any general impressions on the latest intercepts?"

"Well, they already used the bird flu so the *virus* part of, *SON CRITICAL WITH VIRUS* probably means something else."

"Suehad and I were thinking about a *computer* virus."

Nikki is silent as she mulls over the possibilities and slumps back down in her chair. I fill the silence with, "*FINANCE CURE* fits in this somehow."

"I'm taking senior AP economics, and we had a discussion last month on what would make a countries economy go into the crapper."

"We seem to be heading in that direction."

"We aren't even close to countries like Greece, Cyprus, and Italy. They can't just print more money like us, 'cause they're part of the Euro thing."

"But," I say, "the US can't keep spending more that we take in. That's *basic* economics."

Nikki nods. "But the America is the big dog in the world and can always play the military trump card. Like simply tell our creditors, '*we ain't paying you back.*'"

"So did the teacher explain how a super power like the US could go bankrupt?"

"Sure did. Ms. Eagan feels that the most likely way is your basic spend and borrow scenario." Nikki pauses and offers. "But then I asked her for some *unlikely* ways. And that's when it got interesting. The whole class started coming up with ways to bankrupt the U.S. of A."

Somehow the image of a group of seventeen-year-olds discussing world economics struck me as inconsequential. Then I remember that *this* particular generation of high school seniors were weaned on the information highway.

"I'm all ears."

"Well, this kid Scott said all someone would have to do is eliminate our currency."

"Explain that, Nikki."

"Scott said that if everyone had the same amount of money, which is actually no money at all, then there'd be no rich or poor. Even people who hoard gold, diamonds, or silver would starve because as soon as they started trading that stuff for food some bubba would just point a gun and take their crap."

"Makes sense," I say. "So what about my riddle?"

Nikki finishes off her coffee and heads toward the sink. She places her cup down and then turns to me. She concludes. "The United States is about to get hit with a major computer virus which will somehow shut down the economy."

I look down at my notes, which read, SON CRITICAL WITH VIRUS and FINANCE CURE. It makes perfect sense.

North Korea has just given Cairo the 'go ahead' to make it happen. I have no idea on how much time I have to act but know that the clock is definitely ticking.

CHAPTER 28

"Who's gonna believe that cwazy wabbit???"
— Elmer Fudd

"Cripes, Booker, you are nuclear here. I'll get back to you in ten."

Although I call Agent 36 on her personal cell phone, she is prudent not to have this conversation within the FBI walls. The open squad bay area guarantees listeners, even the unwilling ones.

I can only imagine the reprisals for any FBI agent who consorts with the enemy. That enemy is now me. The Bureau has loads of unwritten codes. They are verbally passed down through the generations of law men and are sacrosanct. Some of them make no sense. But cavorting with an agent accused of drug dealing is definitely frowned upon. The possibility of my innocence is not part of the equation.

My cell phone chirps the Marine Corps hymn.

"You *do* know that you are considered a notch below Satan within the FBI family," Gwen says. "And although I have always personally been attracted to the bad boys, you have even gone too far for me. Five kilos of coke, are you outta your mind, Booker!"

"Hi Gwen," I reply calmly. "How's your day going?"

"Talk to me."

"Thanks for showing up in court. I know that probably caused you some heartburn with the boys."

"Sorry to break our goodwill bubble, but I was sent there by Michaels to monitor the court proceedings. In case you said anything sensitive. But," Gwen adds, "I was secretly rooting for you."

Agent 36's brutal honesty brings a smile to my face.

I say, "I'm gonna make you more famous than *Donnie Brasco* and J. Edgar Hoover combined."

"You are now officially creeping me out. You on some *feel-good* meds?"

"Just listen up, Gwen. You take no risk and get all the rewards."

"I don't need any career advice, Booker. I'm a female attorney with big boobs. The only profile better than mine is a black transgender disabled veteran with a lisp."

"Hear me out and then decide."

For the next twenty-five minutes I explain my dilemma. I tell Gwen that she could save three hundred million Americans some severe heartburn if she writes a *simple* memo. She will have no negative exposure and could end up on the cover of *TIME* magazine as a national heroine.

My plan is simple but not without risks. Since I have zero credibility it would be a waste of time for me to prophesize a monumental financial meltdown via a computer virus. But Gwen is the perfect conduit for this mission, for exactly the reason that she *is* a lock for upward mobility within the FBI, namely, *"a foxy female attorney with big boobs."*

Agent 36 fires questions at me in the manner of cross-examination. I answer all her concerns calmly and confidently. Gwen could detect any insecurity or bullshit. One very perceptive observation she makes is, "They are going to grill me on *how* I came to this very dramatic conclusion and I am feeling a bit challenged, Booker."

"Stick to the basic script and don't embellish or deviate. You are a member of the task force, which gives you access to the intel briefings. It's not uncommon for squad mates to share theories."

"The dialogue is a bit theatrical, Booker, but I get the bottom line."

"It paints them into a corner."

"What is it exactly that I'm asking them to do?"

"Send out an alert to every financial institution, state government, the U.S. Treasury, Wall Street, and any other agency, organization, or corporation that deals with moola and request that they alert their IT experts to do something."

"Do what?"

"You are talking to a computer idiot, Gwen. But I *do* know that these IT geeks can take some preventive measures with firewalls or something like that. And let them know that this is NOT going to be your garden variety computer virus concocted by some kid living in mommy's basement. It is going to be monumental."

When I had explained my strategy and soothed all her concerns, Agent 36 sums up her undertaking.

"Booker, let me get this straight. You write a memo under my name, which spells out a tale of some possible super terrorist cell in cahoots with the North Koreans. In that memo, I explain that prior to your arrest: you shared this theory with me. *After* your fall from grace, I continued to scan the intelligence bulletins and now have deduced that America's financial institutions will be attacked with a massive computer virus within the next month."

"That about sums it up."

"And," she concludes, "once I put this fairy tale in writing and feed it up the food chain, then the suits can't ignore or brush it aside."

"You're on record," I add, "and, if a computer virus hits, and I'm sure it will, you'll be the FBI poster child. If nothing happens, your memo becomes one of the thousands filed under '*good try*.'"

"You *do* know that I have to send this memo to Boy Wonder. He's my immediate supervisor and if I break my chain of command on something this major, even *my* boobs won't help."

"Not a problem," I counter. "Just blind copy A.D. Anthony Daniels at Headquarters with a note, '*from your roomie and new hip pocket source*'."

Gwen snickers and says, "I must be crazy because I *know* this is career suicide, but if you're right and I blow it off, then *I'm* in the wrong profession anyway."

"We won't be wrong."

"You are so full of shit Booker, but your heart's in the right place."

"I would trust you to cover my back anytime, Gwen. You are one ballsy FBI agent."

"I know that's somehow a compliment, Booker, but one last question."

"Yeah."

"What happens if I submit this doomsday prediction and the boys in the front office ignore it?"

"Good question," I say. "And, also a good possibility given their propensity to avoid making decisions."

"That wasn't an answer."

"Unfortunately, the answer is that if the Bureau ignores your warning,many good Americans will suffer."

I pull on some faded worn blue jeans and my Marine Corps hoodie. It's nice to go scruffy and not have to shave. My first stop is Steve Sazina's office. It reeks of affluence, garnished with paintings by known artists and lots of glass and plants. A model looking receptionist greets me with a perfect smile, "Can I help you?"

"John Booker to see Mr. Sazina."

A flicker of recognition in her eyes alerts me to the fact that standing before her is the rogue and dangerous FBI agent featured in all the news headlines. The smile has contorted slightly and now has a slight trace of disapproval. I know that murderers and rapist are daily visitors at a major defense firm, so my presence must be especially repugnant.

"He's expecting you."

Government attorneys are generally housed in crowded bleak and austere government buildings. Their desks, chairs and even their computers are *'low bid.'* The call up to a private practice, aka the big league, comes with all the perks of charging clients $400 bucks an hour. Steve is giving me the homeboy discount of $200 per hour, but I still remind myself to get right to the point. My brain conjures up an image of a ticking taxi meter.

Many lawyers merely use their government time as a springboard to the more lucrative private sector. Their journey generally includes cutting their legal teeth on some low-level welfare fraud cases and then onward and upward to the major stars in the criminal hierarchy: organized crime and public corruption.

With that said, Steve Sazini is a different breed. If I had met him during my undercover mob time he'd be called a *stand-up guy*. A small swarthy Italian, Sazini is a down-to-earth guy from Philadelphia.In the courtroom, Steve works like a master mason building his case brick by brick. By the time the opposition came to bat they are already ten points down.

"Okay. John," Steve begins our meeting. "I've spoken to the district attorney and here's their opening salvo. Taking into account your military heroism, your FBI public service which includes the highest civilian awards for valor and your clean record, they offered ten years, if, you give up your drug source."

"Fuck them."

"My sentiments," Steve says calmly. "I told them that we'd consider a suspended sentence, probation, community service and a fine."

"Well then, fuck *you*!"

Steve actually laughs. "I'm merely taking their temperature. Take it easy, John. These preliminary talks are just like philosophy class, all posturing. Actually, they demanded that you go to jail for betraying the public trust, blah, blah blah."

"Fuck him."

"You seem stuck on fucking *someone*."

"I'm innocent!" I protest.

"There's a lot innocent people in jail."

"I'm innocent and won't plea to crap."

"As your attorney, I'll honor your wishes, but I will also present all the options and make recommendations. If you are hell-bent on going to court, it will cost you fifty grand minimum, even with my discount."

"I know the drill. The case won't see a courtroom for two years and in the meantime I will be working at *Burger King* just to pay for your paper clips."

Steve grabs his phone and holds it in front of my face. "Do you want me to brief you aboutmy conversation with the D.A., John, or do I call him and tell him that we'll see him in court?"

I realize that I'm behaving like an ass with the one person who can save *my* ass. "Sorry Steve, it's been a rough few days."

Steve grabs my shoulder and says, "I understand, John, but *you* need to know that I'm on your side. You know the drill better than anybody. They *need* a conviction after making you public enemy number one, but they also realize that their case is not open and shut, so we have some flexibility."

"What're their weak spots?"

"Well," Steve explains, "they've got the physical evidence of the cocaine, but that's all. You have no history of drug use or sales; and I found out that the packaging contained no prints — zero. They *say* it strengthens *their* case since as an FBI agent, you know all the tricks about leaving an evidence trail."

"But they can't have it both ways," I protest. "I couldn't be that much of an expert about leaving an evidence trail if I'm driving around with five kilos of cocaine."

"And that's where reasonable doubt begins to eat away at their case. You don't fit the profile of a drug dealer, have no financial problems as motive, no contact with known drug dealers, and have made many enemies who would have reason to plant drugs as revenge."

"It's sounding better and better."

"Don't get too over confident, John. They'll counter with your years undercover provided plenty of exposure to dope dealers, that you knew you were getting fired, and the drugs were your retirement plan. Then they'll chronicle your behavior lately, which has been erratic, thus making you capable of things like choking out your supervisor *or* selling dope."

Steve's logic sucks the air right out of the room.

"So, what's our next *philosophical* move?" I ask.

"I countered their offer with the probability that a jury would be reluctant to send a bona fide war hero to jail, and we would create so much reasonable doubt that the jury would have no choice but acquit."

"And he said?"

"Plead guilty to one distribution count and take a two-year jail sentence. You'll be out in fifteen months."

"As I said a moment ago, fuck him."

My *'fuck him,'* visit cost me two hundred and fifty dollars, but, was well worth the money. Steve and I agree on a strategy of refusing any offer from the DA and waive the speedy trial requirement. We figure that time is our ally both in terms of my investigation and that the jury pool needed time to forget John Booker.

I head to the Cleveland Clinic to visit with Suehad. Monica shared the good news that her condition had been upgraded from critical to stable. It's just a matter of time until she's transferred to a rehabilitation facility.

As I enter her room, I notice one of the students sitting by her bed. He seems older than the usual fare of undergraduates but many older individuals are back in the classroom these days. Suehad is fast asleep with a full array of monitors and tubes surrounding her.

The student looks at me with a suspicious stare so I smile and say, "Hi, I'm John Booker, Suehad's friend."

I guess his age as late thirties, early forties. There is something distinctly ethnic about his clothes, haircut and body language.

He stares at my hand and says, "And *I* am Suehad's husband."

CHAPTER 29

"Nothing good ever happens without a fight."
— *The Lying Game*

As a whole, most Muslims are just a shade more arrogant than the French. At least they drink good wine, are sexually liberated, and have the good sense to surrender to the Nazis whenever asked.

I am not in any mood to cope with Mansur's attitude but decide to grin and bear his rudeness. This guy maybe may be my ticket back to a normal life. Although I don't believe Mansur is a *member* of any super terrorist cell, I *do* believe he can point me in the right direction. Currently, I am the dog chasing his own tail so any forward direction is welcomed.

"How's Suehad?" I ask.

Mansur maintains his glare as if deciding which way to play *me*. That makes two of us. I decide on developing some rapport and see where it goes. I can always pistol whip him later.

His reply is, "She will live but require around the clock medical care for many months."

"But the doctors say she'll make a full recovery," I offer optimistically.

"That is conjecture," Mansur challenges with a tinge of venom.

I realize that my rapport approach is not going well so I ignore his last comment and approach Suehad. The bandages have been reduced but still cover most of her head. The left side of her face is swollen and for the first time I notice a cast on her left arm.

After a moment I turn to Mansur and ask, "You have any dinner plans?"

My abrupt change of demeanor seems to throw off his confrontation mode.

"Thank you, but I will stay with *my* wife." The emphasis on the possessive, '*my*.'

"Maybe another time," I add. "How long will you be around?"

"I am not sure. It depends on *my wife's* recovery."

"Give Suehad my best when she wakes up," I say. "See you soon."

My first instinct is to do an about face and return to Suehad's room. Leaving her alone and vulnerable with that creep of a husband makes me feel like a deserter. I head to the nurse's station and ask a lady with a stethoscope around her neck to see Suehad's doctor.

"Can I ask the nature of your request?"

"It's personal."

"I'm afraid that the doctor is unavailable but I am the shift supervisor of nurses. Can I help you?"

"Well," I begin sheepishly. "My friend Suehad in Room 24, well, her husband came in from Cairo …"

I am at a loss for words and Nurse Cratchet's stare is not making me more verbose.

"And what?" She finally asks.

"Well, it's just that she may not want to be alone with him."

"Why?"

I think, *Well, for starters, he may be part of a super terrorist group, he forced his wife to participate in orgies,* and, *he is an arrogant radical Muslim* but say, "Can you just keep an eye on him," I plead.

The nurse supervisor looks down on a chart and nods but it is not assent, merely a dismissal. I have nothing left to say that would make sense, so I smile and leave.

The Barking Goose is my favorite spot in northern Ohio. It is a renovated horse stable situated between the Museums and Case Western Reserve University. It is a throwback to the sixties coffee houses and books the best music anywhere. On any given day, you can listen to jazz, folk, blues, and even a Serbian quartet. Goose is a gentle German Shepherd who ambles around the joint with a tip bucket clenched in his mouth, hence the name *Barking Goose....* It's difficult not to ante up to a large smiling dog, so Goose does well for his master.

During the day, it is a college hangout with students occasionally taking the stage to recite poetry or strum a guitar. The drink of choice during the daytime hours is freshly-ground coffee and green tea from places like Ethiopia and Ecuador. I chose the Barking Goose to meet Agent 36 since law enforcement types, *especially* of the FBI variety, would rarely cross the Goose's threshold.

Benjamin, the owner, greets me in his usual laid-back manner, "How goes it John?"

"Been busy Ben, and you."

"At peace. Haven't seen you around."

"Been getting my caffeine fix at *Starbucks.*"

"That's bad corporate karma, John."

I laugh at the old hippies jargon, but could do with some of his peace. Since I'm an hour early, I settle down on the stool next to Benjamin and visit. The knack of visiting is a lost art. It involves actually listening instead of thinking of what you are *about* to say. Human beings have difficulty enjoying the present since it takes effort. We can't appreciate the here and now.

"So," Ben asks. "What's bumming you out John?"

"You can tell?"

"Negative vibes. I can see a red aura surrounding you."

"I take it that red's not good?"

"Stress caused by some evil people nipping at you."

"Pretty accurate shit Ben," I say. "Actually amazing."

"We all have the ability to see things clearly, John," Benjamin explains. "But most people have a shroud that clouds their vision. You just have to lift that shroud."

"How do I lift *my* particular shroud?"

"Difficult question, John, but it involves a cleansing and a belief. We all have bad shit clogging our brain like envy, anger, jealousy, revenge, hate, you get the picture. You have to get rid of all those bad emotions, replace them with love and then believe."

"Believe in what?"

Benjamin smiles and says. "In yourself, in a higher spirit, in goodness."

Someone grabs me from behind and I automatically twist and reach for my pistol. My left hand thrusts toward my attacker's face as my right hand grips my gun.

"We a little tense these days, Booker?" Gwen teases.

I smile and make introductions. "Benjamin, this is Gwen. Ben owns this joint."

Benjamin looks his part of aging hippie with long gray hair tied in a ponytail. Both his jeans and flannel shirt appear well worn. He jumps off his bar stool, bows at the waist and says, "It's always a pleasure to meet a friend of John's."

Agent 36, who is never at a loss for words, hesitates and finally says, "A real charmer, Booker. Your friends usually greet me with a high five and a chest bump."

Benjamin smiles and says, "I'll take that as a compliment, but the chest bump intrigues me."

Gwen blushes for the first time since I've known her. This is rare since she has been trading boob banter with the best of them since *fourth* grade. That is about the time she traded here training bra for the grown up sizes.

"We can discuss that later, Benjamin." Gwen says seductively. "John and I have some business to discuss."

Agent 36 and I find a corner table and order the Ethiopian dark roast. Gwen seems anxious to get going and says, "Well, Booker, it's been an interesting few days."

"I'll bet."

"Boy Wonder received the memo and took a bureaucratic seizure. Told me if I was picking sides, I picked wrong. Went into a long lecture on career development and how something like this memo would end any hope of my advancement."

"Did you fold on me, Gwen?"

"Get real, Booker," Agent 36 objects. "I just smiled and agreed with him."

"What!"

"Calm down. That's your problem, Booker, you're confrontational. I, on the other hand, am devious. Michaels is like most men who have tunnel vision when dealing with females who seem submissive."

"So did he send the memo to Bell?" I ask. "Is the Bureau going to issue an alert to the financial institutions?"

"No."

"No?"

"Michaels told me that he would deal with the memo, and if I went over his head to Bell, he would suspend me for insubordination."

"That indecisive bastard. He's not going to do squat. Same shit he pulled in Idaho that caused the death of two FBI agents. Boy Wonder won't make a decision 'cause if he's wrong then it'll fuck up his career."

Gwen adds. "He told me that there are no super terrorist groups and that there'll be no computer attack on our financial institutions. Michaels said that he'd look like an incompetent fool if he approved my memo and send it to Bell."

"So did you at least send a blind copy of the memo to Daniels?"

"Along with your roomie note and being his hip pocket source."

There is an awkward silence as we both try and digest the situation and determine remedial action.

Agent 36 wonders, "Will Daniels do something?"

"No," I explain. "He can't minus some proof. If Tony issues a country-wide FBI alert on suspected computer terrorism, the stock market would tank and billions of dollars could be lost to investors. It would also negatively affect things like U.S. Treasury notes, gas and food prices, and even our health care system."

"Holy shit, Booker,' Gwen whispers. "No wonder Michaels went jack batty."

"Exactly," I continue. "So, Tony can't act unless he receives an official request from Bell along with a detailed factual report on why he's panickingthe entire world. My roommate is merely our insurance policy when this thing goes down."

"So what's *our* next move?"

"I won't ask you to go over Michaels's head so I suppose that our next move is to sit back and hope I'm wrong."

"But you don't think you're wrong, right?"

"I think that the United States is in for a world of shit."

CHAPTER 30

"It's always darkest before the dawn."

When I was a brand new agent, I did something totally unethical. The FBI had tapped the phones of two Mafia soldiers of the Colombo family in New York. They allegedly had an insider at Yonkers Race Track who could fix races.

After six weeks of conversation involving affairs, diets, and complaints about their mob bosses, Two Ton Tony called Franky the Fish and put in the fix. *"Range Rider in the sixth to win,"* were the *exact* words spoken.

Financially surviving in New York City as a new agent was tough. There were no cost of living allowances back then so we basically ate a lot of popcorn and boiled eggs. Even though the fix was in, the race had to be run to make the case. I figured there'd be no harm in laying down a few bucks.

After my midnight shift, I went to every Off Track Betting parlor in Queens, Brooklyn, and the Bronx and laid down bets. I rationalized that my actions hurt no one individual since *someone* had to win and racetracks were sleazy operations anyway.

Another dirty little FBI secret is that many agents over the years have used wire taps to their advantage. One agent discovered a massage parlor that provided gratis full body massages if a certain Italian name was mentioned.

I reason that if I could not prevent a financial meltdown, I can certainly prepare for one. So, I withdraw money from the bank and squirrel it away in an attic sea bag. That evening while channel surfing I become engrossed in *The American Ninja Warrior.* As I am strategizing my next few moves a *Ninja* is interrupted by a *SPECIAL REPORT.*

It seems that the mainframe computer which operates the New York Stock Exchange has malfunctioned. Although the closing bell occurred some five hours ago, the reporter in front of the Exchange explains that unless technicians can get the system *'back on line,'* trading will be suspended. Experts are confident that the *'glitch'* will be corrected by opening bell tomorrow. They do not suspect foul play and it is not unusual or dire should the market take a day off line.

That's what the experts say but I *know* that this is the work of terrorists. I *know* that the stock exchange is the beginning of a full-scale financial meltdown. I *know* that it could have been prevented and I *know* that no one will believe me. I *know* that my country is in horrible trouble and I *know* that I have to do *something!* But all I can do is *wait!*

I actually sleep well and awake refreshed for a change. I kiss Lorri goodbye and head to Starbucks. Donnie Osmond smiles as I approach the counter and says, "Well if it isn't public enemy number one."

"Fuck off, Donnie," I tease back.

"Why do you always call me *Donnie?*"

"What *is* your name?"

"Fred," Donnie says. "It's gross so I added an 'o', which gives me a mysterious ethnic aura."

"Fredo?" I repeat. "I refuse to call you Fredo, Donnie."

"Whatever. You know, John," Donnie now serious. "that newspaper photo of you wasn't your best, and five kilos of cocaine, *really?*"

"Do I seem like a drug dealer to you?"

"Well, do *I* seem like a gay coffee slinger to you?"

"Yes," I laugh.

"Well my pot hook up raised his price. Can I score some from you?"

"Give me my regular Donnie, before I kick your butt."

"Promises, promises," Donnie says as he shoves a double latte Venti toward me. "It's on me," He says. "You save your pennies, John, now that your drug empire's been busted."

I head to a small table by the window. I settle down with my Venti and mini HP computer nodding to a few familiar faces. The lead story on my home page is the New York Stock Exchange meltdown. The best computer minds are working on the problem and pledge to have it fixed by noon.

I realize that it's too early to call my former roommate, Assistant Director Daniels, with an 'I told you so' since a computer glitch is an isolated incident and has happened before. So I have to wait until the other shoe drops. This is completely and utterly unnecessary, but such is life in today's government since no one will make a decision. Had this bunch of officials been in power in 1941, we'd all be eating sushi and bratwurst.

It is sometime during my third refill of the dark roast when they report that U.S. government computers at the Treasury, Commerce, Securities and Exchange Commission, Federal Trade Commission, and the Social Security Administrations have crashed.

I am about to call Tony when computers at the Federal Deposit Insurance Administration, Farm Credit Administration, The National Credit Union Administration and thirteen of the top banks go belly up.

Perhaps it *is* time to make that call.

Assistant Director Daniels answers his personal cell phone before the second ring.

"No bullshit, no smart ass asides and no smug *I told you so's.*"

"You just used my opening line."

"This is serious shit, John. I need to debrief you as soon as possible."

"Can't," I say. "I am suspended and without official travel orders."

"You are back on the books as of ten minutes ago. Now get to the airport at Hopkins, the Director's plane will meet you, and I'll be on it."

"Can't make it," I protest. "I have laundry to do, then Wheel of Fortune is running celebrity week. Danny Bonaduci and Chubby Checker are bidding on the ceramic dog."

"One hour," Tony says, then terminates our connection.

I head home to pack a suitcase and my notes. It could be sometime before I return to Cleveland. I call Lorri 's office and inform Allison that "The Steelers need a cornerback *and* a middle linebacker."

"John, how are you," Allison says, all serious. "The newspapers were vicious."

"Doing a lot better today," I say. "In fact, that's why I'm calling. Can you leave a message for Lorri?"

"Sure."

"Tell her that I was reinstated to active duty status, but I have to go to D.C. immediately. Tell her I'll call later, tell her that things are working out, and … tell her … that I love her. Gotta run Allison."

Allison says, "One last thing."

"Yes."

"I always thought you were innocent. We Steelers fans may commit a murder or two but we're definitely not drug dealers."

My next call is to Monica, but I connect directly to her voice mail. I leave a message. "Call me as soon as you can." I need a Suehad update.

My mind is racing so I attempt to slow it down with a laundry list of things. They include *things* to take on the trip, *things* to assure Suehad's safety, and *things* I need to do to save our country.

Hopkins International Airport is a mere eighteen minutes from my house and the IX Jet Center is situated at the far end of the main runway. I advise the desk girl that I am awaiting a private plane, and she smiles and points me to the waiting lounge. I recognize the Director's plane immediately as it stops, although no logos or government ID are displayed.

Tony is the first one to appear in the doorway, motioning me on board with a wave. The pilots never shut the engines down and one can almost smell panic in the air. He smiles and gives me a hug, "You are a real pain in the ass."

As I duck into the main cabin, I notice Elizabeth Lewis. She obviously had not taken my advice about the seaweed diet.

Tony says with a trace of sarcasm, "I'm *sure* you remember Ms. Lewis, John." His tone seems to indicate that I was the guilty party during our *last* meeting. Although I am immediately on guard, I smile at the Section Chief and give her a nod. I refuse to utter a single word fearing it will break my emotional dam.

She says, "John, how have you been?"

The dam explodes and I rant, "How have I been!" I repeat raising my voice. "You mean since you tried to fire me for doing my job? Is that a real question?"

Tony attempts damage control with some rational bullshit but I interrupt with, "She asked me how I've been, and the question deserves an answer." I look at Ms. Lewis and say in a quiet rage. "Pretty fuckin' bad. And in a *large* part, pun intended, because you wanted to play cops and robbers, but, you couldn't be a real cop so you have your buddy the President appoint you to the FBI, and then you act like you actually know what *real* FBI agents do. How have I been, Ms. Lewis? I've been fuckin' peachy."

"Cut the crap, John," Tony warns. "This is not the time or place to waste time with hurt feelings. We have much more important fish to fry."

I calm down but ask Tony, "What's she doing here?"

"Ms. Lewis is the FBI's JTTF Section Chief, and if your information is correct, she needs to be in the loop."

"I wouldn't be on this plane if my information *wasn't* correct."

"Good point," Tony concedes. "So let's get started."

I look at Tony and say, "First, some ground rules. I deal *only* with Tony and will not take any direction from Ms. Lewis."

Tony is about to object to my unorthodox demand but Ms. Lewis points a finger at me and says. "I am a senior level FBI official and as such your supervisor. You will *not* dictate how an FBI investigation is conducted. You *will* follow our policies, procedures and guidelines and not take the shortcuts you seem to be fond of. Am I clear on this?"

"Perfectly Ms. Lewis," I quietly concede. "I'd like to apologize for my hurtful remarks and would welcome your direction, given your many years of investigative experience. Don't take this personal Ms. Lewis, but fuck off."

Both Tony and Ms. Lewis are speechless so I use their silence to follow up on my demands, "And, if you don't like my conditions, Ms. Lewis, then turn this plane around. I just hope you can live with yourself when American citizens suffer due to your oversized ego. Pun intended, again."

Now the silence becomes creepy and I decide not to fill the void since my ultimatum was pretty good as delivered. Finally, Tony says, "Let's not worry about chain of command at this time, the clock is ticking so let's get going with what you know and develop an investigative plan."

She reluctantly nods her consent, but I am just getting started.

"I don't think so, roomie," I say. "The boys *and* girls in the puzzle palace didn't seem to be in any hurry when I was screaming, '*the terrorists are coming, the terrorists are coming.*' Now all of a sudden, I'm on the clock. I want some assurances before I cough up my source."

"Be reasonable, John," Tony pleads.

I shrug my shoulders and smile.

Tony relents and says, "Talk to me."

"I want to name my own task force members to work the case. They include Gwen McNulty, Fred Gregory, and Captain Ray Kopka and Detective Tommy Shoulders of the Cleveland Police Department."

Lewis protests, "The two police officers would require top secret clearances to access our files, and we don't have that kind of time."

"We've got all the time in the world," I say. "No cops, no Booker. No Booker, no source."

Tony stands and points a finger at Ms. Lewis. "Our nation is in peril and you're worried about *clearances*. Do you think two Cleveland police officers have ties to al-Qaeda, Ms. Lewis? Do you realize how petty and ridiculous you sound? I don't care how close you are to the President, lose the attitude!"

Talk about your awkward moment. My roomie finally grew his balls back and I am proud to have shared a grubby bathroom with him as new agents. I look at Lewis to gauge her response. She is not the type of individual to be insulted and ridiculed.

Ms. Lewis shifts uncomfortably in her seat and says. "I'll call the President and get the two police officers cleared."

It is the first indication of her humanity. Up until Lewis uttered those words, her voice had always sounded official and angry.

"Thank you, and welcome to the team."

Ms. Lewis now provides the second indication that she is indeed a human being and not an officious angry bureaucratic robot. She smiles and says, "You're welcome, John."

All we need now is a campfire, a guitar, and a chorus of Kumbaya. Since the two HBOs seem to be in the giving mood, I decide to push the envelope. "I also want Michaels far away from me and my team. You *do* know that he could have prevented this entire fiscal meltdown."

"How so?" Lewis asks.

I explain that Boy Wonder had in his slimy hands a memo predicting the computer virus with enough time to alert the financial community but chose to ignore the information.

Tony chimes in with, "It's true. I was blind copied but couldn't intervene or act officially without a field office request."

"That reminds me, Tony." I say. "How did you convince the boys in the puzzle palace I was on the level? After all, I'm a suspended drug dealing insubordinate rogue agent in their minds."

"I figured that they'd have their doubts so I shared the memo with my friends at the CIA. When the computers crashed the Bureau could no longer ignore you. When you called me, I was already en route to the airport to come and get your ass. The President wants action," Tony adds. "The Director came out of the meeting dragging his butt, so he called a meeting of directors, and as they say … the poop rolls downhill."

CHAPTER 31

*"Rome did not create a great empire by having
meetings, they did it by killing all those who
opposed them."*

We land at Dulles and I notice a missed call from Monica. I dial her cell phone and ask, "Is Suehad okay?"

Monica sounds desperate. "You need to get to the hospital immediately."

"I'm out of town. What's wrong?"

"Mansur's complaining non-stop about everything and planning to take Suehad back to Cairo. He says the doctors in Cairo can provide better care. He's having a private jet equipped with all the medical necessities to pick her up day after tomorrow."

"What is Suehad saying?"

"It's strange, John. It's like she reverted back to that Muslim submissive shit. I gave her my best woman's right talk, but she's talking crap like *maybe it's time to go home.*"

"I need you to do something for me."

"I'm all ears."

"Just find out the airport she'll be leaving from. Either Burke Lakefront or Cleveland Hopkins."

"Not a problem, John. You got a plan?"

"Well Monica," I muse. "I *always* have a plan, but they're rarely successful."

"That's not very inspiring," Monica says.

"To use a baseball analogy, it's time to swing for the fences. We either hit a home run or lose the game. You in?"

"To use a *poker* analogy," Monica says, "I'm *all* in."

A large black SUV pulls up to the plane and CIA Deputy John Burke followed by FBI Deputy Director Eddie *'the Exorcist'* Batcheller exit. Both have the guilty smiles of men caught cheating on their wives. I suspect their lack of John Booker support at the *'sex and sea weed'* meeting have smudged their conscience.

"Hi boys," I say nonchalantly. "So happy you invited me back. My last visit was so much fun."

I give Eddie the Exorcist some credit. He grabs me playfully around the shoulders and says, "Tony's right, you *are* a pain in the ass."

Ms. Lewis has been in the background on the phone watching the boys act like boys. She approaches our small group and announces, "The President has authorized the two Cleveland police officers access to all government files."

We enter the SUV and head to headquarters.

"Tony," I say. "Need you to call the Chief of Police in Cleveland and get Kopka and Shoulders temporarily reassigned to the task force."

As my roommate is making the call I tap in Kopka's cell phone number.

He opens with, "Well, if it isn't public enemy number one."

I laugh and say, "Appreciate your sensitivity. You're gonna get a call in about ten minutes from your Chief temporarily assigning you and Tommy to the task force."

"Thanks, but no thanks." Kopka says seriously. "I don't play well with the Feds generally and if I have to work with your asshole supervisor, I'd end up shooting his ass...." Pause. "With a fuckin' arrow."

"Not an issue," I assure him. "You're working with me. Won't even see Boy Wonder." I pause and finish with "I need your help, Ray."

"You back carrying a badge or we going off the books?"

"I'm *officially* in charge of my own little task force so it's all legit," I pause and add, "well, *mostly* legit."

Kopka laughs and says, "Count us in."

"Your first official act is to keep a plane from taking off the day after tomorrow."

"Not a problem."

"It's not an American plane. A private jet coming in from Egypt."

"Not a problem," Kopka repeats.

"Glad you're so sure. Preventing an international flight sounds like it may be a *little* problem."

Kopka laughs and says, "We *are* the Cleveland Police Department."

I promise to get back to Kopka the moment I have the flight information. I feel better already having these two cops on my team. They are men of action and understand that you occasionally have to take a few regulatory shortcuts. Local cops are mission-oriented and will accomplish their objective even if it involves some improvisation. I smile and mentally cross *'preventing Suehad from leaving'* off my 'to do" list. Kopka and Shoulders got it covered.

We reach the situation room at headquarters, which is a beehive of activity. Agents are tracking the financial meltdown with digital images of the effected agencies and institutions. A supervisor approaches Deputy Director Batcheller and provides an update. He mentions things like *'worms, codes, and open windows'* so I ask for the middle school version with drawings if possible.

The supervisor explains that "A worm is a type of computer virus that can reproduce by sending copies of itself to any computer that is connected to the infected machine. Our security experts have designated this worm as *'Amoeba One.'* They describe it as the most sophisticated 'worm' ever created and the first 'worm' specifically targeting real-world infrastructures."

"How does this worm hurt the United States average Joe? Don't we have backups, or can't we just reboot our computers?"

The CIA Deputy Director answers me with, "We have become a nation that is totally dependent on the computer to function. Our government and most employers require electronic transmittals for paychecks, entitlements, bills, and virtually every other type of business transaction. Just using one example, this worm wiped out our entire Social Security Administration database so the elderly and disabled won't be receiving their checks."

"So," I say, "if my Uncle Frank is expecting his pension and social security check to pay his mortgage and buy food and it don't show up in his bank account, then he goes hungry and possibly homeless."

"No immediate danger of homelessness. The government can forestall foreclosures or evictions for a period of time, but buying groceries without money or credit cards is an *immediate* problem."

"No credit cards," I repeat. "Yea, I guess they process directly through the internet for approval so no oatmeal or milk for Uncle Frank."

The situation room supervisor picks up the narrative and says, "After it hijacks a PC, *Amoeba One* looks for Siemens software that runs commercial and governmental oversight systems such as banks. One thing we are sure about is that *Amoeba One* is so sophisticated that only a country with a high level of computer programming know-how would have been able to create it."

"That fits my North Korea and Muslim terrorist connection," I conclude.

Tony clarifies to the group. "John has pieced together an alliance between radical Muslims and the government of North Korea. He reasons that the Koreans have the expertise and resources to supply the Muslims with scientists who can develop these computer viruses. And they leave no footprints back to them."

The situation supervisor says, "Why can't the North Koreans just do it themselves?"

"That's the beauty of this conspiracy," I explain. "As much as the North Koreans like to militarily huff and puff, they could never go heads up with us. So, by using the Muslim terrorists as their shield, they avoid things like economic boycotts or having their homeland reduced to parking lots."

Ms. Lewis asks, "Why is this worm *different* from all the other hackers that infest our computers?"

"Most viruses that are created are normally blasted out like a blunderbuss. But *Amoeba One* is written to only target certain systems. It finds flaws in code and uses it like an open window in a house, like a crow bar to make a bigger gap. *Amoeba One* appears to have been designed purely for sabotage."

"What can we do to kill the worm?" I ask. "And how does my Uncle Frank eat in the meantime?"

Deputy Director Batcheller dismisses the situation supervisor with, "Thanks Jack, I know you need to get back to the problem."

Eddie answers my question with, "We will *eventually* kill the worm. Experts estimate a time frame of around ten days. I won't get into the nuts and bolts of how they do it, but imagine a jigsaw puzzle with a billion pieces."

"Got the visual," I say.

"And as far as the effect of the virus on our economy, that is catastrophic. Your Uncle Frank's life savings have been erased, bank accounts, mortgage payments, savings accounts, all gone."

"So every citizen in the US has a zero net worth?" I ask.

"It's much more involved than that. Our dollar is practically worthless in the world market. The entire economy is teetering since we can't import oil, medical supplies, and even coffee."

"Then we better get going," I say. "I need my coffee."

CHAPTER 32

"Three people can keep a secret ... if two of them are dead."
— Italian Mafia Capo

I follow the group to the Director's suite and directly into his lordship's personal conference room. FBI Director Gary T. McKissock was the U.S. attorney of the Northern district of New York who prosecuted the largest Wall Street scam in U.S. history. He sent fifty-nine of the financial community's movers and shakers to the big house. When they attempted to use their influence and blank checks to slither from justice, McKissock indicted two of his own assistants *and* a federal judge on accepting bribes.

He received a ton of positive ink and a supportive jury. The general public was collecting coupons to buy groceries while these Wall Street guys were collecting bigger yachts. The sympathy factor for a bunch of fit and tanned white males in tailored suits in a bad economy was virtually nonexistent.

He points to the seat next to him and the group fills in the remaining high back leather chairs that surround an oblong glass table.

"First of all, John," McKissock begins. "I'd like to apologize for the previous misunderstanding and have dismissed the OPR investigation against you."

"No disrespect, sir," I say. "But that was no *misunderstanding*. Your staff understood perfectly what I was saying, but it seems that Headquarters has their priorities reversed. Instead of *supporting* the field agents, they go out of their way to *obstruct*."

McKissock shakes his head and says, "It happens, John, but our immediate problem is not a reorganization of Headquarters. We need to figure out how to stop the fiscal bleeding and you seem to have the tourniquet."

"What we've got is a conspiracy between two of America's sworn mortal enemies."

I explain why North Korea would not want any link to an attack on America, so they use a small terrorist cell as their front. Both groups play distinct but vital roles in the operation. Their vile acts are designed to appear as natural happenings, accidents, or common criminal activity such as the mugging and killing of Chief Justice Williams.

"And," I continue, "in that particular incident, the North Koreans had two levels of insulation. They fund the terrorists who then pay some street thugs to whack Williams. And just so there are no loose ends, the terrorists then kill the killers. They also ran a variation of the Williams murder at the Boston Marathon."

CIA Director Burke immediately says, "I can't wait to hear this one."

"Glad to accommodate you, sir. I reviewed intercepts and chatter occurring a few days prior to the Boston Marathon originating in North Korea and they were identical to the types of intercepts on the blackout, bird flu, the Williams murder, and 9/11."

"North Korea was giving the Egyptians the green light for the operation in that communication. Those two idiot brothers and their pressure cookers were actually pawns being manipulated by the Egyptian cell through intermediaries in Chechnya. They were whipped up into an America hating frenzy and believed they were doing Allah's will."

"That *is* a fascinating theory," Burke says incredulously.

"Then allow me to fascinate you to new levels. The day after the Boston Marathon bombing, a fertilizer plant in Texas blew up. Investigators concluded that it was an industrial accident. It was *no* coincidence that these two disasters happened on successive days. It followed the blue print of this secret terrorist cell. They want Americans to be looking over their shoulders, to avoid large gatherings, to sit in their homes with the blinds closed."

Burke shakes his head. "I thought I'd seen it all."

"Not yet," I say, then run down the entire Beck saga involving his CIA field operative and their asset and then a long description of the intercepts and how I connected the dots. For good measure I add my Charter School suspicions, and discuss how numerous Muslim candidates who ran for national and local elective offices were funded by sham organizations that ultimately lead back to North Korea.

I pause to determine if my audience is following the bouncing ball. I continue, "Their goal is to cause maximum and constant chaos and fear in America, ultimately rendering us useless."

The Director nods and offers, "I see. So if they can effect sustained panic with blackouts, computer viruses, bird flu, or high gas prices, then our nation slowly decays by accepting these catastrophes as fate and, we can't fight fate."

"They create their own perfect storm," Tony contributes. "By killing Judge Williams, for example, they tilted the Supreme Court to the left and guaranteed unfavorable decisions for law enforcements war on terrorism. They're in no rush and that's what's frightening. It's like a cancer that slowly spreads until it *can't* be cut out."

McKissock solemnly asks. "So John, since you have the best handle on this thing, I am appointing you the lead agent. What's your next move and how can Headquarters *not* obstruct you?"

I notice the Director smiling at his *obstruction* reference. I can't help but smile back and say, "I see this operation as a two-prong effort, and we're eventually going to need the President in an active role."

"How so?"

"The first phase is proving that North Korea is part of this conspiracy. Once accomplished, the President has a sit-down with the fat juvenile delinquent kid running that country."

The Director says, "That will have to be some strong evidence."

"When I was undercover with the Italians, if we knew that some family mopes had crossed a line, like killing an innocent kid, we'd go to their capo and told him to take care of the problem, or we would. The next day two stiffs would be doing the back stroke in the Hudson."

"I see where you're going but for the President to risk war with North Korea, he'll need 'smoking gun' type of proof."

"I'll get enough proof for the President to back down North Korea. We already have some strong circumstantial evidence," I explain. "The intercepts originate in North Korea with replies from Egypt. The Muslim candidates and their campaigns were funded by secret funds originating in North Korea."

So my first request as case agent is to assign me our best forensic accountants who can trace the campaign money. It may be circumstantial that North Korea is funding Muslim candidates in the U.S. but it certainly raises the question of 'why?'

Ms. Lewis joins the fray with, "Can your source help?"

"I believe so. If nothing else, my source corroborates the existence of a super cell in Egypt and can provide other leads."

"With the permission of the Director, I will support any recommendations made by Agent Booker's task force with the President."

McKissock nods and answers, "Normally, I would discourage my subordinates going over my head, but given your personal friendship with the President, I may need you to whisper in his ear."

I continue with, "The second phase of the investigation is identifying the Egyptian terrorist cell."

"How?" McKissock wonders. "From what you told me, we have no leads on that front."

"Nothing solid, sir. But my source has provided a name that may be the link to the Egyptian terrorists."

It is Tony who asks the sixty-four thousand dollar question, "So *who* is your source?"

I understand that the time has come to cough up Suehad, but I want some assurances. I tell the group that in exchange for Suehad's cooperation, she receives immediate citizenship and a million dollar personal service contract. Since I had the bureaucrats nodding their heads in assent for the past hour, their continued head bobs make Suehad a rich new American citizen.

The Director has heard enough to brief the President. He rises and thrusts his hand toward me. McKissock gives me his assurance that "If for any reason you need to see me, you just walk right in that door. And, anything that you may need, and I mean *anything,* just ask," he says, pointing at his adjoining office door. This last remark was his parting shot and a veiled warning to the others in the room not to fuck with me.

CIA Deputy Director Burke explains that he must return to Langley. He stands next to me and says, "I'm personally sorry that I doubted you. I lost two fine operation officers and all you wanted to do was find their killers. The CIA is at your disposal, Agent Booker."

"Appreciate that," I say. "Can I ask a question?"

"Absolutely."

"How's your covert operations in Egypt these days? Specifically, do you have some assets or undercover officers active?"

Burke says, "When President Mubarak was running the show, we had tacit cooperation to run covert ops against terrorist training camps and use of Egyptian airfields. The new regime is an anti-American and can't be trusted. Why do you ask?"

"I'll need a contact there. Some local who is totally trustworthy and not working both sides of the street."

Burke gives me a sly smile and says, "I just happen to have one of the best assets in the business operating out of Cairo. I'll put him on notice, John. Call me when it's time."

JOHN LIGATO

A moment later, FBI Deputy Director Batcheller stands and gives me a thumbs up. I nod at the Bureau's number two man as he leaves the room and say, "Got it covered, Boss."

Those were my exact words but my confidence didn't match them. It suddenly struck me that I, Johnny Booker of Slippery Rock State College and South Philadelphia, was at the epicenter of an international terrorist plot.

Ms. Lewis is next to leave and her parting words are the most surprising. She offers her hand and says, "Hi, my name is Elizabeth Lewis, nice to meet you."

I understand her sentiment and shake her hand replying with, "Special Agent John Booker, very nice to meet you."

"Agent Booker, it seems that you and I have been at odds from the start. I am not a law enforcement officer as you so eloquently state, nor have I conducted surveillances or made arrests but I can assure you that as of this moment, you have whatever support you need or request and I too wish to apologize for my obstructionist behavior."

I stand and give her a hug saying, "No problem, just smooze the President when it comes time to go to toe-to-toe with Kid Korea."

She walks confidently from the room and I do believe that our paths will cross in the very near future. By mutual agreement of all parties, Tony Daniels is assigned as my HQ contact. I provide Tony a preliminary list of resources. At the top is getting Agent 36 and Fred Gregory physically on board. Gregory is assigned to the D.C. field division, and could be here within the hour but Gwen's plane arrives late, so I send a message to Fred asking him to pick up the lovely Ms. McNulty at the airport.

This will be an opportune time for the two to bond. It's important that we avoid egos and build a team. I have witnessed outstanding agents throw hissy fits over who got the bigger desk near a window. They couldn't get over simple jealousy and put the case first. I chose Thumper because he is smart, tenacious and gets things done and I chose Gwen since she is smart, clever, and has great boobs. They both seem comfortable in their own skin and will challenge authority when necessary.

My second request is an access code for the intel briefings. I was about to say an *official* code but catch myself. I still have no idea who my fairy godmother *or* godfather may be, but without access to that last batch of intercepts, I'd still be crying wolf. Accompanying my access code, I'll need the top ten intel analysts from both the CIA and FBI assigned to my impromptu task force *immediately*. They need to analyze those intel bulletins and prevent the next disaster.

My impressive entourage has gone their separate ways except for my roomie. It's just the two of us and we can be the two wide-eyed new agents bullshitting in our dorm room. Afraid that we couldn't compete with the Ivy League boys and would be booted out at any moment. Tony and I had frequent late night talks about our dreams, and how we'd make the big arrests and partner up like *Starsky and Hutch*. We'd cram for our exams knowing that any two grades lower than an 85 meant instant dismissal. We ran the trails in the deep forest around Quantico and practiced our sight alignment and loading rounds with our red handle revolvers for hours.

Out of the blue, Tony asks. "Who set you up? I know you're a degenerate, but you are definitely *not* a drug dealer."

"Thank you for that vote of confidence. The fuckin' North Koreans did me. They probably used the Muslims to do the dirty work like planting the drugs. But they actually cut me a break since three other people who were sniffing too close got whacked and Suehad is just off life support."

"You talking about the two CIA agents and their snitch?"

"Yep. It was actually a smart move to set me up, because too many dead feds would cause more heat."

"But the three died of natural causes or legitimate accidents."

"So it seems, but none of it passes the smell test," I tease. "You remember the smell test, Tony. Eighteen years ago in the Board Room after three pitchers of beer, two bowls of chili, and a loaded baked potato propelled you to your gaseous victory."

We both laugh and a stupid analogy comes to mind. I say seriously, "Sometimes a fart is loud but doesn't smell, and sometimes you get the silent but deadly variety."

"I know you're trying to tell me something."

"This whole thing pisses me off 'cause I know *who* they are, and *what* they're doing, but, I really don't know *who* they are and *what* they're doing!"

Tony laughs and says, "The weird thing is that I understand what you're saying. This conspiracy has reached the stage of *silent but deadly!*"

CHAPTER 33

*"A good plan violently executed right now is far better than
a perfect plan executed next week."*

– General George Patton

Monica's call comes later.

"Suehad is leaving from Burke Lakefront airport on Thursday at nine. I asked Mansur how long the flight will take and he said about nine hours. Does that help?"

"Immensely," I say. "Burke is not a commercial airport so they have few international private jets filing flight plans to Egypt. I can also find out what class of jet can make the flight in nine hours. You done good, girl."

"So can you get my record, which incidentally that *you* gave me, expunged?"

I laugh and say. "I'll work on it Monica, hopefully not from *my* jail cell."

"I thought everything was forgiven?"

"I wish. The Bureau has forgiven me for some internal bullshit but the drug charges are still pending."

"Bummer."

I change the subject by asking, "How's Suehad?"

"When we're alone, she keeps asking where you are. I tell her that you're out of town on a case."

I'm about to tell Monica that I'll see Suehad soon, but catch myself. I trust my new felon friend but there is no need to spill the beans.

We talk for a few minutes before I tell Monica that I have a pressing matter and promise to keep in touch. I dial Kopka's number. He answers with, *"Wall Mart,* how can I direct your call?"

"The fuckin' arrow department," I tease.

"You got something pressing, Booker? I'm watching *Dancing With The Stars* and that one blond piece of ass from Czechoslovakia is about to dance the Tango."

"I'll be brief." I chuckle. "Burke Lake Front, 9 AM on Thursday. And just so you know, some arrogant Muslim, name of Mansur, will give you a ration of shit."

"Everybody gives me a ration of shit." Kopka says. "How long do you want the plane grounded and do you wish accommodations for this Mansur at the Grey Bar Hotel?"

"I hadn't thought about that possibility but if you can reserve a room for a few days, that eliminates Mansur from squirreling her away to Cairo by some other means."

"Not a problem."

"Ray," I say seriously. "I know I'm asking a lot and I don't want you to fuck up your pension or worst, so be careful."

"Booker," Captain Kopka says, "this is not a big deal, *we are the Cleveland Police Department,* and now I gotta go ... the Tango is about to begin."

I tell Tony that "The wheels are beginning to turn."

"How so?"

I brief my roomie on the Suehad-Mansur front, but purposely avoid discussing my plan. In the bureaucratic world this is deemed, *plausible deniability.*

I look at Tony and ask him, "I need a big one."

He shrugs his shoulders and says, "The Director has ordered us to give you every *legal* and *lawful* request.'

"Well that could be a stumbling block."

"It usually is with you. Shoot."

"I need to get some Egyptian citizen declared an enemy combatant."

"Oh," Tony laughs, "is that all. And I thought you'd give me a tough one." He is no longer laughing as he says, "I just *know* you have a ton of probable cause indicating that this guy is a direct threat to our national security."

"Not yet," I say. "But you can just make some shit up."

"You have lost your mind. Can I ask *why?*"

"Because I wanna put the guy on ice minus attorneys, bond hearings and all that other legal shit that keeps bad guys on the streets doing bad things."

The silence is awkward but I already know my roomie's answer.

"You do know that I have to go to the Attorney General and lie on an affidavit."

I shrug and tell Tony, "Just pretend you're a brick agent again. You remember what it's like to work the streets, roomie?"

"I'll do it, but I get the bottom bunk at the federal pen."

"Well no shit, you can't reach the *top* bunk with those stubby legs."

Tony laughs and asks, "Anything else that his highness needs?"

"I'll need the FBI plane," I say as if I was requesting a paper clip. "Tomorrow."

Tony says, "Twenty four hours ago you were banished from the kingdom and now you want the king's chariot."

"You have no idea how much I'm enjoying this turn of events."

"Enjoy it while you can," Tony says no longer laughing. "'Cause as you know in the Bureau, '*no good deed goes unpunished.*'"

"That reminds me, roomie. I need the head of the Behavioral Science Unit and all his profilers in an hour."

"Suppose he's not around?"

"He's gotta be somewhere and you outrank him."

"Can I ask why?"

"Mansur is our wild card," I explain. "I have a plan using Thumper but first I have to know which buttons to push."

"Do you have any solid evidence that links this Mansur with either the radical Muslims or the North Koreans?"

"No, but my gut says he can give us a lead."

Tony stands and strolls toward his temporary desk.

I call after him. "I also need our top expert on Muslim culture, customs, religion, and line dancing."

My roomie shrugs a look that says, *asshole*, and picks up the phone.

Two hours later the entire behavioral science unit of six agents march into our task force area. The Unit Chief, Dr. Paul Astler, says to no one in particular, "I hope this is a national emergency, since we were working the Colorado serial killings."

I approach Dr. Astler, extend my hand and say, "What we've got is a national conspiracy that could destroy our democracy and we could *sure* use your help."

The good doctor nods and for the next thirty minutes I provide the Readers Digest condensed version of the case, emphasizing as much detail on Mansur as I can.

"By the way," I add, "Mansur is also a sexual deviate."

All eight heads swivel in unison toward me. I explain Suehad's tale of orgies and Mansur's love of sexual interests.

My case brief is interrupted by a young man who enters the room and stands silently observing our group observing him.

Fred takes an aggressive step toward him and asks, "Can I help you?"

"I am Special Agent Mohammed Askari. I was told to report here immediately."

Agent Askari looks like a tenth grader who is the president of the debate club and plays tuba with the marching band.

"Are you our radical Muslim expert?" I ask

"Yes sir."

"How old are you?"

"Twenty seven sir, and please call me Mo."

Gwen approaches him smiles and says, "Tell us a little about yourself Mo."

Mo smiles at the group and says. "After the attacks on 9/11, the Bureau realized that we had zero agents who could speak thelanguage, so they made a concerted effort to recruit agents from the Middle East." Mo adds that he was born north of Cairo in Luxor."

"I am an idiot when it comes to languages, Mo," I confess. "Does each Middle East country speak their own unique language?"

"In my home of Luxor, some 234,000 people speak the Domari language which is an Indo-Aryan language related to Romany. And approximately 77,000 speakers of Beja live in the Eastern Desert and along the coast of the Red Sea. In ancient times, the population of western Egypt was probably made of Berber-speaking tribes. But most Muslims speak Arabic, sir.""

I say, "Welcome to the task force, Mo. I want you to work with the profilers and answer their questions."

"Yes sir."

We wind down around nine and I order coffee and sandwiches for the group. It is critical that Fred, Gwen, and I understand their findings and recommendations.

I nod at Dr. Astler and say, "Paul, the floor is all yours."

The good Doctor begins the profile brief with, "Mansur is a man in conflict. His strict Islamic upbringing is in direct conflict with his western decadent practices, which include abnormal sexual behavior. So this presents a conflict that can be exploited."

Mo jumps in with his cultural analysis of, "But Mansur outwardly must profess an unwavering faith in an Islamic deity whose ultimate goal is to create a worldwide caliphate."

Astler nods at Mo and says, "Mansur is probably ambivalent to any deep convictions or symbols of the Islamic faith. He basically fakes a devout belief in the Koran, given the expectations of his imam father. So if you can exploit these emotional conflicts then Mansur can be manipulated."

"Interesting," I comment. "But give me some practical examples. What buttons can we push?"

Profiler Bill Hagmeir jumps in with, "Power and strength. Mansur is basically a coward."

Astler clarifies, "When *directly* confronted with superior strength or power, he will defer."

"So if I understand you," I ask, "if Mansur can remain in the shadows he's capable of anything, but face to face, he's a wuss."

"In a manner of speaking," Astler expands. "He's a classic bully. Mansur will dominate anyone who submits to his will. He can be very controlling until someone *refuses* to be controlled. He prefers his revenge to be minus risk. The more militant and radical the jihadist, the more paradoxical their behavior. For example, thirteen of the nineteen terrorists who flew planes into the World Trade Center and the Pentagon had frequented cheap strip clubs and regularly viewed pornography."

Gwen interrupts. "Can I ask some specific questions?"

"Of course."

"What can we do to get Mansur to talk if he *doesn't* want to talk?"

"Are you positive that he has information on secret terrorist cell?"

"Nothing positive. But if he *does* have intelligence but doesn't wish to share, what do you suggest we do?"

"That's an operational decision," Astler says. "I can tell you what makes him tick but it's your decision on how to use the information."

"I totally agree," I jump in, sensing that Agent 36 is about to suggest a few torture options, and though I may agree with that tactic, the behavioral science unit should be spared the details. "We'll take it from here. I want to thank you and your team, Dr. Astler, and also you, Mo."

Agent Mohammed Askari smiles broadly and says, "I am at your service, Agent Booker."

"I have you on speed dial, Mo. Your boss has orders assigning you to this task force. You are to remain on standby and report to the intel analysts tomorrow. But I will be calling you at a moment's notice, so have your bag packed."

"So I may get to do some field work?"

"What the hell have you been doing?"

"I basically work T-3 wires on Mid-East targets. Sit in a windowless room all day and translate conversations."

I shake my head and say, "No wonder you're the palest Egyptian I've ever seen. Yea, you'll get to play with us in the field."

After the profilers and Mo depart Tony reappears and asks, "How'd it go?"

"Went well. We now have a starting point."

I check my watch and realize that we've been at it non-stop for ten hours. Any further attempt at coherent work would be futile. I announce that the Bureau is picking up the tab on dinner and cocktails.

When Tony recommends a nearby restaurant I take him aside and say, "Roomie, you ain't invited."

"Why?" Tony whines.

"There are actually two excellent reasons." I explain. "One is your esteemed rank will make us working humps reluctant to freely speak our mind. And there is also the issue of *plausible deniability*. We are going to discuss case strategy and some of our strategy may *not* be Bureau kosher. You need to be able to say you had no idea of what we were up to."

Tony smiles and says, "I understand but am disappointed. I was going to do a reenactment of my Board Room gaseous victory as a team building exercise."

We find a downtown bar that caters to the locals. I take comfort that we are armed but, then I realize that probably everyone in this entire place is armed. Thumper and I discuss our Marine Corps days and build on a bond already forged by scary drill instructors, the confidence course, and earning the title of *Marine*. Sometime during our third round of some drink dubbed *the Coma*, Fred nods toward Agent 36 and whispers to me, "Are those boobs for real?"

I smile and view his lewd inquiry as a sign that our small team is connecting. I give Fred a shit-eating grin and say, "Dunno, ask her."

"Will she get mad?"

"Naw, Gwen is one of the guys, even with *those* knockers."

Gwen holds up three fingers toward the bartender and screams, "Another round of them *Coma drinks*."

We make small talk until the bartender delivers three fresh Comas. Fred calls for a toast raising his glass and announcing, "To the United States Marine Corps, Semper Fi."

"To the Corps. Semper Fi," I repeat touching my drink glass with Fred and Gwen. We chug the unknown concoction and both Fred and I shake our head from the drink's potent kick. No one speaks for a full moment, as Fred works up the courage to ask a virtual stranger such a personal question.

"Hey Gwen," He gets her attention and then points at her chest and asks, "Those things for real?"

"What *things* you talking about?" Gwen says, playing along.

Fred has no idea that Gwen is fucking with him and feels the need to clarify his question. "You know … your chest."

"Why would you ask such a silly question? Of course my chest is real. It holds my heart and lungs. How could a chest be fake?"

Fred looks at me so I say, "She's pulling your chain."

Gwen laughs, touches her ample boobs and tells Fred. "One hundred percent grade A authentic. This one," She says tapping her right breast, "I call Harry. And the other one is named Sally."

Thumper just shakes his massive bald head and holds up three fingers to the bartender and heads toward the bar to await the drinks. I excuse myself and make a head call that leaves Agent 36 unaccompanied. By the time I get back a local DC power drinker has claimed my seat next to Gwen. I smile at the guy in the John Deere baseball cap and neck tattoos. He does *not* smile back so I sit in Fred's seat and anticipate the entertainment.

Gwen is a chronic flirt but that's about the extent of it. She's comfortable in bantering with the male gender because men are constantly hitting on her and rather than be a bitch about it, she deflects the advances with humor. But if the suitor gets too rambunctious then Gwen is capable of going caustic.

The guy totally ignores me and tells Gwen, "You know, I'd really like to get in your pants."

Agent 36 smiles seductively at the guy and takes a sip of her Coma. She tells him, "I'd really like that too."

The yahoo is actually speechless since this particular line had never worked before and Gwen would be his all-time brass ring. As the lecherous dirt bag begins salivating, Agent 36 actually leans into the guy and whispers, "Because if you got into my pants, then, I'd have *two* assholes."

It was never a fair verbal joust and just as the guy is about to become hostile Thumper arrives with the drinks and informs the guy that "You're in my seat."

There is a split second of indecision as the drunk sizes up this massive black guy who is now glaring down at him. Fred flexes a few muscles for effect and says, "Beat it, before I have to *beat* you."

We all laugh and Gwen scolds Thumper with, "Why did you scare away my Prince Charming? I was just about to go back to his trailer."

I figure that this may be the right time to give them my disclaimer and test the water, before these *Coma* drinks render us drooling idiots.

I hold up our fresh refills in a toast. Our glasses meet center table and I say, "To our task force, it may be small, but it *will* be triumphant."

The *Coma* is beginning to taste good, which is probably a sure indication that I've had enough. I lean toward Agent 36 and Fred and motion them to shove their chairs closer. I didn't want the background conversations and television noise to be a distraction.

"Ok," I begin. "And now for the serious portion of the program. You both know our mission and we have some leads, but I may do some things that are not in our rule book. These assholes we're chasing don't have any rules and the stakes are high. I believe the survival of the nation that we know hangs in the balance. You in?"

Thumper sips on his Coma, shrugs and announces. "We gotta do what we *gotta* do."

Agent 36 has this shit-eating alcohol-induced grin on her perfect teeth. She says, "Cut the *Sands of Iwo Jima* speech, Booker, if they can play dirty then we can be *Dirty Boys* too."

CHAPTER 34

"Gentlemen, this is the war room — you can't fight in here."
— Dr. Strangelove

Burke Lakefront Airport is situated on Lake Erie, located a block from both Cleveland Stadium and the *Rock and Roll Hall of Fame*. The runway is framed on three sides by water, giving pilots the illusion of landing on an aircraft carrier. It is city-owned and thus under the jurisdiction of the Cleveland Police Department.

Captain Ray Kopka and Detective Sergeant Tommy Shoulders watch as a Dornier Executive 328JET smoothly touches down. The two had just left the operations center where they confirmed that the flight had originated in Cairo, Egypt. The ambulance carrying Suehad had already come and gone after Kopka pleasantly but firmly informed the driver that their passenger would *not* be boarding a plane on this day.

They observe as Mansur El-Quadir arrives and boards the jet. He deplanes almost immediately and paces on the tarmac. The private ambulance company is getting an earful, as the two Cleveland cops watch from their unmarked car.

"Let's do it Tommy," Captain Kopka announces.

Mansur notices the car heading toward the airplane. It stops a foot in front of the plane's main landing gear. A large man exits the driver's side, followed by a smaller man from the passenger seat. The stocky man points his finger at Mansur and motions him to the car.

Captain Kopka may not have received a psychological brief by FBI profilers on Mansur but the street cop can spot an asshole a mile away. Muslims consider finger pointing a major insult and Mansur's face turns a bright red. He will teach this barbarian a lesson. Captain Kopka is very aware that his finger represents a 'no no' to the Mid-East culture. The cop also intuitively understands that he must establish his control by having Mansur come to the mountain, just like Mohammed.

Mansur storms up to the two men and stands inches away from the big one. The Middle Eastern culture is not big on personal space. Many Americans find their first encounter with someone from India or Syria uncomfortable. Most westerners say or do nothing except to take a step backward. But this is Cleveland, Ohio and Captain Kopka places his big meaty paw on Mansur's chest and shoves the Egyptian like an annoying bug.

Mansur's initial reaction is rage. But when the Egyptian meets the big man's eyes he shrewdly chooses to defer any aggressive word or deed. His anger is slowly dissolving into fear.

"This your plane?" Kopka asks.

Mansur answers with as much bravado he can muster. "I am a citizen of Egypt and have no intention of speaking with you."

Kopka shakes his massive head. He looks Mansur up and down before saying, "Let's try this again. Is this your plane?"

Mansur nods.

"Then I need to see your papers. Passports, manifest, pilot's licenses, log books, registration, and any other document I can think up."

"I am returning to Cairo within the hour," Mansur says with less conviction.

Kopka quietly glares at Mansur who misinterprets his silence as a tacit concession. Although Kopka has not identified himself as law enforcement, Mansur can smell his authority. When the silence becomes uncomfortable the Egyptian almost pleads, "So we are good?"

Kopka takes a step toward Mansur and jabs his index finger into Mansur's chest. "Listen up asshole, you've got five minutes to fork over the paperwork. Because in *six* minutes, I'm hauling your Egyptian ass off to jail where the black Muslims will fill it up with dick."

CHAPTER 35

"Luck sometimes visits a fool, but it never sits down with him."
— German Proverb

We meet at Dulles at nine the next morning, having slept off most of our Comas. There is a nervous anticipation in the air, similar to beginning an exotic journey. Tony Daniels must have directed someone to stock the Director's jet with goodies. It was pure Pittsburgh fare. There were kolbasi sandwiches, pop, candy bars, bagels, and even a six pack of Iron City beer.

It is game time and our trio of crime fighters are sipping coffee and munching on bagels. I provided many of the details of my plan last evening over our *Comas* so I spend a few moments rehashing the more critical points.

The plan includes the information provided by the profilers in addition to a hastily developed Booker subplot that most Muslims view blacks as inferior beings, hence Fred's role. Mansur is a sexual deviate, hence Gwen's role, and although Mansur has a tough exterior, he is your basic coward, hence my role.

Kopka and Shoulders meet us at the plane and introductions are made. I emphasize that Kopka and Shoulders are full-fledged members of our task force. I stress this point for a good reason. Some federal agents view local cops attached to federal task forces as gofers.

They often are assigned the more mundane or tedious tasks, rather than playing to their strengths. Local cops understand human nature better than we Feds no matter how many deviant behavior classes we attend.

I stand back and observe the interactions. Fred is immediately accepted by the two detectives because he spent ten years as a Georgia State Trooper, and likewise Gwen simply because she is smoking hot and cusses a lot. It's a cop thing.

I look around for a jet with Arabic markings. Shoulders solves the problem with, "It ain't here."

"Was it here, and if so, where is it now?"

"Yes and don't know."

"Quit breaking my balls guys."

Kopka relents and explains, "Tommy and I met the plane earlier this morning and asked to see passports, visas, a manifest and I think Tommy even requested to see their library cards."

"And?"

"And, Mansur began screaming that he was an Egyptian citizen and didn't have to comply since I had no authority as a local police officer and couldn't board an Egyptian plane, blah, blah, blah. So I explain that either he forks over some papers or the plane don't leave. He shoves a passport at me and I pretend to act surprised."

"You're killing me Ray …"

"Okay, I tell him that his name is on a watch list and we have to square it away before he can leave."

"How does Mansur handle that curve ball?"

Tommy Shoulders laughs and says, "He has a mild seizure and shrieks that he is *not* on any watch lists, and *demands* we check it again. We slide a finger down our imaginary list and the Captain finally says that '*all your towel head names sound the same.*'"

Kopka continues the narrative with, "He seemed offended by my insensitive remark and tried to grab his passport back. His hand touched my hand so I immediately arrested him for assault on a police officer."

I shake my head and ask, "So Mansur is in jail, but where's the plane and what happened to Suehad?"

"Suehad's back at the Cleveland Clinic and the plane is gone."

"Gone where?"

"I told the two pilots to get out of Cleveland air space or *they'd* be on the watch list. Last I saw, the plane was headed due east. Probably approaching Greenland by now."

"So we got a few days to play with Mansur?"

Kopka nods and says. "He's been trying to call his embassy but for some strange reason, he has phone restrictions."

The five of us pile into Kopka's car and head over to the Justice Center on St. Clair Ave. During the short trip, I ask Kopka why he didn't identify himself as a member of a federal task force when Mansur played the local jurisdiction card.

The good captain laughs and says, "No need, we *are* the Cleveland Police Department."

The Justice Center houses the hierarchy of the Cleveland Police Department and the Sherriff's office as well as Municipal and County court rooms, and five floors of jail cells. Kopka placed Mansur in a cell with three skin heads. Given the white supremists views on mouthy Muslims post 9/11, it's a good bet that Mansur is not praising Allah and reading passages from the Koran.

We meet in Kopka's office and I tell Thumper and Gwen about my time working with the Cleveland Police. During the retelling Kopka interrupts me and deadpans, "Yea, ol' Booker here almost bought the farm in a deadly shoot out at *Wal-Mart*." He pauses for effect and finishes with, "by a fuckin' arrow."

Gwen asks, "What's with this, *fuckin' arrow*," thing?"

I laugh and say, "The bad guys were holed up the sporting goods department and sorta improvised."

"So you two have some history in the trenches," Thumper comments.

"I was actually hiding behind frozen foods," I laugh. "But if my instincts are right, our little task force is gonna have plenty of trench time."

My operational brief to Kopka and Shoulders goes a lot quicker than last evenings Coma brief. Our primary goal is to determine if Mansur has any direct or indirect scuttlebutt on the Egyptian terrorist cell. Sounds simple enough, but the clock is ticking. Any information shed on these ghosts is critical. They've been operating in darkness and Mansur could hopefully shine the light on them.

But first, I have to provide this particular Muslim the motivation to share. Individuals are motivated by a variety of things such as lust, greed, hunger, thirst, and jealousy. But fear seems to be the greatest of all motivators. It could turn the toughest guy into a whimpering soul. Most radical Muslims outwardly appear to be tough guys with their scowls and chest thumping but according to Dr. Astler's profile, Mansur will fold like a cheap suitcase when push came to shove. I just had to determine Mansur's personal tipping point.

Phase One is to soften up the target. Throw him off balance by ratcheting up his anxiety level through terror. God issues all humans the *fight* or *flight* survival mode no matter their ethnicity. And people will do *anything* to survive.

Special Agent Frederick Gregory could intimidate most living creatures. It was much more than the shaved head, twenty-one inch biceps and six-foot-three frame. Fred wreaks of mean.

With our plan in place, Mansur is transferred to a different cell. The white supremists seem disappointed to have lost their object of ridicule. It was about to get much worse. The corrections officer secures the handcuffs on Mansur and guides him to his new cell. The prisoner repeatedly whines, "Where are you taking me?" Mansur is shoved into his new digs and takes a tentative step toward the bottom bunk. A menacing voice warns, "You touch that rack and I will rip you head off and shove it up your ass."

Mansur turns his head toward the voice and is about to utter a challenging comeback until he gazes into the psychotic eyes of prisoner 29371623. Abdullah Husein, better known to his co-workers as Special Agent Fred Gregory.

"You got something you wanna say?"

"Why all the threats, my friend?

Gregory take two steps toward Mansur who recoils and says, "I ain't your fucking friend."

And so begins the Gregory reign of terror. Our plan follows the tried and true brainwashing blueprint of the United States Marine Corps. Sleep deprivation, a few shoves, a punch, and feeling vulnerable each and every second of the day is the process of breaking civilians down prior to rebuilding them as Marines. In this case there will only be the demolition phase.

An hour later, Mansur demands to see an attorney *and* his ambassador. Two hours later, Mansur adds an imam to his wish list and later in the day he is taken to the infirmary with a split lip and bruises on about twenty percent of his body. Even though I doubt Mansur will confess to any direct involvement in terrorism, he unwittingly provides information. Mansur attempts to threaten Thumper with, "*I know some very powerful people.*" When threats prove futile Mansur tries honey with, "I can make you a rich man." Very Interesting.

We set up an impromptu task force space on the third floor adjacent to Captain Kopka's office. My phone chirps and caller ID indicates, *Roomie.*

Tony says. "We've got two connections."

"Talk to me."

Before I left D.C., I had a sit-down with the nine forensic accountants on my new task force. My instructions were simple. "Follow the money!"

There were plenty of leads such as the bank accounts on Mansur's import/export business, campaign funds and PAC monies of the Muslim Congressional candidates, shell corporations funneling the money, Muslim charter schools' article of incorporation, and the individuals on their boards. And once they ID a name, bank account, or board of directors, listed on the legitimate paperwork filed, they develop an intricate web of interrelationships and additional corporations and people. And then they do it again and again and again.

Tony explains, "The accountants traced the campaign funds of two muslim congressional candidates to a bank account in North Korea."

"Outstanding," I offer. "What's the second connection?"

Tony pauses and then nonchalantly says, "Mansur's import/export business receives payments for his products from the *same* North Korean bank account."

"Holy shit!"

CHAPTER 36

"The most beautiful thing we can experience is the mysterious."
— Albert Einstein

"It's not all good news, John." Tony says. "I'm sitting with your intel analyst supervisor and I'm gonna put her on the speaker."

Special Agent Bobbie Geary is the new breed of the FBI. She has a Master's Degree from North Carolina State in Homeland Security and can run a mile in under five minutes. Bobbie is also very good at her job.

"Whatta got, Bobbie?" I ask.

"Well Agent Booker ..."

I interrupt her with, "Just call me John."

"Well John," Bobbie reboots. "A couple of intercepts seem to fit the profile you provided. The wording and syntax are consistent with our previous '*known*' intercepts and also originate in the targeted geographical areas of North Korea and Egypt."

"I'm all ears, Bobbie."

"Two days ago a CIA drone intercepted the single word, *CHINA* over North Korea. In and of itself, it holds no significance, but then just today there seemed to be the reply of *SYNDROME* from a web site used by terrorists to facilitate communication."

"Wow."

She explains, "Our analysts feel that one of our nuclear power plants is in jeopardy. We are ..."

"Which one?" I interrupt.

"We are monitoring all relative intercept options. Nothing specific yet."

"Good job, Bobbie. I want you to keep Assistant Director Daniels up-to-date on *any development*."

Tony explains, "I already called the Nuclear Regulatory Commission and requested they go on their highest alert."

"Two things," I say. "It won't be a frontal attack, like flying an airplane into a reactor. It'll seem an accident or computer failure. Which reminds me, Bobbie. What's going on with the financial meltdown?"

"Good and bad news on that front."

"Give me the bad first."

"That computer virus will cost the taxpayers over one trillion dollars. It could send us into another recession or worst."

"I need the good news now, Bobbie," I say. "You're bumming me out."

"The good news is that they discovered the DNA of the computer virus and will have everything back on line within the next two days."

"Will they be able to recover the data?"

"Yes." Geary says. "*And*, they believe that they can trace the virus back to the creator. Our experts are positive that no hacker, no matter their expertise, could have created this virus. They are positive it has to be an industrialized nation."

"That would be a home run, Bobbie." I say.

"Yes, Agent Booker."

"John," I remind her. ""Call me John."

"John," Bobbie reluctantly repeats and is gone.

Gwen asks, "What's up?"

"Could be a big break in the case. If they can trace that computer virus back to North Korea it'll give us additional evidence that they're linked with the radical Muslims."

"But we still need proof that this secret Muslim cell operating out of Cairo exists, and *then*, we have to prove their connection with the North Koreans."

"Thus, the reason we are working the Mansur end of the puzzle. And now that we have proof that Mansur is involved, we need to ratchet up the pressure."

"That reminds me," Agent 36 says. "Thumper got word that Mansur is a psychological wreck."

Gwen gets serious and asks. "What is your end game with Mansur? I know you want information but we both know that anything he says can't be used in a courtroom."

"This case will *never* see a courtroom," I say matter-of-factly.

Gwen seems confused and asks, "Then how does it end? We're FBI agents and our job is to get evidence to put the assholes in jail. That's what we do?"

"When I was nine," I begin. "Two eleven-year-old kids decided to take my lunch at school. If I told my parents or teacher, it would only get worse and I'd be labeled a snitch. So every day, I simply handed them my food. Those were the *unwritten* laws in South Philly back then and I followed them. Then one day, I realized that since *they* were operating outside the rule book, I could too. And, I was a creative and vindictive little bastard."

"I know this is going somewhere, devious Booker." Gwen laughs.

"So I put rat poison on my food. Not a lot but at the end of a week, both kids were hospitalized and pretty sick. Had their stomachs pumped and didn't come back to school for a month."

"Did you get in trouble?" Gwen wonders.

"No, because I figured that they would have to confess to stealing my lunch and they couldn't prove I put the rat poison on my own food anyway."

"You do know you could've killed them." Gwen lectures me.

"Well, to be completely honest," I reply. "that thought *did* cross my mind, but I simply didn't care. All I wanted was for them to stop stealing my lunch and they wouldn't, so I took the law into my own hands."

"And the morale of this story is?"

"There comes a time in all of us, when rules no longer apply. When the enemy throws out the rule book and the only way to defeat evil is rat poison."

"You're beginning to scare me, Booker." Gwen says with a nervous chuckle. "But allow me to tell *you a* story."

"I can't wait."

"When you gaze at this magnificent body and perfect face, it may be hard to believe that in the eighth grade I was this fat insecure acne-faced loser."

"Oh," I say. "Let me guess, then your knockers sprouted and you became popular and skinny."

"I wish," Agent 36 laughs. "I signed up for the cheerleading squad but at the tryout, the *popular* girls made fun of me."

"So did you punch them out and then sit on them."

"You are such an asshole, Booker," Gwen laughs again. "No, I ran home crying. The next day, I signed up for martial arts and over the next ten months, I got in shape, gained self-confidence *and*, my boobs did their thing."

"So did you beat them up with karate chops then?"

"That option was very tempting, but I came up with something much better. At the tryouts next year, I made the team and was voted cheerleading captain and then I was elected homecoming queen and made all-state forward on the girls' basketball team."

"So how did that get you even with the little witches?"

"You're a frontal attack guy, Booker." Gwen explains. "But whipping someone's ass only hurts them for a little while. What I did was to enter their world and gain control. I figured out that they wanted and needed my approval so I ignored them. Drove them absolutely crazy."

"Know something, Gwen" I say.

"What?"

"That is some elaborate and diabolical scheme, and it impresses the shit outta me. But what's does it have to do with not taking this to court?"

Gwen says seriously. "Well, Booker, there are several ways of going rogue."

Tommy Shoulders interrupts and informs me that I have a call on line two. This is somewhat unusual since the advent of cell phones.

"Booker," I say.

"Hi John, it's Matt Michaels, your supervisor."

"Matt," I say. "Unless you have some information on this case, I am extremely busy, and," I add, "you are *not* my supervisor."

"Well," he whines, "technically I still am."

I hang up the landline and fume. I turn to Gwen and say, "That bastard is gonna try and insert himself in this case."

"Why?" Gwen asks.

"He can't help himself. It's his nature. He smells something big and wants to take the credit.

Gwen observes, "He's an asshole. Why let him get to you?"

"Because he is *not* your garden variety asshole," I clarify. "He is an asshole who got two agents killed."

Shoulders picks up a ringing phone and announces, "Asshole on line two."

I have no idea why, but I pick up the phone and challenge. "What *exactly* do you want?"

"I just want to offer the Cleveland task force if you need support."

"I got it covered."

"Well congratulations on getting your creds back and being reinstated," Michaels says, "I heard you met with the Director himself *and* Deputy Director Batcheller."

"Look Matt," I fume. "You did everything you could to get me fired so quit pissing on my head and telling me it's raining. You don't like me and I think you should've been charged with involuntary manslaughter. You caused the death of my best friend. You would be the *last* person I call, you lazy obstructionist asshole."

"Is that really how you feel?" Michaels asks seriously.

For the first time in years, I am speechless. I slam the phone and punch the desk in frustration. I understand this is a childish reaction, but that guy *really* gets to me. My hand hurts like hell.

Agent 36 sits on my desk crosses her long seductive legs and purrs. "Does my good buddy need a Coma?"

Gwen has a knack for making men smile. Her beauty and body are but a small part of her charm. She's the type of person who can tell you to go to hell and make you happy to be taking the journey.

I laugh and say, "Actually it's time for phase two of this soap opera. I turn to Tommy Shoulders, "Get Fred, Tommy. Make sure Mansur overhears that his cellmate has a court appearance."

Thirty minutes pass and I use the time to jot down the next critical pieces of the puzzle. One miscalculation or misstep and the reign of terror on our country continues. Whenever I think of the magnitude of this case, it temporarily paralyzes me. If I fail it will affect the lives of millions of innocent people.

Special Agent Frederick Terence Gregory, aka '*Thumper*,' enters the room in an orange prison jump suit. He vaguely resembles a pumpkin on steroids. Everything about Fred says, '*Do NOT fuck with me.*'

"How's prison life going?" Gwen wonders.

"Buncha punks trying to act tougher than they are."

"Can I ask a personal question?" Tommy says.

Fred glares at Tommy and says, "I can tell already that your question is gonna piss me off."

Detective Shoulders takes a step back and feigns an injured look. He pauses for effect and asks, "So Fred, we were all wondering. You dating anyone special in prison or just playing the field?"

Fred laughs. "I'm about to throw your scrawny ass over the desk and fill it with a snickers bar."

Sometimes it's the manner in which something's said and *not* the actual words that make it funny. And *sometimes*, it's the situation. The group laughs loud and long, though Fred's threat wouldn't seem as funny under different circumstances. Everyone in our little task force is feeling the enormity of our task and gallows humor serves to lessen the pressure.

Kopka enters the room and asks. "I miss something funny?" He notices Fred and comments, "Orange is *definitely* not the new black."

It's time to get back to business. I motion for everyone to gather around the small conference table.

"We need to speed things up," I say, thinking of a vulnerable nuclear plant. "So let's push the psychological buttons on Mansur. Thumper, you're up."

My cell phone chirps and it's the third call I've ignored in the past twenty minutes from my attorney Steve Sazini. Since I am facing twenty years in prison it may behoove me to take this one.

"John," Steve says. "Been trying to reach you. Seems there's been a development in your case."

I involuntarily cringe since there's a good possibility that they revoked my bond. I take a deep breath and ask. "Okay, Steve. How bad?"

"Bad," He laughs. "It's good. Very good. The prosecutor called me and begins his Monty Hall imitation of *'Let's Make A Deal.'* He whines that he wants the case resolved, that now that the publicity has died down he can be more realistic in your case. So if you plead guilty they are willing to give you a two-year suspended sentence, with a six-month stay at a halfway house, a ten thousand dollar fine and three years of probation … and …"

"We already had this conversation Steve," I fume. "Tell that asshole that we'll see him in court. No deals, cause I will *never* plead guilty. Understand!"

I hear Steve laughing and although I am an irreverent sarcastic individual, his sniggering seems insensitive, *and* out of context with my legal predicament. I ask. "What's so fucking funny?"

"I've been trying to tell you, John. I *did* tell the prosecutor that I'd pass on his offer."

"So then why the call, Steve?" I wonder.

"The prosecutor began to babble about sweetening his offer and that you'd have to at least plead guilty and then he'd *consider* maybe just probation and some drug testing. So I tell him *no thanks* and there won't be any guilty pleas."

"I know you're heading somewhere with this, Steve, and I'm in the middle of some serious shit, so can we get to bottom line here."

"They lost the evidence, John."

"Whatta do you mean?"

"They did a routine evidence inventory and the five kilos of coke were gone."

"Gone?"

"Gone," Steve repeats. "Like in, '*nowhere to be found.*'"

"Does that mean what I think that means?"

"Even if it's found." Steve in legal mode. "They can't use it since the chain of custody was broken. They dropped all charges, John."

"Fuck me." I just realized that I had been sitting at the head of our small conference table and all eyes and ears are riveted on me.

I finish my conversation with Steve by stating, "How the hell can a police department lose five kilos of cocaine inside their own evidence locker?"

Steve has no good answer and we promise to get together soon for a celebratory night out. I place my cell phone on the table and smile at the group.

Captain Ray Kopka locks eyes with me and says, "We *are* the Cleveland Police Department."

CHAPTER 37

"You're not too smart...I like that in a man"
— Kathleen Turner - *Body Heat*

I am a lot of things but naive is not one of them. The look on Kopka's large Croatian mug spoke volumes. When he had first offered his assistance with my legal problems his last words were, 'then, I'll help you in *other* ways."

At the time, I thought the emphasis on the word '*other*' odd and out of context. The way he said it had a sinister ring, as if spoken by Snidley Whiplash. But I knew not to ask questions since I didn't want to hear the answers. Kopka is old school and if he *did* take the evidence he did so alone and feels no need to disclose his felony to anyone.

Another possibility is that the cocaine disappeared through negligence, a clerical error, or someone else stole it. With all that said, my money is on Captain Kopka.

I look Ray in the eye and nod. He raises his hand in a gesture of '*forget about it.*' Or perhaps, he is indicating a case of indigestion. Either way, I have a tremendous weight lifted from my shoulders and my feeling is that Captain Kopka did the heavy lifting.

As I am finally about to restart the meeting, one of Kopka's detectives bangs on the closed door and announces, "Important call for Agent Booker on line one."

"John," Tony Daniels says. "We think we got the nuclear plant identified."

"Fantastic roomie, how'd you do that?"

Tony chuckles and says, "Wasn't me. Remember, I used to cheat off *you*. It was the intel chief assigned to your task force."

"Bobbie Geary?" I ask.

"That's her," Tony confirms. "She's some smart cookie."

"Special Agent," I correct him. "What'd she find out?"

"An intercept of, *NATIVE AMERICAN*, originating in North Korea." Tony explains. "Then some inspired deductive reasoning by our Bobby who figured that nearly half of the one hundred and four nuclear reactors operating in the United States are close to major fault lines, including the Diablo Canyon and San Onofre plants located near California's San Andreas Fault."

"But," Tony expounds,. "the *Indian* Point nuclear power plant in New York is less than two miles from the Pampano fault line, and sits within fifty miles of more than seventeen million people. It is also the *oldest* plant and thus has more safety holes. She parlayed that information with the fact that an Indian is a *NATIVE AMERICAN*, so we're feeling good about our chances. "

"That's fuckin' outstanding work," I interject. "Give ol' Bobby a hug from me and a big FBI cash incentive award."

"I'm not finished. Our Agent Geary then ranked the country's power plant sites based on three equally weighted metrics: risk of natural disaster, safety performance assessments, and surrounding population. In other words, which nuclear power plants are located in the most dangerous physical locations, have the weakest relative operating conditions, and would affect the greatest number of people should an unforeseeable emergency occur. And that would also be Indian Point."

"So what's our plan to prevent an accident that wouldn't really be an accident?" I wonder.

"Been on the phone to Nuclear Regulatory Commission and they suggest we basically shut the Indian Point plant down. They explained that if they pulled some levers, hit some buttons, and tap some switches, they could make the plant bullet proof, so to speak. It will still produce enough juice to power their area, but, it would not be vulnerable to sabotage or fault line manipulation."

"Well, roomie, we're at the turn, and we can *finally* see their asses, tails, and cloves."

"Is that supposed to be a horse racing or Satan analogy?"

"I don't know shit about horse racing but you get the picture," I laugh.

"It's too early to be patting ourselves on the back. We survived the blackout, the bird flu, and the financial computer virus but these animals have no reason to stop now."

"Until we stop them," I add.

Tony in his most serious voice, "I met with the President and Ms. Lewis. Our nation is teetering on a financial and confidence abyss. Americans are terrified about what's coming next. They're purchasing guns and ammunition at a record pace. They're digging shelters in their backyards and hoarding food. If word got out that this was a conspiracy of terrorists there would be widespread panic."

"It's that bad?" I ask.

"The computer virus cost over a trillion, the bird flu cost hundreds of lives, and the blackout brought this country to their emotional knees. But the residual effects of these disasters are heart wrenching and not as obvious."

"What are you talking about, residual effects?"

"When the bank computers crashed, four hundred and sixty one Americans committed suicide. They truly believed that their life savings were wiped out. The blackout reduced our citizens to barbarians and let's not forget the rash of Muslim congressmen funded by terrorists who are now making policies. Throw in charter schools that are brainwashing our kids and have a negative long-term effect on our future leaders, and you have a nation cringing anytime they turn on their TVs."

There is an awkward silence as we both get a visual of an America totally alien to the nation we took an oath to defend. A country that we can no longer recognize. The country our fathers and grandfathers fought to defend and built with their hands.

"Can I ask what's going on in this investigation or are we still playing your game of plausible deniability? I no longer give a shit about having my career protected by some rogue roommate. I'm *ordering* you to give me an investigative update *and* summarize your operational plan."

"You sure?"

"I'm positive. I'd rather be in the loop and able to cover your ass than have to say, '*I don't know what's going on.*'"

"You sure?" I repeat.

"Quit the parrot imitation."

"Okay," I say. "We're probably going to use enhanced torture techniques that are outlawed by our government, and perhaps kill a terrorist or two in cold blood which is capital murder."

"Yea right," Tony says laughing. "Call me when you can quit the bullshit."

"What bullshit," I say seriously. "You wanted to know and now you are *officially* a co-conspirator."

My roommate quickly terminates the connection.

The weird thing is that I am not sure myself if I am bullshitting. Both of those options have been running through my brain lately as viable. We must get Mansur to tell us what he may know even if that includes nothing. *But* unless he has something of value to lose then we can't be sure he'll be telling the truth. The stakes are high so I can't worry about constitutional rights or my career. Mansur *must* believe that his life hangs in the balance if he lies or refuses to answer our questions. And I am not sure how far I will go off course on my own moral compass. We had invested valuable time working the Mansur vein so it is time to shit or get off the proverbial pot.

I look at Thumper and ask, "Tell us about Mr. Mansur."

Thumper shakes his massive bald dome. He says, "Mansur is an asshole. But a slimy, manipulative, and *smart* asshole. He's never slipped up and directly discussed any ties with terrorists but he's made inferences."

"Like what? Be specific."

Thumper briefs the group. It seems that Mansur keeps making noise about knowing some powerful and dangerous folks.

"Alright," I concede. "So Mansur knows some folks, but *what* folks. If they were legit friends like a politician, army general, or major business tycoon, he'd give up a name. So I agree with Thumper that Mansur wanted him to believe that these *'powerful people'* were bad guys."

It is Captain Kopka who reminds us that "The clock is ticking. What's the plan?"

"Here's our move," I say. "Fred goes back to the cell and informs Mansur that his lawyer is outraged at how the city of Cleveland is violating Mansur's constitutional rights and has agreed to represent him. They will file a writ to release him followed by a five-million-dollar lawsuit against the city for wrongful imprisonment."

"How we gonna find a lawyer that we can trust and who'll go along with this charade?" Gwen wonders aloud.

I stare directly at Agent 36 and state. "I believe I see that attorney right here in this room."

Gwen smiles and says, "Duh, I almost forgot that I graduated first in my law school class at Yale."

CHAPTER 38

"We would like to live as we once lived, but history will not permit it."

— John F. Kennedy

Captain Kopka has a point. It *is* time for action. The terrorists have targeted a nuclear power plant and are planning more devastation while we have *discussions*. I run down some options since it's important that the group come to a unanimous decision and feel invested in putting their lives and careers in jeopardy. Each one of these law enforcement officers are in peril by simply *being* on this task force. The bad guys knew that Suehad and I were sniffing their trail, and I went to jail and Suehad's on life support.

"Okay," I begin. "Thumper has given the profile on Mansur. What buttons do we push to get him to talk?"

Shoulders throws out, "Beat the fuck out of him."

"A good plan *but* with a few risks," I say and ask the group. "Any ideas *other* than the *beating the shit out of him* option?"

"Simple," Kopka says. "He *has* to believe that he tells the truth or something very *very* bad will happen to him."

"We've been saying that, Ray," I remind him.

Kopka gives me his *no shit* glance and adds, "There are '*other*' ways than beating the shit out of him that will get his gums moving."

The instant Kopka uttered the word *'other'* my brain again flashes back to our conversation of a few weeks ago. When I had told the good captain that rattling his sabers at street snitches wouldn't help my drug case, his response had been, "Then, I'll help you in *other* ways." And, in a major coincidence, just today, the five kilos of coke, which was the only evidence against me, disappears. Obviously, Captain Kopka is a man of means.

"We're all ears," I challenge him.

Kopka smiles and says, "I've got a plan."

We turn in unison toward Kopka. The good Captain doesn't say much, but when he does, he commands your undivided attention.

"Gwen meets with Mansur as his attorney," Kopka begins. "Gets him released to her custody. She strongly recommends he high tail it back to Cairo until she clears up his legal mess."

While we are waiting for the remainder of the plan, Captain Kopka goes mute.

"And?"

"That's it for now." Kopka says and then as an afterthought adds. "Trust me."

"Trust me?" I ask. "Is that our operational plan? Trust me?"

Kopka feels no need to waste any additional energy on words. So he merely nods. Normally, when someone asks me to trust them on life and death situations, I don't. The few times I placed total trust in anyone, it turned to shit. Perhaps that makes me a control freak but blind faith is a religious belief and I deal in the real world. But Captain Ray Kopka of the Cleveland Police Department is not your average *someone*.

Since it's obvious that he has a plan but little desire to discuss the details. I turn to Agent 36 and say, "Gwen, find a conservative business suit with a little cleavage. Remember that Mansur is a pervert *and* a Muslim, so he'll cycle through conflicting feelings about a *female* attorney. On one hand you're inferior but you can free him *and* he's a typical horny male. Play it business like but throw in some mild flirtation."

"You are hitting all my strong points," Agent 36 says. "I am an expert on dealing with perverts ever since I attended the FBI academy."

"Call Tony and have him order you up an expensive looking web site, business cards, a "hello' line for your office, and input your name in all the government web sites pertaining to attorneys practicing in Ohio."

"Got it," Gwen says. "How can we assure ourselves that he don't disappear once he's free?"

Kopka jumps in with, "Insist he makes the travel arrangements in your presence. You can come up with some legal mumbo jumbo to convince him. Tell him two police officers will escort him from his cell to his plane. Court procedures."

"Let me see if I got this straight," Gwen says. "You release his passport, wallet, money and any other documents to me. I stick close to him until he's ready to board the plane."

I look at Kopka and ask. "And according to your *plan* how much time does Gwen need to keep Mansur on ice?"

"I'm ready to go now. The sooner the better."

"Do you need our assistance in executing this plan?"

"No."

Thumper wonders, "Are we going to allow Mansur to leave with Suehad?"

Kopka responds cryptically with, "Don't matter for now; first step is to *encourage* the towel head to spill his guts."

"Encourage," I tease, "as in cheering him along?"

"You ask too many questions, Booker."

I need to know the bottom line of Kopka's plan. So I say, "One last question. Just so we're clear on *your* plan. Will this *plan* result in Mansur telling us the truth, the whole truth and nothing *but* the truth?"

"Probably."

"Probably?"

"Look John," Kopka says. "It's a good plan and has no downside. So if we're gonna execute it, let's get moving."

There are moments when logic will smack you square in the chops. This is one of those moments.

"Agreed. I'll head to the hospital to take Suehad's loyalty temperature. Gwen and Thumper take care of the backstopping for Gwen's attorney identity. Tell Daniels that we need everything by close of business today. Ray, go take care of whatever you need to do for your *plan*. We meet back here in four hours. Questions?"

There were none and as we were leaving the room Thumper slides next to me and whispers, "Do you trust this guy?."

I look Thumper in the eye. "With *your* life."

Suehad is looking more like Suehad. As I enter her room she is sitting upright and reading. I notice some lipstick and blush and her hair is combed and styled. But the residual damage from her horrific crash is evident when she speaks. She speaks slowly and deliberately and struggles to enunciate the words.

She smiles and motions me to her. Some people smile with their lips and some people smile with their eyes, but Suehad smiles with her heart. She would not do well attempting to bluff in a game of poker. She is genuinely happy to see me.

I lean down and hug her taking in a variety of smells including some perfume.

"How's my favorite jihad terrorist doing?"

Suehad smiles and comes back with, "Fine and how is my favorite fascist?"

I didn't come here with any strategy. If I say too much and Suehad's loyalty lies in Cairo then we lose Mansur and possibly go back to square one. But if she truly views America as her adopted country and Mansur as the evil asshole that he is, then Suehad can help big time.

So I toss out a few feelers to determine her loyalty index. Suehad seems to have come back from the dark side and is ready and willing to betray Mansur. I proceed to the down and dirty details. She actually smiles when I relay how her husband is sharing a jail cell with a psychotic giant.

Suehad nods assent when I ask her to play along with Mansur and act as our *official* informant. So far so good. Although I have specific tasks for Suehad, I can see that she is fading fast. Her eyes are fluttering and she nods off occasionally. The details will have to wait, but for now Suehad is on board.

I give her a hug, peck her cheek, tell her she looks gorgeous and head out into the cold winter afternoon to visit someone special.

As I enter the task force space heads pop up from desks and Bruce Gombar stands and approaches me with a broad smile, "John Booker, the man with nine Bureau lives. You back amongst us?"

We shake hands and I say, "Not quite yet, but soon."

"What the hell is going on?" Bruce wonders. "All we know is that OPR was about to terminate you and you were facing a ten spot at a state prison. All of a sudden, you're in D.C. working some major case, which you get Gwen reassigned to, and then all drug charges are dropped."

"It's long story," I say. "Is Peggy here?"

"Can I get the abridged version?" Bruce chuckles.

"Over a beer later," I say, then add. "I promise."

"C'mon John," Bruce says seriously. "You're in the middle of some major shit and I just wanna know if I can help."

I smile and tell Bruce. "I'm not trying to be an asshole, it's just that shit happened and then it *unhappened*. We'll go for some beers when this is over and you'll get the unabridged version."

Bruce laughs. "You sure you weren't an Ivy Leaguer, Booker, and not a Slimy Pebble graduate?"

"That was *Slippery Rock*," I correct him. "And it was a fantastic school."

Peggy actually does a double take when I turn the corner into her cubicle. Her broad face breaks into a smile and then the tears begin running down her cheeks. She jumps up and smothers me into her ample chest. "Jesus, John Booker, my prayers have been answered.I knew you'd be back. I know a good Christian man when I see one."

I give our squad secretary a peck on her cheek and say, "I wouldn't go that far Peggy, but I appreciate your prayers. How's my favorite FBI gal?"

"Better now that you have come back."

"I'm back in the Bureau but am temporarily detached to headquarters." I explain and hand her a bag containing a Reuben sandwich and a bag of barbecue potato chips.

Peggy looks inside and hugs me again. She says, "I love you John Booker."

"I only have a few minutes and wanted to see you and ask you something."

"Ask away, John Booker."

"I found an access code to the intelligence briefings in my desk." I say with a smile on my face. "Any idea how it got there?"

"The Lord works in mysterious ways." She says with complete seriousness, but the smile in her eyes tells me that it was Peggy who had risked her job to help me, and in some small way had probably saved a nuclear power plant.

Individuals make a difference in life. If you believe that all doctors or FBI agents are interchangeable pieces, just imagine *your* child kidnapped. If Agent X is assigned the case you should immediately make funeral arrangements because your kid is a goner. You'd want Agent Y on the case.

"I gotta go, Peggy."

"I'll keep praying for you, John Booker."

"And I'll need *all* those prayers," I say then add, "You haven't cursed me out once Peggy, don't you love me anymore?"

"Three weeks ago I went to a healing revival. The visiting minister prayed and laid hands on me and I haven't cussed since. My Tourette's symptoms are gone, praise the Lord."

I congratulate Peggy on her miracle cure and thought about asking for the name of that particular minister. I may need this guy to lay some healing hands on me in the very near future.

As I turn to leave the office Matt Michaels is standing directly in my path. This scene strikes me as an eerily similar to our last encounter. But I have no stomach for another confrontation so I say, "Hey Matt, how's it going?"

The smile on his face is a cross between the Joker and Mike Tyson. He asks, "Do you have time to give *your* supervisor a case briefing?"

I fight my immediate response which is to put two slugs in his goard. I realize that I require my energy on *positive* things like Mansur so I politely say, "Can't right now Matt, in a hurry, but maybe later."

Of course Boy Wonder won't allow this mild rebuff to go unchallenged. He says with an edge in his voice, "Maybe you can *make* the time, since you're evidently working a terrorist case in *my* jurisdiction and I *am* the supervisor."

My blood pressure rises like the tachometer on a sports car driven by a teenager. I say in my most calm voice, "You are going to step aside and I'm going to leave now Matt. Do you understand what I'm saying?"

Michaels drops his eyes to the floor and takes a step to his left. As I walk past him I whisper, "Good move, Boy Wonder."

Agent 36's attorney outfit includes a tight skirt with a white blouse and a matching jacket. Her massive perfect mammary glands are high and tight. She completes her motif with a pair of black horn rimmed glasses. Gwen looks like a porn star librarian in a seedy movie. Not that I ever saw that particular movie.

"Love the look," I say. "A little overdone but who am I to judge what constitutes *sleazy*."

Tommy Shoulders enters the room waving some papers, "Good shit." He says. "Boobie Geary sent some financial documents on Mansur's import/export business in Cairo. Scumbag is receiving massive amounts of money from North Korea. We're talking millions of dollars."

"Does it describe what product Mansur is peddling?"

"No, but some recent transfers total over three million bucks, and the interesting thing is that the money doesn't stay in Mansur's account for long."

"Give me an example," I ask.

Shoulders runs his finger down a column of numbers and says, "On February fifteenth, two million three hundred thousand dollars was wired into his account from some bank in North Korea. On February twenty-first, Mansur withdrew all of it except for three hundred grand."

"Where did it go?"

"He took it in cash."

"I guess Egyptian banks are a trusting bunch."

Kopka looks at me and says, "Know what happened on February twenty-second?"

"I have no idea what year it is, been a little busy." I say and ask Captain Kopka. "So tell us what happened?"

"Let me give you a clue." Kopka says. "We were ducking fucking arrows at Wal-Mart."

That was the day of the great American blackout.

CHAPTER 39

Between two evils, I always pick the one I never tried before."
— Mae West

Mansur is seated behind a metal desk as Attorney Gwen McClanahan enters the interview room. He makes no attempt to stand or extend a greeting.

The snub is not calculated but rather standard behavior for Muslim men who follow Sharia Law. Women are considered necessary evils to clean, cook, and screw. In that *one* regard, they are not much different from Italian men.

"Mr. El-Quadir." Gwen says as she tosses her briefcase on the desk and offers her hand. Mansur makes no attempt to take her hand but does reply with a "Yes."

Gwen's first inclination is to smack Mansur across his chops and sing two verses of, *"I am woman, hear me roar."*

But playing her role perfectly, she just smiles and takes a seat across the desk from his highness. Two correction officers stand outside the half glass walls and peer inside to assure that everything remains kosher.

"Abdullah has told me of your situation and I find it outrageous," Gwen begins her spiel. "I also reviewed the police reports from your arrest and it reeks of police misconduct."

Mansur suddenly becomes animated and adds, "The big cop struck me in my face. In my country I would have his head. I demand my release immediately!"

Gwen shakes her head sympathetically and writes furiously on her yellow legal pad. She says, "I will make a formal complaint with the police internal affairs unit and file a writ of habeas corpus for your immediate release. Then once you are a free man, I will file a five-million-dollar lawsuit against the city for wrongful imprisonment and pain and suffering."

Mansur's eyes are cleavage scanning but he eventually forces his eyes level with Agent 36 and asks, "When can I leave this barbaric country?"

"I have an appointment with Judge Cullison in one hour." Gwen says and then lowers her voice barely above a whisper. "The judge is a *personal* friend of mine. If you get my meaning?"

Mansur smiles and once again lowers his pupils onto Agent 36's boobs.

She slides a document across the desk and says, "This is an authorization for me to represent you. Sign the bottom and I'll go see the *judge*."

Mansur scribbles illegibly on the form and Gwen rises and seductively straightens her blouse. He asks with a confrontational tone, "Why would you come here and help me? What is in this for you?"

Gwen patiently explains, "I get a third of that five million dollars and *that* Mr. El-Quadir, is why I am here."

As she is about to leave Mansur shouts, "Hey, you."

Gwen turns and playfully scolds, "My *name* is Miss McClanahan."

"Whatever," Mansur dismisses her. "How do I know if I can trust you?"

Gwen coos, "Because I'm the *only* hope you've got."

CHAPTER 40

"It is a characteristic of wisdom not to do desperate things."
– Henry D. Thoreau

"It went well," Gwen briefs the team.

"Tell us about Mansur. What's your take on him?"

Agent 36 laughs and says, "He's just your typical arrogant, horny, egotistical, frustrated, radical, Muslim terrorist."

"Did you two get along then?"

"We did but sadly Mansur realizes that I won't qualify as one of the seventy-two virgins awaiting his arrival in Mecca."

"Thank you for that in-depth psychological profile," I say. "Is he on board with the program?"

"No problem. He totally bought the fact that I'm an attorney."

"You *are* an attorney." I remind her.

I shake my head and turn to Captain Kopka. "I just wanna be sure we understand your *plan*. Do we *really* want Mansur getting on a private plane heading to Cairo?"

Kopka shoots me a frustrated look and says evenly, "Listen to me carefully, John. My plan is for Gwen to *convince* the asshole to get his plane to Cleveland."

Just as I am about to rephrase my question convinced that Kopka must be confused, it hits me. The good captain *totally* understood my reservation and has been basically hinting that I '*shut the fuck up.*' I have no idea of his plan, but I now know that he is strongly discouraging *any* inquiries. For now, it's good enough for me.

"Gwen, you go back and give Mansur the good news."

I turn to Captain Kopka and announce, "Ray, you do whatever you gotta do to make your plan work."

"We *are* the Cleveland Police Department."

Kopka and Shoulders wander into the outer room with a "Be right back."

Thumper is having his recurring doubts, "I *know* that you trust Kopka, but how can you trust a *plan* that you know nothing about?"

I turn to Gwen and ask, "Whatta you think?"

"Kopka reminds me of my father." Agent 36 says. "Solid, quiet, dependable and a man of his word."

Kopka and Shoulders reenter the room and Thumper announces, "Hey, Captain Kopka, Gwen has some perverted daddy complex on you."

The big Croatian cop smiles and simply says, "I'm honored."

"Okay," I remind the team. "Back here in two hours. Good luck Gwen, the ball is now in your court."

My cell phone caller ID indicates that the Assistant Director of the FBI has the business of the government to discuss.

"Your makeshift task force has hit a grand slam."

"I need some good news," I say.

"They tried to sabotage the *Indian* Point nuclear power plant."

"You are shittin' me."

Tony explains, "Indian Point would have experienced a major incident had the NRC not heeded our warning and powered down. It seems that an electrical failure prevented the main feed water pumps from sending water to the steam generators that remove heat from the reactor core." Tony pauses for a second and says, "I'm reading this so bear with me."

He continues, "This would have caused the plant's turbine-generator and then the reactor itself to automatically shut down and the pressure in the nuclear portion of the plant to increase. If we hadn't alerted the inspectors then the nuclear fuel would've overheated to the point at which the zirconium cladding would rupture and the fuel pellets melt. The core would have melted and released radiation equal to fifty times that of Hiroshima.

"Holy shit," I interrupt. "What's the bottom line, roomie?"

"Well," Tony concludes. "The radiation fallout could have been Chernobyl-like in scope with New York City suffering the greatest number of casualties."

When the impact of what I hear registers in my brain, I can only respond with a "Wow."

"Any suspects?" I wonder.

"That's the interesting point," Tony says. "Had your task force not alerted Indian Point to possible sabotage, the series of malfunctions would have been chalked up to an *accident*. There is no real evidence of any sabotage. We are conducting a massive investigation, looking at every employee, visitor, vendor, cleaning crew, phone records, and I ordered our Evidence Response Team to dust every inch of that facility."

"But those bastards *really* fucking exist and we stopped a massacre of thousands of innocent Americans."

"Hundreds of thousands," Tony corrects. "The experts told me that due to the long-term effect of radiation, individuals in the fallout area not *immediately* killed would contract fatal radiation poisoning and cancer over the next two decades."

"Well," I reason, "We stopped the attack but we haven't stopped the *attackers*. Hell, we don't even know who *they* are. We almost have enough evidence to get the President to back down the North Koreans but the Muslim piece of this puzzle is still missing most of the pieces."

"Keep plugging away," Tony encourages me. "The President and the Director wanted me to pass on their personal congratulations on the Indian Point piece and Ms. Lewis is now your biggest fan here in Headquarters. She wanted me to tell you that she is on that seaweed diet."

"Our government is a fucked up thing," I muse. "A week ago, I was under indictment, about to be fired, but suddenly I'm the golden boy."

"Don't get too self-important," Tony warns me. "Remember that a week from *now* you could easily be dog shit again."

"Thank you for that reality check, roomie." I say. "Tell Ms. Lewis that when we get the time, I'll take her to a place near HQ for some *Comas*."

"*Comas*?" Tony asks.

"Yea, Comas." I reply. "A mysterious booze concoction that will make Ms. Lewis giggle and horny."

"You are one fucked up person," Tony laughs and tells me that the Director desires his presence immediately.

"Tony becomes serious and signs off with, "John, you're doing great but be careful, these people are mass murderers and you are now officially a pain in their ass."

"I'm a pain in *everybody's* ass."

My cell phone chirps in my hand and I notice Monica's name on the caller ID.

She is hysterically screaming and crying.

Monica gains a moment of composure and sobs, "Suehad is dead!"

CHAPTER 41

"INDECISION is the key to FLEXIBILITY"

Monica can't provide many details other than something about a major stroke caused by the accident.

I arrive at the hospital and Monica is only *slightly* less hysterical. She explains that Suehad experienced a massive stroke about an hour ago. Doctors went through their arsenal of life saving steps but couldn't resuscitate her and pronounced her dead. We both avoid the obvious question of Suehad being murdered by terrorists. Of course, there would be no evidence of a murder just as there was no evidence of sabotage to the Indian Point Nuclear Plant, Beck's aneurysm, the blackout, and Suehad's original car *accident.*

"Where is she?" I ask.

"Don't know," Monica says through her sobs. "A student sitting with her called me and I immediately called you. I got here five minutes before you."

"Where's the student?" I ask.

"Downstairs in the lobby."

"Go get them while I try to find someone to speak with."

I walk out into the hall and stop the first nurse I see. "I am Suehad's brother and need to know how she passed," I say.

She wants to be sympathetic but ICU nurses have an extra layer of emotional skin that insulates them from the constant strains of their job.

She informs me that I'd have to go to the nurses' station for that information. I thank her and follow the hallway where I find my friend the head nurse. She immediately says, "I'm sorry for your loss."

"Thank you," I mutter and ask, "Can you tell me what happened?"

"Of course. Suehad suffered a traumatic brain injury in that car crash." The nurse pauses as if measuring her words carefully. She asks, "Are you a football fan? As hard as they try and prevent concussions in football with space age helmets and stricter rules, they still average the same number of concussions as they did thirty years ago. That's because the helmet, like the skull, can't really protect the brain from major trauma. It's the *violence* of the hit that jars the brain regardless of any outer protection."

Once again the nurse pauses and finally says, "I'd rather not get into graphic descriptions of what happened to your friend's brain during that accident but let's just say she sustained significant damage to areas of her brain that may have healed in time, but proved to be a virtual ticking time bomb."

I ask, "Were there any unknown visitors, any doctors who you didn't recognize, anyone or anything out of the ordinary in her room?"

She shakes her head at the strange nature of the question.

I try a different approach. "Well, can you tell me the *official* cause of death?"

The nurse flips through some papers until she comes to a particular form and reads it aloud, "The doctor listed cerebral edema as the cause of death."

"Can you explain that in laymen terms?"

"It's the swelling of the brain," She continues, "no one can accurately predict whether a person with a head injury will die. There are two critical periods. The initial period is in the first day or two after the injury when the injuries may be so overwhelming as to cause death in the face of the most intensive treatment. Those who survive this period face another critical period beginning a few days later and continuing for two weeks or more. This critical period results from swelling of the injured brain. This swelling cannot be controlled and caused Suehad's death."

"Thank you for that explanation," I say. "Can I ask just one more question?"

"Of course."

"Where is the administrative offices located?"

"Third floor."

I thank the nurse supervisor and as I turn toward the elevator bank I run into Monica and Rose Eagan. Rose is a junior at Cleveland State and was with Suehad when she passed. She resembles Pollyanna with blonde hair, freckles, and a 'aw shucks' attitude.

We shake hands and I ask that they accompany me to the third floor. During our trip I ask Rose, "Tell me what happened?"

Rose informs me that she was sitting with Suehad and everything seemed fine. Suehad was in good spirits as Rose read loud A Tale of Two Cities by Charles Dickens. When Rose went to the restroom, Suehad suffered a stroke. Upon her return to the hospital room, Suehad was surrounded by doctors and nurses attempting to revive her.

I walk into the administrative offices and ask the receptionist that I want to see who's in charge. Before she can reply I add, "No, I don't have an appointment. Yes, I realize he or she is very busy."

To avoid further useless dialogue I flash my creds and announce in my most official tone, "FBI, this is a national emergency. Get your boss now please."

The receptionist stands and quick walks through glass doors. A moment later the doors open and she motions me inside. I tell Monica and Rose to meet me in the cafeteria in half an hour.

My meeting with the head administrator is short and sweet. I go through a vetting process answering a variety of questions and which culminates in her contacting FBI Headquarters. When Ms. Janelle Mann is finally satisfied with my authority she asks, "Now what can I do for you."

I smile and say, "First off, I need the body of Suehad Fasaid ready for transport to a government morgue for autopsy. A court order will be delivered to you within the hour. In the meantime, I need her body immediately segregated and copies of all her hospital records. The court order will also include a request for the personnel records of all employees, a patient list for the past three weeks, all private doctors who have patients at this hospital, a list of vendors, and any and all records of visitors." I pause and add, "I'll need this information by tomorrow morning."

Ms. Mann nods and says, "I'm not happy about this, Agent Booker, especially on such short notice, but I will obey any lawful court order."

"Thank you," I say. "Just know that it's very important and I do appreciate your help."

On my way to the cafeteria, I call Tony and give him the abridged version of Suehad's death. I ask that he secure the court order within the hour."

"Anything else?" Tony asks. "Maybe you want me to realign the solar system. I've got five minutes to spare."

I tease, "You don't want me calling the Director and diming you out now, do you?"

"I'll have the court order ready to go at the U.S. Attorney's office. Have someone pick it up and serve it."

I hang up and am about to enter the hospital cafeteria when suddenly the hairs on the back of my neck bristle. I suddenly remember that Suehad's car had mysteriously disappeared after the accident. I half trot back to Ms. Mann's office and bypass the receptionist. The hospital administrator seems surprised as I enter her door minus a knock.

"Sorry for the interruption," I say. "But I need you to call the hospital morgue and tell them I'm on my way. Where is it located?"

"We don't have a morgue per se. We *do* have a temporary holding area in our basement that can accommodate up to ten bodies for a few days. This need arises occasionally when the deceased or their family are from out of town and require a few days to make arrangements."

"Call down there and alert them on who I am and will be there in a minute."

She nods and grabs the phone as I head toward a stairway and run down four flights of stairs to the basement.

After a few wrong turns into confusing hallway mazes I ask a custodian where the bodies are stored. He points to a door and I half run toward a door marked 'Employees Only."

An elderly gentleman in a lab coat looks at me and says, "You must be the FBI agent."

"That would be me sir," I respond. "And I'm looking for the body of Suehad Fasaid."

"Well she is no longer here."

"Well where the hell is she?"

"The funeral home people picked her up."

"*What* funeral home people?"

The man checks a log and holds it up for me to see. He says, "Right here. Cunningham Funeral Home in Berea. Left about half hour ago."

CHAPTER 42

"It's not what you look at that matters, it's what you see."
— Henry David Thoreau

I call Sgt. Shoulders and ask him to get to the Cleveland Clinic pronto. I'll assign Tommy to lead the investigation into Suehad's death and body snatch. The problem is that this type of investigation requires numerous interviews, painstaking review of hospital surveillance cameras, hospital logs, personnel files, additional subpoenas, and hundreds of other time-consuming details as yet unknown.

Agent 36 is busy and Kopka and his *plan* are up to bat. I can call Tony and have him gather a gaggle of agents from other divisions, but we'd lose a day or two that can make all the difference in the investigative world. I need bodies and I need them now.

"Supervisor Michaels speaking."

I asked that Peggy put me through to Michaels minus any identity to avoid gamesmanship by the immature asshole.

"Matt," I begin. "It's John Booker. I am calling to take you up on your offer to assist me in this case.

"I knew you'd eventually need *my* help."

I take a deep breath and resist any caustic comeback. "Matt. I'll need five agents from the task force and Peggy."

I provide an explanation of why I need the manpower and what they'll be doing. "Peggy," I justify, "will be busy typing subpoenas, court orders, and reports."

When I conclude my explanation Boy Wonder actually whines, "Well, I don't know if I can spare that manpower. You already took Gwen. Let me get back to you after I study caseloads and how I can reassign leads. But Peggy is out of the question; she does all my work and is invaluable to me."

I actually bite my lip. Blood trickles down my chin and if this meeting had occurred in person, I probably would have pummeled Michaels to near death. Instead I say, "I understand."

My next call is to the Director of the FBI. Mr. McKissock provided me his personal cell phone number and promised immediate access day or night. The Director is true to his word as he answers before the third ring. "John," he says enthusiastically. "Great work on the Indian Nuclear Plant, great work."

"Thanks." I reply. "But I'm calling because I need something and I need it ten minutes ago."

"Name it."

I quickly describe Michaels's history and remind him of Boy Wonder's role in the Idaho incident. There is no need to embellish Michael's arrogant and egotistical antics as an FBI supervisor. The Director listens quietly and at the conclusion of my diatribe says, "You will have as many agents or other personnel that this case requires immediately. I'll call you back in five minutes."

I would like to confess a minor pang of shame for breaking the unspoken rule of diming out a fellow agent but my only emotion is a perverse pleasure. Michaels has no business being in command.

My phone rings and caller ID indicates the top G-Man. "John."

The Director begins pleasantly. "Supervisory Agent Michaels won't be able to help you.

My brain attempts to process this information. Did it mean that even the Director couldn't move Boy Wonder off his throne?

The Director clarifies his statement with, "Michaels has been transferred to the Dothon, Alabama office to conduct research on the migratory bird act, which as you know, is one of our most important violations."

So the head guy has a sense of humor and is fucking with me. Touché, McKissock. I chuckle along with his satirical comment and commiserate with, "Yeah, I personally feel that my FBI career is lacking since I never worked that particular violation."

The Director continues with, "I promoted Special Agent Bruce Gombar as acting supervisor of the task force and personally spoke with him. He promised to provide you with *whatever* you may need."

"I appreciate the quick action," I say and can't help but add, "You *really* need to reevaluate your management program, Mr. Director. There are too many guys like Michaels obstructing guys like me."

McKissock laughs and says, "Well, when this case is over I just may promote *you*, John."

"Thanks, but no thanks. I don't play well with others in an enclosed environment."

"Anything else I can do?"

"No sir."

"Well then, go get 'em, Tiger."

I have never been one to require any accolades or verbal cheerleading to do my job. I feel comfortable being an FBI agent and with all the duties that job entails. In other words, I *know* how to do my job so butt out.

The function of supervisors, in my humble opinion, is that of an enabler. So when the Director asked, '*Anything else I can do?*' he was enabling me to be successful by offering his assistance. The new Bureau supervisors offer equal parts of criticism, condemnation, and finger pointing, but *little* actual help. I understand their oversight responsibilities but many in management are too busy covering their ass to care about cases. They put their careers ahead of our mission, which is to simply put the bad guys in jail.

Tommy Shoulders arrives at the hospital a mere ten minutes before Bruce, S.W.A.T. Boy and the remainder of the task force. We hold an impromptu briefing in the lobby. I make it clear to Bruce that Tommy Shoulders is in charge of this investigation, and he is to support him in any way possible. We discuss details around Suehad's death and steps to find her body. Shoulders is already assigning leads to the agents as I say my goodbye. As I about to leave, Bruce asks to speak to me privately.

"Word is that you got Michaels shipped to Alabama to count wild birds," Bruce whispers.

Since I don't have time to indulge in Bureau gossip, I simply nod my head and say, "Bruce, you'll be a good supervisor. Take care of the troops and don't get in their way."

He smiles and says, "*Sure* you didn't go to an Ivy League school?"

I find Gwen and Kopka back at our office. They both express their condolences over Suehad and we discuss the distinct possibility that terrorists had murdered Suehad and disposed of her body. We have no *proof* of murder but rather everything points to a stroke caused by the massive injuries sustained in the auto accident that was *no* accident.

"Talk to me, Gwen. Did you get Mansur to arrange his departure?"

Agent 36 sits on the desk, still decked out in her lawyer garb. She is equal parts fashion model, tomboy, and prom queen. She says, "Mansur is scheduled to leave Burke Lakefront airport tomorrow afternoon at three."

"What's his mood?"

"Well as I suspected, when I informed him of the judge's order he said that he was sorry to leave his wife behind but he must get back to Cairo immediately."

"Did he say why?"

"Not directly, but it seemed important, like he was on the clock. And one more thing." Gwen concludes, "Dr. Astler was right about Mansur. He is a coward and would sell out his mother or father to save his own skin. He'll be on that plane tomorrow."

"That's very interesting Gwen," I say.

"What's interesting?"

"The part about selling out his mother and *father*," I muse. "Because phase two of my plan is for Mansur to do *exactly* that."

"What?" Gwen wonders.

"I'll share the details when and *if* Captain Kopka is successful on phase one." I turn to Kopka and announce, "The ball is now officially in your court."

Kopka smiles and simply says, "We *are* the Cleveland Police Department."

It's been a long day with many twists and turns. Tomorrow promises to be even more intense and unpredictable. I check in with Tommy Shoulders who updates me on his investigation. Not surprisingly, Cunningham Funeral Home had a hearse stolen two hours prior to Suehad's abrupt departure from the basement of the Cleveland Clinic. The team is in the process of gathering the hospital surveillance film from several hundred cameras and interviewing Suehad's direct care staff. It will be a long night.

My instincts are to head over to the hospital and help in the investigation but my lack of sleep and consequent fatigue has reduced me to a near vegetative state. I decide to go home, see my family, and sleep in my own bed.

Lorri and Nikki are in near shock as I stroll into the kitchen from the side door. I've had a few conversations with my wife and daughter over the past few days but nothing of substance. I called them immediately when the district attorney dropped all drug charges and then again when I arrived in Cleveland.

I give both my girls a big hug and can feel tears roll down my cheek. As we pull away, I notice Nikki sniffling and Lorri dabbing her eyes. I'd put my family through sheer hell with months of moodiness and irrational anger fueled by the prospect of being jobless *and* imprisoned indefinitely.

The shame of being indicted, for any citizen, is both embarrassing and frightening, but to a law enforcement officer it is emotionally devastating. Our sense of right and wrong is sharp and defined. I considered suicide but am not sure how seriously. My thoughts went as far as how I would off myself. Most cops swallow their pistol but that never appealed to me. I also vetoed jumping off anything high, cutting my wrists, or hanging. Too violent.

An overdose of pills appealed to me but then I thought about Nikki and suicide was off the table. I visualized her finding me lifeless and attempting to wake me. I'd always been her strong and invincible dad who could slay dragons and make scraped knees feel better. So whenever the suicide demons crawled into my cranium, I'd feel Nikki's disappointment.

We sit at the dinner table as a family. The talk is light and inconsequential, with no mention of terrorist, drug cases, or bird flu.

As I enter the bedroom, Lorriis decked out in some flimsy lingerie. In the law enforcement world this is considered a clue. Normally my beautiful wife is sporting neck high flannel pajamas with an army of pillows vertically running down her demilitarized zone. I am totally exhausted but my meat puppet has its own agenda. We make wild passionate love reenacting moves from our college days. Evidently I was in better shape back at Slippery Rock because I awoke the next morning with an aching muscle pull. As I limp to the coffee pot, I seem to recall attempting a modified back flip during an especially passionate moment. Back in college, I had perfected that particular move.

I grab some coffee and several Advil. Today is critical in determining the success or failure of our case. If Kopka's plan misfires my backup strategy is basically duct tape and a Brooklyn psychic. As I am pouring my second cup of java Nikki shuffles into the kitchen and says, "Morning pops, pour me one."

I grab her Brad Pitt coffee mug and fill it to the brim. We sit in silence waiting for the connection between coffee and brain.

Finally Nikki wonders, "So, is everything alright in your world, Pops?"

I smile enjoying the way my daughter turns a phrase and uses our language. I say, "My world is your world, and it's pretty darn good right now."

"That's good to hear 'cause I actually went to church and prayed for you and mom."

Her words stike a sensitive chord so I asked, "Why both mom and me?"

Nikki sips her coffee searching for the right sentiment. She says, "Well Pops, you are a tough Marine and macho FBI agent who eats bad guys for lunch. So I never worry about your *physical* safety because you can handle yourself. But you and mom have always been a team and I worry that if you guys split, you would fall apart *emotionally*."

"Wow," I say. "Am I *that* fragile?"

"No offense, Pops, but she's the glue and without her you'd come apart like a cheap watch."

I hug my daughter and assure her that "Well, we're both good. We just had a minor blip on the marital radar but it's all smooth now."

Nikki gives me a shit-eating grin and says, "I know."

"Well, I want you to stop worrying about us, okay?"

She smiles again and offers, "I already have."

"That's good honey," I say. "So our little talk was good."

"Yea, but it had nothing to do with our talk," Nikki now barely holding back a giggle.

"What convinced you then?"

She looks me square in the eye and says, "All that noise last night coming from your bedroom."

Nikki is chuckling as she leaves the kitchen. I'm speechless and embarrassed but also good knowing that my daughter feels loved and secure. But I make a vow to *never* be the cause of my daughter feeling vulnerable as long as I breathe air.

My phone is chirping as I maneuver north on I-71. It is almost nine, which is a late start for such an important day. Agent 36 announces that Kopka has been humming in the office. The big Croatian cop is definitely *not* a hummer so this development is either a good or bad sign. His mysterious plan is a game changer either way it breaks. I tell Gwen to use all her womanly guile to extract some information from the Captain.

"Now how far should I go?" Gwen wonders.

"Well, you may have to take one for the team," I say. "I would feel a whole lot better if I knew the plan had a chance of working. We have no idea what happens if it goes bad. Am I putting the team at physical risk, do we have the right equipment, do we need some outside help, is it legal? Hell, we don't even know if he *has* a plan."

"Well," Gwen taunts, "I'll just sweet talk him since he reminds me of my dad. And if that fails, I'll arm wrestle him for the information."

"Good strategy," I agree. "No man can resist a woman with big biceps."

My three cohorts are present when I arrive with a quick apology for my late arrival. Detective Shoulders stares at his watch and says, "Actually it's a bit early for a Fed."

I look at my watch and counter with, "Just in time for a coffee break."

Tommy briefs us on his investigation into Suehad's murder and disappearance. "We got squat."

"Nothing with the surveillance photos, no suspicious people working in ICU, anything on the visitor logs, anything at all?"

"Well, initial background checks on the entire ICU unit produced some minor bullshit arrests and four bankruptcies. We still have a few hundred interviews left but nothing's jumping off the sheet."

"Anything stick in your gut?" I ask.

"Well the orderly is a mutt. Typical ghetto trash with a pea brain. He definitely is not the master mind of any terrorist organization but the guy had access to Suehad and motive."

"Motive?" Gwen asks.

"Yeah," Tommy explains. "The guy had people chasing him for cash and enjoyed playing with guns and drugs."

"I like your thinking, Tommy," I say. "Full-court press his ass."

The group discusses a variety of potential leads concerning the visitors log and the funeral home. I head to the coffee pot followed closely by Agent 36. She pours herself a cup of coffee and whispers, "I got Kopka to open up about his plan."

"No shit," I say. "I never thought you'd break him. How'd you get him to talk?"

"Well," she explains, "I told you he reminds me of my dad, so I just whined and nagged him. It *always* works."

"It usually does. What'd you find out?"

Gwen leans closer and says, "Captain Kopka promised me that the plan poses no physical risk, we won't need any outside help or special equipment and he's almost positive that it'll work."

"But did he tell you exactly what the plan was?"

"No," Gwen dismisses my question. "But he did answer all your questions."

"So did he say anything about the legality of his plan?

"He did," Gwen volunteers.

"And what exactly did he say."

"He said, '*You don't wanna know.*'"

Tommy Shoulders screams, "No fucking way!"

Both Gwen and I turn in time to see Tommy speaking on his cell phone.

As we reach the table Tommy tells his caller, "I'll be right there."

"What was that all about?" I ask.

"Our fuckin' orderly," he explains. "The gun toting drug dealing bankrupt asshole."

"What about him?" I ask. 'Did he take a powder? Is he on the run?"

Tommy looks at me and says, "No, but he *is* dead."

CHAPTER 43

"I'm a slow walker but I never walk back."
— Abraham Lincoln

Shoulders will conduct a thorough investigation into this orderly's life but it will be in vain. Whatever drugs or money he was paid will be long gone except for the heroin needle still dangling from his skinny dead arm. Though the overdose scenario is a repeat of Chief Justice Williams mugging gone bad, it has no loose ends. It will not lead us any closer to the terrorists.

I look at my watch and realize that it is almost time for Mansur to catch his flight to Cairo. I turn to Captain Kopka and say, "Ray, you're on. Do you need Tommy or can he work the Suehad end?"

Kopka smiles and says nonchalantly, "No, Tommy needs to get to the crime scene and do his stuff."

Shoulders leaves the office with the disclaimer of, "Hey, Ray. You and I've been through ten years of working the streets. If you need me, I got your back."

Kopka says seriously, "Naw, Tommy, this Mansur thing is a piece of cake, but if I need you, I'll call."

Shoulders makes me promise to call him as soon as Mansur is gone. He confides in me that he has no idea of Kopka's plan, but assures me that *whatever* it is, *it will work.*

Thumper is back in his cell with Mansur to gauge his mood and perhaps gain some last minute intel.

"So Ray," I say. "Where do you want Gwen and I during your *plan?*"

Ray seems to give my question some thought and finally responds with, "Here's how it'll go down. Gwen stays here. The airport will call me as soon as the plane lands. I instructed two Cleveland coppers to wait for my call before they take Mansur from his cell and to the airport. I'll go in my car and you follow me. That's it."

I challenge him by saying, "I don't mind some creativity and fly by the seat of your pants operation but you need to at least let me know some very basic things."

"Shoot," Kopka says calmly.

"Do we need an S.W.A.T. team?"

"No."

"Will I be involved in the operation?"

"Yes."

"How?"

"Mostly observing."

"Observing what?"

"The plan."

"What will I see by observing?"

"The plan working."

"Where will I be observing from?"

Kopka gets downright gabby and explains, "Mansur arrives with my two coppers in a black and white, they escort Mansur on board his plane. I check passports, flight plan, manifest and licenses. You are parked by the plane. Wait ten minutes and then board the plane."

"So *that's* your fucking plan?"

"Yep."

I lock eyes with the big Croatian. He is asking me to take him at his word. I announce, "It sounds like a great fucking plan to me."

Gwen smiles and adds, "I *always* loved your plan, *whatever* it is, but *now* I've got one concern."

Kopka nods and says, "I'm listening."

"You know I love you, *Dad*. But, if I even *think* you're keeping me in the office to protect your little helpless girl, I will personally drop kick your fucking balls into that fat gut."

The big police captain laughs and responds with, "I'd never piss you off, daughter. Mostly because I value your friendship *but* I also value my balls."

Kopka's phone rings; he looks our way and simply says, "Showtime."

The distance between the Justice Center and Burke Lakefront Airport is less than a mile. As I follow Kopka's unmarked police car I strangely experience a sense of calm. When faced with some crisis my Sicilian mother would say, Que sera, sera, which translated means, *'What will be, will be.'*

That about sums up my sentiments as we enter the most critical stage. I say aloud, "What will be, will *fucking* be."

Kopka pulls up to a jet with Arabic markings. The side door is opened and I observe at least one pilot sitting in the left seat. Kopka exits his car and strolls up the steps and into the cockpit. I check my watch for the ten-minute countdown.

I notice the pilot rise and walk back toward the cabin. Eight minutes pass and a marked police car arrives, stopping some twenty feet from my car. I see Mansur in the back seat and two uniformed officers in the front. One cop gets out and makes a call on his cell phone.

I wait my ten minutes, exit the car and head toward the plane. As I make my way on the tarmac I notice that Mansur is being escorted toward the plane in handcuffs.

He actually nods at me as if we are old friends bumping into each other at the grocery store. I give a half-hearted head bob in return and curse Kopka since I have no idea if I'm the good cop or the bad one. Perhaps I should give Mansur my evil eye or maybe a fraternal slap in the back and a happy bon voyage.

I make the decision to board before Mansur just in case Kopka wants to give me a *'heads up,'* on some last minute strategy. But Kopka merely smiles a shit-eating grin my way and stays mute.

Kopka instructs the uniformed cop to, "Uncuff him and you can go."

The cop joins his partner on the tarmac and they leave the airport. Mansur stares at Kopka but says nothing. The good police captain calls the two pilots into the coach section of the luxurious private jet. We stand in a semi-circle, all awaiting some sign from Kopka.

He finally says, "Gentlemen, just a few routine procedures before you take off. Just like last time, I'd like to see your pilot's license, flight plan, visa and passports and your airworthiness certificate."

The two Egyptian pilots nod and wander off to gather the requested paperwork. Mansur can't help himself and tells Kopka, "My attorney is suing you and your Zionist police department."

Kopka smiles and answers, "That's nice."

Mansur ratchets up his bravado with, "You will be ruined. I will take your home and job."

"That's also nice."

The two pilots return with a handful of papers and hand them to Kopka. I notice that he *pretends* to inspect each document thoroughly but in fact his eyes are erratically scanning the papers. He will later confess to me that he has no idea on how to read a flight plan or air worthiness certificate.

He milks the inspection process for several minutes and finally pronounces, "All your papers seem to be in order."

Mansur and his two pilots seem to take a deep sigh of relief and their shoulders relax.

Mansur is practically sipping the champagne being chilled in a bucket of ice sitting on the nearby table. He waits a moment and says to Kopka, "I will see you in court, now leave my plane."

"I'm practically gone but I am required to ask a few exit questions."

Mansur's face is a cross between anger and fear.

"Ask your questions quickly and leave," Mansur says with a false bravado.

Ray turns to the pilot and says, "Who owns this plane?"

"Mr. El-Quadir, sir."

Kopka turns to Mansur and says, "That'd be you right?"

"Yes, yes." Mansur is impatient. "My corporation owns this plane."

"And what is the nature of your corporation?" Kopka asks.

"I am in the import/export business."

"And what exactly is it that you import and export?"

"A variety of items." Mansur now guarded. "Items such as artwork, gems, and even electronic goods."

"Is that all?"

Mansur angrily says, "Stop your games and allow me to return to a civilized nation."

Kopka gives Mansur a smirk and says, "Do you import and export drugs?"

"What!" Mansur incredulous. "Your own country is infested with drugs. Your children consume them as if they were milk. Muslims bodies are temples for purity as Allah commanded. You insult me with that question, now get off my plane."

"So," Kopka calmly concludes. "The fact that this is *your* plane presents me with a serious problem."

"And what is this problem?" Mansur demands.

Kopka takes three steps toward the bar area and opens a cabinet. He says, "During my routine inspection of this plane I came across something very interesting. Import/export businesses are often used as fronts to import and export drugs."

The big Croatian cop reaches inside the cabinet and pulls out a shopping bag with Arabic markings. He places the bag on the table and extracts five rectangular packages secured with duct tape and announces to no one in particular, "I believe what we have right here on *your* plane is five kilograms of cocaine."

CHAPTER 44

"Everyone has a plan until they get punched in the mouth."
— Mike Tyson

Okay, so the drugs look familiar, but dope is often packaged similarly and secured by duct tape. Am I sensing that Kopka's plan *never* included Mansur leaving Cleveland. Yep. Did the thought cross my mind that Mansur's five kilos of coke was in fact *my* five kilos of coke, which originally was *the* terrorists' five kilos of coke? Yep. Was I morally offended by this maneuver? Nope, in fact the words *sheer fucking genius* come to mind.

I suppose my lack of outrage speaks volumes about my *own* ethics but at this very moment I feel only sheer admiration by the simple complexity of Kopka's plan. It accomplished a goal, nobody is hurt, and in a manner of speaking, justice is served.

Mansur did not take his round trip ticket back to jail with calm or stateliness. "You fucking infidels will die; you will die a slow death," was one of his many editorial asides. Kopka has this shit-eating grin on his craggy mug as Mansur threatens him with everything from bombing to beheading.

After depositing Mansur back in the grey bar hotel, Agent 36, Kopka, and I reconvene back in our office. I am careful not to put

Kopka in a position to have to confirm or deny how five kilos of cocaine *appeared* on Mansur's plane.

"Well," I say with an amusing inflection in my voice, "that all worked out well."

I provide Gwen the broad brushstroke of the airport happenings, but she insists on the minute details such as, "And what did the pilot say?" followed by, "And what did you say?" and "Was the plane nice inside?"

She looks at Kopka and asks, "So what made you look in the cabinet, did you suspect Mansur was into drugs?"

Ray gives a cryptic, "Yep."

I interrupt her inquisition. "We need to be able to use this unexpected good fortune to our advantage."

Kopka smiles and says nonchalantly, "I believe that the federal penalty for five K's of coke is a mandatory 20 with a 10 kicker for the airport."

I look at Agent 36 and say, "I do believe the good captain is correct."

Gwen begins spouting out the federal sentencing guidelines. "Mansur is looking at a long vacation, but is it enough time for him to give up a group of international killers?"

"Dr. Astler's profile says it is. Mansur will roll big time."

I meet Kopka's eyes and recognize the brilliance of his plan. Our Mansur mantra all along had been that he wouldn't cooperate *unless* he was seriously motivated. Thirty years is some pretty serious shit.

Kopka laughs and hoists his size twelves on the desk. "Hey, daughter." He says. "Can you figure out why I wanted you to stay in the office?"

It suddenly registers and Gwen punches Kopka, "I'm his attorney and will be the one to officially inform Mansur that he has limited options."

Kopka observes, "We still may have a problem even if he rolls. It'll take us days or weeks to follow up on any worthwhile information he gives, so once we leave Cleveland, how do we keep him from calling half of Egypt and warning them to beat feet?"

"I got that covered," I say. "And, it doesn't even involve cutting his tongue out."

"You want to share?" Agent 36 taunts.

"Not at this time. Let's get his gums moving first." I remind the team, "Remember the profile provided by the Behavioral Science Unit? Mansur is a classic bully who will submit to power and authority. Mansur *must* believe that he will spend the rest of his life in an American hell hole prison."

"Then what?" Gwen wonders.

"I will make him an offer he *can't* refuse."

Gwen's visit with Mansur is short and sweet. She is all business and warns, "Proving your innocence will be difficult. The FBI has entered the case and you're now looking at federal time."

"I hear from the prison underground that I am facing many years in your prison system."

Gwen performs an award-winning dramatic pause and speaks in a somber voice, "I'm afraid that they're correct. The amount of drugs on your plane requires a mandatory minimum sentence of thirty years."

Mansur slumps further in his chair and seems on the verge of tears. "There was an FBI agent on the plane who has been seeing my wife. He may be behind this whole affair to get me out of the way."

"This only complicates your case unless you have some proof that those packages were not your drugs."

"So what do we do?" Mansur asks dejectedly.

"I'll meet with the federal prosecutor and see what we can work out."

He gains a minimum of composure and confides, "I have access to a great deal of money. Can we pay off the big cop?"

"Normally I would have no problem with that course of action, but now the FBI is involved. Captain Kopka would probably just take the money, but you are about to be indicted by a *federal* grand jury and they don't play around. If I even insinuate 'bribe' I'll be disbarred and jailed."

"Contact my embassy," Mansur insists. "They will demand justice and contact your president."

Agent 36 acts as though this is a grand idea and says, "That just may work. I hadn't thought about political pressure. I'll get right on it."

Mansur nods his head in affirmation and offers, "My government will make them pay for this."

"But," Gwen says bursting his bubble, "that process will take years and in the meantime you'll be incarcerated and," she continues while going for the jugular, "given your crime and being Muslim, they will place you in a Level One facility."

Mansur's eyes get wide as he works up the courage to ask, "What is this Level One?"

Gwen shakes her head and with a grave expression explains, "Level One facilities are where the murderers and rapists reside. They employ the most sadistic guards and the conditions are horrible. Unsanitary, cold, with no regard for your religious diet needs, and you will be subject to racial cruelty on a daily basis."

Mansur is speechless so Gwen continues. "I'll leave you now so I can contact your embassy and the prosecutor. Will you consider a guilty plea?"

"What are my chances if we go to trial?"

"Not good."

"I will never plea to thirty years. At my age it is the same as a death sentence."

"Well," Gwen says with just a tint of hope in her voice. "Maybe there *is* something that can help you. That FBI man who is hitting on your wife ... he's involved in this case somehow and is probably the *only* person who can save you."

The seed is planted and now it is time to water. When Mansur asks how Booker can help, Gwen rises and heads for the door. Just as she is about to walk out the door, she turns back to Mansur and says, "Do *whatever* he wants."

Back at the office Agent 36 briefs us on her meeting. "Are you positive he used the word, *access?*" I push Gwen.

"Positive. His exact words were, 'I have *access* to a great deal of money, can we pay off the big cop?'"

Kopka laughs and adds, "I'm open. How much we talking about?"

"What's our next move?" Gwen wonders.

I use my best Marlon Brando voice and say, "I'm gonna make him an offer that he can't refuse."

CHAPTER 45

"Whether you think you can or think you can't, you're right."
— Henry Ford

I arrive at the Justice Center at seven somewhat bushed. I left the Center near midnight after a strategy session with Gwen and Ray. My meeting with Mansur is for all the marbles so it is critical that I play our encounter with just the right balance. Mansur must absolutely believe that I am his *only* hope but I also have to make his betrayal seem palatable.

We finally agree on my interrogation demeanor and I head home. As I am departing the Justice Center I overhear Agent 36 ask Kopka, "Know any places that serve up a *Coma?*"

"What the fuck is a *Coma?*"

They are almost out of hearing range but I *think* Gwen answers with, "Four or five of those babies and you're *in* a coma."

I shout out to them, "We gotta an early start tomorrow."

The two never acknowledge my warning but Agent 36 may have wagged her middle finger my way.

Early in the morning Agent 36 and Kopka stroll into the office. The fact that they arrive together can be chalked up to a timing coincidence. They look like shit and Kopka being people savvy immediately says, "Don't fucking get any ideas; Gwen crashed on my couch."

Even hung over Gwen can't pass on a softball pitch tossed her way and says, "But I did wake up naked and sore."

Kopka laughs but wants to assure me that nothing unseemly happened and says, "My girlfriend lives with me."

Gwen is incorrigible and adds, "So we had a threesome. Tried to find a circus midget but it was late."

"And I went home, had a hamburger and played with the dog. If you two party animals are able, let's get this party going."

It's show time and I head to the jail. I instruct Kopka to get rid of the two officers who normally stand outside. Mansur will feel less vulnerable minus prying eyes. As I enter the interview room he actually rises. I smile inwardly taking this gesture as a sign of respect and in keeping with his psychological profile.

My demeanor is all business as I take a seat opposite him and stare. I wait for Mansur to speak. This subtle interrogation technique will indicate someone that is anxious, fearful, *or* subservient. Mansur blinks first.

He asks, "How is Suehad?"

His question indicates that he is attempting to build rapport, which is also consistent with Dr. Astler's profile. Rapport is just a fancy word for brownnosing.

Alerting him to Suehad's murder has no upside so I tell him that she is recovering nicely.

I have been conducting these types of interviews for decades and am aware of their predictable path. As soon as the suspects realize that you're asking them to betray friends or family their first instinct is refusal. If your hammer over them is not ample enough, they will lawyer up.

But *if* they are facing the end of their life as they know it, they will either cooperate *or* conduct damage control in their brain while *pretending* to cooperate. In other words, they'll toss a load of insignificant bullshit your way. The bullshit option presents problems and is time-consuming. Mansur is both totally exhausted and a psychological shock. His inability to think clearly is to my advantage. It's like studying for an exam when exhausted. You keep reading the same paragraph repeatedly but not comprehending a word. The brain recedes toward a more primitive stage with sleep *or* survival as your most critical impulse.

"So Mansur," I ask. "How are you holding up?"

He leans forward placing his elbows on the metal desk and speaks in a whisper, "I have been beat up for the past two days by my cell mate. He hits me for no reason."

I almost smile but give Mansur my most disgusted look and say, "I don't give a shit about you getting your ass kicked."

Mansur looks both surprised and injured by my demeanor. I say, "I'm busy, let's get down to business. Your attorney says that you wanted to speak with me."

"She describes my case as hopeless and predicts I will spend the remainder of my days in an American prison."

"She's right," I confirm. "And I'll make sure that it's some dump. I'll put the word out that you're a terrorist that had some involvement in 9/11. The prisoners will put one jar of Vaseline in your mouth and one in your ass. They'll make you grow tits and you'll be passed around like a stuffed pig.

Mansur is speechless. *Did I go too far?* I think.

He regains some composure and says. "My attorney said that I may be able to resolve this grave matter by speaking with you."

"She's right."

"Well, I may be able to point you to some smugglers who deal with my company. They are importing cheap electronic imitations from China and selling them to warehouse operations in California."

I bang my hand violently on the desk. Mansur jumps a foot in the air and visibly cringes. He stares at me with wild frightened eyes.

"Do not insult me and, do *not* waste my time," I hiss. I rise and begin to leave saying, "Have fun tonight with your little pajama party."

Mansur jumps up and grabs my arm. I stare at his hand until he releases his grip.

"Please don't go," he pleas. "What is it that you want? I am willing to help you in any manner that I can."

I stare him in the eye and warn, "Here's the rules. I ask a question and you give an answer. But I must caution you that some of the questions that I ask, I *already* know the answer, so, one lie and I walk. One lie and you will rot in prison." I pause and ask, "Do you understand me?"

Mansur nods but I emphasize. "I want to hear you say the words, Now do you *understand* me!"

"Yes."

"Does your corporation deal with the North Korean government?"

"Yes, but it is legal to do so in Egypt."

I realize that this is going to be like pulling teeth with Mansur deflecting, minimizing, justifying, and qualifying each answer.

"Is your father an imam in Cairo?"

"Yes, a very religious man, as am I."

"Now I want you to take a moment before you answer this next question. If you lie to me, I will leave and you will be raped and brutalized for the remainder of your life. I *need* the truth."

Mansur is nodding his head like a bobble doll. I'm hopeful he does the right thing but it could go either way, so I add. "If you answer me truthfully, you will walk out of here a free man."

I realize that I am fibbing but all's fair in love and war.

"And I can go back to Cairo?"

"Tomorrow."

"Can I bring Suehad with me?"

"Yes." I say and think, "*If we can find her body.*"

"Do you know, or are you aware, of a group of a Muslim terrorist cell operating in concert with the North Koreans?"

I know the answer to my question before Mansur opens his mouth. His eyes are as big as saucers. He is attempting to balance his survival against a major betrayal. His words are measured and he walks the line between deceit and truth.

Mansur says, "I believe that I have heard of such a group."

"I am going to count to five," I say calmly. "To allow you the opportunity to clarify your response. I will *not* play verbal gymnastics with you Mansur. Last chance."

I begin to count and when I get to 4 I rise and head toward the door.

Mansur quietly acknowledges, "I know this group."

I sit back down and ask, "*How* do you know them?"

Mansur lowers his head and it all comes out. In dribs and drabs at first and finally the dam breaks. And when Mansur has told me all, after he has betrayed his family, friends and religion, he quietly begins sobbing. I feel zero sympathy and it takes all my composure not to crush his head on the desk. This religious hypocrite is part of a conspiracy that kills Americans. My precious daughter Nikki could have died from bird flu because Mansur was both ideologically fucked up *and* greedy.

It takes several hours for me to write up a legible statement that contains sufficient facts that can be corroborated. Mansur discusses the North Korean bills of lading along with the physical description and name of the bogus businessman who over pays for Mansur's goods. He probably downplayed the amount of money flowing between Mansur and his father, but it was still significant. My best guesstimate is somewhere north of 40 million dollars over the past decade.

I spend a fair amount of time reviewing Mansur's bank accounts paying particular detail to current balances, routing and account numbers, and bank locations. Many of the bank accounts are located in non-Muslim countries like Belize. These tax havens will not cooperate with the United States government so I demand that Mansur sign a power of attorney naming yours truly as executor. I purposely exclude this information from the formal statement as the seed of a plan roots in my brain.

Although the signed sworn statement will never be entered into evidence in a court of law, it may prove critical in proving to our President that this grand conspiracy exists and that the United States of America is the target.

On one hand, I am elated that I have confirmed the existence of a super terrorist cell exist being supported by the North Koreans. But even after Mansur has spilled his guts, I still have no idea on *how* to stop them.

CHAPTER 46

"What doesn't kill you, will still fuck you up"
                                        — Dick Vercauteran

"Hey Sully, how's it going?"

"Getting too old for this shit. You?"

"How many years has it been?"

"Too long."

"Sometimes it seems like yesterday."

"And sometimes, like a million years ago."

"Congratulations on the promotion. One of our guys sent me an email."

"Colonel James T. Sullivan *does* have a ring to it."

"The Marine Corps is stingy with their rank, you should be proud."

"If you hadn't been a rocket and bullet magnet, you'd be a General by now."

"I need a big favor."

"Anything for you Booker. I owe you for saving my ass outside Baghdad."

"If you have any reservations just say no and this conversation never happened."

"Quit the civilian disclaimer bullshit."

"Okay. All you gotta do is pass the word to the general population."

"Is that it?" Colonel Sullivan chuckles. "And *I* thought, you were going to ask me to kill someone."

"I am."

CHAPTER 47

"You talking to me!"

— Taxi Driver

On the way back to office I stop for a cup of coffee and make two phone calls. My first call is to CIA Deputy Director John Burke. He had previously provided me his personal cell number with the promise, "Anything you need, call me."

"Hello Director Burke," I begin. "Remember when I asked if you had a trusted asset in Cairo?"

"Clearly," Burke confirms. "We have the best asset in the business in the Cairo area."

"Can you give them a call and ..."

My next call is to my former roommate and the Assistant Director of the FBI.

Tony answers his cell phone and says, "A little birdie told me that you had a very important meeting today. How'd it go?"

I laugh and say, "I pretty much figure that Gwen is your birdie. What'd you do, promise her a promotion?"

"Promised her that if she keeps me informed, she will be my personal assistant. I never bought your *plausible deniability* bullshit so I needed a pair of eyes and ears to make sure you didn't get too far off track."

"Gwen's got eyes, ears, and a fabulous pair of boobies, you pervert." I laugh and say, "I need a favor."

"Shoot."

I explain that it is vital that Mansur be transferred immediately to the Marine Base at Guantanamo Bay and placed in the prison population with the rest of the radical Muslim terrorists."

"That should present no problem," Tony assures me. "I already have him designated as an enemy combatant per your request and Ms. Lewis can call the President and expedite his travel."

"The sooner the better," I say. "I've got him on ice for a day, but it's critical to the case that he's in Cuba tomorrow."

"The Director has his plane on standby *just* for my roomie. I'll call Ms. Lewis as soon as I hang up. The plane can be in Cleveland by tomorrow morning."

"The Director's plane is for *my* group," I clarify. "Mansur will need separate transportation."

Tony laughs and laments, "So you want *two* planes. Can I ask where *your* group is headed or should I wait for Gwen to inform me?"

"Cairo."

"You can't just fucking jet off to Cairo and run wild." Tony agitated. "We *have* to notify our ambassador. Egypt is critical to the entire balance of power in the area. As an FBI agent you represent our government and can start a fucking war if you pull your Rambo shit."

"You worry too much," I respond. "I've got it covered and besides, no one will know we're there."

"And just how long do you think you'll *remain* anonymous? As soon as you begin poking around the populace, the police *and* army will scoop up your group and there ain't no due process in Egypt."

"We're going undercover as tourists. They've got plenty Americans and Europeans roaming the streets in Tommy Bahamas shirts," I say. "So quit the Aunt Rita over protective act. We'll wear our seatbelts and drink our milk."

"The Director ordered me to assist you in any way possible, and I will but John, this going to Egypt is some serious business with some serious consequences." Tony pauses and offers, "I wasn't going to tell you because we haven't confirmed it."

"Confirmed *what?*" My interest peaked.

"Just yesterday Bobbie Geary intercepted a communication originating from the same region in North Korea as the rest of the pertinent intercepts. Not good roomie, not good. The words were, *HOLIDAY IN ONE MONTH, BRING SUITCASE.*"

I haven't been playing the Jeopardy game in a while," I say. "So just tell me what the fuck is going on."

"Remember when the Soviet Union collapsed?"

"Of course President Reagan kicked Gorbachev's ass."

"Well the down side of that collapse was that before they held elections and pretended to be a democratic society they lost a chunk of their nuclear arsenal."

"Lost," I interject. "How can you *lose* nuclear bombs?"

Tony explains that in the 1970s the KGB developed a nuclear suitcase bomb. In 1988, General Alexander Lebed, of the Russian Security Council confirmed that he could only locate 48 out of the 132 suitcase sized nuclear devices. The missing 1 kiloton weapons are especially dangerous because they can be transported by a single person and kill one to two million people if detonated in a large city. Tony concludes with, "The Russians have no idea where 82 nuclear suitcase bombs are."

"Wait a minute," I challenge. "The intercept *can't* be referring to a nuclear bomb, because that goes against their total game plan. Remember, their genius is that none of the disasters can be tied to a deliberate attack. They all appear to be accidents, natural disasters, or acts of God. Why would they show their ass now?"

"Think about what would happen if a nuclear device exploded in New York City."

"The United States would act in kind and kick ass."

"Who's ass?"

The way he framed his question alerted me that the answer is not as obvious as I think. "Well," I say. "We'd do an investigation and find out who's responsible. But," I conclude. "We already *know* who's behind it."

"Knowing and proving are two different things." Tony pauses and asks. "Russia was the only country who developed the suitcase nuclear bomb, so who's the likely suspect if a suitcase bomb detonates in America?"

"But," I protest. "What probably happened is that North Korea either provided the Muslims the bomb or the money to buy the bomb."

"*Probably,*" Tony concedes. "But if two million New Yorkers are killed by a Russian nuclear bomb who do you think we will go after?"

Tony's logic hits home. "Fucking ingenious bastards," I mutter and add, "The American public and Congress will force the President's hand in striking back at Russia."

Tony agrees with, "The terrorists drag us into a limited nuclear war with Russia and just sit back and watch."

"*But* we now *have* proof that North Korea has been secretly funding Muslim candidates in the U.S. and that those same shell corporations are funneling money through Mansur to the Muslims."

"I meet three times a day with the FBI and CIA Director, the National Security Advisor, Ms. Lewis and the President. The bottom line is that the President will give North Korea an ultimatum *if* you can identify the Muslim terrorist cell. He'll warn North Korea that if the Statue of Liberty so much as stubs her toe, their entire nation will be reduced to ashes."

"Why can't he just do that now?"

"Because," Tony explains, "without proving the Muslim end of this conspiracy, all we've got is North Korea funding political candidates overpaying Mansur for counterfeit iPads, neither of which justifies nuking a few million citizens."

"But Mansur provided a sworn statement that his North Korean money *is* used by the Muslim terrorists to kill Americans."

"Mansur's statement is hearsay since he's never even *met* the terrorists. He's a third party idiot being manipulated by his daddy. Mansur is just a *bag* man at this point."

We are silent as the reality of the situation settles in my brain. "Okay," I mutter with a weary and resigned voice. "I'll find the maggot Muslim terrorists but we both know that the kind of proof you want is impossible to get. I can't bring them to justice in a US *or* Egyptian courtroom and I probably can't get a taped confession."

"Look roomie," Tony says, "Just verify they're a living breathing entity with direct ties to the North Koreans. Give me something I can take to the President."

"So I'm on the clock with that *clock* attached to a nuclear fuckin' bomb."

I enter our makeshift office and the entire team is present. They actually freeze, like characters in a movie after hitting the pause button on a VCR. Fred remains in his orange jump suit and Gwen in a pink sweat suit. My initial thought is what a hideous clash of colors followed by *do I tell my team that millions of Americans are dependent on us to find a ticking nuclear bomb within the next four weeks?* Perhaps not, since it will accomplish nothing but put additional pressure on an already stressed group.

Tommy Shoulders says, *"Well,* did the asshole roll?"

My smile provides them the answer but they want the details.

"It was like pulling teeth at first," I say. "But the bottom line is that Mansur is the bag man between the Cairo terrorists and the North Korean government."

"Does Mansur deal directly with the North Korean government?" Gwen asks.

"No, but the wall between his contact in Korea and the government is real thin. An alleged businessman who buys goods from Mansur and overpays."

"I'm not totally getting this," Shoulders comments.

I explain, "Say some shell company in North Korea orders a thousand widgets from Mansur's Cairo corporation. He delivers some worthless shit to Korea and gets paid millions of dollars. There's a paper trail and all seems kosher. Mansur then funnels the cash to the Cairo terrorists and takes a commission."

Thumper jumps in with, "So did maggot face cough up some names on his North Korean contact?"

"He did and that information, along with identifying all their shell corporations, will be used to *convince* the North Korean government that we have the goods on their entire conspiracy."

"I see a major hole in the timing of all this," Kopka observes. "You told Mansur he can head back to Egypt while we are in the middle of this operation. And unless we kill him, once he has access to a phone, then we can end up as mummies in some Egyptian tomb."

"I have no intention of allowing that to happen," I assure Kopka. "And I also have no intention of *personally* harming Mansur to prevent him from talking. You asked us to trust you and I'm asking the same thing. I got that angle covered."

"What'd you find out about the Cairo terrorists?" Kopka says to change the subject. "Are they connected to al-Qaeda or the Muslim Brotherhood? Because if we go to all the trouble of eliminating that particular cell, then some other camel jockey can just get in their saddle."

"That's a possibility," I concede. "But Mansur *swears* that the Cairo group consists of four members who have totally insulated themselves from all terrorist cells or any other affiliated Muslim extremists. They are virtually invisible and not on *any* radical radar screen. They realize that they're way ahead of the terror game with North Korea as their partners so they have no need to fraternize with local cells."

"You mean to tell me that even their relatives and friends don't realize they're into bad shit?" Kopka says.

"Supposedly they're good family men who use Mansur's corporation as a front to justify a salary and their travel. That's the reason they're so lethal." I explain. "They correctly figured that such a small group reduces their exposure to infiltration." I pause and emphasize that "Our bottom line is that we have to eliminate *both* ends of this conspiracy or we're just having a circle jerk.

Shoulders asks if Mansur coughed up the names and location of the Cairo terrorists.

I shake my head. "No, but he told us who can."

"Who?" Agent 36 wonders.

"His father," I say then add. "Mansur has never personally met the terrorists and his father has never met the North Koreans. It's a clever way to insulate each group. Mansur receives money from North Korea in a supposed legitimate business deal. He'll deliver the money to daddy who then passes the money along to the terrorists." I pause and conclude with, "Mansur is positive that his father will *never* betray them."

Agent 36 seems to be offering an editorial opinion and says, "So we essentially got squat. Daddy evidently didn't give his balls to Mansur. His son is a punk who would sell his soul, but how in the world can we get his father to talk?"

"I agree that it isn't the home run we were hoping for." I concede. "But there's another wrinkle that we may be able to exploit. Mansur is expected to deliver three million dollars the day after tomorrow."

"Okay," Kopka says back on point. "What's our next move?"

"Our next move is to pack sun tan lotion and enough clothes for a few weeks."

"So we finally get a boondoggle on the government arm," Gwen being facetious. "So is it Jamaica, Tahiti, or Bermuda? Should I bring my string bikini or we going topless?"

"That's a lovely visual," I say. "But you'd be better served to bring your gun and lots of ammo." I pause for effect. "Tomorrow morning we're heading to Cairo, Egypt."

This is the first time since we've gathered as a task force that I can recall absolute silence.

Tommy Shoulders finally utters, "Holy fuck. Can we see the pyramids?"

"We may not have the time, Tommy," I say and caution, "and it is absolutely critical that you do not bring *any* identification in your name. No badges, cop T-shirts, FBI pens, or any other item that connects you to law enforcement. Undercover IDs will be furnished on the plane and there'll be plenty of time to get comfortable with your new identities."

I turn toward Agent 36 and say, "Call Mo and alert him that the Director's plane is coming to Cleveland in the morning. Tell him to be on it and to bring clothes that will blend into the streets of Cairo."

"Who's Mo?"

"Special Agent Mohammed Askari," I remind her. "Our Egyptian linguist and cultural expert."

"That cute little Egyptian agent we met in D.C.," She laughs. "He looks fifteen and has never been in the field. You sure you want me to call him?"

"Yep. We'll need his expertise if we have *any* hope to stop these bastards."

Agent 36 puts a damper on our party by saying. "But realistically, we're back to square one with the same problems. Mansur's daddy is our *only* connection to the terrorists and he definitely ain't talking. We'll be on a foreign and hostile soil, have a language problem, and don't have the time or ability to profile or panic Mansur's father."

Thumper piles on with, "Gwen's right. This guy's a cleric who doesn't trust anyone *including* his own son. And *we* can't trust the Egyptian government. Our target has nothing to lose since we've got no hammer over his head." Thumper pauses and looks directly at me, then concludes his evaluation with, "Am I on the money with this shit or am I missing something?"

"Unfortunately you've covered it all and though it may *appear* that we've hit a wall," I pause and smile at our little task force, "permit me to throw out some very ambitious initiatives."

Thumper laughs aloud and responds, "Booker, the last time you spewed that line of bullshit, I end up sharing a jail cell with some smelly Muslim."

"And, I'd like to award you an Academy Award for your psychotic performance, though some police detective with the initials of Tommy Shoulders called the part *'type casting.'*

Before Thumper can issue a threat of bodily harm to Shoulders, I alert the group to my *very ambitious initiatives.*

"Here's my plan."

CHAPTER 48

"Some have been thought brave because they were afraid to run away."
— Thomas Fuller

I promised Mansur his unconditional freedom if he'd spill the terrorist beans. There is plenty of motivation for Mansur to speak the truth, but there are also several thousand jolly fat guys who spend the entire month of December lying to little children. My final words to Mansur this morning were that it would take a day or two to square away the paperwork.

"After the judge signs the release form," I pledge, "a private government jet will fly you directly to Cairo."

Mansur was going to board a plane alright but it was not headed to Cairo. Do I feel bad about the deception? No. Fuck him and the camel he rode in with.

Additionally, if I cut the Muslim loose he'd warn our targets, which *now* include his father. Hell, I would warn *my* father had the roles been reversed, so I have to put him on ice for a few weeks. And the one place to make someone invisible is the detention facility at Guantanamo Bay.

Mo arrives at Burke Lakefront Airport in the Director's jet. Tony briefed the pilots that they would be at my disposal indefinitely and they should plan for international travel to the Middle East.

"Hey, Mo," I say. "Welcome to Cleveland."

Special Agent Mohammed Askari is smiling as he shakes my hand, "I am at your service, Agent Booker."

I nod my head at a black briefcase at Mo's side and ask, "Director Daniels give you that?"

"Yes sir. He said that it should never leave my person, and I was to personally hand it to you."

I take the briefcase but make no reference to its contents. We turn toward my car and without much preamble I get right to the point. "Ready for some covert ops?"

"I'm not certified to work undercover," Mo says dejectedly. "I never attended the school."

"I just certified you."

"You can do that?"

"Yep."

"Then I'm good to go, sir."

On the way to the jail, I furnish Mo a case update and alert him that he's about to monitor a phone call that can make or break the case.

"You have to use all your training and cultural expertise," I caution him.

"What will I be looking for?"

"The truth."

Mansur awaits us in the interview room. Captain Kopka reconfigured a telephone with a separate head set which allows Mo to scrutinize Mansur's call.

He gives a weak smile when he sees me and asks, "So when can I return home?"

"Soon," I lie. "But first we have to make a call."

"To who?" Mansur now guarded.

In keeping with Mansur's psychological profile I eliminate any wiggle room to protest or negotiate.

I say forcefully, "Here's what's going down today, Mansur. You are going to call your father and tell him that you're sending a trusted associate with the money." I nod toward Mo and clarify, "Mo here, is your trusted associate."

"That is *not* the way it is done," Mansur protests. "He has always dealt with me alone. My father will be very suspicious."

"Does your father know you're in Cleveland?"

"Yes. My father is aware of my affection for my wife."

"Then tell him Suehad's condition is critical and the doctors warn that she can pass at any moment."

Mansur finds some hidden resolve and warns me, "Calling my father is *not* part of our agreement!"

I stand and walk over to Mansur. He is seated and I lean down so my mouth is next to his left ear. In my most ominous voice I hiss, "Our deal is *anything* I tell you it is. Are we clear on *that*?"

Mansur has difficulty holding his tongue and I can practically sense his brain calculating some form of double cross. This is where Mo will earn his stripes. I require not only a linguist but also someone who is attuned with cultural subtleties and colloquial nuances.

I repeat, "Are we clear on that Mansur?"

Mansur nods minus any conviction and then attempts to regain my sympathy by changing the vibe with, "Thank you for transferring my violent cell mate. I slept well."

"Protecting you *was* part of our deal," I say to remind him who is in charge and that I can keep my word.

"My father may call the hospital to verify Suehad's condition," Mansur observes.

"That's fine," I say, "and they will tell him exactly what *you* tell him."

"If I make this call, when can I leave and what will happen to my father?"

I purposely soften my eyes and lean forward in a gesture of intimacy.

"I normally don't share investigative plans with civilians, but, you have been cooperative and I feel I owe you. You can leave tomorrow."

I pause and finish my sham with, "We have *no* intention of harming your father or placing him in jeopardy with the terrorists. We just need to *identify* the terrorists and we'll let the Egyptian government take over."

Mansur likes what he's hearing since he is fully aware that the Egyptian government supports *any* terrorist activity aimed at the U.S and will probably throw a parade for father and son. Mansur barely suppresses a smile and is suddenly cooperative. "I understand now," he says, "let's make the call."

Mo settles down next to Mansur and plugs his head set into the phone system. We conduct a test call to Kopka and Mo gives a thumbs up. Dirty little FBI secret is that our electronic equipment often malfunctions so it's important to conduct a dress rehearsal *prior* to the actual show.

For the next fifteen minutes Mansur and I verbally rehearse several possible conversational scenarios with verbal contingencies for each one.

When I feel comfortable that Mansur is *comfortable* with his mission, we dial daddy's number. My CIA contact already verified that the number Mansur provided me during the debriefing is indeed subscribed to Jabar El-Quadir, an Egyptian name meaning *brave.*

Evidently daddy has been awaiting this call because Mansur's voice alternates between frenetic staccato to hushed and defensive tones. Mo is furiously taking notes and concentrating on his mission. The call lasts for three minutes and forty-seven seconds, and Mansur actually sighs and his shoulders slump at its conclusion.

I'll debrief Mo later but it's important to hear Mansur's version and conclusions. He begins with, "My father is not happy."

I nod and say, "I gathered."

Mansur explains that his father has been frantic in his attempts to reach his son and scolded him for his lack of respect. The money is crucial to the fatwah and *must* be delivered to him without further delay.

"Did he buy your Suehad excuse?" I ask.

"I am not sure since my behavior is inconsistent and not in character."

"Well, is he expecting your personal courier with the money?"

"Again, he is not happy but has no choice since the money is critical to the war against the infidels."

"Where and when will the delivery take place?"

"In our mosque, tomorrow following afternoon prayers."

Mo and I spend the next two hours debriefing Mansur on the '*who, what, where, and when*s.

Who is Jabar El-Quadir and what makes him tick? Is he dangerous, paranoid or timid? Will he likely have counter-surveillance? Does he have weapons, any vices, a car?

What is Mo's backstory? Where and when did Mo meet Mansur? What is Mo's role in Mansur's business, and should Mo be privy to personal details of Mansur's life? What will Jabar do once he receives the money, will he go directly to a bank, and does he deal with all four terrorists or just a single contact?

Where is the location of the mosque; is it located in a residential or commercial area, where does his father live, will there be other individuals present during the transfer of money, where inside the mosque will the meeting take place?

When do these money transfers normally take place, are they on a regular schedule or tied to a specific event?

Mansur's replies are robotic and I can't get a read on the veracity of his answers. My gut tells me that the shock of prison, lack of sleep, and dietary problems has taken a collective toll. Mansur appears to have mentally surrendered and simply wants this nightmare to end.

As we are about to leave I drop the other shoe and say, "Mansur, I have one last question and it is absolutely crucial that you answer truthfully."

Mansur jerks his head toward me indicating that he grasps the seriousness of my tone.

"Before I walk out that door," I warn, "is there *anything* that you want to change, correct, add, or subtract from your statements?"

He nods and says, "May Allah rip the tongue from my mouth if I have uttered one untruth."

"Well," I conclude. "if anything goes south tomorrow Allah will be the *least* of your problems."

As Mo and I start for the door, Mansur calls out, "So I will leave soon for Cairo, Agent Booker?"

"Tomorrow," I lie as we exit the room. It is my last word ever uttered to Mansur.

As Mo and I stroll over to our Justice Center office he asks, "Aren't you concerned that Mansur may alert his father *before* we arrive in Cairo."

"What?"

Mo repeats his concern and I realize that I hadn't briefed him fully so I say, "He ain't going to Cairo anytime soon."

Mo digests the information and says, "Wow, you are totally believable when you're lying. I only hope that I can be as good as you."

"Thank you for that compliment," I chuckle. "You married?"

"No, sir."

"Well it would've helped your undercover work had you been married since lying is a staple of any good marriage."

CHAPTER 49

"The door of opportunity won't open unless you do some pushing."

Mo is anxious to give me his take on Mansur. There exists a multitude of false impressions among ethnicities. When I first took Lorri to my home in South Philly, she experienced culture shock. At the dinner table my new girlfriend was mute as my mom, dad, sister, aunts, uncles and a few neighbors animatedly discussed a wide variety of topics. They shouted over each other, pointed, gestured and made guttural sounds to emphasize a particular point.

My mother later asked, "What's matter with this girl, she no gotta tongue?"

I shrugged and said, "She's just a little shy, mom."

Lorri really isn't shy by nature but wondered, "Why is your family so angry?"

I patiently explained that Italians customarily communicate in a loud and animated way and added that "If they were *angry* then they'd be throwing stuff at each other."

Thus, I need Mo to give me his cultural take on Mansur. Were there any red flags in the communication between father and son? Were there any signs of deception in the information Mansur provided regarding the, who, what, where and when? Did Mansur afford his dad a subtle sign or warning?

Mo is silent as he shapes an opinion to my series of questions. He finally says, "In many ways, we Muslims reflect other cultures and ethnic groups. Some are liars, some thieves, but most are honest and ethical. One reason the West has difficulty in dealing with terrorists is that they cannot comprehend that *most* Muslims do not consider the slaughter of innocent Americans as wrong. It is *not* considered a criminal or evil act when Muslims engage in Jihad and kill Americans."

I interrupt him with, "How can they logically or morally defend that position?"

"Easily," Mo continues. "Because they are simply practicing their religion and abiding by the Koran thus fulfilling Allah's will. This teaching or indoctrination takes place at birth and continues through adulthood."

"But," I challenge, "The two brothers who planted bombs at the Boston Marathon had been practically raised in America and adapted to *our* culture. They were living the American dream with college scholarships, jobs, and the freedom to speak their minds."

"Actually," Mo says. "Dzhokhar and Tamerlan Tsarnaev are excellent examples of *my* argument. The brothers partook of the benefits of America but they could not rise above a *hatred* of America. Their brains were programmed and though most Muslims living in America may not directly take up arms you can rest assure that they did not feel sorrow or remorse when the Boston bombs exploded."

"But you didn't answer my question. Do you believe Mansur?"

"I believe *most* of what he said."

"And what part was he lying about?"

"I am not sure if it was lies or merely half-truths."

"Can you be a little bit more specific?"

"No, but we should be careful."

"Hey Mo," I say with a sarcastic bent. "We're about to fly covertly into a hostile nation to unearth a major terrorist cell and your advice is, '*be careful*.'"

Mo laughs and says, "Perhaps that was understated."

We plan to meet our CIA contact at nine tomorrow, Cairo time. This will allow us some nine hours to plan the transfer of the money to Jabar. I inform the FBI pilots of our time constraints and they calculate the flying time between Cleveland and Cairo as twelve hours and thirty minutes. Allowing for the five-hour time zone change, the pilots estimate that we need to leave Ohio no later than one today.

The group is packed and ready to go. Gwen sports dress sandals, tight white pedal pushers and a sleeveless blouse. She justifies her outfit with, "I checked the weather and it's hot in Cairo. Thumper is nattily attired in dress slacks and an expensive silk shirt. The two cops are in their standard fare of worn blue jeans and golf shirts with alligator logos. We will likely stand out as some developmentally disabled tour group from Duluth.

Our CIA contact has made arrangements for our plane to land at a private airport which eliminates custom inspections and allows us to transport weapons, ammunition and assorted secret squirrel shit.

We take off and head east. Our pilot in command is a former Navy top gun, FBI special agent Bob Dupuis. His co-pilot is a former Air Force B52 jockey, John Canley. We are in good hands and the pilot/agents have stocked the plane with an assortment of food and liquor. The mood is light and jovial as are most beginnings of long flights, but I know that the excitement will eventually burn off and we'll require sleep. Our little task force has been functioning on nervous adrenaline and we are reaching critical mass in the case.

Mo and I spend an hour reviewing his backstory until he is comfortable and can reply to my questions minus the slightest hesitation.

"How did you meet Mansur?" What's your position in his business? Where are you from? What did you do prior to …?"

The young agent is a quick learner and seems to have a talent for being a convincing impostor.

"Maybe it *is* time for me to get married," he laughs.

We eat hoagies and drink a few beers. The group is loose but there is a nervous anticipation. FBI agents have no authority to conduct operations on foreign soil minus that country's approval. Hell, Cleveland cops can't even conduct operations *outside* of Cleveland, yet we are headed to Cairo, Egypt to stalk super terrorists and are operating totally off the grid.

"I suggest we get some sleep," I say after our meal and a short operational brief. "We've got a big day tomorrow."

The inside of the plane is configured like a cozy family room with seats that recline horizontally. Captain Kopka and Detective Shoulders are snoring within a few minutes. Thumper bites the slumber dust next but Agent 36 and Mo are engaged in an animated discussion. Although they attempt to mute their voices, I gather the topic is the subservient role of women in Muslim society. Mo attempts to calmly explain the historical and religious rationale, but Gwen's repeated refrain of *'bullshit,'* is not conducive to any meaningful dialogue.

As I enter that opaque dimension between sleep and consciousness, my father appears. He was a tough Philadelphia police officer back in the Rizzo days when being a cop had some cache with the public. The cancer that ravaged his body reduced his once robust frame to a skeletal body but could not reduce his inner strength.

He smiles at me the way he did when he was about to make a point and says, "Are you doing okay, son?"

"Been a rough few months but things seem to be improving."

"Take better care of your family, John."

I feel the subtle stab of my father's disappointment and promise. "I'll do better, dad."

"And your work," he says. "Are you confident in your mission?"

"I am, Dad. It may not be perfect but it's better than doing nothing."

"Do good, John. Do good."

My dad's image fades and is replaced by a rocket propelled grenade slowly making its way directly at me. I can actually see the fins and attempt to run but my legs won't move. It hits and as I begin to feel the surge of pain, my body begins to shudder and I cry aloud. I open my eyes and see it is Thumper who is gently shaking me. He asks, "You okay, Johnny?"

I shake my head and mumble, "I'm okay, Thumper."

Thumper smiles, pats my shoulder and as he heads back to his seat says, "I'm right over there if you need me."

As I am attempting to calm myself back to sleep I hear Agent 36 ask, "You wanna cuddle Booker?"

I smile and answer with, "A minute ago I may have jumped at that offer."

"What happened a minute ago?" Gwen wonders.

"I promised my father that I'd be good."

CHAPTER 50

"I see dead people"
— The Sixth Sense

Our pilot, Bob Dupuis, awakes me around eight Cairo time. He informs me that we'll touch down in 58 minutes. The two pilots were issued covert pilot licenses and assorted identification cards to include library and credit cards. I open the Tony Daniels brief case that Mo delivered and hand John several additional documents. They include registration papers indicating ownership of the airplane to a U.S. corporation that sponsors tours.

I extract five scuffed and frayed wallets containing various alias identification papers for my task force. These documents will withstand the toughest scrutiny since the biographical information has been entered into computer data bases such as DMV and credit bureaus.

Quwaysina Airport is located close to Cairo. CIA Deputy Director Burke had greased the covert skids with stamped entry documents for both airplane and occupants.

Thumper is already awake and sipping on coffee. He smiles and says, "You sleep okay?"

The question concerns my noisy nightmare last night.

I nod and say, "Okay."

"I heard you saw some shit," Thumper says referring to my combat experiences.

"You can't go through life these days without seeing *some* shit."

"I suppose," Thumper agrees. "Because our world has turned to *shit*, but that's a discussion for another time."

A short man of an indeterminate age with pointy ears and wise eyes awaits us at the airport. He bows before our little group and announces, "My name is Anpu Astennu Minva. Most people call me Pu. I am your official tour guide." Pu resembles Yoda from the *Star Wars* trilogy.

My verification script requires me to answer with, "A pleasure to meet you, sir. We are very excited to tour your lovely country."

Pu bows again and says, "My *pleasure*, sir."

"What's our itinerary, Pu?"

"We have planned a grand tour of Egypt. Five days exploring Cairo and Alexandria, an overnight in Tripoli, and then a trip the pyramids."

Pu's location sequence proves him to be our CIA asset and just as I am about to acknowledge my recognition Tommy Shoulders says, "I always wanted to see the Pyramids."

I shoot Tommy a nasty glance for interrupting this bad scene from a *Get Smart* episode and tell Pu, "That sounds terrific. Let's get started."

We board a large van and Pu remains in his role as tour guide commenting on the history of Egypt. About forty-five minutes later we enter the outskirts of Cairo and maneuver through narrow crowded streets for another twenty minutes. Pu turns down an alley way barely wide enough for the van and stops at the back door of a three-story building.

The bottom floor is configured with one large room that reminds me of any travel agency office in Cleveland, Ohio. Posters of exotic Egyptian locations with chubby tourists teetering on camels litter the walls. There are four desks with papers strewn atop and a few plastic chairs along the walls. The front of the room reinforces the travel agency motif with a large glass window littered with more travel posters and beyond that window, a busy Cairo street.

The group follows Pu to the center of the room and stands in a semi-circle awaiting some signal to end the charade.

Pu turns and announces, "Mr. Burke sends his regards."

I clarify to the group that CIA Deputy Director John Burke has been our conduit in this most perilous part of the operation.

Pu explains that some thirty years ago a young CIA operations officer turned a young revolutionary and a funny thing happened. They became friends. It turned out that they had more in common than either believed possible, including a love for classical music, animals, and a core conviction of what constitutes good and evil. The CIA financed Pu's education at Oxford and provided him seed funds for this modest travel agency.

It proved a perfect CIA front operating in the most critical powder keg region of the world. Pu's tour guide backstopping permitted him to move around the country freely without suspicion. As the business grew, Pu gained status within the community as a successful businessman. He joined the local mosque and made modest tithes to his imam.

After a decade of cementing his cover, the donations increased and so did his position within the community. This newfound standing afforded him access to the movers and shakers that included *players* with alleged ties to al-Qaeda and The Muslim Brotherhood.

In many ways, religious extremists in the Middle East are no different than a Baptist zealot in Tulsa, Oklahoma. They will gently twist the arm of anyone in the congregation who has money. Pu was visited one day by a mosque member and in very circuitous manner was given an emotional pitch to use his money in a crusade against the infidels. With CIA financial backing, Pu became invaluable in providing information that thwarted many a terrorist plot.

I ask Pu directly, "So what do you know about this super-secret terrorist cell?"

Pu pauses. "Not much," he finally says. "Even the most radical extremists speak of this group in hushed and revered tones."

"But can the extremists confirm that this secret cell exists?" I press. "Are these guys flesh and blood?"

Pu gives us a Yoda-like smile and says, "They exist in much the same manner as Big Foot. Although there is no *proof* of their existence, there are individuals who swear they have met with this group, or have an associate who is a member. The group has taken on mythological proportions and are credited with the more vile terrorist attacks, whether deserved or not."

I interrupt Pu with a question, "Are you speaking of traditional terrorist activities such as bombings, or hijacking airlines, or is this group more clandestine in their terror?"

"I do not understand your question," Pu says.

"In the past six months," I explain, "America has experienced a major power outage, the bird flu, outrageous gas prices, the murder of a Chief Justice of the Supreme Court, and an assortment of other disasters that *appear* to be accidents and unrelated."

"So you speculate that this group could be orchestrating these misfortunes?"

"Yes."

Pu tilts his head in thought. "Existing jihadist cells do not possess the sophistication to conduct such complex operations. So it *would* take an exceptional group such as our ghosts...." Pu pauses as he rethinks his position. "*But*, minus financing and other resources, even this super cell could not conduct the terrorist acts you describe."

I ask, "If they *had* unlimited financing and *any* necessary technical support could they pull off the cataclysmic events I described?"

This time, Pu does not equivocate his answer. He says, "Then they are capable of much destruction."

Following that sobering prediction, we climb the stairs to the third floor, which is a modest apartment and Pu's living quarters. He offers us tea and as he boils water the group makes polite conversation.

Gwen tells Pu that she was accepted at Oxford but chose Yale law school instead. The two discuss a variety of topics as we drink our tea and munch on some local pastry. It seems that Agent 36 and Pu have made a connection based on their opinion of reincarnation. They are completely simpatico on the belief that after death we get to return to resolve our flaws.

Being Italian, I understand the bonding value of small social talk but there is a nuclear suitcase bomb lurking out there so I say, "First off Pu, we want to thank you for risking both your cover and your life."

Pu smiles and tells me, "Mr. Burke stressed that I am to assist you by any and all ways possible. That is a request that I am bound to honor."

I begin with a synopsis of the case up to the present. When I conclude my summary I look at Pu for a comment. His eyes are wide and he says, "Your scenario is both frightening and plausible. I had always feared that *some* extreme group would evolve from the more primitive terrorist techniques to this level. It is quite ingenious were it not so hideous."

"Tell us about the imam, Jabar El-Quadir."

Pu gives me a sly smile and offers, "So you have already made that connection." He explains that Jabar is the most powerful religious figure in Cairo. He is rumored to be the spiritual guide to a group of Muslim terrorists who are considered ghosts. "I have had limited conversations with Jabar at the mosque."

Pu pulls his cell phone from a pocket and taps a few keys. He hands me the phone and says, "A photo of Jabar." I pass the photo around to the group and comment that "Mansur's father resembles an angry black bear."

Pu stresses that unlike religious leaders in the West, Muslim clergy *encourage* the slaughter of the unbelievers since it is Allah's will. They are not bound by the ten commandment edict of "Thou shall not kill."

I outline our plan, which consists of Mo fronting as Mansur's money courier. We discuss the mosque location, and I ask Pu to draw a diagram of the inside rooms. Kopka wonders about the surrounding area concerning traffic patterns and potential areas to observe the mosque. Mo inquires if Jabar may search him or threaten him in some manner.

Pu's replies are thoughtful and incisive. He feels that Jabar will not engage Mo in small talk but is an impatient and brusque individual. "I do not feel that Mo is in imminent danger but you must expect him to be followed once he leaves the mosque. There is also a risk that Mo can be kidnapped once he leaves the mosque and tortured to confirm that he is indeed simply a courier."

Mo gulps but bravely says, "I would not talk."

I pat Mo playfully on his arm and assure him, "We'll have your back covered. No one's gonna torture you, unless it's Gwen asking you stupid questions."

I explain that Mo will be wearing a pair of glasses, which contain a micro transmitter. Standard undercover operational procedure dictates that the undercover and his team have a code word indicating that things have turned to shit. Pu's tour van will be in the area of the mosque during the money transfer and monitoring Mo's conversation with Jabar.

Thumper asks several questions about Mansur. He begins his inquiries with, "Excuse my language, Mr. Pu, but I spent a week with Jabar's son in a very enclosed area and I just can't imagine that *asshole* being involved with super terrorists."

Pu laughs aloud and agrees with, "Mansur was a source of embarrassment to his father as a child. He is basically a coward who uses his father's power to bully others."

"Is Mansur *capable* of being the money conduit between the North Korean government and his father?"

"Mansur does not lack intelligence," Pu states. "He is lacking in character and integrity. He is quite capable to follow the explicit orders of his father."

"Here's the rest of our plan," I tell Pu. "I need your input and feel free to tell us that we're full of camel dung."

Pu smiles and nods.

I clarify that Mo will deliver the Tony Daniels briefcase to Jabar in the mosque. He'll keep any conversation to a minimum and get in and out as quickly as possible. My roomie included the money in Egyptian currency with several bills embedded with a GPS microchip. Undercover FBI agents learned the hard way that sophisticated criminals will stay a step ahead of the law enforcement curve. It's no great secret that law enforcement hides electronic devices within articles such as brief cases, hence the embedded cash.

The end game of this entire exotic vacation is to follow the money to one or more of the secret terrorists. Then it gets kind of fuzzy after that. Although I don't require proof beyond a reasonable doubt, I need some strong evidence that the Muslim bogeymen are genuine.

Afternoon prayers generally conclude at five. That time frame allows our team approximately six hours to conduct a preliminary surveillance of the mosque, conduct tests on our electronic equipment, load our weapons, finalize plans for an emergency extraction, and *pray.*

I hadn't prayed in quite a while but my mind drifted back to first grade at Saint Thomas Aquinas when I first memorized the words to the Act of Contrition , "O my God, *I am heartily sorry for having offended thee, and I detest all my sins ...*"

At first I have no idea why my brain went instantly to *that* particular prayer and then I recall that the Act of Contrition is the prayer to cleanse your soul from all sin following confession.

Catholics desire to be in a state of grace when death is imminent.

CHAPTER 51

"Do one thing every day that scares you."
— Eleanor Roosevelt

The choreographed chaos of Cairo hits you like a ton of bricks. It is a wall of noise, snarl of traffic, cry of hawkers, and a blanket of exotic smells. Pu, Gwen, Tommy, and I board Pu's eight-seat tourist van and head toward the mosque.

Mo, Thumper, and Kopka will depart the travel agency once we are in position near the mosque.Our primary method of communication is satellite cell phones, which have been encrypted and are not subject to intercepts.We also have backup walkie-talkies also with encrypted frequencies, but with a limited range.

Cairo is the capital of Egypt, with a total population in excess of seventeen million people and one of the largest cities in both Africa and the Middle East. It is also the nineteenth largest city in the world, and among the world's most densely populated cities.

Located on the Nile River, Cairo is famous for its own history, preserved in the fabulous Islamic city and Coptic sites in Old Cairo.

We head toward the district of *Islamic Cairo*, the name commonly given to the core of medieval Cairo, a part of the city remarkably different from the modern Downtown district and the suburbs to the west

The Sayyidna al-Hussein Mosque is not accessible to non-Muslims. One of the most sacred Islamic sites in the country and the Middle East, the mosque hosts the shrine in which the grandson of Muhammed the Prophet is alleged to have been buried.

I plan this undercover operation using standard FBI covert techniques. The cover team of Thumper and Kopka will follow Mo to the target location. They visually hand him off to a second surveillance team who are stationary with an eye on the target location.

The stationary team will observe Mo enter the site and that's when things can get dicey. We'll depend on a transmitter to assure his safety while out of our direct view. But, if Mo utters our pre-determined emergency code word, then all covert bets are off and we storm the mosque.

We bantered about several suggestions regarding Mo's "*Oh shit*" word. The code has to be somewhat unique and hardly ever uttered, but distinct enough not to be confused with similar sounding words. Thumper threw out '*Mickey Mantle,*' Gwen recommended '*Zumba,*' and Captain Kopka proposed '*Siberia.*' It dawned upon me that if shit hits the fan and we need to extract Mo quickly, our code word need not be too fancy. I instruct Mo to simply holler '*HELP!*'

"Team one in position," I tell Thumper on the phone. Pu and I are located with a fixed stationary view at the front entrance to the mosque

Thumper, Mo, and Kopka hail a cab and head toward our location. They get within five city blocks and exit the cab. Mo goes it alone on foot with Thumper and Kopka discreetly following. Since none of us have been in Cairo till today we are not concerned with counter-surveillance at this stage of the operation. Mo is dressed in an eclectic combination of west meets east garb. It fits his backstory as an Egyptian Muslim who left the region to make some money.

I emphasized to Mo that "You ain't there to make friends, so get in and get out."

Mo nods but I know about the temptations that undercovers suffer when they come face to face with the enemy. Most feel a need to converse and build rapport with small talk. They fill in any silence with nervous babble that will *eventually* out them as counterfeit.

Thumper's voice alerts me to the fact that "Mo is in the area, do you have an eye?"

Pu's van has the requisite tour guide advertisements covering three sides of the van. It blends perfectly within the hectic and crowded streets of Cairo. I sit in the passenger seat and we are parked near the square with a view of the front entrance of the mosque. As Mo's transmitter enters our receiver's range I hear street noises and Mo humming. It's a nervous reaction to his situation but it also assists me in identifying him. Mo climbs about eight steps and pulls open a fifteen-feet-high door.

Agent 36 and Detective Shoulders, Team 2, are strolling near the rear area playing the happy western tourists exploring Cairo. Their assignment is to cover the exit to the back of the mosque.

"We have the eye," I alert our teams. "He is inside location."

Thumper and Kopka, Team 3, transition into a mobile foot surveillance team attempting to detect any *counter-surveillance* in the immediate area.

I can hear footsteps echoing on a tiled floor for about thirty seconds and then a sustained quiet. Almost a full moment passes which seems like an hour before the footsteps continue. Mo's utters a standard Arabic greeting and receives an identical reply.

Pu sits next to me with instructions to provide me the broad strokes of the conversation, breaking it down to the basics of, *good* or *problem*. He gives me a thumbs up and mouths "Jabar."

Jabar mumbles' something in a gruff tone and there is more echoing footsteps ending in a door being closed.

The imam begins the conversation with what sounds like a sermon. I may not understand one word of Arabic but I've been the focus of a bunch of lectures from nuns, priests, drill instructors, and my wife. I can recognize an ass chewing when I hear one. I look at Pu and he gives a shrug and says, "Jabar is angry at his son and Mo is taking the brunt in his absence."

Mo sounds apologetic and subservient which is consistent with his backstory and culture. An imam is a powerful individual within the Muslim community and their status transcends spiritual matters. A position similar to the capo of a mob family.

Jabar uses his silence as an intimidation tool. He eventually jabbers a short burst of what sounds like pig Latin and Pu alerts me to the fact that "Jabar is inquiring about the brief case."

"He knows what's inside, so why ask?"

Pu holds up a silencing finger at me and says, "Mo tells Jabar that he does not know the contents, but was instructed by Mansur to deliver it."

Mo evidently recalls our contingency for this exact storyline and according to Pu says, "Sir, I am a mere messenger for your son, who is *also* my employer. My instructions were to deliver this briefcase. I am not aware of its contents nor do I wish to know. I now desire to leave."

Jabar's tone is severe as he reacts to Mo's mild insubordination. An awkward silence ensues and our imagination runs the gamut by our inability to view the combatants.

The silence is broken by the shouts and screams of several new players. Pu can only babble, "This is not good."

"No shit."

I desperately need information to make a decision. If we rush into the mosque with guns blazing and discover some innocent reason for the loud voices then we blow the entire case. But if we ignore this unanticipated development then Mo can bite the big one.

While my brain runs through options I hear Mo, in perfect English, state "Do not point those guns at me."

CHAPTER 52

"Houston ... we have a problem."

—*Apollo 13*

"Stand by," I alert the surveillance teams. "We have party crashers."

Thumpers voice crackles over the phone, "We going in?"

"Negative," I emphasize. "We need more information. Stand by in close proximity to target location."

"Roger that."

I verbally toss out a variety of observations trying to wrap my brain around the situation.

"Well, he didn't give the panic word."

"But he spoke in English so maybe that *was* his call for help"

"Those guys have guns so he's in obvious danger."

"*But* maybe they're just bluffing and if we bust in there with guns blazing, Mo gets shot anyway and possibly several more of us."

Pu ignores my ramblings and concentrates on the dialogue inside the mosque.He finally says, "Please be quiet, I am attempting to assess the threat level."

I shut my yap and listen as Mo reverts back to the Arabic language. It appears that there are several intruders inside the room in addition to Jabar and Mo. There is persistent shouting as the men talk over each other in what sounds like an angry interrogation. Mo's voice remains calm as he appears to be countering a barrage of questions and accusations.

Pu turns to me and informs me, "They are accusing Mo of being a spy and are demanding to know who sent him. Mo is sticking to his cover story."

I press Pu. "Do we need to get in there?"

Pu waves a dismissive hand and says, "My feeling is that they are testing him and do not have proof to the contrary."

"*Why* do you think that, Pu?"

"Their accusations lack detail and specifics."

"I hope you're right, Pu. I promised that boy I'd cover his back."

"That *boy* is an FBI agent and a tough Egyptian," Pu says then adds in a softer tone. "This intimidation tactic is commonplace with Muslim extremists. But they will not risk hurting someone who can be of value to them and Mo has just handed them three million dollars."

Pu listens intently for a full minute and observes, "Our dilemma involves not knowing the extent of their brutality in determining Mo's true identity."

"What?" I ask.

Pu explains in a calm voice that "They are striking Mo and threatening him with a sword."

I cue my phone and alert both teams to be ready for extraction.

Both teams acknowledge the preparation order. Their innocent looking tourist bags include MP5 submachine guns. We had previously rehearsed our extraction plan using diagrams Pu supplied of the inside of the mosque.

Pu implores me, "Do not rush this action. Mo can handle their menace."

"I hope your right. Give me a running dialogue so I can make this decision."

"Yes," Pu responds as he concentrates intently on his mission.

All I can decipher is shouts, yells, and shrieks, but am unable to distinguish if any of them involve pain or are merely bluster. I must

JOHN LIGATO

trust Pu to make the extraction call due to his home team insights of the players' culture and tactics. Had this been the Italian Mafia, I'd be able to sense immediately their true intentions by listening to their voice inflection, words, and hidden meanings. But this is a much different culture and I am at the mercy of some guy who resembles Yoda that I met this morning.

"What's going on?" I ask.

"They have stripped Mo naked and are examining his clothes and wallet for wires."

"Did they take his glasses?" I ask, knowing that the transmitting device is secretly inside the frame. A quick inspection would not expose the listening device but the glasses could never withstand a more thorough scrutiny.

"Not sure," Pu answers. "They are also running his identification papers through contacts that have access to data bases."

"That should all check," I say feeling slightly better. "We backed up his identity to the hilt."

"Jabar has either left the room or he is being mute," Pu advises.

We have given Jabar the code name of *Daddy*. Both surveillance teams have a photo of Jabar so I transmit the instruction to, "Be on the lookout for Daddy. He may be leaving the mosque."

Both teams acknowledge with a "10-4."

My combat experience ingrained in my brain is that in crisis situations two basic scenarios unfold for the combatants. Either things slow down, and one can make sensible and judicious decisions, or speed up and the combatant enters survival mode. My instincts have always tilted toward action but that style has gotten my ass in worst jams. I am fighting my basic instinct to do *something*!

"Daddy exiting rear door," Gwen says on the phone line. "On foot heading westbound."

"Is he carrying anything?" I wonder.

"That's a 10-4. A large cloth-type bag over his shoulder. Do we follow?"

"Affirmative. Team two on Daddy. Team three, assume Team two's position near rear exit of mosque."

A multi-team surveillance makes it much easier to avoid detection. The agents can trade positions on the eye should one become *'hot.'* But I just reduced our team by one third and may need that manpower at the mosque if Mo requires extraction.

My decision to split the teams goes against any normal safety considerations given the circumstances. I now have two law enforcement officers with no legal jurisdiction operating in a hostile environment with a language barrier and no earthly idea of where they are. It is a tactical decision that can have dire circumstances. I realize that my decision is based more on gut feeling than standard operating procedures.

My self-reflection is interrupted by a loud scream. I recognize this agonizing wail having heard it many times on the battlefield. It is a cry of physical pain.

"What's going on, Pu?" I ask sharply.

"Standby," He replies as he leans forward gesturing closer to the audio.

Pu is intent and motionless for several moments as I fidget and feel absolutely neutered. My feelings alternate between a frontal charge on the mosque to a *'wait and see.'*

Agent 36 reports, "Daddy still westbound on foot. Approximately five blocks from mosque."

"10-4," I say automatically, then remember to check the GPS monitor to see if Jabar is transporting the money. In all the excitement, I totally forgot that the money has separate transmitters woven within the fabric of the bills. A green triangular shape blip is moving westbound in the same direction Agent 36 described.

Pu monitors the transmitter, while I communicate with Gwen and Tommy and use the limited range walkie-talkies for Thumper and Kopka. It's actually your standard law enforcement three-ring circus surveillance.

Pu turns to me and says, "We may have a development."

He turns back toward the receiver and listens intently. "They seem to be satisfied with his identity."

"Are they releasing him?"

"It appears so."

I cue the walkie-talkie and say, "Team three, Mo may be exiting target location."

Our plan calls for Mo to exit the mosque and proceed on foot for at least a mile before hailing a cab. Thumper and Kopka will discreetly follow to detect any counter-surveillance. Mo will direct the cab in a circuitous route to clean his destination, which is a fruit stand three blocks from the travel agency. If all seems kosher, Thumper and Kopka will meet Mo at the fruit stand and all three will separately stroll back to Pu's building.

"We've got a problem," Thumper says. "Stand by."

A moment elapses before Thumper says in a strained voice. "Mo is injured. We need to get him to a hospital. Recommend you stay put rather than burn Pu. Injuries don't seem life-threatening but he's lost a lot blood."

"How you getting him to a hospital?"

"Cab," Thumper replies. "Kopka already hailed one down. We can keep our cover as concerned tourists helping out. Stay put," Thumper says, now adamant.

"Roger that," I reluctantly say. "What is the extent of his injuries?"

"Stand by."

I hear voices and realize that I can overhear the conversation between Thumper, Kopka, and a very subdued Mo. This alerts me to the fact that Mo has somehow maintained his eyeglass transmitter.

Four minutes elapse and the frantic cab conversation conjures up so many bad scenarios that I can no longer contain myself. "What are the extent of his injuries?" I repeat.

Three additional minutes slide by with no response. Just as I am about to ask a third time, Thumper tells me, "He's been beaten badly and has cuts over his back, legs and stomach."

"What kind of cuts?"

"They appear to be sword cuts," Thumper says, then adds, "stand by. We are attempting to stop the bleeding."

I rationalize that they are in a cab headed to a hospital. The wounds, according to Thumper are *not* life-threatening and no cover was burnt. All told, I can live with these consequences.

I can hear Captain Kopka ask Mo repeatedly, "Where do you think it is? Is it back at the mosque? Where can it be?"

"Thumper," I scream. "What the hell is going on? What did Mo leave back at the mosque?"

In a weary but resigned voice Thumper informs me that "They cut off his fucking finger."

CHAPTER 53

"Leave the gun but take the cannoli"
— The Godfather

Pu and I sit quietly in his van for a moment, trying to digest the two separate tracks that this runaway train is travelling. I fight the urge to rush to Mo's side and assure myself that his injuries are not life-threatening. There's a certain amount of guilt attached to that feeling since I was the one responsible for sending an untrained undercover into an international nest of trained killers.

But I rationalize that I can't do anything worthwhile at the hospital except pray and wait. There are more pressing considerations that need my immediate and undivided attention. Two members of my task force are tailing a subject who may be leading them to members of a super terrorist cell, but even more critical is neutralizing a nuclear bomb that can kill millions of Americans. Mo will have to wait.

I tell Gwen, "You can back off a little. We have an electronic connection with Daddy. He must be carrying the cash."

Agent 36 responds with, "Well, he isn't carrying the briefcase so he must've transferred the cash to this cloth sack."

Ten minutes later Gwen advises that "Daddy's entering a café."

"What's the name of the café?" I ask.

"Al Ammor," Gwen answers. "It's a small local joint."

"I know that café," Pu chimes in.

Gwen tells me that Tommy's checking out the back for a door.

Pu advises me that Al Ammor is a meeting place for influential peddlers in the nation's capital. Visitors include politicians, religious leaders, and rumors of individuals associated with terrorism. It is the Egyptian equivalent of Fryman's in Cleveland, and I *suppose* in every other town on earth.

Gwen transmits the message of, "Instructions?"

I ask Pu if it would be unusual for two American tourists to stroll into the café.

"Al Ammor does not normally attract westerners. They offer no menu selections other than local fare, Arabic is the only language spoken, and it is not up to the cleanliness standards expected by tourists."

"Is there a back door?" I ask Gwen.

"Negative. Tommy advises that the back area is a cluster fuck of windows, trash, and either cats or rats as big as cats."

"Set up somewhere with an eye on the entrance and I'll get back to you." I ask Pu, "Do you think that the members of the secret cell attacked Mo?"

"No," Pu answers. "They would never risk exposure for something as primitive as a physical attack. I believe that Jabar paid some local thugs to do the dirty work on Mo."

"I agree. So identifying them would not accomplish much in the bigger scheme of things."

"No."

While driving to the Al Ammor café, I call Thumper. It had been some forty-five minutes since we last communicated. Thumper answers and informs me "Mo is in surgery. That's all I know."

"Did he go into shock?" I ask. "Was he conscious?"

Thumper actually chuckles and says, "That is one tough boy. He felt bad that he cried out when they cut his finger off. Mo never gave us up after the punches, the kicks, the sword cuts, and even the amputation. Jabar finally told the attackers to give Mo his clothes and let him go.

"Call me immediately once you get word."

I smile, thinking back to my first meeting with Mo in FBI headquarters. We thought he was some college summer intern lost within the maze of hallways. He had spent his entire career inside the confines of the office and craved fieldwork. My gut instinct had been firm that Mo had big balls and would do the right thing. I am both surprised and awestruck by just how big those balls actually are. Could I withstand intense torture including loss of limb? Don't know for sure, but I do know that it took an incredible amount of courage.

Pu alerts me to the fact that "We are about to pass the café."

I ask Pu to do a drive by to acclimate me to the area. As we pass the café, I can see that the Al Ammor is a local dive with dirty windows and a coarse hand-painted sign. It is well lit and crowded.

We park west of the café. From this angle it is difficult to determine Al Ammor's door from the many doors and street chaos of pedestrian and motor traffic. The signal from our GPS monitor indicates that the money is stationary somewhere inside the café.

"Pu," I say. "Take a leisurely stroll past the café. No need to go inside, just see if you can spot Jabar with someone."

"Sure you don't me to go inside?" Pu asks. "I am local and would not stand out."

The Al Ammor café is the equivalent of an Italian social club where the same wise guys meet each day. If an unexpected lone male suddenly appears at the same time that a deal is going down that person is immediately suspect. It had taken Pu over a decade to solidify his cover and I couldn't risk his exposure.

"I'd rather you just walk by and glance inside."

Pu nods and exits the van walking toward the café.

I tell Gwen, "We are in the area, and Pu will be making a pass of the target location on foot."

Gwen answers, "We saw you go by."

354

"Well we didn't see *you* and it'd be hard to miss a tall blonde with big tits on this particular street."

Gwen laughs and says, "I've been walking around hunched over. The hunch hides my boobs and makes me shorter. And, I'm wearing a scarf on my head. Tommy and I are sitting in a sidewalk café located across the street. We've got a good eye on the entrance. What's the plan and how is Mo?"

"Mo is at the hospital. I'll let you know as soon as I hear something. If Jabar leaves, you and Tommy follow him and we'll stay put with the money."

"10-4," Gwen says. "We've got an eye on Pu."

Our van is parked some sixty yards from the café. With the heavy street traffic of vehicles and people, I intermittently lose sight of Pu. A full fifteen minutes elapse before Pu returns to the van.

He informs me, "Jabar is meeting with an individual at a back table. The man's age is early to mid-forties, clean shaven, and Egyptian."

"Anything else?" I ask.

"I could not linger at the window," Pu explains. "Several men were standing just inside and looking out."

"Any ideas?"

Pu squints in thought and asks, "Do you wish to retrieve the money?"

"I'm not worried about the money," I emphasize. "My *only* goal at this point is to somehow prove the existence of this cell of super terrorists."

"What constitutes proof for you?"

"Good question," I say then add. "The best proof would be to capture Jabar and the four terrorists, have them confess, and bring them to justice."

"That scenario is highly unlikely."

I nod my head in agreement. "So the next best thing would be to somehow document their existence."

"What form can this documentation take?"

"Well," I say while thinking of an answer, "it can be written, or even oral. But, if it's oral then it has to be from someone inside the conspiracy, and they would have to give me some facts that I can verify."

"But," Pu wonders, "if you don't kill or capture the terrorists why will they stop their activities?"

"Because the United States will cut off their access to cash, scientists, weapons, and all the other advantages that make them so devastating. They will be reduced to your garden variety zealots.

A moment of silence passes before Pu makes an observation. "The only member of the conspiracy that we can identify is Jabar."

And with that simple declaration a plan hatches in my brain. I ask Pu if he has another vehicle.

"Just a motorcycle. Why do you ask?"

I tell Pu, "I don't want your van burnt. It's tied to your cover." Pu smiles, walks to the back, and holds up several signs with images depicting plumbing objects. He tells me that "These signs are magnetic, and I can actually fix a toilet if required."

"Next question," I say, laughing. "Do you have access to a somewhat private location?"

"No such location exists within the confines of Cairo. But there is a CIA safe house just on the outskirts."

"Perfect," I say. "Here's some things I'll need. Nothing too complicated."

CHAPTER 54

"The brave don't live forever, but the cautious don't live at all."
— The Princess Diaries

Pu programs the address to the safe house into the GPS and then hails a cab, leaving me alone inside the van on a hectic Cairo street. I tell Gwen that I will be joining them at their location in a minute.

As I approach the outdoor café, on foot I can't help but notice that Agent 36 indeed has a scarf covering her head and *seems* slightly hunched forward. It is not a burka but does cover much of her hair with a few golden locks straggling from the sides.

I sit and notice two small coffee cups with a thick black substance resembling espresso but only thicker.

Gwen offers that "The menu is a bit of a confusing, but I'd recommend the stuffed fateer."

Tommy Shoulders chimes in with, "This koshari shit tastes like monkey puke."

I order a cup of the sludge coffee and say, "Here's the plan."

Like I said, my plan involves some creativity, some improvisation and an abundance of luck. I figure that we can always track the money and in fact rationalize that the café is not a final destination. I also figure that the terrorists aren't going to deposit the money in a bank, so I choose to wait, see, and *hope* that we can track the money later.

What we *can* do is become proactive in this investigation and quit being observers.

I am back inside the van situated behind the driver's seat. The right side of my brain is filled with doubt and fear, but the left side of my brain is screaming, '*you fucking pussy, do something, asshole.*'

I usually listen to the left side of my brain, which explains my current situation. My plan depends on timing and an Academy Award-winning performance by Gwen, my Agent 36.

"Daddy's exiting the café and heading back toward the mosque."

"Showtime," I say. "Is he carrying anything and is he on the same side of the street as the café?"

"No and yes," Gwen says.

"That corroborates the GPS signal, which indicates that the money is still inside the café."

I accelerate the van into the frenzy of Cairo traffic that includes everything from buses to rickshaw-like carts. I actually pass Jabar as he leisurely strolls down the street. I'm looking for a parking space on the north side of the avenue which will place Jabar some fifteen feet from the van as he strolls pass.

I find a spacious parking spot and advise Gwen, "In position. Approximately six blocks from the café."

"Be there in five."

I see Gwen fast walking down the street directly toward me. She tells me that Jabar and Tommy are about one block away.

"Ready?" I ask.

Gwen gives me a seductive smile and says, "Ready, Teddy."

I never could figure out what that meant but I *do* know that Agent 36 is one fantastic FBI agent. She strolls down the street in the mosque direction and pretends to be window shopping. I sit in my van with one eye on Gwen and one scanning my side mirror looking for Jabar. Gwen's body language alerts me that she has spotted Jabar. Agent 36 must time the encounter to coincide with Jabar's proximity to the van.

Gwen begins to stroll back toward my location and adjusts her gait to Jabar's progress. I notice that Tommy Shoulders has closed the gap behind Jabar to virtually a foot. All is in order but that means nothing in law enforcement.

Jabar is now less than twenty yards from the van, which is about the same distance as Gwen, both on a collision course. Ten yards till touchdown and Tommy moves even closer, holding an object in his right hand. The two Cleveland cops told me they were packing this particular item for the trip and my comment had been, "Don't see the need but it's your call."

Well, we now have a *desperate* need for a Taser.

Gwen is face to face with Jabar, separated by five feet of Cairo sidewalk. Jabar notices the tall westerner in the scarf but his Muslim arrogance toward women will not permit him to step aside. Gwen pretends to trip and plunges head first into Jabar's chest. She continues her descent to the ground while grasping his leg and making it impossible for him to scurry away. As Gwen slowly attempts to rise using Jabar for support, Tommy Shoulders joins the fray. While pretending to assist Gwen he discharges the Taser. A Taser works to disrupt the body's electrical pulses that are sent from the brain to the limbs. They send one to three milliamps, which temporarily paralyze the brain and the various muscles. The brain is confused and shuts down for a moment.

Jabar jerks violently and falls to the ground. I jump out of the van and pretend to examine him. I say to no one in particular, "Help me to get him in the van, I'll take him to the hospital."

Tommy, Gwen, and I half lift and half guide the massive Jabar into the side door of the van. He is not unconscious but basically incapable of any coordinated movement of his muscles. His incapacity will not last, so we move quickly. Gwen and Tommy frame Jabar on each side of the bench seat. Tommy cuffs Jabar's left wrist but is having difficulty joining the right side of Jabar's ample girth with his left wrist to lock the cuffs. Agent 36 grabs Jabar's shoulder and pushes toward Tommy. The three of them seem to be engaged in an amateur wrestling match. I say, "You guys look like a bad ménage a trois scene in a cheap porno."

I believe Shoulders mutters, "Fuck you," but I'm not sure. They finally cuff the imam, and then Gwen wraps her scarf around his eyes. Pu had switched the Garmin to the English language mode and a female computer voice is pleasantly directing me to turn left, turn right. A red arrow visually guides me along a green pathway toward our destination.

About ten minutes into the trip, Jabar regains the use of his limbs and raises his cuffed hands to remove the scarf. Tommy anticipated Jabar's recovery and Tasers him again.

I yell back, "Jesus, Tommy, we don't want to kill him. He may have a heart condition."

Tommy seems offended and informs me, "I put the Taser on low voltage, or whatever the hell this thing uses. He'll be okay."

Five minutes later the arrogant Muslim begins screaming at us and he once again reaches for the scarf, which covers his eyes, so Detective Shoulders Tasers him once again. Pu figured it will take us a good hour to reach the safe house and I'm starting to worry how many jolts this asshole can endure.

It turns out the answer is five jolts. So we now know that Jabar will not fold easily like his wussy son. I figure we'll have to step up our efforts and maybe get creative. Or, just maybe a sixteenth century technique will encourage him to move his fat lips.

CHAPTER 55

"Every now and then, you just gotta say, Fuck It!"
— Risky Business

We receive the good news that Mo is resting comfortably at the hospital. Though his wounds are not life-threatening, they *are* severe. The loss of his middle finger up to the second joint will probably reek more psychological than physical damage. Thumper relates to us how Mo handled his injuries with composure and courage. An hour after surgery Mo, held up his bandaged right hand with the missing middle finger and asked in his most serious voice, "Now how am I going to express my feelings in D.C. traffic?"

I desperately need Thumper and Kopka for any hope of carrying out our mission. "Can Mo be left alone?" I ask.

Thumper chuckles and replies with, "The boy will *not* be alone. Mo has a bunch of young cute nurses sniffing around him."

"Did the police come to question him?"

"Evidently getting carved up like a Thanksgiving turkey is not that unusual in Cairo. These doctors are much too busy patching people up to care."

"Good news," I say. "When we get out of this rodeo, I'm writing him up for the FBI Medal of Valor."

"I'll sign my name to that."

"Okay," I say back to business. "I need you and Captain Kopka. Here's where you need to be within the next hour."

I have no idea on Jabar's ability to understand English so I turn to Gwen and Tommy and inform them that "Mo is doing great, no problems."

Due to the circumstances, we violated a basic law enforcement rule when we snatched Jabar on the crowded Cairo sidewalk. Any law enforcement rookie knows that you should search the suspect immediately, but that wasn't an option.

I remind Tommy that Jabar needs a good pat down. "Secure his phone, wallet and anything else on his person."

The folks back at the FBI may be able to match phone numbers on his phone to one of the terrorists or decipher a piece of scrap paper with scribblings. We reach the safe house and at first glance it seems to afford us the privacy we require. The structure is surrounded by a wrought iron gate and sits in one of the few wooded areas I've seen since arriving in Egypt. Pu greets me at the door and asks, "I suspect it went well?"

"Yeah, Pu, it did."

He hands me a cloth hood and instructs me to, "Place this securely over his head. He will be in darkness but the hood is porous as you requested."

"Is everything in place?"

"Yes."

Tommy and Gwen maneuver Jabar up several steps into a large room with modest furniture. There are a few lamps sitting on end tables and a sofa. The cloth mask seems to envelop his head. Jabar appears compliant but still maintains a defiant posture and is muttering.

Pu whispers, "Jabar has threatened us with Allah's most severe revenge."

"And what's that?"

Pu smiles and informs me, "Allah calls for the disembowelment of the great unbelievers."

"No offense, Pu," I smile. "But after eating the food here, my bowels *need* to be disemboweled."

Pu directs us to the kitchen area and opens a louver door to a small pantry. It is an innocent looking area approximately five by six foot. There are food products on shelves and some mops and brooms hanging on hooks. He reaches under a shelf and pulls a hook upward, then sideways. The back wall opens and accesses a lower level windowless room.

"It is sound proof," Pu says referring to the room. We shuffle single file into the room. My first impression is an American 1970s finished basement with dark paneling and indirect lighting. The kind of place where teenagers played spin the bottle. Situated in the middle of the room is a ten-by-three-foot wooden board with leather restraints, and off in one corner is a mini jail cell.

As late as November 2005, water boarding was on the CIA's list of approved "enhanced interrogation techniques," intended for use against high-value terror suspects. It is no longer approved and definitely frowned upon by the bureaucrats. Since water boarding would violate several international laws, I needed to take the liability temperature of my team. I discussed the water boarding possibility on the plane and their comments didn't particularly indicate any strong opposition.

Thumper just smiled, Agent 36 wanted to know if we would torture her, and Detective Tommy Shoulders offered, "We do a lot worst shit than that back in Cleveland."

Captain Kopka chimed in with, "We *are* the Cleveland Police Department." Then added, "Why waste water, let's shoot him with a fuckin' arrow."

The arrow joke never seems to get old.

In a nutshell, water boarding makes a person feel like he is drowning. Their gag reflex kicks in as if they were choking on the water falling on his face. To my thinking, it is the perfect way to make someone talk. There is no physical damage, or genuine pain. I actually attempted to self-water board myself in the bathtub a month ago by tilting my head backwards and under the water. I think of myself as a Marine, a tough FBI guy who can withstand some serious discomfort. When the IED exploded, I remained calm and attempted to stop my own bleeding with direct pressure. I was scuba-certified and have held my breath for close to two minutes underwater.

But I lasted a grand total of *five seconds* in my simulated water boarding scenario. So either I *"ain't"* so tough or this enhanced interrogation technique is extremely effective.

Abu Zubaydah was Osama bin Laden's senior lieutenant and involved in every major terrorist plot carried out by al-Qaeda. He was also one of the planners of the September 11 attacks. After his capture, Abu's initial interrogation by the FBI produced nothing of value. That's when they decided to use enhanced interrogation techniques. My FBI classmate, John Hyler, was part of the team of interrogators who witnessed Abu *man up* to some serious suffering. John's *exact* words to me were, "That is *one* tough mother fucker."

First, they beat Abu Zubaydah, as authorized by the torture memo. Interrogators wrapped a towel around his neck and smashed him repeatedly into a wall. He was left confined in a tiny, pitch-dark box for hours; he was suspended naked from the ceiling, and he was not allowed to sleep for days on end. Abu never uttered one word.

But when they water boarded his ass, Abu began singing like a parakeet on speed. Water boarding has been around for centuries. It was a common interrogation technique during the Italian Inquisition of the 1500s.

I instruct Pu to, "Tell Jabar that we have *proof* of his involvement with the four-person terrorist cell operating out of Cairo."

The more specific facts we provide Jabar, the more he'll *believe* that we actually know. We throw in the Al Ammor café as the drop point and that his son Mansur is the North Korean bagman. At the mention of Mansur, Jabar becomes animated and spews out a tirade of fatherly love, "My son is responsible for this betrayal and he will suffer the wrath of Allah."

I give the big guy credit for immediately figuring out their leak, though Mansur would've also been my first choice for betrayal. Jabar's brain is also conducting damage control. He needs to determine just how much *we* know and how far we'll go to extract additional information. Jabar seems to be gaining his bravado back. After all, in his mind he is a powerful man and we are merely common thugs. His voice is gaining its usual authoritative arrogance so I need to bring him back to a terrified state.

I ask Tommy to give me his Taser and whisper, "Sure this thing is on low?"

Jabar is sitting in a chair and keeping up a steady dialogue of threats and demands from beneath the hood. I approach Pu and quietly ask him to tutor me on the Arabic words for "Your mother fucks pigs."

Pu smiles and rattles off some guttural sounds. I parrot the phrase until Pu is satisfied of my limited proficiency. I then approach Jabar who is still woofing away. I lean down and whisper into his ear, "*Your mother fucks pigs.*"

This great insult has the desired effect as Jabar strains at his restraints but before he can utter an angry syllable, I Taser him once again. I wait for the body contortions to subside and his breathing to become regular. Then, I lean down and once again whisper, "*Your mother fucks pigs.*" Jabar's immense body tenses so I Taser his fat ass once more.

The room becomes eerily silent as we wait for Jabar's brain to communicate with his muscles and become one big happy family. This last Taser application seems to have taken a toll on Jabar. His body requires almost fifteen minutes before it calms so I decide not to tempt fate by inadvertently killing our goose with the golden eggs. The original plan was to have Mo conduct the interrogation but he is currently unavailable. Our only remaining option is Pu. But Pu's previous conversations with Jabar at the mosque could compromise the identity of a major CIA asset.

It is Pu who resolves my dilemma. "We have neither the time nor resources to worry about my cover." Pu says solemnly. "I will interview Jabar. It is my destiny."

I nod my agreement and we begin the interrogation in earnest. I supply Pu the questions and he translates them into Arabic for Jabar.

"Are you aware of a terrorist cell operating out of Cairo?"

It is a relatively simple question requiring a relatively simple answer. Basically, it's a verbal polygraph since we already know the answer and are merely attempting to establish a base line.

Jabar's reply of "*no*" tells me that he has not been adequately motivated by the Taser to share even the most *basic* truths.

It's time for Jabar to go to the beach.

We strap Jabar to an inclined board, with his feet raised and his head lowered. Tommy and Gwen bind his arms and legs so he can't move, and rearrange his cloth hood. Since we can't see Jabar's face it is difficult to gauge his level of anxiety and fear. I would suspect that the imam may have deduced our intentions buthe probably had never experienced the sensation of drowning.

"Last chance, Jabar," Pu says on my prompt. Jabar suddenly becomes mute.

I pour water onto the cloth hood, which seeps through into Jabar's nose. You can close your mouth but need hands to close your nose. Jabar jerks his head violently in an attempt to avoid the water. I motion for Thumper to hold Jabar's head.

I look at Pu and say, "Let's try this again."

Just as I am about to simulate some more drowning on Jabar, he begins to excitedly scream and babble something. There's something in this particular rambling discourse which gets Pu attention.

I ask, "What's he want?"

"He wants us to immediately release him," Pu says.

"Oh really," I smirk. "And if we don't?"

"Then he will reveal my identity as a traitor to Allah."

"Do you mean what I think you mean?"

"I am afraid so," Pu says calmly. "He recognized my voice as Anpu Astennu Minva, the travel agent."

"I'm so sorry, Pu."

"Do not be. It was an acceptable risk and it is better that we know."

Everyone in the room understands the consequences of what just happened. Immediately following this operation, Pu will have to leave his home in Cairo and retire as an active covert asset for the CIA. There's no telling how many active CIA operations, field officers and assets have just been compromised.

Gwen approaches Pu and rests her hand on his slender shoulder. She says, "It'll work out, Pu. I promise you."

Jabar continues his threats as I attempt to reboot my brain. Pu is burnt and we can't put that genie back in the bottle so it's time to get serious. I have Pu repeat the question, "Are you aware of a terrorist group operating in Cairo?" Jabar continues his ignorance on the existence of *any* terrorists group operating in Cairo. I would imagine we'd get a *no* on Santa Claus and the Easter Bunny too.

It takes five additional water boards before Jabar finally admits that he may be vaguely aware of *some* group. I do realize that a person being tortured may say *anything* to stop the torment. So I incorporate into my plan the words of President Ronald Reagan. In response to Russia's promise to reduce their nuclear arsenal a reporter asked, "How can you trust the Russians?"

Reagan smiled and said, "*Trust*, but *verify*.'

I need information that can be been verified before the President will approach the North Koreans and threaten them with extinction. Perhaps, not much confirmation, but enough to make me feel warm and fuzzy.

It takes four additional deep sea dives to encourage Jabar to provide the names of the terrorists. I ask Gwen to contact our intel genius, Agent Bobbie Geary, and run the names by her. While Gwen is on the phone, I ask Jabar if the North Korean government is supplying funds and aid to the Cairo terrorists. This question seems to test

Jabar's new role as our snitch. His body tenses and Jabar shakes his jowls back and forth. It is an incorrect reply either way, so we water board him until he begins to string sentences together and quits the monosyllable pissed off replies. Interrogations are unique but all share some common ground. The subject realizes that they must provide *some* variation of the truth, so they tend to minimize their liability.

Agent 36 whispers in my ear that our intel files *hit* on all four names with numerous references as terrorist *sympathizers,* but no indication of *direct* involvement was noted. In other words they had successfully flown below the radar.

Both Mansur and Jabar advised us that these men have families, bogus jobs, and attend the mosque. So, I reason, they must have *someplace* to lay their head at night. Gwen is gabbing away on the phone as I approach and ask her, "Give Bobby the pedigree on those mopes, I want their addresses."

Pu overhears my request to Gwen and informs me that I will be able to obtain those addresses in an expeditious manner.

Agent 36 concludes her phone conversation and actually grabs my arm.She warns me that "Tony Daniels needs to speak to you *immediately*. He stressed that it concerns a critical case-related matter and *emphasized* that he means *now*."

I've got a good idea why Tony requires my ear and I am not ready for that particular conversation. It will also be a mistake to allow Jabar time to mentally recuperate now that we had broken his will.

"Gwen," I say. "*You* call Tony and find out what he wants."

She gives me a look of concern and says, "What happens if he insists on speaking with you."

"You just tell him the truth." I laugh.

Agent 36 gives me a confused glance and asks, "The truth?"

"Yep." I confirm. "Tell him I can't talk with him now. I'm in the middle of torturing a terrorist. Just like I briefed him."

CHAPTER 56

"What great things would you attempt if you knew you could not fail."
— Robert H. Schuller

It takes four-and-a-half hours before I feel that Jabar has been properly debriefed. Sometime during that period, Gwen must've spoken with my roomie because she literally pulls me aside and informs me that "Mansur's been murdered."

I realize that her statement requires a reaction so I say, "And *how* did that happen?"

"Had his throat slit by some detainees. The word at Gitmo was that Mansur was a government snitch."

"No shit," I say and realize that Gwen is no dummy so I add, "when we come up for air, I'd like all the details, but right now Mansur is old news."

Agent 36 gives me a sly smile and with an accusatory tone says, "You *knew* he was dead. I can tell, you knew!"

"Don't be ridiculous Gwen," I counter. "How would I know?"

She laughs and says, "You can't bullshit me Booker. I *always* know when men are lying and *you* just fibbed big time."

"If you know when men are lying then why did we waste a day torturing this fat arrogant asshole? You could've just interviewed him."

Now Agent 36 goes for any man's Achilles heel. She says, "What's the matter, Booker, don't you trust me? I thought we're partners. If you can't trust me, who you gonna trust?"

"Gwen," I say seriously. "I love and trust you *and* if I really knew about Mansur, I'd tell all."

As I walk away Agent 36 observes, "You just lied *again*, Booker."

During the four-hour interrogation Jabar confessed to being the money conduit between the North Korean money and the terrorists. He admitted to some twenty-five exchanges over the past fifteen years. Jabar initially denied any knowledge of specific terrorist acts but upon some additional deep sea adventures recalled sketchy details of the terrorists funding Muslim political candidates, their introduction of the bird flu in America, the blackout, and the manipulation of oil prices.

But Jabar emphasizes that these discussions always occurred *after* the terrorist actions and never before. I tend to believe him on this one point. Jabar's admissions constitute solid evidence since only someone involved in the conspiracy would know these details.We had not mentioned these acts of suspected terrorism during our questioning, so Jabar's confirmation makes our suspicions a reality.

Pu sits in the corner preparing a written statement in Arabic that contains the factual details of Jabar's admissions. We include Jabar's pedigree and history, how he became involved in the conspiracy, the North Korean support of money and resources, Mansur's role as a bagman, several specific American disasters that Jabar cited, and the names and contact information of the four terrorists. I take particular time having Jabar provide physical descriptions of the four terrorists. As their spiritual adviser, he has led them in prayer on many occasions. The imam suddenly becomes absentminded on things like height, weight, and eye color, so I Taser his fat ass.

And when he continues his vagueness *after* the tasing I water board him, which produces a much more detailed description right down to a mole on a forehead. Other interesting tidbits that result after Jabar's latest deep sea dive include the leadership in the group of four.

Jabar identifies Akil Adofo as the brains and balls behind the small cell. The group has been together since primary school, some thirty years ago. They are educated men with Akil attending UCLA. It seems that while at college he met and befriended the son of a North Korean government official and over their four years in America, hatched this sophisticated and deadly conspiracy.

"Where can I find this Akil?" I push Jabar.

"He frequents the Al Amoor cafe."

The nuclear suitcase is front and center in my brain so I attempt to determine a time frame. I push Jabar, "What's the money for?"

"They do not disclose any of their plans," Jabar pleas. "When their deeds are done, we will praise Allah and the details emerge, but *never* before."

"What did Akil say when you delivered the money?"

"He inquired why it was late, and I explained Mansur's difficulties."

"Think Jabar, think!" I scream. "What did Akil say then?"

"He was grateful that the money had arrived."

"What else?" I push.

"Only that they required it by Wednesday."

It is now 2311 hours on Sunday so that leaves us three days to get the evidence to the President and have the North Koreans put a kibash on the Muslims. A day later and Muslim terrorists will have a nuclear bomb.

We point a video camera at Jabar and record him reading the statement aloud. At the conclusion of his verbal confession he signs the written statement with Gwen, Thumper, Kopka, Shoulders, and I signing as witnesses.

The team is both exhausted and excited by our success. But there are too many loose ends in my mind for me to start any celebratory back slapping. There is the question of the money blipping away on our GPS somewhere in Cairo. *And* the chances are good that one or more of the terrorists are sitting in close proximity to that money. Also, Pu's question to me earlier had placed an investigative burr up my ass. If we pack up our tent, then these four terrorists will still be out there operating in the ether world of monsters who want to destroy the USA. And, this particular group is *not* your run of the mill screaming jihadists who indiscriminately fire a few rounds in the air to impress the cameras. These guys are smart and devious.

So after Jabar reads and signs his confession for the camera, I break the news to my team that "We're not finished just yet."

"Don't we have enough for the President to back down the Koreans?" Thumper wonders.

"Probably," I say. "But we can't leave anyway till Mo's ready to travel and I personally can't sit on my ass knowing that these maggots are a few miles from here with 3 million dollars of our tax money."

It takes about 3 seconds before Thumper says, "Well, lets rock and roll."

Pu's private subterranean den includes a mini jail cell that is where we stash Jabar. Although I briefly consider a more dire option, we may require the imam alive for use as a hostage.

It's off to the mosque. Our immediate goal is to bag Jabar's office, searching for any documents or other evidence that further proves the existence of this conspiracy. My secondary goal, though as yet unspoken, involves something far more perilous that will either cut the heart from the monster or kill us in the process.

Captain Kopka has periodically checked the location of the money via the GPS monitor inside the van. Two hours ago, the signal moved from the café to a location near the mosque.

On the way to the mosque Tommy wonders. "What are we looking for?"

I give his question some thought. Searching Jabar's office at the mosque is a long shot but it just seems like the thing to do. I say. "We'll know it when we see it."

It's almost midnight before we reach the mosque. Pu feels that the building *should* be empty, but can't be sure. Even at this hour the streets have small groups of people milling around. We park near the rear door and use Jabar's key to enter. It is a cavernous structure with the center ceiling some forty feet in height. Some equivalent of a Catholic altar is off to one side and marble statues of religious icons are sprinkled along the walls. Pu leads us through an open alcove to a series of doors. He indicates a particular door and Tommy begins the elimination process with Jabar's key chain.

The office is western standard fare with a wooden desk piled high with papers. Two filing cabinets, two chairs, and a computer terminal complete the inventory. Normally I'd have a search warrant in my pocket and conduct a systematic time-consuming search itemizing each item seized in a log.

Those necessities are not possible tonight so I instruct the group to seize the computer hard drive and every piece of paper in Jabar's desk *and* filing cabinet. I ask Pu to quickly eyeball the folders as we pile them into trash bags. The FBI cryptologist will scrutinize every word later. Even this abbreviated process takes several hours. I decide to leave before people show for morning prayers. The back of the van is totally filled with our booty and I feel that there's a nugget of gold somewhere in that pile of shit.

We still have about an hour before sunrise so I tell Pu to take us to the money. The GPS blip seems to directing us somewhere between the mosque and the Al Ammor café. Pu says that "It is a residential area."

The signal leads us down a street reminiscent of Jerome Avenue in the Bronx. No telling how many human beings per square foot inhabit this one city block.

"There," Captain Kopka says pointing at a particular building.

"Suggestions, ideas, or comments?" I ask the group.

Tommy Shoulder offers, "Yeah, we break in the place, take the money, shoot the assholes, and cut the dough up six ways."

"Quit fucking around, Tommy," I say. "We don't have much time."

"He ain't fuckin' around," Captain Kopka replies.

I laugh and say, "Under different circumstances I'd give that scenario some serious thought, but for now maybe we need an alternate plan."

"What's the goal?" Agent 36 asks.

"Is it just me," I begin. "Or is anybody else pissed off that these four terrorists have killed, maimed, bankrupted and ruined the lives of millions of Americans, and they get a pass? I mean they're right up the fuckin' block."

"You said if we get the *evidence* of the conspiracy, we *stop* the conspiracy," Gwen challenges. "Why risk everything for some revenge?"

An awkward silence ensues. Gwen's logic is solid and responsible. We already have the goods proving a conspiracy between North Korea and Muslim terrorists. The President of the United States will force the North Korean government to cut off all support to these jihadist and they become impotent towel heads. We can risk the big picture now by acting like cowboys, so I'll do the adult thing. Revenge is not justice.

But the group's silence takes me back to the hospital where my daughter lay ill with the bird flu. These assholes tried to kill my Nikki.

It's really scary when you have a moment of temporary sanity.

So much for responsible adult behavior.

CHAPTER 57

"It's always too soon to quit ..."

– Unknown

As we make a second pass of the apartment building, Kopka scans the GPS and announces, "Bottom floor, first unit to the left of the entrance door."

Gwen clarifies, "So if we walk inside the main door and turn, it's the first door on the left?"

"Yes."

Thumper looks at me and asks, "Wanna go now and get this thing over with?"

There are additional unknowns that prevent an all-out cavalry charge. We have no idea if *any* of the four terrorist are with the money, so why risk a gunfight to retrieve 3.5 million dollars of Uncle Sam's unlimited booty, get someone hurt, *and* possibly lose all our evidence.

We discuss options and some are pretty creative, but *all* involve needless risk. I settle on a wait and see approach. While we are waiting and seeing, we call the hospital and speak with Mo. He is wide awake given the early hour, and reports that he may be in love with his nurse. I warn him that Demerol has that effect on people and ask if I can serve as best man.

I pass the phone around so that the team can offer their personal words of encouragement. When the phone is back in my hand I ask Mo, "Why the hell didn't you give the signal, son?"

"I was not in grave danger," Mo explains calmly.

"Not in danger! They cut off your fucking nose picking finger!"

"They were merely testing me and could have killed me at any moment. You must understand the jihadist mind-set. A finger is an insignificant piece of flesh." Mo pauses and finishes with, "Besides, I was enjoying my time as a field agent and didn't want it to end."

I can't help myself and laugh. "Are you physically able to make the trip back to D.C.?"

Mo's tells me that he can indeed travel. "But," he qualifies, "only if I can take the nurse."

I chuckle and say, "You can bring anyone you want."

The group's spirits are buoyed by Mo's courage and the mood in the dark van turns light. Everyone's exhausted but alert and motivated. It's not every day that one can prevent a plot to destroy your country. We'll rest later.

Agent 36 takes the opportunity to grill me about Mansur's murder at Guantanamo Bay. Her beauty can lull a guy into overlooking her Mensa IQ. She begins her subtle cross-examination by rubbing my neck and saying, "Poor Johnny Boy, you've been under a lot of stress."

The massage is relaxing and I can feel the tension melt and my shoulders droop. But more importantly, I let my guard down.

"Feel good, Booker?" Gwen asks.

"Ahhh," is the only sound that escapes my mouth.

"So, Booker. You never told us that Mansur was at Gitmo."

"Must've forgot." I say still in an altered state. "Had to put him on ice so he couldn't make calls to Cairo. Didn't I?"

"Why there?" Gwen innocently wonders as she continues her massage.

I feel like the tourist hypnotized by the Python who can only stare ahead in a trance. "Why *not* there." I say.

"Didn't you tell me a few weeks ago that your old Marine Corps buddy was the CO at Gitmo?"

The fangs insert the venom and I am now in deflection mode. "Did I?"

Answering a question with a question may work with a wife, but *'ain't* going to cut it with Special Agent Gwen McNulty.

"Yes you did," Gwen replies. "And don't you *think* it's a coincidence that Mansur is murdered at the same facility that your friend commands?"

She just turned the tables on me and answered my question of her question with another question. God, she's good. I counter with, "What is it that you're trying to say?"

Gwen laughs and continues the interrogation with, "You tell me."

Touché', I think, and tally up six consecutive questions with not one answer. I wonder how far this can go on.

Thumper interrupts this cat and mouse game with, "We've got some movement."

The entire group stiffens and jerks their head down the street toward the target building. Two figures exit the structure and begin walking our way.

I ask Kopka, "Is the money moving?"

"Nope."

"What's *our* move?" Thumper asks me.

I say, "Stand pat."

Odds are that the two people are not connected with our group of four.

Pu informs us that "There are most likely six apartments which utilize that particular exit door, thus the probability is less than twenty percent that these individuals are part of the conspiracy."

It's still dark outside but dawn is beginning to soften the horizon. The two figures continue walking toward our van. Six people sitting in a plumbing van in the early hours of the morning is somewhat suspicious, except in certain parts of Brooklyn. The two figures are about fifty yards from the van and I make a command decision to move.

Pu shifts the gear into reverse and is just about to back up when Tommy says, "Wait! They're getting in a car."

The two figures are no more than twenty yards from our van, which is tightly squeezed between two parked cars. The angle and darkness works to our advantage. They would need to be within ten feet of the van to notice Pu, who sits motionless in the driver's seat. I sit in the front passenger seat but my view of the sidewalk is obstructed by cars.

The two have come close enough for me to note that they are most likely Egyptian males. Pu has a better view of the driver as he turns full face toward the van just before he enters his car.

They pull out and everyone breathes a sigh of relief.

"A false alarm," Thumper says.

"Yep," Captain Kopka agrees. "Money never budged. Those two must've come from another unit."

A full minute later Pu announces to us, "I'm pretty sure that the driver of that car was Akil Adofo."

"Who the fuck is that?" Tommy wonders.

I inform him that, Akil Adofo is the leader of the Muslim terrorist cell that wishes to destroy America.

CHAPTER 58

"The shit is gonna hit the fucking fan now."
– Nick Carangio - Hue City 1968

"Are you sure?" I ask Pu.

"He fits the description of Akil provided by Jabar and ..."

"No offense, Pu," Thumper interrupts "but the majority of guys in Egypt match *that* description."

"And," Pu continues unfazed. "This is the same man that Jabar met with at the Al Ammor café."

"Fuck me," Tommy Shoulders utters.

My immediate reflex is to follow Akil's car. But, due to the sparse traffic and distinctiveness of a plumbing van, we'd probably get burnt. And if we are spotted by Akil, he may go underground. The old adage of, *'a bird in hand,'* makes sense so I decide to stay with the money, because if we abandon the money *and* lose Akil, we've got squat.

I ask the team for "Options?"

Jabar provided us a time frame of three days before the money is needed. Although I don't verbalize it, the cash will likely be used to purchase a nuclear suitcase bomb. The clock is ticking.

Tommy immediately wants to "Knock the door down, snatch up whoever's there, *and* the money."

Kopka adds, "If we take their money, they can't use it for terrorist acts."

A simple and accurate assessment but only a temporary fix since Akil constitutes the serpent's head. We can likely carry out that exact scenario since we are well-armed law enforcement officers that have executed hundreds of search warrants with bad guys on the opposite side of the door. The fact that there are probably armed terrorists guarding the money is not much different from armed drug dealers guarding ten kilos of cocaine.

But while this option is a viable one I ask, "Any thoughts on how to capture the money *and* neutralize Akil?"

It is Agent 36 who begins a rambling and complex plan. It addresses both issues of money and Akil, though there is significant risk involved. Of course, *that* risk pales in comparison if we do *nothing* and a nuclear device explodes in America, setting off a war with Russia.

When Agent 36 completes her monologue she pauses, looks at the group and asks, "So what do you think?"

The group is momentarily silent and it is Captain Kopka who finally says, "I like it. Let's rock and roll."

Gwen's plan involves timing *and* luck but that's been a main stay of our existence lately. We head back to the CIA safe house to fine tune the plan and prepare our equipment. The sun has risen and the temperature is climbing. We arrive and Gwen asks Pu for the keys to Jabar's cell saying, "I better go check on Jabar."

I tell her to "Take Tommy with you."

Agent 36 laughs and says, "The guy is blindfolded, his arms and legs are strapped down, and he's in a cell. I can handle it."

Just as I am about to express my concerns, Gwen turns on her heels and walks away challenging me with, "Don't be a sexist pig, Booker."

She's right, I think and turn my attention to more pressing matters.

Back inside the house, we suddenly feel the hunger pangs of not eating for some eighteen hours. Our group sits around the kitchen table as Pu busies himself with preparing food while Thumper, Kopka, Shoulders, and I decide on equipment and weaponry.

A few minutes later, Agent 36 strolls out of the pantry that connects with the hidden room and calmly announces that Jabar is dead.

Still tightly strapped to the chair Jabar's body is slumped and still. Pu loosens the restraints and we take turns trying to find a pulse but to no avail. Thumper throws out the possibility of performing CPR, but that suggestion is met with blank stares and a Tommy Shoulders comment of "Fuck him, I ain't touching those fat greasy jihadist dead lips."

Kopka rationalizes, "No big loss. He's no longer of any use to us and he's definitely no longer a threat to Pu."

That possibility *had* crossed our minds. Jabar could have done some real political damage by reporting an American operation on the sovereign soil of Egypt which included torture, kidnapping, and the desecration of a mosque. Shoulders couldn't find a bathroom and took a leak on some statue when we were bagging the mosque last night.

Pu kneels over Jabar's large carcass carefully examining his carotid artery, chest, and wrists. His movements seem to indicate some expertise in the human anatomy. My impression is that Pu is looking for something specific as he continues to prod and probe Jabar's corpse.

Pu slowly stands and locks eyes with Gwen. He pronounces with some assurance that "Jabar has suffered a heart attack."

Then Pu does something that strikes me as odd. He pats Gwen's shoulder in a comforting manner and says to her, "Jabar's death is good karma, no matter the cause."

Kopka teases Tommy with, "You fucking killed the imam with the Taser. You're gonna go to hell."

"Shit," Tommy laughs. "Booker Tased his ass a lot more than me."

We have a brief discussion while standing over the deceased and conclude that Jabar's unexpected demise is a blessing. It would have been one major loose end with the real possibility of Jabar recruiting new jihadists to kill Americans. His death also saved me from making some tough choices.

Pu tells us, "I will dispose of the body in a manner that it will never be discovered."

"I'll bet you will," Thumper laughs.

Gwen breaks the awkwardness of the situation by saying, "I'm hungry, let's eat."

Agent 36 having hunger pangs while straddling some dead terrorist eight thousand miles from home confirms my suspicion that she is indeed one tough cookie. Many females would be somewhat unsettled about their proximity to submachine guns, torture, or an occasional corpse, but Gwen seems totally at ease. Perhaps she *is* my female clone. After a not so hearty breakfast consisting of some type of pastry, the sludge coffee and mush that resembles baby vomit, we take naps. We'll need our wits about us and without sleep the human brain will shut down. We find several bedrooms, couches and futons on the second floor.

I set my cell phone alarm for three Cairo time, but am fully awake at two. Caffeine is one of my addictions and I approach the sludge coffee with some trepidation. I add some honey and milk to the sludge and heat it on the stove. *Not bad* is my immediate reaction and I can't wait to tell Donnie Osmond back at Starbucks. Maybe we can christen the concoction with some catchy name like *A Double Jihad Venti.*

Thumper awakes next, followed by Kopka, Tommy Shoulders, and Gwen. Pu enters the kitchen from an outside door and announces that Jabar has left the building. We avoid any direct questions on Jabar's current whereabouts, though we are all tempted to ask. It would be unprofessional to put our host on the spot.

Pu informs me, "I have Akil's address, as well as the other three."

"That's great news, Pu." I praise. "I'll make sure to tell Mr. Burke how invaluable you've been."

"I have a deep respect for both John Burke and America," Pu says. "Sharia law disrespects the sanctity of life and cannot be the instrument of a just god."

I ask him, "Did you get another vehicle?"

He nods and says, "It is parked near the travel agency."

"Building layout?" I wonder.

Pu places a diagram in the center of the kitchen table and points to a particular square. "This is the unit with the money."

We all lean in to get a better look.

Pu continues, "It is typical of this area of Cairo. One main room that functions as both kitchen and living space. There is one bedroom here." He points to a separate room. "There are only two outside windows, which open up to the main living space."

"So the bedroom has no outside access?" Kopka asks.

"Correct. There is also a bathroom next to the bedroom door, accessible only through the main room."

This information is critical to our plan and I make a mental note to tell CIA Deputy Director Burke that his longtime friend is the finest asset and gentleman I have ever worked with.

"So while *we* were snoozing," I say. "You arranged for another vehicle, acquired the terrorist addresses, the floor plan for the apartment, *and* disposed of a body. I'm impressed."

Pu gives the group a Yoda-like smile and waves a dismissive hand through the air. He says, "It is my pleasure to assist you in such an important matter."

I look at the group. "Ready?"

A few nods and smiles provide me my answer and I say, "Good, then let's saddle up and go kick some terrorist ass."

We pile into Pu's van, plopping down in our usual seats. There's a comforting feeling attached to ritualistic behavior. The booty from Jabar's office has been replaced by eight heavy-duty nylon bags containing a variety of items ranging from stun grenades to breeching tools.

An hour later we reach Pu's travel agency. "Any questions?" I ask.

There's a very unique look on individuals going into harm's way. I've seen it on the faces of young Marines prior to battle and it is equal parts of fear, courage, determination, anger, and righteous indignation. "Okay, then. Let's do this." I say.

We transfer the GPS monitor into Gwen's car per our plan. Captain Kopka, Tommy Shoulders, and Gwen jump inside the car while Pu, Thumper and I follow them in the van. A mile later our van turns southbound while their car continues west.

The money has stayed put during our siesta, which is important to our plan but not critical. If the money *had* moved, we planned to execute at the new location. Pu maneuvers the van through the late afternoon Cairo traffic as we transition from a commercial district to a residential area. Akil's residence is located in a modest but well maintained neighborhood. It is a notch or two up the residential food chain from last night's location. The residences are attached single row homes with cars parked on both sides of the street.

"That one," Pu says, identifying Akil's house. The homes seem identically reproduced down to the color of the doors. We circle around the block in concentric circles looking for Akil's car.

I grew up in a row home in South Philly which was devoid of driveway, garage, or designated parking. You parallel-parked your car into tiny spaces on the street. If you returned home after ten or eleven, chances were you'd be parking a few blocks away. We spend a valuable half hour searching the area for Akil's car to no avail.

Frustrated, I contact Gwen and say, "No joy here. Going to secondary location." Our back up position is the Al Ammor café.

"10-4," Gwen responds. "We're in place. Package stationary. Will stand by for your call." The package that Gwen refers to is the money.

Jabar informed us during his debriefing that "Akil frequents the Al Ammor." This was corroborated by the fact that Jabar met with Akil *at* that very location just yesterday. Pu adds credence by describing the cafe as a gathering place for Cairo's underground power brokers.

We drive past the café's front windows but do not eyeball Akil. It's Pu who alerts us and points, "There."

Akil's vehicle is parked some fifty yards down the street. It is not far from where we parked our van yesterday.

Akil's modest black Daihatsu compact is sandwiched between two large SUVs.

Thumper exits the van to keep a loose eye on the car while Pu and I find a parking space. Thumper blends well into the Egyptian landscape with his newly grown goatee, dark skin, and arrogant sneer. He sports a tourist style shoulder bag that holds a variety of weapons as well as a GPS transmitter mounted inside a magnetic shell.

The goal is to attach the GPS device to Akil's car. If successful, we can loosely account for both the money and main player. The odds are that Akil, the money, and his three cohorts will hook up later and then the fun begins. The streets are crowded with rush hour traffic, tourists, and street vendors. We just can't stroll up to Akil's car and bend down to secure the GPS under the bumper. There are too many eyes behind these windows who may know Akil.

"Ready," Thumper announces over the phone.

Pu smiles at me as he climbs down onto the Cairo pavement and heads toward Thumper. He walks slowly and when he reaches Akil's vehicle, he begins to cross the street between the parked cars. Pu stumbles on a phantom object and falls next to Akil's back bumper.

Thumper hurries over to the old man and bends down, pretending to give some first aid, and deftly attaches the GPS device to Akil's car. He assists Pu to his feet; both men smile and walk off in opposite directions.

I monitor our new GPS signal on my hand held monitor inside the van. The signal is strong and should last a few weeks. If that time frame proves insufficient then millions of Americans are probably dead.

"We've located subject vehicle," I alert Agent 36. "Signal is strong."

"10-4. No movement here."

Pu and Thumper make their separate ways back to the van where we sit and wait, *and* wait. Surveillances are art forms. Most law enforcement officers become adept at pissing into jars and paper cups, eating a variety of processed fast foods while driving at high speeds, and learning how to be patient.

We take turns keeping the *'eye'* on the target whether it be a car, house, store, intersection, or a telephone pole. When you're not on the *'eye'*, you learn to be patient. Patience is not a virtue normally associated with hard charging cops and agents, so we learn how to pass the time. Some agents do cross word puzzles, some read, some eat, and some just stare.

After a few hours my brain begins to power down so I ask Pu if he can grab us some of that sludge coffee. A few sips will recharge our mental batteries and I've somehow acquired a taste for the pungent potion.

"What the fuck's he doing in there?" Thumper wonders aloud.

As a pretend wise guy I would "hang out" at the social club or some diner for hours. These places act as wombs for groups who are bonded by some common purpose. The Italians would have heated discussions on a wide variety of topics such as sports, women, cars, kids, food, and the occasional criminal activity. The group in the Al Ammor café may not be aware of Akil's terrorist activities, but they knew he was *'somebody.'*

It is almost seven before the GPS signal begins to blip itself away from the Al Ammor café. The sun is starting its descent and the consensus among our group is that Akil will head toward the money.

Football teams, FBI task forces, and even terrorist cells share some common traits. The successful ones are detail oriented. They conduct strategy sessions and discuss possible communication, control, and command issues. They'll likely take time to inspect their equipment, drink sludge coffee, break each other's balls and tell stupid jokes to ease the tension.

If I was in the middle of a big operation I'd be in constant touch with my co-conspirators. So if our reasoning is sound, then Akil is in route to join the boys guarding the moola for some plotting and brotherhood. Just like last evening. But here's where it gets dicey. Bad guys in a car plus bad guys in an apartment equal many unknowns. We have no idea of their weaponry, counter-surveillance abilities, or timetable to move. The one thing that we *do* know is that our prey are stone cold killers.

Do we wait and get them all in one place or take down the car and *then* the apartment? It's easier to divide and conquer, plus neutralizing the car is a safer option. *But* if we fail to engage the car in a timely manner then the car guys call the apartment guys and we blow *both* ends. I make an executive decision to wait until all the players are in one location. It's a riskier play with an all or nothing outcome.

We follow our GPS arrow but already know its destination. Every few minutes I alert Gwen's team, "Still headed your way."

"10-4," Agent 36 replies. "Our location is three blocks east of target."

We can afford the luxury of a loose eye and avoid the risk of being burnt since we now have *two* GPSs. These devices allow us to lay back instead of heating up a *hinky* and dangerous subject. When people think of large metropolitan cities like New York, London, or Paris, they visualize an anonymous mass of humanity aimlessly bumbling around like ants. That image may be accurate for the tourist areas but once you get into the neighborhoods, strangers become immediate suspects. In my old South Philly neighborhood, I was familiar with every individual and that individual's cousin or grandmother *and* the cars they drove. If three strangers were planted in front of my house for more than twenty minutes, they were either cops or thieves.

I turn to Pu and say, "It would be nice if you can eyeball Akil as he enters the apartment."

Thumper agrees with, "Yea Pu, you're the *one* person who can identify him and also our only native who both speaks the lingo and looks like he belongs."

Pu nods his assent and nudges the accelerator. We veer away from the GPS signal and turn on a parallel course.

A moment later Pu stops the van and jumps out and says, "Drive straight and locate a parking space. I will find you."

I jump behind the wheel and do as instructed. The area *looks* familiar but then again, the streets of Cairo give new meaning to déjà vu. From my right side mirror, I notice Pu take a right on a side street. I locate a rare parking space and begin my attempt at parallel parking.

"Pu is making a pass on foot," I tell Gwen. "We're hoping to eyeball the main guy."

"Got it."

Twenty five minutes elapse before I recognize Pu's Yoda-like figure walking toward the van. He tells us, "Definitely Akil, and I believe accompanied by Ziaul-Haq."

"That's two confirmed members of the cell of four," I say. "If our luck continues, the other two are sitting with the money."

We did some beer math at the safe house attempting to figure out the best time to hit the apartment. The consensus was that the later the better, since there'd be less chance of civilian interference and a less clogged escape route.

As the time slowly ticks, we are all hopeful that Akil stays put because plan B is not as finely tuned as plan A. At a few seconds before midnight I ask everyone if they're ready.

Agent 36 replies with, "Booker, I was born ready."

This is our plan and we're sticking to it.

Phase One:

Pu exchanges the magnetic plumbing signs for Cairo Police insignias. He climbs into the back of the van and dons the uniform of a Cairo police lieutenant. Captain Kopka and Sgt. Shoulders exit the car and walk toward the apartment carrying tourist type shoulder bags.

Phase Two:

Kopka and Shoulders enter the apartment building. Once inside they cue their radios twice, which alerts us that they are in position. Thumper and I exit the van and head that way. When we are in sight of the building I tell Gwen, "Good to go."

Phase Three:

Gwen leaves the car and now we are all on the same collision course with the terrorists. The front of the apartment building is offset with a few scraggly bushes and devoid of any illumination. The few light casings have long ago been damaged. These two conditions offer Thumper and I the cover and concealment we'll need at this late hour.

Agent 36 alerts the two Cleveland cops that she's inside and they join her in the hallway. Thumper and I frame the two windows holding a collapsible metal baton in one hand and a stun grenade in the other.

If you've ever been on the receiving end of a stun grenade, you'd know that the effect of the surprise, intense noise, concussion and smoke is near paralysis. But unfortunately, that inability to act last for only about twenty seconds.

That's really not a lot time to save the world.

CHAPTER 59

"Things do not happen - things are made to happen"
— John F. Kennedy

Agent 36 and Captain Kopka keep their radio frequencies open so we can monitor the action.

The team had vigorously debated one critical piece of this puzzle. How do you get four sophisticated terrorists to open the door to their criminal lair? Thumper, Kopka and Shoulders all wanted to play the sex card using Gwen as the bait.

Grant Beck told me that I had a gift to think like the bad guys. Though he intended it as a compliment, it kind of hurt my feelings at the time. But, perhaps he was right because I envisioned myself inside that apartment and thought, "What would make *me* open that door?"

A seductive female materializing at a late hour, *and* this close to D-Day, would peg my suspicion meter. I can always get laid later. We came up with several viable scenarios but only one that would get *me* to open that door. And, *if* Akil was as good as he seems, it will be that scenario or nothing.

Gwen spent 30 minutes with Pu memorizing the Arabic words that are the equivalent of "Open Sesame." The irony of this magical phrase from the story of *Ali Baba and the Forty Thieves* is that it opens the mouth of a cave in which forty thieves have hidden a treasure.

Gwen pounds on the door. A gruff male voice barks something in Arabic through the closed door.

Agent 36 mouths her memorized words that translates to, "Jabar has sent me. There is a problem."

Two specific words in that short sentence provide this late night visit plenty of credibility. "*Jabar,*" is their trusted spiritual guide, and "*Problem,*" is never good when doing stuff involving nuclear bombs.

I chose Gwen because of her gender and *not* her beauty or boobs. Muslim men consider women subservient, weak, and fearful. A woman knocking on the door lowers the suspicion level and it could be enough to make the difference.

The brusque voice inside the apartment rattles off another burst of Arabic. He is not a happy man and Gwen has already exhausted her entire repertoire of the Arabic language. I had anticipated some give and take so I emphasized that Agent 36 keep repeating the mantra of, "Jabar has sent me. There is a problem."

The terrorists basically *have* to open the door for two reasons. Jabar has *trusted* this messenger and divulged the address of the secret location. And, they simply could not risk ignoring a *problem* so close to D-Day.

A few more gruff and staccato challenges and then I hear the code that the door has opened. Gwen says in a very serious tone, "Hi, I'm Vanna White and you guys get to play *Wheel of Fortune.*"

I allow this seemingly silly code for two reasons. The first being that it is unique and couldn't be easily confused, and secondly, because Pu had casually mentioned that the game show, *Wheel of Fortune* is the top television show in Cairo. The image of macho terrorists sitting around the television set screaming, "Buy a fucking vowel, camel dung," struck me as hilarious.

Thumper and I break out the glass windows with our metal batons and toss the stun grenades inside the main room. We duck back down and use the outside walls for cover. The noise is deafening and a few screams can be heard over the noise. The plan calls for Kopka,

Shoulders, and Gwen to enter the apartment immediately after the explosions and for Thumper and I to provide cover.

But the *best laid plans,* as they say, rarely work. As I pop up to cover their entry several bullets hit the window frame inches from my head. Debris fly into my eyes and I fall backward. We obviously hadn't anticipated that the bad guys would automatically react in the direction of the stun grenades and broken glass.

"You okay?" Thumper asks.

I squint and wipe some of the crap from my eyes. "Fine," I say as I pop back up more cautiously. It takes a split second for my brain to analyze the chaos inside the main room. Shots are ringing out in all directions and the noise is deafening. Target identification is critical in close quarter fighting. I see an unknown male crouched in the corner by the kitchen table and as he raises his arm, I fire off a few bursts with my submachine gun. I must have hit him center mass because he falls backward into the wall and slumps to the floor. A second terrorist lays prone and motionless near the bathroom door.

I notice a flashing blue light in front of the building. It is Pu with his bogus police van. I tally up the bad guys since our exit clock is ticking. Terrorist One is lying still and bleeding by the table, Terrorist Two ditto by the bathroom door, and Terrorist Three has retreated behind the kitchen counter, firing what sounds like a large caliber pistol. That leaves one terrorist out of four MIA, if in fact there were four in the apartment.

We need to neutralize the asshole still slinging lead behind the counter. Kopka and Gwen have taken up positions behind a couch, opposite the kitchen counter guy. Tommy is using the entry doorway for his cover, while Thumper and I form the right side of a four-point diamond.

There is a lull in the firefight. The kitchen counter is barely six feet long so any movement to either side exposes terrorist three to either Tommy or Thumper and I. We need to nudge him to one side or the other.

I motion for Gwen and Kopka to lay down some cover fire from their frontal position. Number three can't safely pop up and return fire so his options are to pick a side. Thumper and I aim low waiting for a body part to appear and it is Thumper who gets the Kewpie Doll by grazing the left side of the asshole. Terrorist #3's weapon falls forward and his choices are now seriously limited. He'll either have to leave his cover or start throwing butter knives.

The terrorist chooses to surrender by raising his hands above his bleeding head and standing. Tommy Shoulders runs into the room and tosses the guy to the ground. All eyes are now on the closed bedroom door. I radio Pu to enter the apartment.

We all have our weapons trained on the bedroom door and realize that one of us will have to eventually breach that doorway. I instruct Gwen to cover the hallway against unwanted intruders and position Kopka next to the bedroom door. Then I tell Tommy Shoulders to check out the three fallen terrorists since many a cop has been shot by a wounded perp playing possum. Two shots ring out from behind us and we jump.

"Sorry," Shoulders says. "Asshole was making some kinda move, so I put two in his head."

I begin to breathe again and say, "Good going, Tommy."

As Detective Shoulders moves to the wounded terrorist laying by the kitchen table, two more shots ring out. "Fuck, Booker." Shoulders whines. "Now *this* asshole was trying to grab something, so I had to put two in *his* head."

This time my, "Good work," has less conviction, but who am I to say that Shoulders hadn't just saved all our asses. I realize that Tommy may be pushing the truth envelope but at this particular time and place, I'm relieved he's on my team. I'll worry about any morality issues later.

My gaze stays riveted to the bedroom door as Tommy moves to the counter guy who is laying prone on his stomach and holding his bleeding head. Shoulders leans down and suddenly jumps back and puts two rounds in *his* head.

"Sorry," Shoulders says somewhat apologetically, "but these fuckin' Muslims won't stay still."

Gwen screams, "Coming in!"

I'm happy that Detective Shoulders had completed his terrorist inventory before Pu arrived.

Pu pokes his head around the corner of the doorway and we wave him inside. He surveys the room and smiles at the dead terrorists littering the floor. I tell him that we possibly have one more inside the bedroom.

Pu inspects the faces of the three dead men on the floor and whispers, "Akil is our missing man."

I ask Tommy rhetorically, "You done fucking around?"

He nods as he clicks a fresh magazine into his MP5 submachine gun.

"Check this room for the money."

As Shoulders is tearing apart the room Pu asks, "Allow me to speak to Akil through the door."

I nod and say. "One minute then we go in."

Although it seems an eternity, it has only been three minutes since the stun grenades had alerted this entire city block of some occurrence that requires emergency services. The Cairo Police Department is basically an untrained corrupt organization so their response time may not be up to speed with American standards. My hunch is that we have ten minutes minimum. But they'd get here eventually and we really couldn't explain our presence or the three dead locals.

My plan is to take Akil alive and transport him back to the states for intelligence debriefings. That is the adult thing to do since Akil can be invaluable in identifying not only his North Korean contacts but also the terrorist hierarchy in Egypt. Since he is considered an enemy combatant in the war on terrorism, kidnapping his ass would constitute one of the *few* of our actions that didn't violate both the constitution and the Ten Commandments.

Pu joins Captain Kopka aside the bedroom door. Kopka has positioned himself so that anyone opening the door presents themselves as a target to the Cleveland cop. Using the wall as cover, Pu raps on the door and speaks in a command voice. I gather from his demeanor that he is representing himself as a Cairo police officer and asking Akil to surrender. I have major doubts that this approach will work with this particular terrorist, but then again when Saddam Hussein was cornered in his rat hole, he pissed his pants and beat the world surrender record.

From inside the bedroom a voice provides the confirmation that *someone's* inside. The math says it's Akil since Pu observed him enter the apartment building and the magic number of terrorist has always been four.

Pu replies to Akil and they begin a dialogue that seems almost conversational in nature. As my one-minute deadline approaches Pu turns to me and announces, "He will come out but believes he will be assassinated."

I can hear *real* police sirens from somewhere in the distance so it's go time. "Tell him he has five seconds to come out with his hands up or we go in and we *will* kill him."

Pu's voice now has urgency as he relays my ultimatum. We maintain our cover and train our weapons on the door. My five-second deadline is firm since we are risking not only our lives, but the lives of many Americans. We need to get our proof into the President's hands so he can confront North Korea and put an end to the systematic destruction of America.

Akil's voice now seems resigned. Pu tells us that he is coming out.

Shoulders pauses his search for the money and joins us as we snap into our shooting positions. Chances are that Akil won't go quietly. I learn later that Pu had assured Akil that the police now controlled the situation. This ploy is pretty Yoda-like since Akil is outgunned. The smart move is to surrender and play the victim card with the cops. A few phone calls to the politicians plus a donation to the Cairo Police Benevolent Society and life goes on.

As the door knob moves my finger begins the trigger pull ready for some aggressive move. I tell Pu, "Tell him to come out with hands high."

Pu translates my words and Akil slowly shuffles into the main room. The man that emerges from the bedroom is *not* the man I expect. My image of crazed terrorists is from the cable news network. Some angry, screaming, chest-pounding bearded asshole.

But Akil resembles your friendly Chemistry professor at some state college in Iowa. He appears to be in his mid-forties, average height and weight, clean-shaven and wearing pressed trousers and a dress shirt. He takes a few steps forward and scans the room going from Kopka to Pu, to Shoulders, to Thumper, to Gwen, and finally me.

And when our eyes meet the image of the innocent academic completely dissipates and is replaced by evil. This is a man who has killed innocent men, women, and children and is about to incinerate several million more. These are actions that transcend ideologies, religious beliefs, and revenge. These are the actions of an individual who has no soul.

Our eyes are locked in some weird type of recognition. Akil somehow knows that I hold his life in my hands. I tell Gwen, Shoulders and Thumper to search the bedroom. Akil must recognize that I hold his life in my hands because he maintains eye contact.

I look at Pu and tell him to ask Akil, "Where's the money?"

Akil shrugs his shoulders and I already know how this thing ends. But I really need Akil alive so my preference is to Taser him and toss his spastic body inside the van and boogey. The money is expendable since the entire terrorist cell would be eliminated.

"Ask him again."

Pu repeats the question and Akil repeats the shrug.

I appreciate the need to move things along so I take two steps toward Akil and point my weapon at his head. I nod at Pu who repeats the question, "Where's the money?"

Akil blinks and it's the first chink in his armor, but we really don't have the luxury of time to wait for the remainder of his suit to fall.

Initially, the gun to the head threat was to be my last move before I gather the troops and boogey back to the safe house with Akil in tow.

Gwen appears in the bedroom doorway holding the decorative cloth bag Jabar delivered to the Al Ammor café. It is the money bag. She smiles and says, "Found it in the laundry basket below some really moldy skivvies. I had a boyfriend who would hide shit there, so it's the first place I looked." Agent 36 taps her prize and says, "Money's inside."

I can hear Shoulders complain in the background, "You mean to tell me that you gals know about that hiding place."

CHAPTER 60

"You want me on that wall, you NEED me on that wall."
—A Few Good Men

"Good work Gwen," I say. "Everyone to the van."

Pu suggests that he lead the group to the van. "It will appear that the police are in contro.l" Pu enters the hallway and uses his command voice to alert anyone within listening range that the police have arrived.

"Okay," I say. "Maintain your weapons but file out in a surrender shuffle."

Nobody moves a muscle and it dawns on me that this entire group is totally comprised of alpha males, *including* Gwen. Their DNA prevents them from being the first to leave a hot LZ.

"Gwen," I say. "Cover Pu's back. Thumper, take the point and make sure we're not heading into a trap. Shoulders, out the window and cover us to the van. Ray, bring up the rear." I pause and finish with, "Akil and I go last. Now move it!"

The group responds and begins the getaway procession back to the safe house. We'll regroup there and collect Mo tomorrow for the return trip to CONUS. (Continental United States)

Shoulders hands me the Taser and alerts me that "It's on the maximum level so don't be shy."

Akil and I are now alone in the room surrounded by the carnage. I would imagine that the three dead men on the floor had been more than passing acquaintances. Jabar told us that *"The group have been friends since childhood."*

The fourth terrorist maintains eye contact with me and smiles. It is totally out of context with the situation and sends a chill down my spine. A few silent seconds elapse and we can hear shouts in the hallway. I suspect that some occupants are emerging from their apartments and verbally challenging the strange mix of people with guns.

As our eyes remain locked, I suddenly grasp the implication of Akil's smirk. It's his acknowledgment that we are more *alike* than different. Grant Beck was probably right and Akil recognizes me as his kindred spirit. Perhaps we are *both* bad guys doing what comes naturally. Akil justifies his actions from some deep-seeded ideology and I, from an equally powerful but opposing belief system.

I smile back and know that Akil will *never* cooperate nor be rehabilitated. His DNA prevents him from being a snitch as did mine. Perhaps we are both lost causes *but* at least I have the gun.

If i get Akil back to the States, there is the distinct possibility that Akil would eventually gain his freedom in some international trade of hostages. If he reaches the States alive then he will be in the control of politicians and their irrational actions are often as evil as terrorists.

I can actually hear Grant Beck's voice imploring me to use my gift of *"thinking like bad people."* So I tap into that part of my brain and the grey matter quickly concludes that I need to make a business decision.

After all, when you cull away intangibles like patriotism, morality and conscience, then the choice is obvious. *"It's strictly business,"* as the Italian mob likes to say. My bad guy persona is screaming that Akil must be destroyed to prevent any further misery that this animal will wreak on mankind.

But I am an FBI agent who took an oath to uphold the Constitution. Killing Akil in cold blood will simply make us different sides of the same immoral coin. It will reduce me to his rung on the depraved ladder.

I smile back and point my weapon at his head. Akil is measuring me, struggling to decide if I have the stomach to kill someone in cold blood. This terrorist is wondering if I will take the *final* step.

As I enter the empty hallway, I can see a few heads leaning out the doorways of two apartments. I raise my gun to discourage any potential heroes and rush out into the night air. I jump into the passenger seat of Pu's bogus police van and ask, "Everyone present?"

"No." Gwen says. "Where's Akil?"

I turn to face the group and announce, "Akil had *other* plans."

CHAPTER 61

"Out here ... due process is a bullet."
— *The Green Berets*

Our van passes the first Cairo police car arriving on scene. Although we are still in a vulnerable situation, no one seems concerned. The team is quiet as we slowly weave our way through the late night. The silence is comforting, each of us immersed in our own thoughts. No one in *this* van will ask me about what happened in that apartment. I wouldn't insult their intelligence with some bullshit and wouldn't place them in a legally compromising situation by revealing the truth. These individuals are realists who can distinguish between vigilantism and patriotism.

They could truthfully recount that *"When we left the apartment, Akil was alive."*

Our options were limited given the circumstances. Capture them and hope the Egyptian government does the right thing? Not likely. Kidnap them and bring them back to the States for justice? That scenario would turn into a media circus with pro-Muslim groups demanding their release, and American politicians all too willing to appease.Or, simply cut the head from the serpent.

I chose this team because I somehow knew that they would unanimously select door number three. Whacking Akil really wasn't a difficult choice given the options. America *needed* us on this mission because we were prepared to do their dirty work.

Akil accepted the risks when he decided to kill people in cold blood. His death can be chalked up to an occupational hazard. Though I killed *him* in cold blood, I have no pangs of hypocrisy. My lack of remorse is not rooted in any high moral ground of good versus evil. It was simply a sensible decision.

Akil understood my predicament, and if the roles were reversed, I'd be lying on that dirty apartment floor. So maybe we *are* more alike than different, except on this occasion, *I* had the gun.

Even though we eliminated the most dangerous terrorist cell on earth and thwarted the North Korean government's sabotage, America's politicians are ideologically incapable of connecting the dots between due process for animals and a nuclear bomb devastating some American city. Though this was a clandestine operation, enough people back in the puzzle palace have knowledge of our actions. We need to reduce this entire operation into a neat administrative bow. You can bet that the FBI hierarchy will want a sanitized account with a happy ending. It is their version of a bureaucratic hand job. So, that's what we'll provide in a single post op report signed by each team member.

The team will likely take turns testifying before some closed door Congressional committee who will leak our testimony to the press. All of us will stick to the script and omit any accounts of blood and gore. It's all predictable bullshit that will end with a barrage of new regulations to prevent it from happening again. But it will happen again because we are imperfect human beings and there will *always* be bad guys and good guys. There will always be an Akil *and* a John Booker.

Okay, so maybe I shouldn't have been both judge and jury but sometimes a moral line in the sand is murky. As an FBI agent, I was simply doing my job but as a father, it became personal. These savages deserved their fate because they hurt my daughter Nikki. Fuck them and may they rot in hell. I may join them there, someday, but for now, I'll just drink some celebratory whiskey and smoke the stogie I stashed in my pack.

When I was a rookie agent, I once flippantly began an official report with the nursery rhyme introduction of, *"Once upon a time."* Some senior agent didn't find it funny, telling me "You can fuck with a report but don't ever rub anyone's noses in it, dickwad!"

Another dirty little secret, FBI agents will occasionally skew a report to tidy up some loose ends. They won't fabricate evidence to make the innocent guilty but they might nudge the guilty along.

My report will state that *"I had to use deadly force on Akil since he presented a threat to myself or others."*

That phrase is taken verbatim from the FBI's deadly force policy which justifies its use. Although my statement is pure bullshit, the HBOs will be sympathetic and nod in agreement. That's what they'll do because they can't accept that we are in a war with terrorists who do not abide by the niceties of the Geneva Convention. They kill indiscriminately and like the scorpion, will kill again and again. Killing is part of their DNA and doesn't include a conscience or remorse. They fight dirty but had just met their match. We beat them on their turf and will claim the title of *Dirty Boys*.

We arrive at the safe house and sit around the kitchen table. Pu finds a bottle of Jack Daniels and some local pastries. The group sits around the table and the mood becomes festive.

Captain Kopka asks Pu, "I thought you Muslims didn't partake in liquor."

Pu says, "When I was at university in London I acquired a taste for good sipping whiskey."

"So," Kopka concludes, "you Muslims are a lot like Catholics."

Pu laughs, "I suppose, but not *quite* as strict as Baptists."

Thumper raises his glass and announces, "A toast."

We raise our cups and Thumper says, "To Pu."

Tommy Shoulders offers, "A stand up guy."

Kopka adds, "Fuckin' aye."

The whiskey goes down smooth especially after the events of the last three days. As certified *thrill junkies,* our team works hard and plays hard. They deserve America's gratitude but will be lucky to receive a *form* letter in their personnel record. I'll coerce Tony Daniels into treating the team to an expensive dinner at a D.C. bistro, but we won't be entertaining the rank and file agents with exotic tales of our trip to Egypt.

There's one team member who will *remain* in the shadows and receive *no* recognition. "You saved America's bacon, Pu," I say as Thumper pours a second round. "We can never thank you enough."

Pu nods and holds up his cup of whiskey and says, "I would like to thank all of you for ridding my beloved country of the likes of Akil."

Thumper asks seriously, "You have no problems killing brother Muslims?"

"I am a devout Muslim." Pu says while holding a shot glass of whiskey in his hand. "Well," he laughs recognizing the religious contradiction of drinking shots of liquor. "Perhaps not quite as devout as I believe."

We laugh and Pu becomes serious. "A true Muslim is a peaceful soul. Allah was a wise compassionate prophet. I am saddened that Muslims like Akil justify the killing of innocent people in Allah's name."

"John Burke will be very proud of you. He knew what he was doing when he put us all together," I add.

"What will you do now?" Gwen wonders.

"Continue my work," Pu says. "It appears that my cover has remained intact, thanks to all of you."

I couldn't detect any irony in Pu's expression of gratitude since the scoreboard tallies six dead terrorists who can tell no tales. He never eyeballed any of the deaths and *never* asked for details. Mansur was murdered at Gitmo, Jabar dead of a coronary, and Akil and his three friends in the apartment shootout before Pu arrived and *after* he left.

Pu looks at Agent 36 and asks, "And what about you, Gwen?"

She giggles and confides, "I enjoy being an FBI agent."

"You are quite proficient in that role," Pu says. "You remind me of my own daughter."

This last tidbit is news to us but I suppose Pu has a life in addition to his CIA world. He had never mentioned children or a wife but it had never come up. Pu fills in the silent pause with, "She is also bright, beautiful and quite unique in her thinking."

"That is so sweet, Pu."

I observe. "Maybe the *unique thinker* part is *not* a compliment."

Pu laughs. "Allah said that some things just *are*. They do not require a value judgment. Both my daughter and Gwen can see things clearly."

Shoulders comments, "You totally lost me, Pu."

Agent 36 rises and walks behind Pu, who is seated. She bends down and they exchange a few words. Gwen kisses his cheek and returns to her seat.

I've noticed a connection between this unlikely pair since our first day in Cairo. It seemed to reach a new level when Jabar died. Some unspoken message passed between them immediately after the imam suffered a heart attack and Pu confirmed his death from *natural* causes.

Gwen had been troubled when Jabar identified Pu. This disclosure would have seriously changed Pu's life. Aside from being hunted down by trained assassins, Pu would be required to flee his beloved Egypt and live his remaining years in fear and hiding. Agent 36 felt particularly strong that Pu's cover remain intact.

I have my own ideas on what happened when Agent 36 went to check on Jabar in the basement cell. That's because I was seriously contemplating a similar course of action. Gwen took pleasure in constantly reminding me that she and I were alike. So, it wouldn't be that far a stretch for her to do what I would have done. Dead men tell no tales.

I ask Thumper to call Mo and determine his health status for the long flight home. Thumper informs me that Mo is ready to go but insists on taking his nurse.

"Is he serious?" I ask.

Thumper repeats my question to Mo then turns back to me with, "As a Jabar heart attack."

"Ask him if she has a passport," I tell Thumper.

Thumper gives me a thumbs up. "Okay, we'll call his bluff." I say. "Tell Mo to have his nurse packed and ready to go at nine with her passport."

I turn to Gwen. "You're an attorney. Can we take an Egyptian citizen back to the US without breaking too many immigration laws?"

Agent 36 gives my query a thoughtful moment and concludes, "Well, she should have a VISA if she intends to stay awhile along with forms I-49 I-30, N-410, green card, a job, and a bunch of other forms, but what's one more illegal alien in the states?"

I contact our FBI pilots and advise them to, "Gas it up, boys. We roll out of here at eleven. We might have one additional passenger."

My dreams that evening are a jumbled version of the Iraqi war meets Disney World. I sit on some roller coaster type ride, speeding wildly around while rockets explode on the tracks. Distorted fun house images of Mansur, Jabar, Pu, Agent 36, and Akil alternately appear blocking my path. Akil is laughing like a maniac and pointing a skeletal finger in my chest. He is shouting something but I can't hear a thing.

The next morning I rise early and head to the kitchen. Gwen is sitting at the table with a cup of sludge coffee and the remains of last evening's pastry. She smiles and shoves the pastry in my direction.

"You know, Booker," She says, "I had a lot of fun here. When can we do it again?"

I shake my head and tell Agent 36, "It has been an honor and privilege to know you. I would trust you cover my back any time."

At around eight, Pu and Thumper head to the hospital to gather up Mo and his Egyptian squeeze. My money is that she won't follow through on such an impulsive act, but then again I'm no expert on the behavior of this generation.

Two hours later, the tourist agency van rolls into compound with Mo, Thumper, Pu, *and* Mo's nurse Anippe Femi. Her name means *"love of the Nile,"* and she is a stunning young lady. Femi's arrival cost me twenty bucks on a bet with Gwen. I was positive that the nurse would be a no show.

The group takes turns hugging Mo. He raises his bandaged hand, sans finger in the manner an athlete hoists his trophy in victory. The young FBI agent seems to consider his missing digit as a badge of honor. Mo is a hero and I will do everything in my power to see that he receives the FBI Medal of Valor. He introduces Femi to the group and she speaks surprisingly good English. She studied basic nursing at Edinburgh University in Scotland and followed up with a specialty in trauma care at Cairo's School of Medicine. Femi has traveled extensively throughout Europe and Asia has no current love interest or cat, thus this move is *not* that impulsive.

Our pilot in command, FBI special agent Bob Dupuis, greets us at the remote Quwaysina Airport. The location caters to local air traffic and offers a much lower profile after last evening's shoot-out. Dupuis gives me a hopeful thumbs up and I respond with a smile and a "Horaah!" I follow up with, "Mission accomplished, details once we clear Egyptian airspace."

I make some quick introductions with the pilots to Pu and Femi. It's time to bid goodbye. Pu wrinkles his nose and squints his eyes and I ask him, "Has anyone ever told you that you look like Yoda from the Star War movies?"

"Often," Pu laughs. "As Mohammed once said, you are what you are."

"Wasn't that Popeye?"

Gwen holds back while the group communicates their personal good buys to Pu. She slowly approaches him and hands him a small object. They embrace and exchange a few words, then Pu heads toward his tourist agency van. As we board the plane, Agent 36, is wiping away a few tears from her green eyes. It doesn't seem like the right time to ask what she handed Pu.

We settle into our seats and about forty minutes later our co-pilot, John Canley, strolls back and announces that we have entered international air space. He pops the cork from the champagne and hands me the bottle. I take a pull and pass it on to Thumper. Even Femi partakes and I'm beginning to wonder if *any* Muslim obeys their religious dogmas regarding alcohol abstinence.

We spend the first few hours of the flight in a celebratory mode. The group high fives, chest bumps, hugs and guzzles champagne, before slipping into a semi-exhaustive stage. After things quiet down I take the seat next to Agent 36 and tell her that she had done good, then qualify my remark with, "For a *female* agent."

Gwen laughs and informs me that at new agent training she finished first in academics, firearms, and physical training.

I ask, "Is that with the modified female push-up?"

"One hundred manly push-ups so fuck you, Booker."

"Hey Gwen," I say seriously. "Can I ask what you gave Pu at the airport?"

"It's personal."

"Okay. I understand. Can I ask another question?"

"Fire away, Booker."

"Have you had any medical training?"

"Just a CPR and first aid course. Why?"

"Nothing."

As I am returning to my seat Agent 36 adds, "But *my* father was a physician."

I ask, "What kind of doctor?"

"A heart surgeon."

EPILOGUE

"It ain't over, until I say it's over."

— Animal House

Tony is meeting our plane at Dulles airport sometime around five in the morning. He is aware of the broad strokes of our Cairo painting but wants the down and dirty. Somewhere over the Atlantic last night, the team agreed that I'd take the lead on any debrief. We spent an hour to fine tune and memorize our story just in case one of us gets bushwhacked.

This is our story and we're sticking to it.

"Once upon a time ..."

Mansur confessed to being the money conduit between the North Koreans and the terrorists via his father Jabar. He supplied bank account information that provides a paper trail between the North Korean shell corporations and Muslim candidates in the United States. Additional account information indicates money transfers that coordinate within the time frame of American disasters.

Jabar suffered a fatal heart attack. He was overweight and it would have happened sooner rather than later. At the time of his coronary, he was cooperating and we were "chatting." In fact, Jabar *voluntarily* provided both a signed and video confession that supports our narrative. Jabar implicated his son Mansur as the bagman between the North Koreans and the Muslims.

Akil and his buddies decided to shoot it out rather than discuss their involvement in global terrorism. The fact that the FBI electronically marked money was found inside their apartment is further proof of their guilt. Their identities and terrorist activities were confirmed by Jabar, who also provided their names and physical descriptions.

The remainder of our post-op report includes several simple mantras which include:

"No bad guys were tortured."

"We followed the Attorney General Guidelines on foreign '*shit.*'

"They shot first."

And lastly, "God Bless America."

I omit some of the details contained in Mansur's sworn statement regarding his bank accounts. The official statement includes specific account numbers but neglects to mention that Mansur signed a power of attorney designating John Booker his representative in all financial matters. There was a cumulative total of $28,470,000 US dollars sitting in four different bank accounts in Belize, Belgium, Aruba, and Switzerland.

That money was stained with American blood and I had no intention of allowing it to remain on foreign soil. I also had no intention of turning it over to our *own* government since they would simply pass it on to illegal aliens, welfare queens, and third world nations who hate America. So I made an executive decision.

I left a few million in each account as evidence for our President to convince the North Koreans of their complicity in the conspiracy. Our federal geek squad somehow traced the financial computer virus to North Korea. That discovery, along with the evidence we gathered, makes our President's chat with North Korea somewhat one-sided.

The remainder of the money was donated anonymously to The Cancer Society, Hope for the Warriors, The Developmental Disabilities Council, MS Society, and the ASCPA.

Our Secretary of State told the President that although the North Koreans never admitted their complicity in the terrorist plot, they clearly understood the implications of an armada of America's nuclear warships sitting just outside their territorial waters. "It's merely a training exercise,' the Secretary of State said with a straight face.

Thumper returned to the D.C. field office and was offered the violent crime desk but declined. We spoke weekly and made plans to get together soon. We never did meet and one year after our Cairo adventure, Thumper was killed in a shootout with two fugitives from Philadelphia.

Thumper's widow received full tuition from an anonymous donor for her three kids to attend any college of their choice. Detective Shoulders somehow won a contest with the grand prize of a condo and boat in Key West. Case Western Reserve University received an annual stipend for four scholarships in the name of Dr. Suehad Fasaid for students majoring in Homeland Security.

Gwen's townhouse was paid off and an Audi convertible appeared on her driveway, compliments of a secret admirer. She gave me the third degree about this strange series of events but I know when to stifle my pie hole.

Captain Kopka retired from the Cleveland Police Department and went into a silent partnership on a restaurant specializing in Croatian fare which he named, *The Arrow Cafe*.

Okay, I'll admit to a minor deity complex but there are zero pangs of guilt concerning my actions.

Mo and Anippe Femi are living together in Alexandria. Femi mysteriously received a back dated work visa with additional immigration documents placing her on a fast track to citizenship. She works as a trauma nurse at the Walter Reed Hospital and is considering medical school. Their wedding is scheduled for June and I will walk the bride down the aisle. Gwen is the maid of honor and Captain Kopka the best man with Detective Shoulders serving as usher.

The reception will be held at Rock's bar in Parma, Ohio and the wedding, honeymoon costs, in addition to a $75,000 incentive award are compliments of the FBI Benevolent Society in recognition of Mo's heroism. This society was incorporated as a non-profit within the past month designating Deputy Director Anthony Daniels as the individual who recommends recipients for an annual award, for Bureau personnel who distinguish themselves.

Mo received the FBI's highest award for valor. His commendation described his courage under the most extreme hostile conditions. It read in *"Agent Mohammed Askari endured sustained torture in an attempt to elicit information that would have compromised a covert operation of world-wide significance. Agent Askari sacrificed his finger rather than disclose his connection with law enforcement to known terrorists ..."*

Following his award ceremony, Mo was promoted to supervisor of the Middle East desk in FBI Headquarters.

There is a bittersweet irony involved in Mo's promotion. This is an FBI agent who desperately wanted field work but had tasted its seductive allure on one brief occasion. His missing trigger finger precludes any further excursions into that world.

Tony Daniels is promoted to Deputy Director and we eventually took that family vacation to Myrtle Beach. He spent the majority of his time on his Bureau cell phone until I tossed the Samsung in the ocean. For the remainder of our long weekend at the beach, we drank gallons of rum while Tony complained about the bureaucracy. When I remind him that *he is* the bureaucracy, he threatened to retire and play golf. But my roomie is a lifer and will probably die at his desk while bleeding FBI blue blood.

Although Pu and I have no direct contact, Deputy CIA Director Burke serves as our middleman. My Egyptian friend is doing his thing in the most tumultuous and perilous region on earth. I read in our intel bulletins just last week that a major Muslim Brotherhood operation was thwarted by the CIA in Cairo. The Brotherhood planned to kill three busloads of American tourists. Somehow, I see Yoda's fingerprints all over this one.

Nikki is a sophomore at Ohio State and has changed her major three times. She mentioned a passing interest in law school. I'd rather

Nikki become an aromatherapist in Estonia than add to the ranks of that ambulance-chasing group of sleazy con artists. No offense to my attorney Steve Sazini.

Boy Wonder quit the Bureau after his demotion and now works as a real estate agent in Vegas. He somehow blames me for his fall from grace and I only wish it were true. At least he can no longer wreak his misery on good law enforcement officers. That is, unless he sells a condo with mold to some Vegas motorcycle cop.

Agent 36 rejected a supervisory offer to head the Joint Terrorism Task Force in Los Angeles. "I'm not ready to sit at a desk all day," was her reasoning. That sentiment has been my personal mantra throughout my FBI career. Gwen *has* always contended that she and I were cloned.

We work cases in Cleveland and have discovered that there *are* some bona fide terrorists in northern Ohio. In the past year we've arrested 9 Iranians, most of whom were students at the University of Toledo, who were planning to place pressure cooker bombs at the Saint Patty's Day parade. Bruce Gombar, our supervisor, mentioned that Harvard would never admit terrorists.

Lorri and I are behaving like newlyweds. She told me that one definition of a good marriage is the ability to fall in love with the same person, over and over. I suppose that's true because of the smile on my face whenever my wife enters the room.

As for me, I feel good about my career in law enforcement. Not just some of it, but *all* of it, and that includes my three days in Cairo.

A very wise man once told me that "*You have an ability to think like the bad guys.*"

Human beings are wired at birth so the *bad* guy side of my brain has served me well. My demons are *mostly* vanished and I sleep well these days minus exploding rockets and monsters.

I understand that some folks could view my actions as vigilantism. Murdering unarmed terrorists, skimming illegal money which rightfully belongs to the government, lying on official government reports, and breaking a slew of regulations and laws are but a *few* of my sins. The full list would be a source of both embarrassment and pride.

But whenever those ethical considerations creep into my mind, they are immediately countered with, *"Fuck it!"*

ABOUT THE AUTHOR

John Ligato is a South Philly native who was involved the 1968 TET offensive. In 1994, as a deep undercover agent for the FBI, he orchestrated the largest public corruption case in U.S. history. He has three Purple Hearts and has been inducted into the Marine Corps Museum.

The 2006 movie *10ᵗʰ and Wolf* was loosely based on his life. He is the author of a fictional account of his undercover experiences, *Lerza's Lives*. He's been a pilot who flew missions for the FBI special operations group, hosted a radio talk show for nine years, been a motivational speaker for the US Marine Corps, and has appeared on television series such as A&E's *Runaway Squad*, and The American Hero Channel's documentary series, *Against The Odds*. John has worked as a deep undercover FBI agent for eight years.

John Ligato has been a college professor for the past eleven years, teaching courses in Homeland Security, Organized Crime, Covert Operations and Constitutional Law. He currently resides in North Carolina and is at work on his next book.